The
Wartime
Nanny

Lizzie Page

Published by Bookouture in 2020

An imprint of Storyfire Ltd.
Carmelite House
50 Victoria Embankment

London EC4Y 0DZ

www.bookouture.com

ISBN: 978-1-83888-208-2
eBook ISBN: 978-1-83888-207-5

The
Wartime
Nanny

To Miranda, my wonderful blue-eyed girl who has taught me so much about being brave and daring.

'We are nicely honeycombed with little cells of potential betrayal[…]the paltriest kitchen-maid with German connections is a menace to the safety of the country.'

Daily Mail, April 1939

PROLOGUE

2012

Natalie had tried to find Hugo Caplin three times before and three times she had failed.

The first was in 1952. She'd thought about him often before that. He was always somehow there, buzzing in the background, but in 1952, he came into focus. He was part of the Olympic team, rowing, in Finland. She saw the name in a newspaper, knew it was him. She contacted the British Olympic Association but didn't hear anything back. Whether they passed on her message to him was anyone's guess. It was better to think they didn't.

The second time was when Patricia went on a skiing trip to Austria in February 1967. While she was away, over those terrible ten days, Natalie ignored the advice of friends and went through the telephone directory. She had nice but ultimately fruitless conversations with a Hugh Caplin, a Harriet Caplin and a Heather Caplan.

Then, about five years ago, while she was driving on the motorway to Norwich, she thought she heard his voice on one of those radio show phone-ins. It was a replacement presenter, and they were talking about refugees. The replacement presenter, who had a pleasant, melodic voice, said, 'And now we have Hugo Caplin from London. Hugo, what do you have to say?' Natalie had pulled onto the hard shoulder to listen and after he'd spoken, she called right in, surprising herself with her efficiency, and the radio people told her they would try to reach him but even as they said it, she had a feeling she was going into the pile of 'crazy callers'.

She was ready to try again. She knew it would probably be her last chance but this time, Patricia might help. Guilt is a powerful thing. It can sink you but when used properly, it can propel you to great things. And Patricia was feeling guilty, because Natalie had told her some time ago she was feeling poorly, yet Patricia didn't take her to the doctor for some weeks. Patricia now thought that if only they'd gone sooner, things might have been different. She didn't say it aloud, but Natalie saw it written all over her face. Patricia had thought her mother was a hypochondriac. Natalie *was* a hypochondriac, but even a stopped clock is right twice a day. Poor Patricia.

Natalie was in a care home now, but it was a nice home in Westcliff-on-Sea and her room overlooked the estuary and there were different views at different times of the day. In the morning, you might have mudflats, flat land, all the way to beige factory chimneys; after lunch, the sea might be blue, green and pulsing gently at the sand; and by late afternoon, you might have a vista of a dark grey sea pummelling the sea wall, tipping over it and making puddles on the pavements.

They did a good variety of events in the home too – it wasn't just staring out the window. Karaoke, knitting, and Natalie's favourite – 'chair-based exercise'. There was a debating club, which was dominated by the same men who always sang Neil Diamond songs at karaoke, and there was scrapbooking, which Natalie was sniffy about at first, until she discovered it was mainly flicking through old *Hello!* magazines and cutting out pictures of the Queen and Princess Margaret. There was something surprisingly warm and collegiate about life there. It reminded Natalie a little of the lounge at work. And if she was too tired for company, Natalie watched *The Sound of Music*, ignored the Baroness and had vivid dreams about Captain von Trapp.

It was a Jewish care home and the security was tip-top: a code, followed by a buzzer to which you had to declare yourself, then a second door that opened automatically. Natalie had been told off twice for letting people in without checking who they were first. One more time and she'd get a warning. Patricia said it was the best place in the area, and Patricia did nothing by halves. She'd have gone through the paperwork, interrogated the staff, tested the emergency cords, before committing Natalie there.

Natalie had had to stop driving and that was painful, but Patricia's children visited once a week. Sundays were Anthony, Tuesday afternoons were Sharon. It was Sharon who noticed that the elevator was manufactured by a company called Schindlers. It was Anthony who christened it 'Schindler's lift'. If the great-grandchildren had too much homework to visit or were being ferried between tennis classes, guitar lessons, or bear-making parties, they sent home-made cards. *We love you, Gigi* – it was short for Great-Grandma.

Natalie had made new friends: nearly-bald Maisie, who was originally from Poland, and nearly-blind Andrew from Finchley. The staff carers were from all over the place, which Natalie enjoyed; she liked finding out about their lives. There was a German boy whom Natalie was very fond of. Patricia snorted, 'He's not a boy, he's twenty-five,' but he was a child really. They all went some way to compensate for the losses she had incurred by moving into the home.

When the doctor said there was nothing to be done, Natalie found herself staring at the calendar behind him, a mixture of filled squares and squares left blank, and she realised nothing applied to her any more. She was all the blanks. There would be no more filled-in squares, but it was not too terrible.

Patricia was speechless in the consulting room and not a lot made her speechless. Finally, she found her words: 'Not even tests?' Even Natalie understood they were saying 'no point doing tests on this one', but Patricia didn't get it, refused to get it, and kept arguing the case.

'If only I had made an appointment last month,' she kept saying.

Her dearest girl, Patricia, was sixty-three now. A grandmother, but she'd always be Natalie's little girl. The girl who saved her.

'Hindsight is a wonderful thing,' Natalie said. But she was thinking, *it isn't, really, no, it isn't.*

A few days after the diagnosis, Natalie said to her daughter, 'I want you to try to find Hugo Caplin for me.' She tried to imagine Hugo as a man of... what? Eighty? She was never very good at visualising what was not right in front of her.

'Really, Mum? I don't think it's a good idea.'

Natalie knew Patricia wouldn't like it.

'Does everything have to be a good idea? You find him, ask him – he can decide what he wants.'

Would he come? He probably wouldn't want to see her. He probably hated her.

'If you must,' said Patricia reluctantly. 'I'll look into it.'

Patricia was a person who kept to her word, which was something Natalie had always admired about her ever since she was a little girl. It was probably the way Mama had felt about Natalie once. As the pains in her stomach that had drawn her to the doctor tightened and deepened, she looked up at Patricia, who was staring at her, looking quite afraid.

'You'll have to be quick.'

CHAPTER ONE

1936

Natalie had heard that English people were less punctual than Austrians, so she was surprised when a middle-aged woman galloped over and grabbed her suitcase from the platform floor before even a porter had appeared. The woman was wearing a charming hat that looked like the kind of boat you'd make from folding paper. Although it wasn't made of paper, obviously, it was made from something midnight blue and furry. She had a thrown-together, careless look and a friendly smile.

'Natalie? Is it Natalie Leeman? Oh, I am so pleased to find you here.'

Instead of kissing her, the woman shook Natalie's hand up and down. *Ah*, Natalie thought gleefully, *this is England. People are more reserved about kissing here.*

'It is I,' Natalie responded delightedly. 'That is me. I am Natalie Leeman. And these are my first steps in London.'

The woman had rosy crab-apple cheeks and small, kind eyes. She explained the refugee agency was exceedingly busy – as Natalie could surely imagine – so she had volunteered to collect her herself. Natalie couldn't imagine, but she agreed politely. The woman grabbed Natalie's suitcase – Mama's honeymoon suitcase – and set off at quite a pace. Natalie followed her through the station past one ticket office, several commuters with briefcases and a crocodile of schoolchildren.

The sky was white-grey and sunless, and rain came down in fat droplets. For the first time, Natalie was glad that Mama had insisted on the less attractive but sturdier leather shoes and the warmer coat-for-all-seasons.

The woman continued talking as they walked. 'I'm Mrs Sanderson. Beverley. And I'm so sorry but my German is very bad.'

'It's ordinary,' Natalie excused her breathlessly, then said the line she had been going over and over on the train. 'I need to practise my English like a hole in my head.'

At that, Mrs Sanderson gave Natalie that lovely smile again. 'Right then!'

Natalie told Mrs Sanderson that she admired her furry hat tremendously, and Mrs Sanderson told Natalie that indeed, it was her favourite. She also said Natalie had good taste, a phrase that threw Natalie slightly. She had no idea what she – or the hat – would taste like. She decided it was a colloquialism, so she committed it to memory.

She should have mentioned the weather first. Natalie's etiquette book said to do so immediately with English people, so she quickly announced that she had anticipated the weather to be much more pleasant – it being April and all the best poems being about how lovely April in England was.

Mrs Sanderson admitted she was constantly surprised by rain. 'A sensible person would always carry an umbrella on their person – unfortunately,' she said with a sigh, 'I am not a sensible person at all.'

Realising that this was the much-fabled English sense of humour (Chapter 5 in her etiquette book), Natalie laughed loudly so Mrs Sanderson would know she appreciated her effort.

Natalie saw her first policeman. He was wearing a fun hat like a singular breast. There were cars, much like those at home, and trams, which were a different shape and colour to those at home – they even sounded different. And trees, again much like at home; but the paving stones were a different shape and size, and dirtier, yes, it was grimier, and the people, their clothes, their hairstyles and hats were different, but not remarkably so. There were more puddles here perhaps. If you looked for similarities, you would find them easily enough but if you looked for differences, you'd find them too.

There were fewer horses and carriages, less granite, less magnificence maybe, but there were, surprisingly, street sellers, and occasionally cafés with long colourful awnings. Rachel had warned Natalie the English hardly drank coffee in cafés and Aunt Ruth had advised that she didn't go anywhere called The Rising Sun or The King's Head because these were public houses or, 'places of ill-repute'.

Then, a beautiful sight. A bright red, brighter than you can imagine, double-decker bus passed in front of them. You could go upstairs and the conductor went after you to give you your ticket.

'Well I never!' Seeing one in the cold light of day was quite different from learning about them in a textbook and Natalie was awestruck. Laughing, Mrs Sanderson grabbed her hand. 'You're going to love it here, Natalie, I'm sure.'

Only three days previously, Natalie had been so firmly planted in Vienna, she might as well have had her feet buried in concrete – and it seemed incredible that she was in London now. Only two nights earlier, her family had held a farewell party for her. There were speeches, dancing, drinking, cousins, more dancing. Natalie tasted slivovitz for the first time; she wanted to like the 'adult' plum brandy so much, but would it be immature to say it did nothing for her? Even her younger sister Libby had been made to wear a frock, although from the moment she was buttoned up at the back, she had begged Mama to be free of it again. Her older sister Rachel *Goldberg* was glowing as though it were her party. She was just back with Leo from their honeymoon to the Italian lakes and she was full of the *utter majesty* of it and preferring to talk to the aunts and uncles now and not the cousins. Leo Goldberg was his usual self, expounding on the merits of some obscure composer. Rudi Strobl, Natalie's neighbour and private English tutor, hadn't come because he was on a university field trip. He had never missed a field trip in his life, and he wasn't going to start now. It was awkward when people asked her where he was: Natalie could see that, for some, his excuses didn't add up.

Uncle David, who had a good memory, said, 'Still planning to be a translator, little one?'

He had laughed the first time she told him and told her that in five years' time, everyone would be speaking Esperanto. This time he slapped her on the back: 'Good plan.' She was about to tell him of the idea she had to translate the children's book *Making an Elephant out of a Mosquito* by Kurt Brunner from German into English but mid-question, he drifted over to the sideboard to 'help' Mama decant the whisky. Later, after all the helping had been done, and his nose was rose-petal red, he re-approached her. She braced herself for Esperanto but he said gruffly, 'Your father would have been very proud. Pauly was fearless too.'

Between inhaling her American cigarettes, Great-Aunt Mimi said, 'I don't see why you don't go to Palestine,' while Great-Uncle Ben said, 'Stay and get a good education here. You'll never catch up if you don't.' Great-Aunt Mimi and Great-Uncle Ben never agreed on anything.

That night, once the relatives had gone, shouting and laughing into the moonlit street, Mama had followed Natalie up to her bedroom. As Natalie got changed into her nightdress – 'Look away!' – Mama knotted her fingers together tremulously and sighed.

'It's not for ever, Mama.'

'You will be good, won't you, Natalie?'

'Good?'

This was quite the departure, since Mama had spent almost the entirety of Natalie's childhood telling her to 'be herself'. She had never told her to be good before. Not once. Not even when Natalie had that 'antagonism' with a now-retired teacher in kindergarten.

'I didn't mean anything by it.' Mama said. She had tears in her eyes, which she wiped away resolutely. Parties always made her cry. She gave Natalie a big smile. Papa used to say that Mama had a smile that launched ships. Mama would reply, 'Sank them, more like!'

'It's such an adventure. I'm so proud of you, Natalie. You're going to learn so much about the world.'

'But, Mama, be *good*? Really?'

'Well, if you can't be good, be careful,' Mama said lightly, kissing her on the forehead. 'No really, sweet pea, just be yourself.' She smoothed down Natalie's quilt – she hadn't done that for years; Natalie wouldn't usually let her – then smiled tenderly at her.

'The English won't know what's hit them.'

Now Mrs Sanderson led Natalie to a fine-looking black motorcar, with a roof so shiny you could have skated on it. When Natalie realised that Mrs Sanderson was going to drive it herself, she was even more delighted. Natalie had long encouraged Mama to learn but Mama was too anxious, and Natalie had encouraged Rachel to learn but Rachel just said that since Leo could, brilliantly, what would be the point?

Natalie wanted to learn to drive as soon as she could. Now she wondered if it mightn't be part of her job?

Mrs Sanderson set off on the wrong side of the road. After a few seconds, when she still didn't pull over to the right, Natalie let out a surprised 'oh.' She really was in England. They *did* drive on the wrong side of the road here.

Mrs Sanderson said, 'You did very well, that long journey all by yourself,' which made Natalie feel prickly. The border checks had not been onerous, both train and ship were quite comfortable and an elderly woman on the way to Manchester had shared her dried sausage with her. *And* she was not a child, she was nearly seventeen, for goodness' sake. Still, it was nice to be complimented so Natalie said, 'It was straightforward, even though I sneezed every time the train went through a tunnel.'

Mrs Sanderson explained that she was a lecturer at university. Her subject was philosophy. Natalie had never met a philosopher, and this filled her with excitement. What greater introduction to English life?

'Fantastic! I love to read... philosophy.'

No sooner were the words out of Natalie's mouth than she realised this was an abject lie. She didn't, hadn't, *never once* had read philosophy. Why had she said that? Her mouth always ran away with her. Rachel said it was her biggest fault.

'Wonderful!' said Mrs Sanderson, more pink-cheeked than ever. 'And which philosophers do you read?'

Natalie could backtrack or push on. She chose to push on. 'I like... Richmal Crompton...' She began explaining the many-layered pleasures of her *Just William* books. Mrs Sanderson was so kind; she just nodded and didn't point out that children's writer Richmal Crompton wasn't in the philosophical canon just yet.

After she had gone on about William and Violet Elizabeth Bott for what seemed like for ever, Mrs Sanderson interrupted. She managed to do this delicately somehow, so that it was more of a nudge than an interruption:

'So, Natalie, won't you tell me about your family in Vienna?'

Keeping in mind Rachel's advice before she left – *You don't have to tell everyone everything* – Natalie launched in. Rachel was the family musician: violin, viola and superb at everything really; she was also the family beauty. Men literally fell over when they caught a glimpse of her (it had happened at least twice). Libby was the youngest, a proud sportsgirl, running mostly the 400 and 800 metres – and the relay – and wasn't that unusual in a girl? Mama, Dora Leeman, the family matriarch, was a wonderful storyteller. Kind and forgiving, and with a smile that would launch ships or sink them...

It sounded too pat, too pigeon-holed somehow, so Natalie added, 'But actually my family are wonderful at everything they do. They are complete all-rounders.'

She gulped. Now that just sounded immodest, which was not good etiquette either (Chapter 8 – 'Things that offend the English').

Mrs Sanderson said, 'I'm sure they are,' giving Natalie that warm feeling that someone liked her. 'And your father?'

'He died four years ago.'

'I'm sorry.'

'It's not your fault.' Natalie used the sing-songy voice she always felt obliged to use when the subject of Papa came up.

'But tell me, Natalie, didn't your sisters want to come to England with you?'

'Oh… well, Rachel has only recently married Leo – only two weeks ago. And you should have seen the magnificent wedding, he's from a very distinguished family – Mama says they are actually the poshest people she's ever met. They play in the orchestra together, you see, he's brass, and there will be tours and…'

She was doing it again. Rachel, who was a master at keeping herself to herself, would want to kill her.

Mrs Sanderson had driving glasses, straight at the top, curved at the bottom. When she came to a stop because of traffic – there were horses ahead – she looked over them curiously.

'You know, there are wonderful orchestras in London.'

'Ye-ss.' *Where was this conversation going?* 'I imagine there are.'

'And Libby? She could have come, couldn't she?'

'Well, she'll be representing our district soon. She's awfully fast. You wouldn't think so if you looked at her, she looks just like a little rat, really. No, not a rat, um, or a pretty rat, do you know what I mean? And she's… she's just turned things around at school. It would be a shame to have her… go through more upheaval. She does struggle with her schoolwork, you see. So we want to keep things… simple for her. She's always said the letters swim. I've never seen swimming letters. Have you?'

'I haven't.'

'And she used to be quite the bed-wetter so…'

There. She had done it again.

'But the discrimination?'

So, that was what Mrs Sanderson was getting at.

'We haven't noticed anything new. It's not like Germany. We have so many things in common with Germany, but we are quite a different country as well, you know. And it's forbidden for Germany to try and unify with us and we wouldn't want to anyway… well, *I* wouldn't want to. Some people would.'

Natalie thought of her Great-Uncle Ben, family maverick. He might.

She continued. 'Anyway, you see my family are not even very Jewish. We don't do anything. We don't go to the *shul* even on high days or holy days. Papa disagreed with organised religion. He was…' Natalie trailed off. Rachel really would be shaking her head by now. *You told her what? Blabbermouth.*

'A communist?'

'A social democrat. He worked very hard for social justice. That was kind of his religion. And Mama is the same. No, she is worse… she doesn't even believe in God at all!'

'But aren't you worried?'

Should she be more worried?

A couple of months ago, someone had attempted to paint a swastika on the optician's shutters, but a little run of paint had dripped off each point, it was a mess. Everyone gathered in the street and had agreed it was awful, awful that it would happen *here in Vienna! Of all the places!* and they decided unanimously it had been kids. *Just kids. Kids like to shock, that's all.* For a while, Natalie had kept an eye out to see if she could catch the perpetrators, but she soon forgot.

'If it gets too bad,' she started again, 'we'll reconsider. But we are confident that it will pass. I'll be back next year so I'll see how it is. These things happen. We were a powerful empire and then we were not. We had a royal family and then we did not.'

Natalie knew she sounded much older than her years. She continued, feeling quite profound.

'There is deprivation, unemployment and homelessness now – possibly more than before – but it won't always be like that. It's like our Ferris wheel in Prater Park – we rise, we fall. It's what we have come to expect.'

Natalie looked at Mrs Sanderson for approval. No matter what Rachel said, people *do* love to share information. Mrs Sanderson, however, continued to frown at the road ahead. Perhaps she did not agree but was too polite to say? Natalie decided to take control of the conversation and to steer its subject to the thing she preferred talking about.

'I do have a special friend back home, who I'm going to miss awfully.'

Mrs Sanderson's expression softened. She eyed Natalie indulgently. 'Ah, a *special* friend? A boyfriend, you mean?'

'He's not *quite* a boyfriend as such. His name is Rudi Strobl. S-T-R-O-B-L. It's a strange spelling, right? Nothing has happened between us yet. We haven't *declared* our feelings as such. But is it odd to say that I feel we are together? No, that's wrong. We're not together, quite clearly we're very far apart, never further, but in my mind, it is as though he is mine and I am his.'

That wasn't exactly it, but it was the best Natalie could come up with. This was her third language after all. Perhaps it could be explained better in the more romantic French?

'I *think* I know what you mean. I had a sweetheart like that once.' Mrs Sanderson patted Natalie's cold knee. 'And it was wonderful.'

'Oh, it is!' Natalie thought of the time he kissed her over the kitchen table, so soft, so adorable, and the way he shook his head, 'we shouldn't…' just as Libby had come bowling in.

'How do you know this Rudi Strobl then?'

'I know him very well,' Natalie told her, misty-eyed. 'Maybe better than anyone else in the world.'

Mrs Sanderson cleared her throat. 'I meant, how did you meet?'

'Oh! Not only is he one of my neighbours but he's also been helping me improve my English.'

They were old friends. They used to shine their torches into each other's bedroom windows, late at night when the moon was high in the sky and back when the age difference – only three years – didn't feel so large. But then, overnight it seemed, Rudi grew up, and became a student at the University of Vienna. For a couple of years, they didn't see each other much. Her torch remained ready on the top of the closet, but he never flashed the light over at her. Recently though, Mama had paid Rudi to tutor Natalie. He was a scientist, a biologist, but he was skilled at languages too, and over the last six months, a fondness – dare she say, an intimacy? – had grown between them while they were knee-deep in dictionaries.

Rudi had pushed her about England. He had a theory that a translator must have lived in a foreign country to be taken seriously. You had to get under its skin. Put it under the telescope. And Natalie intuitively knew that if Rudi was ever to take *her* seriously then she would have to live in a foreign country too. Rudi had lived in France as a boy and he rhapsodised about it. It wasn't just Paris that he loved, he said, it was coming back home and seeing it all with fresh eyes: *you look around and see what you have and—* Natalie knew she would feel the same.

He and Mama used to talk about England sometimes, after their lessons, when Mama was looking for her purse. One time, Natalie had gone into the hall, where they were talking so animatedly it sounded like they were arguing; but when they saw her, they laughed.

'We were agreeing,' they protested. 'We both think England would be fantastic for you!'

Mrs Sanderson started the car again.

'And does your mother approve of Rudi?'

A question only a mother would ask.

'She likes him.' Natalie decided she wouldn't mention that, with the exception of Rachel who knew *everything*, her family had no idea that feelings had 'progressed'. Rudi wasn't Jewish – Mama didn't mind that, she always said 'you can't help who you fall in love with' – but she preferred another neighbour, Arno, who also wasn't Jewish but was 'more the right age' and 'a sweetheart' and 'Natalie, *he* would never try to tell you what to do'.

'I don't think she would want us to marry, necessarily or...' Natalie paused, 'immediately, but she always respected him. She says he'll go far.' She nodded fiercely to herself. 'And he will. Rudi is extremely clever.'

Far cleverer in fact than Leo, Rachel's boyfriend – no, her *husband* – who was rather soft and insubstantial. It was painful to think that Rachel was married now. It was wrong but Natalie did feel slightly abandoned – it was just that they used to be such a *team* and she had expected for them to be a team for many more years, but Rachel had cut that short. Rachel had had different plans. And Rachel was not just married, she was married to the upper crust. The Goldbergs had more staff than Natalie's family had hot dinners. The Goldbergs were one of Vienna's finest families.

'Please tell me about *your* people, Mrs Sanderson?' She had done exactly what Rachel had told her not to do: she had blathered her mouth off to a virtual stranger and now this poor woman knew her entire life-history while Natalie knew approximately nothing about her. She would make a lousy spy.

'Well, my husband works away but I have two daughters at home, Isabella and Catherine—'

Isabella and Catherine? They sounded wonderful. 'I'm looking forward to meeting them,' Natalie interrupted. *Here I go again.* But she *was* looking forward to meeting the Sanderson girls. If they were anything like their mother, she envisaged them having a fine old time together.

The car stopped abruptly. Mama's suitcase, which had been on the bench behind them, clattered onto the floor. Mrs Sanderson looked shocked. 'I'm dreadfully sorry, Natalie,' she said. 'I should have been clearer. Forgive me.'

She was not Natalie's employer; she was Cousin Leah's employer. Leah, who wrote every two months or so that Natalie or her sisters must plan to come to England. Leah, who had been in London working as a cook for three years. Natalie's employer would be Mrs Caroline Caplin, who couldn't be here today. Family crisis or whatnot. Mrs Sanderson looked so embarrassed; and there was something else – an edge to her voice – that Natalie couldn't place. She kept touching her boat-hat even though it looked perfect.

'I should have explained properly. I am so sorry.'

'Oh well, that's more friends for me then.' Natalie didn't want Mrs Sanderson to feel more mortified than she evidently did. 'If Mrs Caplin is only half as nice as you then I'm sure she is nice.'

This made Mrs Sanderson smile, revealing all her lovely yellow teeth. She looked Natalie directly in the eyes. 'You will be happy with the Caplins, I assure you. And you will love their little boy.'

It's a boy! At this Natalie's heart really did sink. How was she, the middle of three sisters, to know anything about the care of small boys? But Natalie didn't say that. She had to be good. She could manage it for the first few days at least, surely?

In Vienna, on Kartner Strasse, there is a toy shop where you can buy a marionette of just about anything. Soldiers, ghosts, the Grim Reaper without a face. In one section, which Mama kept steering her away from, there were naked bodies complete with hair in *all* the right places. Natalie was pulled towards the sea-themed area, where the pirates and mermaids vied for attention. 'Everyone loves a sailor,' Mama said, laughing, pulling the strings to make the little fella kick his heels. On the rare occasion Natalie managed to get Mama all to herself, they both became exuberant and silly.

The selection had been narrowed down to two: a princess and a – Natalie wasn't sure what she was – a lifelike woman in a fitted suit and high heels. Perhaps she was a translator, like Natalie aspired to be, or a secretary? Her fingers were spaced out and as you moved the strings, it was like she was typing. She was adulthood personified. The princess was adorable too. She had a tiara, a ball-gown and a tiny pearl necklace, and she looked like a fantasy figure far from everyday life.

Mama had stared at Natalie's choices. 'What if it's a boy, though? Do you think he would prefer these?'

'Good grief, it won't be a boy,' Natalie had told her confidently. 'There's no way anyone would want *me* to look after a boy.'

'I have presents for the child,' Natalie said now. On that shopping trip she had eventually selected a third puppet that hadn't been in the initial running at all. It was a grey horse with the most magnificent teeth. It had curly acrylic eyelashes and a tail made of crinkly wool. It was perfect. If the child didn't like it, there would have to be something wrong with him.

Mrs Sanderson nodded. 'Hugo will be thrilled.'

'I hope so.' Natalie stared out the window at the English rain, the English trees and the English cars. She had been so pleased with Mrs Sanderson. And now this. A small boy. 'I spent most of my pocket money on it.'

Mrs Sanderson glanced at her sideways. 'If there are any problems, you will let me know, won't you?' But it was as though all the air, the lightness and the fun, had gone out the car. And all Natalie could think was, *what problems are you expecting?*

'You must be looking forward to seeing your cousin.'

'Very much,' lied Natalie, looking guiltily at her fingers in her lap. Then, when she was sure Mrs Sanderson wasn't looking, she bit the tip of her thumbnail clean off.

The rain continued. English had all the best words for rain: pelting, drenching, drizzle, chucking it down. Natalie related them to Mrs Sanderson, who admitted she hadn't thought much about it, but yes, oh yes, isn't that something! The neighbourhoods were becoming more residential, like the outskirts of Vienna, where the bigger houses are and the more elderly people live.

Mrs Sanderson brought the car to a halt in the street. You could tell she was proud of her house from the way she said, 'Welcome to my home.'

It was the stuff of picture books. Rose trellis up the front walls, fresh-white-shuttered windows; it looked happy and inviting. It was not a mansion; it was not a classic home for debutante balls or banquets, but it was where the nicer characters in Jane Austen's novels might have moved to in harder times.

And then Cousin Leah, who Natalie wouldn't have put in a picture book, appeared from a side gate and kissed Natalie briskly on just one cheek as though the effort of two was quite beyond her.

Mrs Sanderson surveyed them both happily and rubbed her hands.

'Well, I'm running late as usual.'

'Ha!' Natalie said. They both turned to her. Leah had one eyebrow raised and the other eyebrow seemed to be saying *shut up*.

'Sorry! I just… No, nothing.'

Mrs Sanderson shook Natalie's hand again. 'I'm going to the track, Leah. Do give your cousin some food and drink. Poor girl must be famished.'

*

Leah was as unemotional as Natalie remembered her. Tall and busty – Natalie only came up to her chin – and her hair was pulled back so tightly that all you could see of it were a few sparse, sweaty tendrils on her forehead.

Rachel would love to hear this.

Their mothers were sisters, but they had fallen out over Natalie's father. The Bergman family did not like the radical young man, Paul Leeman, who Natalie's mother had fallen in love with twenty-five years previously. They still saw each other, but both sides of the family had been hurt. Leah was an only child of older parents and her mother, Aunt Ruth, was Natalie's least favourite aunt. Leah was the most stodgy and annoying of all her cousins (and she had a vast number of stodgy and annoying ones to choose from). Leah was spoilt – Rachel and Natalie were convinced she thought the sun and the moon revolved around her. A Leah-centric view of the universe. At family do's, weddings and bar mitzvahs, Leah would hunch over the buffet and explain how the dishes could be improved on. She was fastidious about seasoning. At Seder nights while poor Libby, as the youngest, was entreated upon to read aloud, Leah's eyes would glaze over and she would absently pick at the unleavened bread until Aunt Ruth slapped her hand.

Leah was quite possibly the last person you would ever have expected to go overseas or even to leave her family home, but she apparently wanted to open an English restaurant in Vienna one day. According to Leah's mother, there would be an infinite demand for her daughter's English lamb stew and dumplings.

Mama was very fond of Leah and, although it seemed a mysterious affliction to her daughters, she wouldn't hear a word against her. Every two months or so, letters from Leah would stir in Mama some strange mix of excitement, pleasure and fear. 'Leah says you must go to England, girls,' she would announce. 'She will find you domestic work.'

Rachel would raise her perfect eyebrows, for she was destined for one of the country's top orchestras. 'Uh huh, Mama, maybe one day.' Then she would mouth at Natalie, 'No way!'

Natalie might also make a face, but Mama had eyes in the back of her head when it came to her and invariably, she was caught. 'Natalie, stop it.'

'It wasn't just—'

'Stop it, I say! Leah is very generous to think of you. And this is an opportunity. Think about it. Please.'

Leah led Natalie down some concrete steps to a basement kitchen where there was a vast stove with three saucepans cooking on it and a long wooden table laid for ten. Natalie's first impression was how cosy it was. The second was – *Leah is in charge of this? Impressive.*

Leah explained that she had arrived on the day of the Jewish festival of Yom Kippur, and the Sandersons had lit a candelabra here for her. It was the loveliest welcome she could have imagined. And the Sandersons did their best to find her kosher food even though she had more or less given up on it here. Natalie was surprised at this detail because while her family ate just about everything – Mama drew the line only at a pork chop – Aunt Ruth was very devout.

'The Sandersons treat me as one of the family.'

'Are they Jewish then?' Natalie asked. Mrs Sanderson hadn't given her a sign. (Not that there *was* a sign – they weren't the Freemasons – but still.)

'Good grief, no,' Leah said. But they said – no, insisted – she must feel at home and it was good for the children to learn about different cultures and ways. Mr Sanderson, like his unusual wife, was an academic, but he lived during term-times in Calcutta, India, so it was mostly Mrs Sanderson and the children, although there were always friends from the university calling over. Philosophers, historians, scientists, writers. Once, even J.R. Tolkien came for tea.

Natalie's heart was still thumping wildly.

'And my people, Leah? What are the Caplins like?'

Leah looked even more serious than usual. 'You'll find out soon enough.'

The teapot was dressed in the kind of woollen hat Rachel always wore ice-skating. Even stranger was the tea itself – imagine Libby's reaction if anyone had dared serve this! (Libby did not suffer milk gladly.)

Leah said, 'This is how the English like their tea.'

Natalie heard: *you ought to know.*

'When in Rome…' Natalie said, bringing cup to mouth. Leah looked like she wanted to explain something further but then changed her mind.

Natalie had brought a letter for Leah from Aunt Ruth, which Leah scanned unemotionally. Then they caught up on other family affairs. After about an hour or so had passed, Leah announced she would take Natalie to the Caplins' house.

'You're allowed to borrow the car?'

What Natalie meant was, *you can drive? Wow.* Another exciting piece of information to tell Rachel.

'When Mr Sanderson is away, yes.'

Leah fixed on large driving goggles and then driving gloves. She looked like a studious fish. 'And he's often away. I've been lucky,' she finished sternly.

It had stopped raining, Natalie noted approvingly, as they walked out to the car. This sky was a far more appropriate colour for the time of year.

'I hope we can see each other lots.' Natalie surprised herself by meaning it. There was something unexpectedly soothing about Leah's assured company. And although she hadn't been nervous about meeting her family, the Caplins, before, now the time was approaching, she really was.

Leah placed a gloved hand on Natalie's elbow. 'This *isn't* a jolly, you know. Life in England is hard, and you are here to work. The Sandersons are good people, but I still work from six most mornings to nine at night. And you will too at the Caplins'. Possibly more.'

'I'm not afraid of hard work,' Natalie said, trying not to sound sulky. She thought of the time she had forgotten her chemistry homework and it took her until three in the morning to copy out the periodic table.

'Natalie, you *do* understand why you're here—'

'Yes.' That was another thing about Leah. She always thought everyone was more stupid than she was. 'I'm going to be a nanny.' Natalie still couldn't get over the fact that she had been lumbered with one small boy when she had been looking forward to two or three older girls. This didn't seem fair.

'And?'

'And…' *What did Leah want from her?* 'I'm here to improve my language skills.'

Natalie wasn't going to share with Leah her plan of translating Kurt Brunner's children's book *Making an Elephant out of a Mosquito*. Leah wouldn't appreciate it.

'It's *not* just that,' Leah said. 'I've been begging Aunt Dora to send you for months. The situation for the Jewish people is worsening—'

'In *Germany*,' Natalie interrupted impatiently. She could be fierce too. 'Things are fine in Austria, Leah!'

'Fine? Our chancellor was assassinated by Nazis.'

'Yes, but—'

'Backed up against the wall. They wouldn't even send for a priest! State-sanctioned murder. And the anti-Semitism is rising… you know it is, you *must* know. So many paths closed to us too. So many restrictions.'

'It's always been like this. Don't you remember the reign of Karl Lueger?'

Natalie didn't *personally* remember Karl Lueger, and Leah wouldn't either, it was before their time, but this was what Mama said. Mama was just a girl when Karl Lueger became the Mayor of Vienna, but she remembered seeing the nasty cartoons in the newspapers where the bankers were always Jewish people portrayed counting money, the crude headlines, the whispered conspiracies, the university students thrown out. The restrictions on jobs. The never-ending red tape. The aftermath of the Dreyfus Affair. But there were too many of them now. Too many Jews, too many professionals. They *were* the Viennese middle class now. So, what could the right-wingers do? They couldn't *all* lose their jobs. They'd be no doctors left, nor dentists. Everyone in Vienna would have rotten teeth!

Leah looked annoyed. 'People think trouble will come to Austria soon, and I do too. We must plan.'

Natalie thought, *what does she know?* Leah hadn't even set her unfashionable brogues in Vienna for the past three years. And again, this was so typical of Leah. She had to be more of an expert than anyone else. She was always so black and white and strident when the rest of them were wading around in grey nuance. Mama always made excuses for her, but it was exasperating.

Natalie didn't say that though – she had to be good – so resentfully, she held her tongue. She had a sudden new realisation that this might be what being good meant. It was not saying what you wanted to say for fear of offending someone; it was chewing back words.

'You're here because it's safer.'

'I hardly think London is safer than—'

'If it gets worse back there, you will be able to help.'

Natalie wanted to snort. Her interests were mostly linguistic. How could she possibly help? *By telling everyone how the present participle works? Or the past perfect of a gerund?*

'It might not come to anything, but it might, Natalie. I tried to persuade Aunt Dora to come as well, but she wouldn't. She would only agree to send you.'

'Well then, it can't be *that* bad!' Natalie couldn't let Leah have the final word, she just couldn't. 'If they're staying. Don't you see?'

*

They pulled up outside an elegant double-fronted, cream-coloured house. The Caplins clearly had serious money. More money than the Sanderson family. This was a level of wealth probably on a par with Leo Goldberg's family. The house was detached and had an air of emotional detachment too. There was an extended drive and a lawn – as big as a school playing field – which extended around both sides of the house and towards the back. The hedges were trimmed – one even seemed to have been shaped into a cat, but it was a bit of an unclear cat, with only two legs and one ear. At one end were rose bushes, all different colours, and they were in bloom. A wooden sign swung on the iron gate: 'Larkworthy'.

In Austria, Natalie's house did not have a garden – you opened the front door directly onto the street – but so few people there had gardens that she had never aspired to one. Gardens seemed to require an awful lot of attention that might otherwise be spent on books. This was impressive, though. On the front lawn, which seemed, impossibly, to be striped, there were at least twelve or so knee-high stone men. One of these was fishing, one was reading, one was smoking a cigar. All were grinning. *A religious thing?* Natalie looked for the one with the elephant head that she'd learned about last semester in school.

'Ganesh?'

'Garden gnomes.' Leah shrugged. 'The English like them.'

Looking at the creepy figures with the red hats and long beards, Natalie raised her eyebrows: 'What's not to like?'

Now she had reached her destination, Natalie was in no hurry to get out. She could have sat in the safety of the car all day long. Leah put a stop to that though: 'I really do have to make dinner. Mrs Sanderson has guests later – scientists from Cambridge,' she added proudly.

'Mrs Sanderson said she was going to the track? Does she ride horses?'

'She races dogs,' Leah said.

'Dogs?'

Leah shrugged again as if to say: '*That's the English for you.*' Then she hauled Natalie's Mama's honeymoon suitcase out of the car and placed it at Natalie's feet with a terse, 'Good luck.'

Natalie imagined a twinkly-eyed Mrs Caplin, full of apologies for not being at the station. Like Mrs Sanderson, she might compliment Natalie on undertaking such an arduous journey; she would also compliment her on her sophisticated level of English. Natalie would confide in Mrs Caplin about her hopes of translating *Making an Elephant out of a Mosquito* and doubtless Mrs Caplin would say she couldn't wait to read it and that she was a prolific reader or had friends in the publishing industry—

The door was swung open by a short, angry-looking woman with round spectacles and a handkerchief of a hat on her head.

'I'm the nanny. I've come from Austria,' Natalie said, proffering her hand. 'So far!'

The woman looked at it. Perhaps she was more of a kissing sort? 'The Caplins are away.'

'Away, where?' said Natalie before remembering her manners. 'My name is Natalie Leeman. And at least it has stopped the drizzle.'

'Makes no difference. They're not here.' *No, she was not a kisser.* 'What do they expect me to do with you?'

Natalie considered going back to the car. If the Sandersons were as generous as they seemed, surely they'd put up with a little stranger for the night? She would be more at home with scientists from Cambridge than with gnomes and this rude hanky-wearing lady. But no, the way Leah was waving so firmly from the driving-seat window made it more than abundantly clear that Natalie was to remain.

Finally, the woman huffed, 'I suppose you could help with the housework – just until they get back.' Out in the road, Leah sounded the horn, then drove away.

'Absolutely!' Natalie said, but her heart sank. *Housework? As if being a nanny to a small boy wasn't bad enough!*

CHAPTER TWO

The next morning, after a dispiriting breakfast of gluey paste – porridge, no syrup – Mrs Monger the housekeeper, the woman who had met Natalie the day before, shuffled her out the back door with a sack of potatoes, a saucepan of water and a knife.

'I thought the family were away?'

Mrs Monger guffawed. 'We still need to eat, child. There's you, me, Mol' and Alfie to feed today.'

Natalie's domestic incompetence was a family joke. She was a thinker, someone who was constantly ruminating on politics, psychology, the meaning of life. It had never once entered her head that she might have to peel vegetables. Mama was also a progressive, a woman's liberator; women did not have to do the chores. Women should not be chained to the kitchen sink. Besides, they paid their lovely Helga to help every day.

At home, Natalie did have some tasks; she was in charge of overseeing laying and clearing the table, but this was a task she never took seriously. Instead of putting the knives and forks in their rightful place, she poured them in the middle of the table and told everyone to pick a weapon. If there were books stacked there at mealtimes, and there usually were, she merely swept them aside and then, after dinner, restored them to their rightful place.

If you wanted something cleaned up or cooked or ironed, you'd ask (in this order): Helga, Mama, Libby, Rachel. You wouldn't ask Natalie.

Natalie sat down gloomily on the back step. A grey long-haired cat came to watch her and as soon as she saw it, Natalie knew it would make her sneeze. Animals were another thing she never had much success with.

Natalie tried to work out how many potatoes she had to do. Mrs Monger had been so vague. There were four of them eating, would they have four each? Sixteen? Possibly – who knew what the English liked? One. She had done one. Out the bag it had come, big and bold, but now it was feeble and tiny. She had taken off most of the skin, but most of the white part too. They'd need way more than four each of these tiny specimens. She tried another. To distract herself, she thought about her translation and all the interesting words she could use. It was a shame Kurt Brunner never mentioned rain in his book: Natalie could have written a thesis on that.

'That took nearly an hour,' Mrs Monger said accusingly when Natalie took the pan into the kitchen.

'How long should it take?'

Mrs Monger thought that was cheeky. Her eyes said she had never seen anyone so stupid in her life. Her *entire* life. She thrust a second sack of vegetables at Natalie. 'Ten minutes.'

It was Saturday morning, which meant Libby would be coming back roasty from a practice run, peeling off her damp socks, her plaits swinging like they had lives of their own. Rachel, by contrast, would be swanning in from a rehearsal, untouched – the girl with the world's smoothest hair. The most unblemished skin. The envy, if not of every girl in town then certainly of all Natalie's friends. Or perhaps Rachel didn't go home any longer; she most probably went back to the fashionable apartment where she and Leo Goldberg were now living and did whatever newlyweds did.

And Mama, the heart of them all, framing her morning as a funny anecdote: 'Well, you'll never guess who I saw at the shops today…' Always an incident, always some fat, fulsome tale to relate.

Later, Natalie looked up the word for *Heimweh*: 'Homesick'. Half a day in and she was sick for home. To cheer herself up, she imagined her dazzling return. She would be fluent in English, accent-less if possible, she would also be slimmer yet bustier, sophisticated and way more worldly. Mama would throw a party, where Natalie would regale her family with pithy observations about English culture and colloquialisms. She would charm Elizabet Steiner, Lena Schwartz and everyone at school by admitting that actually, she preferred Vienna all along. Overwhelmed with admiration, Rudi Strobl would ask her outside, they would talk about her work, Rudi would slowly kiss her…

At lunch, Natalie met the other members of staff. Alfie was a bad-tempered young man who looked after the garden and the motorcars. He lived in a room in the back of the garage. His hair was cut too short, which made his large purple ears look like handles on a jug. Natalie hoped she wasn't the cause of his bad temper – she certainly didn't seem to be helping. He came in, pulled off his muddy shoes and then stood by the fire, ranting.

'What language is he speaking?' she asked Mrs Monger.

Mrs Monger cackled while Alfie scowled furiously. 'That's the King's English!'

There was also a girl there with red hair and pale blue eyes who looked a bit like Libby's schoolfriend, Mina. She must have had some of Mina's spirit too, because when Mrs Monger asked her to budge along the bench, she refused.

'I was here first,' she said.

'Natalie sits where I can keep an eye on her,' Mrs Monger said firmly.

The girl still refused. 'We should take care of our own,' she muttered. She wouldn't look at Natalie, but kept her eyes on Mrs Monger. 'There's too many of 'em over here.' But Mrs Monger wasn't having it. She got to the girl in three strides and grabbed her by the arm.

'Ow! Aunty!' she cried.

'You're over there where I don't have to look at you,' Mrs Monger growled. Reluctantly, the girl gave up her seat.

'Natalie, this is my niece, Molly. Molly, this is Natalie. Respect, please.'

'You've got a funny accent,' said Molly. She was as pristine as a freshly made bed. Her hair was neatly styled, her shirt collar was gleaming white, and her black skirt fitted impeccably.

'I think *you* do,' Natalie retorted.

'At the house my sister is at, they've got a Jewish nanny from Germany. I guess you people like nannying.'

Natalie narrowed her eyes at her. 'I guess so.'

'She sings these brilliant songs. Everyone likes her.'

'And everyone may like Natalie too, eventually!' said Mrs Monger encouragingly as she brought the mashed potatoes to the table.

Mrs Monger looked at them all, then said, 'For what we are about to receive may the Lord make us truly thankful.'

Natalie raised her glass. 'Yes!'

Alfie and Molly mumbled, then tucked in. Natalie sawed at the meat on her plate. There was a pride to be had in watching everyone eat the potatoes and carrots she had laboured over, but before she had the chance to point that out, Alfie said, 'Blimey, large chunks today, Mrs Monger, are you trying to choke us?'

Natalie knew blimey was a derivative of 'blind me', but she didn't expect Alfie wanted someone to put a fork to his eye, tempting though it was.

Ignoring him, Natalie told Mrs Monger how she couldn't wait to meet the Caplins and that they would be enormous friends.

This cheered everyone. Alfie the miserable laughed the loudest of them all, and Natalie wished she hadn't said anything. They were probably jealous.

'You have no idea!' Mrs Monger said, dabbing her eyes with her napkin.

'How do you mean?'

But no one said.

*

That afternoon, Natalie mopped the floors of the hall and the dining room and then she swept the fireplaces – then she realised logic dictated she should have cleared the fireplaces before mopping, so she mopped all over again. Then she took the stick with the feathers at the end and proceeded to wag it around all shelves and tables. This was dusting.

The drawing room was filled with books. The Caplins simply had to be wonderful people! There was a ladder to reach the books on the higher shelves, which was something Natalie had seen and envied at the Goldberg family home. The furnishings in the drawing room were elaborate, with ornaments precariously placed towards edges – Natalie didn't knock any down and it was disappointing there was no one to witness how well she'd done. The only one interested was Tilly, the damn cat, and *she* made Natalie's eyes water.

She had been doing dusting without knocking over for some time when she spotted the day's newspaper. There was a lovely picture of the English King on the front, the handsome King Edward VIII. All English kings seemed to be unimaginatively called George, Henry or Edward. But then that was the same in Austria: they were all Ottos, Ferdinands and Leopolds.

The best photo was one of the King with his brother Albert, Duke of York, where he looked less formal, as though a friend had taken the shot. The brothers were both wearing enormous wide trousers and flat caps. Was this normal fashion or royal fashion? The King was smiling his heart out in this picture. He had an air of Hollywood heart-throb about him. Would it be better to be the King or the brother, Natalie wondered? The heir or the spare?

This was the kind of discussion Natalie would have *all* the opinions on when she returned to Vienna.

She was so immersed in the royals that she didn't hear Mrs Monger sidle up beside her.

'It'll be back to Mr Hitler for you!' the housekeeper bellowed, grabbing the duster and making as if to stick the feathers right in

Natalie's face. Although Natalie had suspected the woman had a temper, she hadn't anticipated this. Mrs Monger shouted that Natalie was not here to read but to make herself bloody useful. *How dare she? Pre-sump-tuous!* If Natalie wasn't bloody careful, Mrs Monger would put her on the first bloody train home again.

Mrs Monger seemed to think going back to Vienna would be Natalie's worst nightmare. Once behind her back, Natalie sniggered.

Natalie's bedroom was a good-sized bright room with a sash window that overlooked the striped front lawn. Natalie was not one to pay a great deal of attention to her surroundings, yet she knew it could have been worse. The furnishings comprised a single bed, which had some spring in it, a dark wardrobe that opened and shut nicely – an improvement on her squeaky one at home – and a chest of drawers that was presumably to double as a desk since a chair was facing it. The blankets were scratchy, a bit like those Mama had donated to the homeless soldiers, and Natalie yearned for her far more pleasant duvet. It was spring but the nights were unexpectedly cold. Later, she would come to realise there was no central heating in the house, none at all. It was still rare in England then, but she would get used to it – like she would have to get used to a lot of things.

Mama's suitcase sat open on the floor between bed and door. Natalie didn't know what the washing arrangements were in the Caplin household, but she suspected it wouldn't be easy. *Nothing* was going to be easy here. But worse, it was as though everything was somehow *deliberately* difficult. It was as though they liked things to be harder, the blankets to be scratchier, the vegetables to have less flavour.

What would her family be doing tonight?

Mama would be sewing, eyes lowered, smiling at some secret thought or squinting at the newspapers or dreaming up a funny story. Rachel would be entertaining guests, eyeing up Leo playing the cello with his soft hands. Libby would be snoring after an afternoon's vigorous exercise in the programme for gifted girls.

And Rudi Strobl? What would he be doing?

He *had* knocked at their house before she left, apparently, but Natalie was out with Elizabet Steiner and Lena Schwartz – they were swearing to be best friends for ever – and unfortunately it was Libby who had opened the door. 'He said he will think of you,' Libby had reported vaguely. Out of all of them, it had to be Libby who had been at home (Libby had many talents, but message-passing wasn't one of them).

Was he thinking of her now?

CHAPTER THREE

Natalie's first week continued in much the same fashion as her first day. An unedifying combination of dusting, cleaning, peeling and mopping. She and Molly grew acclimatised to each other if not great friends. Molly's favourite topic was 'chaps'. She had an impressive array of words for men – almost as many as there were for rain. Alfie was not a gentleman, Molly declared, laughing, and Natalie agreed, for he remained sulky and bad-tempered towards her. She thought about asking him what his problem was, but the direct approach didn't seem to come under being 'good', so she refrained.

Molly lived out, so most of Natalie's time not working was spent alone. Sharing a room with her older sister in Vienna, Natalie had always thought she would love solitude, but instead she found it surprisingly lonely. She ached to share her thoughts with someone. More than once in those early days, Natalie contemplated returning to Vienna, *that would show Mrs Monger!* Only the thought of navigating her way to the train station and beyond, then facing the twin prongs of Rudi and Mama's disappointment, was too much. Naturally, Mama would wear her stoical face, but she wanted Natalie to make something of herself and this was the path Natalie had chosen, so this was the path she should walk.

One Thursday morning, after Natalie had been in England for ten days, she heard a shriek from the hall.

'They're on their way!' Mrs Monger screeched, breaking her own rule about shouting between floors.

'How long have we got?' Molly shrieked back.

'Thirty minutes at most?'

They whirled around like bluebottles. Dusting, straightening, shining, reordering. Mrs Monger took yesterday's flowers away – even though there was nothing wrong with them – and replaced them with fresh ones in vases in the hall, the dining room and the drawing room.

Natalie went up to her room to spy on the arrivals. It wasn't long before a beautiful modern car, more modern even than the Sandersons', had pulled up onto the shingle.

A boy hopped from out the back. He had dark brown hair cut in an unnatural circle shape. He was not chubby exactly, but looked chunky and strong. Three steps out from the car, he tripped over the gravel. Even from up at the window, Natalie winced, expecting tears, but he got himself up, brushed himself down and carried on towards the front door.

Mrs Caplin took her time to emerge. Cigarette in hand, neat handbag dangling from her wrist, she was what Great-Uncle Ben would call 'shapely'. Whether she was pleased to be back after her time away, it was hard to tell. She did have a serene, satisfied look about her as she glanced towards the house. She must have sensed she was being stared at, for she looked up to Natalie at the window. Natalie cowered as Mrs Caplin waved.

Natalie dashed downstairs and stood excitedly between Mrs Monger and Alfie in the long, cool hallway. Molly had disappeared.

'Brace yourself,' Mrs Monger said, more to herself than anyone. 'Here we go.'

Alfie snorted, then whispered some swear-words Natalie couldn't catch. Mrs Monger pushed her hair into her cap. Natalie arranged her feet on the black-and-white checked tiled floor so they didn't cross any lines. She *was* going to be *so good*; Mama wouldn't recognise her.

'You-know-who hasn't come back then,' Mrs Monger whispered, but before Natalie could ask what she meant, the door opened.

'I'm Natalie Leeman from Vienna. Which is in Austria. So excellent to meet you at long last.'

Alfie was silently shaking with laughter next to her.

Mrs Caplin smiled and blinked. Her hand was softer than feathers. Natalie liked her enormously – and her first impressions were rarely wrong. Here was a friend. Somehow, it was clear: Mrs Caplin was going to change her life.

'Hello Natalie Leeman,' she said pronouncing the words clearly and loudly as though Natalie was hard of hearing. 'I'm Mrs Caplin. How excellent to meet you too.'

'What a gorgeous automobile! I've never seen one of those before. That type, I mean, not the automobile itself, we have them in Vienna. And isn't the weather pleasant for the time of year? When I arrived, it was raining.' This didn't seem worth mentioning on its own so she added, 'cats and the dogs.'

'She likes to talk,' said Mrs Monger.

Mrs Caplin laughed. 'Some people have a lot to say. Now, has anyone ever told you that you look like someone from the Bible?'

Natalie touched her curly hair. There she had been thinking she came across as quite the modern thing.

'Which one?' she asked. *Adam? Eve? Job?*

'I mean that as a compliment,' Mrs Caplin laughed again. 'Black eyebrows are fashionable and that little bit there in the middle… nice.'

Mrs Monger and Mrs Caplin went to the living room while the boy jogged upstairs. Natalie wasn't invited, but then neither was Alfie. She was about to ask him what to do, but he shrugged his annoying shoulders and sloped off down towards the kitchen. Natalie stayed behind the shut door. This wasn't as she had expected. She wondered whether she should run upstairs and fetch the horse marionette that was dangling from her wardrobe, but she didn't want to miss out on anything here.

Silence. Then Mrs Monger's voice.

'To be honest, she's not a great cleaner, ma'am. Molly does a better job.'

Mrs Monger sounded different to usual. Almost pleading or appealing. 'She's fourteen, but a super hard worker. She'll have more of a clue in the kitchen than Miss Hoity Toity here.'

'It's not settled what she does though, is it? She'll have to do what needs doing.'

Mrs Monger's voice was strained. 'So, are you suggesting we get someone else in for Hugo?'

'I'm not *suggesting* anything, I'm just pointing out that it might be less... controversial if she cleans? For now, I mean. Given the situation. We never know how the master is going to react, do we?'

Mrs Monger said something that Natalie didn't hear. It was frustrating.

There was another pause. A very long pause. Then Mrs Caplin said something, also too quiet for Natalie to catch, and Mrs Monger added something that might have been, 'Shall we wait for Mr Caplin?' and finally, Mrs Caplin spoke again. Natalie couldn't tell if she was agreeing or not.

Mrs Monger came out first, closing the door carefully behind her as though sealing in a fire. When she saw Natalie standing there, she startled, then tried to make her face look stern, but she only looked concerned.

Mrs Caplin came out of the room next, moving briskly. Her mint green dress made a shushing sound like reeds brushing. Ignoring Mrs Monger, she reached out and took Natalie's hands between hers. Her blue eyes were clear and searching; Natalie told herself to remember this. It felt like an important moment.

'I don't know how things are done in your country,' Mrs Caplin said. A tremor of anxiety ran through Natalie. *I don't know how things are done in my country either. I've only ever gone to school.* 'But I want you to know you're *very* welcome here. I am a great friend of the Jewish people. A great, great friend.'

Natalie didn't know whether that was the moment to tell her she wasn't religious. She didn't want to let her down in any way.

'I was having a small discussion with Mrs Monger about the exact nature of your role.'

Her lashes were long and curled. You could see each individual one of them. Her eyeballs were like gemstones. Her cheeks were smooth and pale like a china doll that Libby used to cart around.

'I... I thought I would...' Natalie tried again. 'I came to be the nanny. That was the idea.'

'And so you will be,' Mrs Caplin said, shooting a glance at Mrs Monger. 'I expect.'

'I don't want to create any problems,' Natalie felt tearful suddenly – *where did she stand?* It seemed she was the cause of a dispute. Should she go home? But now the thought of returning to Austria early – in under one month! – would be a disaster. A humiliation. She could imagine her family gossiping: 'They sent her home!' No, the sympathy would be worse than the gossips. Rachel and Mama putting their arms around her: 'Well, you did your best... Not everyone has the gumption to do well abroad.' Rudi, arms crossed: 'Really? Oh, such a shame, Natalie, shame!' She flushed red, just thinking about it.

What *would* the master say? Was Mr Caplin so unpredictable? But Mrs Caplin, oh so kindly, reached out for her hands again, squeezed them and with great passion declared, '*You* are not the problem, always remember that. Let's see how we get on, shall we?'

Hugo was waiting for her apparently, in the nursery. Natalie walked up, aware that Mrs Caplin and Mrs Monger were watching her every step. She wanted to do this right. The door was slightly ajar. She opened it and a cushion fell slap bang on her head. She had fallen for the oldest trick in the book.

'Owww!' To be fair, it was the indignity of it that hurt most. That and the shock. But she knew she mustn't react, not with everyone listening. She had to be good.

The boy pointed and said, 'Ha ha! You should have seen your face!'

'Very good,' agreed Natalie. 'Super fun. You must be Hugo.'

'Must I?'

Natalie wished Molly had warned her. Or Mrs Monger. A little advance information would have helped. When Natalie had thought about working in England – and to be fair, she had given it little in-depth consideration, it had been arranged so quickly – she had pictured looking after a child about Libby's age. Ten-year-old Libby required little attention; she was as self-contained as a cardboard box. She was an enigma, always out running or swimming or training.

This boy was a fidget. His feet kept tapping and his fingers were all over the place, scratching, picking, digging up his nose. His cheeks wobbled. He pushed his weird hair from his forehead.

He threw himself on his bed. 'London is the absolute pits.' *What did he mean?* The boy's face was such a picture of grumpiness it was impossible not to laugh. This made him worse. He kicked his feet against the mattress.

'I'm far too old for a stupid nanny.'

'Excellent,' she told him. 'Because you don't have a stupid nanny, you have a clever nanny.'

He sat up and stared. Then, like his mother, he blinked slowly. Natalie never knew a blink could be so powerful.

'Says who?'

'Says me.'

'Says me and whose army?'

From that moment on, Natalie adored Hugo Caplin.

CHAPTER FOUR

Mrs Caplin wanted Natalie and Hugo to breakfast in French and dine in German. Natalie said, 'That's fine, *d'accord, bien.*' Hugo, however, had different plans. He wanted them to breakfast with dinosaurs and dine in jungles while throwing cushions and beanbags at Natalie's head.

Hugo was not a bookish boy. Reading for him was not escape but a prison. He hated being indoors, wanted to go back to Dorset, where he was free to play with the animals, observe insects and put his head in the water tank. He also had no aptitude for languages or music. The only time he would sit still was for drawing, tongue out, crayon gripped. He loved art. He also loved his horse marionette, and this thrilled Natalie. Few things warm the heart like a successfully chosen present. She made Mr Horsey dance for him with the strings. She became adept at manoeuvring the two sticks of wood to make Mr Horsey trot, canter and gallop or all three, one after the other.

For all Leah's warnings that it was unrelentingly hard work in England, Natalie enjoyed her days. Sometimes she found it hard to believe that she was getting paid for playing noughts and crosses or battleships. (She wasn't getting paid a great deal, after food and board, but it was more than your average sixteen-year-old student in Vienna could be expected to earn.) Hugo was not what she had expected or hoped for, but he was charming company, easy to be with and he liked to have a go at everything. She told him that he had springs instead of feet. She understood that the English phrase was *live wire.* Or as Alfie said after Hugo surprised him with a beanbag over the banisters: *little sod.*

Natalie had only two disappointments in those early weeks. One was how little everyone back home wrote. She had not expected much from her family – none of whom were *particularly* keen correspondents – but she had hoped better of her friends, and especially of Rudi. Their relationship – if they even had a relationship – was an elastic being constantly stretched, and it was now stretched so taut, it cut into one's fingers.

About one month after she arrived, she got a note saying: *I'm thinking of you,* but *I'm thinking of you* wasn't a lot to go on. Rudi was probably occupied with test tubes or student politics, she knew that, but still. *I love you* might have lasted. *I want to marry you, come home* would definitely have caused a stir, but *I'm thinking of you?* What did that evoke? It was the exact same words Natalie had written to Aunt Ruth after her latest bout of gout.

Impetuously, Natalie had dashed off a note saying, *I wish you would write more,* but after she had sent it, she wished she could fish it out of the letter box. *An English lady doesn't court attention,* said her etiquette book. Or, as Alfie said when she asked him to move his shoe polish from the doorstep because she had carrots to peel, 'Nobody likes a nag.'

The other disappointment was how rarely Natalie got to see the fragrant Mrs Caplin. She had hoped that they might spend time together, the three of them, but Mrs Caplin disappeared most days from about eleven in the morning until about two and then again in the evening. She hardly ever spent time with Hugo. If Hugo was disappointed, he didn't show it, although occasionally he drew pictures of Mrs Caplin waving from motorcars.

'Where does she go?' Natalie asked Mrs Monger.

Mrs Monger shrugged, but Natalie knew the way Mrs Monger worked now. She would say nothing, nothing, nothing, then she'd crack. Eventually, she would 'spill the beans'.

'Auditioning,' Mrs Monger said finally.

There was a Steinway piano in the drawing room, but Mrs Caplin didn't touch it. If Rachel had been there, she would have been playing Bach all day long. Natalie was supposed to encourage Hugo to practise but he was terrible, and she didn't know how far she was supposed to push him.

'Shows.' Mrs Monger explained that Mrs Caplin was an actress. Mrs Monger also told her Mrs Caplin was twenty-four. Which meant she was only eight years older than Natalie.

'She had Hugo young,' Natalie said.

Mrs Monger raised her eyebrows.

Natalie waited.

'We don't say that in England.'

'Oh.'

Two minutes later, Mrs Monger leaned across the table with her spatula. 'Very young and very soon after they married, if you get my drift.'

Hmm, thought Natalie. She knew what Mrs Monger was insinuating and she knew Mama would say, 'Don't judge, Natalie, unless you've walked a mile in their shoes.' But Natalie was not as restrained as Mama.

'And what's he like?'

'What's who like?'

'Mr Caplin.' She remembered Mrs Caplin's words – *it might be less controversial if she cleans? For now, I mean… We never know how the Master is going to react, do we?*

'He works hard.' Mrs Monger slung the tea towel onto the hook over the sink. She had an excellent aim. 'But he's complicated.'

'Isn't everyone?' said Natalie. She was glad when Mrs Monger smiled.

*

The walk to Hugo's village school took thirty minutes, but Natalie allowed forty-five. It wouldn't do to be hurried. On their way, Hugo and Natalie discussed what to do if Tyrannosaurus rex came back to life – run, fight, surrender? – and which were the worst of the biblical plagues (first locusts, second frogs).

The first time they parted at the gates, Natalie didn't know what to do (this wasn't in her etiquette book), and Hugo didn't either. He had explained that no one talked about his previous nanny any more.

Natalie devised a secret goodbye handshake just for them that became longer and longer until the person on playground duty blew a whistle next to her ear: 'Time, please!'

Back at the house, Natalie tidied, mopped and dusted Hugo's room, which often inexplicably resembled a jungle or a forest. She washed his nightclothes and bed linen every two days and prepared things for after school. Lunch was usually taken with Mrs Monger, Alfie and Molly and would usually be a sandwich – a slab of corned beef, Spam or cheese. For Natalie, lunchtime was invaluable – a lesson not just in English food and table manners but colloquialisms and anecdotes too. When she went back to Austria, she would hold court about the scandals she'd heard here. Mrs Monger caught her grinning once, and told her she looked like 'the cat that got the cream'.

At two thirty, Natalie left the house for the school and from then on, she existed solely for the amusement of Master Hugo. Playing with Hugo, arguing with Hugo, getting Hugo to do his languages, his music, and eat his supper.

One afternoon, Natalie found Alfie polishing shoes on the back doorstep, whistling and smiling to himself.

'Good, aren't I?' Alfie said, admiring his work. *Annoying man.*

'What was the nanny before me like?' Natalie had been mulling over her mystery predecessor for some time and Alfie seemed to enjoy being useful. The answer would give her a better picture of how this house worked – or rather, her place in it. Alfie gave a low whistle, then held the shoe up to the light.

'She was all right.'

'What happened to her?'

Alfie packed his tins and grubby cloths away. His fingers were black at the ends.

'Found her coming out of Mr Caplin's room when she shouldn't have been.' Alfie raised his eyebrows at her and simultaneously his earlobes waggled.

'Oh, I see,' Natalie said, blushing. Ah, so *that* was it. This was a twist she would write about, not to Mama, but to Rachel, who loved a romantic intrigue more than anything.

The weekends were the longest, since Natalie had to care for Hugo from when he woke up until his bedtime and overnight. However, once or twice a month, the Caplins took Hugo away to visit friends or family members and this was her free time. On those occasions, she went to spend lunchtime with Leah, a twenty-minute walk away, where Natalie would sit and watch her cousin slaving over a meatloaf or an apple crumble.

Leah's routine was more fixed. Mrs Sanderson didn't like her to work on Sundays and she had a half-day most Saturdays. Natalie couldn't decide if her own more ad hoc arrangement was preferable. Natalie probably had more time off than Leah did, but she never knew in advance, which meant planning could be tricky.

'Shouldn't you be doing chores?' Leah always greeted Natalie suspiciously, confirming Natalie's disloyal opinion that Leah was indeed a 'strange fish'.

Natalie thought of her suitcase still lying on her bedroom floor and how she needed to ask Mrs Monger about what to do with her own laundry. In the meantime, Natalie wore her knickers inside out and wished she weren't so ill-suited to domesticity.

'Not really,' she told Leah.

The Sandersons' kitchen had low lighting – Leah complained it was terrible for the eyes – and everything about it was warm and cosy, from the cushions tied onto the wooden chairs to soften the seat to the stripy tea towels.

Natalie enjoyed her time with Leah, although she was never sure Leah enjoyed it as much as she did. She always had something to grumble about, and she never asked Natalie how she was; nor would she engage in polite talk about the weather but barrelled straight in, asking how Natalie's mother was.

'Aunt Dora should come here,' she kept saying. 'I can see her here. And Libby and Rachel, of course. Wouldn't it be good?'

'What about Aunt Ruth?'

Leah would scowl. 'You know that she has her house in South of France, she will go there if things get worse.'

'*If*,' repeated Natalie daringly. She had forgotten Aunt Ruth's second home, although it had been the cause of much uproar when she had first inherited it from a forgotten French uncle.

'*When* they get worse,' pronounced Leah.

Natalie hated not seeing her family, but on the other hand, there was something quite wonderful about forging her way on her own in the world and having her own adventures. If Mama wanted to come here it would be joyful but seriously, why would she? Everything she loved was in Austria. Mama was no linguist either. She didn't have the ear or the enthusiasm. And you couldn't imagine Mama without her Austrian newspaper, her coffee, her pastries and her sewing machine. She would look positively underdressed! And Natalie would be home soon anyway.

Then Leah would inevitably say something absurd about how Vienna was 'finished'. *Over. Kaput.* And Natalie never knew quite how to respond to that.

Half in, half out of the family Caplin was a slightly strange place to be. Natalie's status – if that was the right word – was clear when she was cleaning. Then she was a member of staff, the lowest rung of the ladder. But she was also nanny, which was a rung or two up from domestic staff, so she was *kind* of part of the family. Oh, it was confusing. It made Natalie think of Helga. Natalie wished she could have gone back and said nicer things to the housekeeper – what a wonderful cheesecake, how do you iron so nicely? – instead of taking the dear woman for granted.

Maybe it was confusing for the Caplins too. It must have been confusing for Hugo – or maybe the children of the wealthy didn't find that sort of thing confusing? Often, Hugo called Natalie 'Mama' and then corrected himself, looking mortified. Natalie told him that she had once said 'Mama' to her French teacher, and worse than that, called her own Mama 'Herr Kramer', her most hated maths teacher.

'What did your mummy say?' Hugo asked, wide-eyed.

'She laughed and pretended to be Herr Kramer all afternoon!'

Leah had a bike, and Mrs Sanderson kindly offered Natalie hers, so the girls went out together in town. Wonderful to be pedalling around the streets like she used to back home. Natalie struggled with directions and never knew where she was going, but so long as she kept an eye on Leah's broad back, she knew they would be fine. Throughout April and May they did this every weekend if Natalie didn't have to mind Hugo. Week by week, Leah was softening towards her like butter – Austrian butter, not the dreadful margarine that Mrs Monger liked.

One Sunday, Natalie followed Leah on her bike down a narrow riverside path, away from the shopping area. Leah called out that she knew a place where they could sit and eat the bread pudding that she had made for them.

Natalie hoped Leah wouldn't start on about Mama again. Leah was obsessed with National Socialism. Rudi had been similar, but at least he read books and listened to public debates. He knew what he was on about, whereas Leah just seemed to have an itch that she was determined to publicly scratch and scratch until it bled. Natalie didn't know if Leah talked to everyone about these sorts of things, or if it was saved up just for her. You had to be firm with her: she was like a rolling pin sometimes, subduing everything in its path.

As they cycled slowly, Natalie noticed a crowd of youths nudging each other ahead. Boys about their age who had them in their sights.

'Hello ladies.'

Leah paled. 'Don't speak,' she hissed, but it was too late. 'Hello boys!' Natalie had returned.

'What accent is that?' one said.

'It's a Nazi accent,' another responded.

'Keep going,' Leah whispered. 'Ignore them.'

The ringleader was a scrappy dog of a boy, shirt hanging out of his shorts, straggly hair in need of a good wash. He was all mouth.

'Go back home, Nazis.'

The boys started throwing stones at them. Natalie was willing to ride at them if they had to, but Leah had ground to a complete halt and was covering her face with her hands. Natalie wasn't frightened at all, and would remember that later; nothing about it worried her, she just had a detached sensation of wanting to see what would unfold.

One of them, the biggest one, came up to Natalie on her bike, grabbed her handlebars and shook. Natalie swung off to one side, into the mud. Her palms saved her fall but not her dignity. Yet her foot was still attached to the bike, caught in the spokes, and it twisted. Now she yelped in pain.

Leah ran over to her and picked her up. But that left her own bike unattended. One of the boys moved quickly towards it.

'Filthy Germans,' he said although he seemed to have no compunction about grabbing her filthy bike.

'*Austrian.*' If he was going to insult her, at least he could insult her correctly.

'You're never Australian!' one of them shouted.

He spat at her. Natalie hated him then. She put weight on her foot. It wasn't broken, or was it?

The boy threw Leah's lovely bike into the water. It stopped halfway and then, in terribly slow motion, which seemed to make it all the more tragic, fell in.

'How dare you!' Natalie wanted to slap their ugly faces. The boys burst into laughter.

'Leave them,' said Leah quietly. 'Please… come on, Natalie, let's go.'

A small man, red-faced and perspiring, appeared suddenly from behind them. Launching into the group, he identified the ringleader at once and pushed him hard, two hands on his chest. The ringleader stumbled backwards, shouted, 'Oy, Nazi lover'. Fists were raised.

Natalie realised with alarm as much as relief that it was Alfie from the Caplins' house.

'You idiots. These aren't Nazis!' Alfie was shouting. '*You're* the fucking Nazis! They're innocent in all this.'

'We'll get you, German girls.'

'I already told you, we are Austrian!' Natalie called out. Now the cavalry had arrived, she couldn't stop herself.

Alfie wiped his face; he'd been punched at, but ducked in time. One cheek was bright red. He was out of breath. Small and fiery. He was just taller than Natalie, about three inches shorter than Leah.

Leah's face was glowing almost as much as his was.

Alfie sounded animal-like: he was in a right fury. Natalie didn't understand what he was saying, but Leah responded, 'Yes, it's my bike, but please don't worry.'

Alfie dropped his cigarette, then ground it into the pavement with his boot. He certainly could swivel his hips, she'd say that for him. Then he strode off to the riverside, pulling off his shoes and socks in one vigorous swoop.

'What on earth was he saying?' Laughter bubbled up inside Natalie.

'For goodness' sake,' Leah scolded, 'I understood him, why can't you?'

Natalie looked on with interest as Alfie now rolled up his trousers. Even she had to admit he came across as quite... well, masculine. Even more interesting was the way Leah was staring at him. Her lips had fallen open. She had something of a pigeon about her. She was transfixed.

Alfie waded to the bike out in the river. His pale blue trousers went dark blue up to his thighs. 'Please be careful!' yelled Leah. She knotted her hands together plaintively. 'Please!'

'I will,' he said, turning to smile at her before losing his footing in the mud and turning all his clothes several shades darker.

'Take care!'

'I am...'

'Earth calling Leah,' Natalie said in German, waving a hand in front of her cousin's eyes. Leah grabbed her hand and pushed it out of the way. Natalie was obscuring the view. This time Natalie did laugh. '*Ex-cuse me*!' she said.

'It's stuck,' Alfie yelled back, pink from exertion. 'But I'll get it.'

'Oh, please don't worry, I will manage—'

'No way, I'm getting it.'

'Oh, oh,' Leah called out encouragingly. 'Thank you so much.'

Alfie heaved and heaved like a pirate then he had set the bike free. He pushed it hard up the riverbank as they took the concrete steps down to him, Leah first, moving faster than Natalie had ever seen her move. She was also looking quite uncharacteristically emotional.

'This is *so* good of you. So helpful.'

'I'll make it look like new for ya.'

'Oh no, you don't need to, it wasn't new to begin with.' Leah was purring. Her eyes were shining.

Natalie couldn't help but gape. They were both blushing like a pair of schoolgirls.

'I want to,' Alfie said. 'I do.'

'Let me help then.'

Leah knelt at Alfie's feet, reminding Natalie of the Renaissance paintings she had studied at school. Jesus washing the disciples' feet? Leah was unrolling the bottom of Alfie's trousers. She was so committed to her task she probably wouldn't have noticed if the boys came back wearing Nazi uniforms and goose-stepping.

What would Aunt Ruth say to this?

'Did the bread pudding survive?' called Natalie. They ignored her.

After the incident in town, Leah stopped nagging Natalie about persuading her family to come to England. Or rather, whenever Leah mentioned Nazi Germany now all Natalie had to do was raise an eyebrow – *England's just the same* – and Leah would pipe down. What could she say? In a horrible way, those boys by the river had inadvertently proved Natalie's point. *Nowhere* was safe. London wasn't better than Vienna. Idiots were everywhere.

The other result was that the next day, over breakfast, Alfie said, 'Next time you ladies go out, I'll come with. Make sure you don't get yourselves in any trouble.'

'Like a bodyguard?' Natalie smirked. King Edward VIII had bodyguards, burly men in suits; she had seen them in the photos. Meeting Leah didn't seem to have warmed Alfie towards Natalie though. He scowled at his porridge. 'Not like a bodyguard, no.'

'It's no trouble, Alfie.'

'It's no trouble.'

'I mean no, it's fine, we don't want you.'

Natalie reported the entire conversation back to Leah because it had made her laugh. But Leah didn't laugh, she said, 'Oh tell Alfie, yes, please. What a dear!'

Natalie made a face at her, but unlike Rachel, who understood everything Natalie said without her even saying it, Leah simply pretended she hadn't seen.

CHAPTER FIVE

Even though Natalie had many misgivings about her sister Rachel marrying into the Goldberg family, Rachel had expressed a reservation only once. It was a few nights before the big wedding, when they were lying next to each other in their beds at home, and Rachel had said: 'How will I ever fit in with people like those?' Natalie remembered consoling her: 'You fit in with them? They're lucky to have a girl as beautiful, gracious and kind as you joining them!'

Rachel had laughed and had fallen asleep. Natalie hadn't slept though. She was worried that the Goldbergs would swallow up her lovely sister. In a way, Rachel's most recent letter revealed that they had.

Natalie,

I hope things are going well in England. Is the work too awful for words? I have to say, the thought of you cleaning makes us laugh! Mama said you are quite attached to the little boy though. Is my little sister getting maternal feelings?!

I can't believe Leah is getting so 'friendly with the natives'. How hilarious! Aunt Ruth would have a fit, wouldn't she? It would be enough to bring on her gout. As for your master, the mysterious Mr C, my advice to you is **Steer Well Clear**!! I have read far too many stories where the young ingénue is taken advantage of by the wealthy good-for-nothing, please don't let that be you.

I'm so sorry I haven't written much. I have been rather preoccupied! Married life is idyllic. No, I don't have any regrets, you pest! Leo is perfect for me. We performed five nights in a row at the *Konzerthaus*. I was picked to play over Irena Metz. You should have seen her face.

I've been rowing and playing tennis, and I have been to more parties than I have ever been to in my life; and my goodness, everyone loves to wear fancy dress! Leo and I held our own Masked Ball and Leo's brother Nathan, he plays clavichord, do you remember? He joked that we should dress up as German SS officers! (He came as a Roman senator instead!)

Of course I look after Mama. No need to remind me – she is doing very well. Leah really thinks Mama should plan to come to England? My goodness, can you imagine her there?

Hot on the heels of Rachel's letter came an envelope from Libby. Libby's writing was still pretty dreadful: her a's looked like fallen fruits, her e's resembled c's and the t's were like something a slug had dragged a leaf through in ink. But this time Libby had just sent a photo, which was thoughtful since Natalie hadn't brought any photographs of her family with her – an oversight.

The photo was not yet a year old; it was from last September, when they had gone to the photo studio on Wilhelminenstrasse. Leo's mother, Mrs Goldberg, had recommended the photographer and if Mrs Goldberg recommended something, you did it. It was a command. It was where Rachel and Leo had gone for their engagement photos. When they had arrived, they were told to put on Chinese outfits. Natalie had argued – they were Japanese, not Chinese – but no one cared. So, there they were, the four of them, wearing kimonos and jet-black wigs that were heavy as crowns. Libby was scowling. She loathed dressing up (she would hate life with the hilarious Goldbergs) and would have turned up in running kit if she could. Mama was turning towards her youngest daughter, as if to tell her off, (only in Mama's gentle way). Rachel looked more beautiful than ever, the silly outfit another (slightly bizarre) frame for her beauty. There Natalie was, caught in the middle, her hands raised as though saying, *What the heck are you making me do?*

Natalie had been in England just over two months when, returning from delivering Hugo to school, she found a man standing in the hall staring at himself in the gold-framed mirror. He was wearing a black fur coat and a black hat, and he was twirling a black umbrella in one hand and a cigar in the other. Natalie was determined to get to know every facet of English life, but he was not someone she'd particularly want to look at under a microscope.

Her nose involuntarily twitched from the smoke.

'Mr Caplin?' she nervously addressed the man in the mirror.

The man put the cigar to his mouth, inhaled deeply, slowly, then removed it. His lips were wet. He sized her up.

'Do I *look* like Mr Caplin?'

For a moment, Natalie was lost for words. The cigar smoke made her eyes sting.

'I don't know what Mr Caplin looks like, so it's impossible to say,' she said tartly.

Come to think of it, there were no pictures of Mr Caplin on the walls or on the sideboard. Back home, their shelves were lined with photos of Papa, Papa and Mama and all of them: studio photos and some less formal. There was even one of baby Papa with his family, newly arrived from Russia.

'You know what Larkworthy means?'

Natalie shook her head.

'Enclosure of people who netted the birds.' He laughed, flashing a gold tooth.

Fortunately, Mrs Caplin now arrived, dramatically, as though sailing through a sea-mist. She was wearing tall going-out shoes, a camel-coloured coat and a small cloche hat, and she looked beautiful, as always. She gazed between the two of them, saw Natalie's confused expression and laughed.

'Ah, Natalie, this is my agent, Mr Freeman. Michael, this is Natalie. The famous nanny from Vienna.'

Natalie was about to protest that she was not at all famous, but Mr Freeman only blew out more industrial quantities of smoke at her and said to Mrs Caplin, 'Let's go.'

He opened the door and stepped out into the sunshine.

Before following him, Mrs Caplin hesitated. She leaned into Natalie's now smoky hair and whispered hotly, 'He's one of your people, Natalie!'

It took a while for Natalie to work out what she meant.

That was the same day Natalie got a postcard of St Stephen's Cathedral – it was the kind of card a first-time visitor to Vienna might send, so her first reaction was, *why would anyone be sending her that?*

Dear Natalie,

The city is teeming with tourists, I pretended to be one and went up to everyone, asking where the cathedral is. The things you do when you are alone and bored! My friends are all away. I have a field trip in October, so it seemed too much to absent myself twice. Papa is in and out of the hospital a lot now while poor Mama rarely gets out of bed. They try to be cheerful though and they send you good wishes.

Do well, Natalie. You may be wondering if opportunities would be better for you back here, but I can assure you they wouldn't be. You are in the right place.

Yours,
Rudi

(How I wish we were still shining a light through each other's windows!)

How I wish we were still shining a light through each other's windows? This *was* sentimental, and Natalie welcomed it as a metaphor of something beautiful – although of what she was not quite sure. Later though, she thought: was it normal for lovers to go on about opportunities and locations so much? She read the postcard again and again. If you could wear something out by reading it, that little card from Rudi would have evaporated.

CHAPTER SIX

The next time Natalie, Leah and Alfie were free they met at the New Piccadilly Café in the centre of town. At first, Alfie sat at a neighbouring table glowering at anyone who came near. Even the poor waitress with the crumpets was subjected to his glare. *By the power of his eyes, Alfie will protect us,* Natalie wanted to say with a smirk, but Leah was not in the mood for smirking, or at least not for smirking at Alfie. She was dressed up to the nines. She did scrub up nicely, even Natalie had to admit. Simple clothes: a long black skirt, a pretty white blouse and a shawl. They suited her, perhaps because she was tall. If Natalie tried a similar look, she would look like she would be better suited to picking potatoes in Gdansk. The hat Leah was wearing also seemed to set off her face, making it look 'interesting' as opposed to 'wide'.

'Join us, Alfie, please.' Did Leah have something in her eye or was she fluttering her eyelashes? Natalie kicked her under the table, but Leah ignored her. 'We owe you our lives!' she continued.

'Our lives? Our bicycles at the very most,' objected Natalie.

'It's a figure of speech,' explained Leah as if Natalie was a very silly girl. 'It's an exaggeration. They do that here. Try it.'

Leah was incredibly solicitous to Alfie, and she had also developed a ridiculous laugh, a hiccupping sound that went on far too long. Natalie could hardly hear herself think between Alfie's guttural grunts and Leah's hiccups, and she wondered if the family on a nearby table daintily eating sandwiches might complain.

Leah and Alfie quickly established they had something in common: they both hated the National Socialists. Natalie agreed that Nazism was a pernicious ideology but felt that if they could contain it, and they *were* containing it, then it wouldn't last long. It was like when she had measles – they had kept her in her room so she couldn't spread it. Natalie got loads of reading done and it had soon passed. These things do. She thought about saying this to Leah and Alfie, but it seemed like she would be interrupting an elaborate mating ritual.

After they'd finished their pot of tea, Natalie stood up, disgruntled with the pair of bores. She wanted Leah to leave with her but instead, Alfie and Leah looked at each other.

Alfie said, 'Shall we?' and Leah hiccup-laughed, 'Oh why not? It's payday!'

Natalie went home alone.

The second time they went to the New Piccadilly Café, one month later, Alfie joined them at the table *before* they had ordered; and the third time, another month later, he was sat at their usual table when they arrived. Natalie's heart fell. She still barely understood Alfie. His English was so straggly, like it had been through the mangle; however, his adoration of Leah was growing. There was no getting away from it.

When Leah went to the bathroom, Natalie leaned across the table: 'Are you falling for my cousin?'

He looked back at her and did his smug Alfie grin.

'I like her,' he said. At least that's what she thought he said. 'She's far nicer than you!'

'Brace yourself for disappointment, Alfie,' Natalie told him. There was no point not being clear about this. She tried to be like the wise sister, the Rachel of the situation (although Rachel probably would not have got involved at all).

He glowered at her. 'What's she said?'

'Well, nothing,' Natalie admitted, 'but don't get too attached.'

Natalie thought of Aunt Ruth and her disdain for the 'shopkeeping class'. Alfie was someone even shopkeepers would look down on. He was a Jack-of-all-trades, a dogsbody, a no-hoper. That morning, she had watched him prune the hedge with massive shears. A wonder he had any fingers left.

He slurped his tea loudly. 'I'll thank you to keep your advice to yourself, Miss Hoity Toity.'

'Just saying, Alfie. Honesty *is* the best policy, wouldn't you say?'

His face was thunder as he wiped his mouth and stood up. 'Tell Leah I'm off.'

One sunny morning, Natalie had just come back from taking Hugo to school when Mrs Monger frantically intercepted her in the hallway, her hands covered in flour. 'Chop-chop, Natalie.'

Natalie gazed at her. *Vegetables?*

'Quick-quick. He's upstairs.'

'Mr Freeman?'

Mrs Caplin's agent was often in the house in the mornings. He took Mrs Caplin for auditions, or out for lunch. While he was waiting, he smoked, stared in the mirror or stroked Tilly, calling her 'Prettypuss' as though it was all one word. The fact that he was sweet to the cat surely meant he couldn't be all bad, but Natalie couldn't bring herself to like him and, despite their having *something in common*, Mr Freeman wasn't interested in Natalie either. He barely raised his head to return her wish for a 'good morning' and he didn't even respond the day it was raining and Natalie had announced that, 'It was a nice day for ducks' (a new favourite saying).

But there was no tell-tale cigar smell now.

'Not Mr Freeman, you fool!' said Mrs Monger, exasperated. 'The Master. Tell him he has a telephone call. I don't want to go in the middle of baking.'

Natalie knocked on the door of the bedroom that she knew was Mr Caplin's. She had never been inside – although she could well imagine the kind of things that had gone on there with him and her predecessor.

There was no answer. She knocked as loudly as she could. Still nothing.

She chewed her nails. She thought of reporting back to Mrs Monger, 'He's not there', but didn't like to give up. Mrs Monger often insinuated Natalie gave up on everything too soon or that she was slapdash with her work, so she wouldn't, not today.

Natalie tried the handle. The handle moved. The door opened. Inside the room, Mr Caplin was fast asleep. Naked. His sheets pushed to the floor. Natalie took in his whole long body. She saw his penis. She couldn't help it. It drew the eye. She gasped, then backed out, silent as a nun. How was she to know Mr Caplin was in bed? How was she to know Mr Caplin wore *nothing* in bed? Was this the British custom or a Mr Caplin custom? What on earth was wrong with pyjamas?

She shut the door, then knocked loudly, and loudly again. She made a cacophony of sound. She knocked to the tune of 'When the Saints Go Marching In', she knocked to the tune of 'Für Elise'. Finally, she heard signs of life within.

'There's a call.' Her voice was embarrassingly shrill. Finally, there came a muffled reply. *He had heard. He was coming. Thank you.*

Mr Caplin was still on the phone when Natalie gathered herself enough to go downstairs, ten minutes later. He nodded at her as she walked towards the kitchen.

He was in a maroon dressing gown, tightly belted with the same kind of golden rope that held back the velvet curtains in the drawing room. He had fair hair and a long, rather sad face. He looked neither like King Edward VIII nor Mr Freeman. He brought to mind Eeyore from *Winnie the Pooh*. He must have been about forty-five, although Natalie was never good at guessing the elderly. And she had seen him naked. This was the man of the house. The one glamorous Mrs

Caplin had picked and married. Natalie was building up a picture and it was no masterpiece.

Poor Mrs Caplin, she thought.

'They're certainly growing in numbers in the city,' he was saying. 'We'll soon be infested.'

Natalie knew instantly what he was talking about. She blushed, then leaned against the wall in horror. He was talking about the Jews. He had to be. Talking about people like her, like they were nothing but vermin. She could just about make out the other man down the wire. He said something like, 'I don't know if we can hold back the tide.' And Mr Caplin responded: 'We've just got to hope for the best, expect the worst. Makes me uneasy though.'

Awful, awful man.

Later, when Natalie was tidying up Hugo's room, Mr Caplin popped his head around the door. It was like he couldn't bring himself to enter the room. Perhaps he thought she was contagious. Natalie remembered, *I don't know what Mr Caplin is going to say about all this, do you?* and she disliked him more than she disliked Mr Freeman (and she was no fan of Mr Freeman).

'Apologies, we haven't been properly introduced.'

'It's fine.' Natalie put Hugo's tennis balls and shuttlecocks up on the shelf where they lived next to his noseless bear and his untouched collection of Charles Dickens books. 'We know who we are.'

'How are you getting on at Larkworthy?'

Natalie kept her eyes lowered.

'Quite well.' She paused. 'Thank you for asking.'

'Getting used to the weather?'

'It's very English,' she said and he laughed. She hadn't meant it as a joke.

Even if she hadn't overheard him, why did she have to see his penis? There was no way she was ever going to be friendly with this man. She knew too much. She knew the nasty things in his head – and in his pants. It was so mortifying that she couldn't even write about it to Rachel or Mama, the thought of committing the words to paper was too much. She tilted her head away from him. Had he intended it as a trap? Or worse, an invitation?!

'Good-good,' he said eventually. 'Well, if you need anything, Mrs Monger and… and… I will endeavour…'

'I won't.' Natalie told him firmly. 'Thank you.'

When Mrs Caplin returned from her gallivanting that afternoon, she was even more giddy and excited than usual. Natalie arrived in the drawing room as she was unbuckling her shoes.

'I might have good news soon.' Mrs Caplin admired herself in the mirror over the fireplace. As usual, she looked beautiful. Mrs Monger said the mistress hated getting sun-kissed, but it did suit her.

'I auditioned for Juliet.'

'Juliet?'

'*Romeo and Juliet* – Juliet…' explained Mrs Caplin.

Mrs Caplin was too old for Juliet, wasn't she? Natalie tried to conceal her surprise, but it couldn't have worked, for Mrs Caplin said, 'I know, I know, but show-business years are different from normal years, darling.'

'I will keep my finger crossed,' Natalie said. It was one of her favourite expressions and the English were crazy about superstitions. Hugo was always 'touching wood' and if he couldn't find a wood surface, he liked to tap Natalie's head.

Natalie waited. Should she say Mr Caplin was here? She didn't *have* to mention the nudity.

'Mr Freeman *is* brilliant, isn't he?' said Mrs Caplin to her reflection.

'I… yes.'

'He's one of your people.'

'You said.'

'Did I? Oh well, he's a *wonderful* agent. Best in town. He believes in me. He believes I can be as big as Mae West. He thinks I could go far – Pinewood to Hollywood. There is no end to his talents—'

'Can I just...' Natalie interrupted. 'It appears that, I'm afraid... your Mr Caplin has returned.'

'Oh, has he? Back like a bad penny, eh? Well, thank you, Natalie. I hope my husband hasn't...' she paused, 'been any bother?'

Natalie shook her head and smiled to let Mrs Caplin know she knew *exactly* what she meant, and she was always on her side: 'I can handle myself.'

'Don't worry, he never stays for long.' She slid her shoes back on and squeezed Natalie's hand. 'Good girl,' she said as she marched from the room.

CHAPTER SEVEN

There was a dance the following Saturday night. Natalie was keen to go, until she found out who had invited her and Leah.

'Really? A dance with Alfie?'

Leah had flushed pink. 'It's just a dance, Natalie. I'm not going to marry him.'

Still, Natalie liked dancing and an opportunity to go to a real-life English dance was not to be turned down. She fretted about whether she was free or not until finally, on Saturday afternoon, Mrs Monger told her that she had permission to go.

Later, she was in the nursery putting Hugo to bed when Mrs Caplin came in.

'Are you… are you wearing that?'

Natalie stood up. She was wearing the pale blue blouse that she had travelled in from Vienna, and her usual daily tweed skirt. She wouldn't have chosen to wear it, but needs must. She had a dress – the one she had bought for Rachel and Leo's wedding – but that was far too fussy and she regretted bringing it to England.

'Pretty Natalie,' said Hugo shyly, hanging onto his marionette.

'She *is* a pretty little thing,' said Mrs Caplin, 'but she needs to learn to make the most of herself. And,' she said sternly, 'stop biting those nails. Come, borrow an outfit, darling.'

Mrs Caplin's bedroom was a frothy feminine place. The blankets were pale blue, the cushions were pale blue, and the curtains had pretty birds in flight on them. There was a view of the back garden, where Natalie could see the trees gently waving in the breeze. Some were in blossom and some had lost blossom, leaving pink heart shapes like pretty thumbprints all over the grass.

Together, they flicked through the dresses in the closet. How lovely to feel the different materials through her fingers. Natalie didn't yet have much of her own style, but she somehow knew none of them were quite for her, although she could imagine Rachel would look wonderful in any one of them. They were all so sophisticated, Natalie would look a little girl trying to look grown up in dress-up clothes. Eventually, she chose a skirt, a light blouse and a red tank top that gave the outfit a bit of oomph. It was quite possibly the plainest thing in the collection. Mrs Caplin giggled, and said she still looked like she was going to work, but Natalie liked it. Then there were party shoes to worry about. Mrs Caplin, who looked dainty, had surprisingly large feet, so none of them worked, but a friend had once left some shoes and these, cream heels with a buckle, couldn't have been more perfect.

Such kindness. Such grace. Natalie was so lucky to have Mrs Caplin on her side. She was like her mother in England really. Mrs Caplin sat her at the dressing table and swiped at her cheeks with the powder puff. It tickled.

'Sometimes, I feel I am Jewish,' said Mrs Caplin suddenly. Natalie was going to laugh again, but she realised the woman was being serious. Natalie tried to keep her expression in the reflection unperturbed. Her heart was beating so loudly, she was sure Mrs Caplin would hear it.

'It's like deep down inside I am one of your people.'

Natalie swallowed loudly. 'I don't know what you mean.'

Mrs Caplin made Natalie stick out her lips and dabbed on some lipstick.

As she did that, she said, 'I just feel like I was a Jew, maybe in another life.'

'Were either of your parents?'

'No,' Mrs Caplin said, 'and neither am I… It's just a *feeling*,' she went on, patting her flat stomach. 'You know what I mean.'

Natalie didn't know what she meant. Natalie didn't feel Jewish. She *was* Jewish.

The conversation puzzled Natalie, maybe for longer than it should. Natalie couldn't tell if they were throwaway words or sincere analysis. Why did it feel strange – as if Natalie's Jewishness was something Mrs Caplin coveted, something she could wear? Perhaps Mrs Caplin was saying it to make them feel closer, but unlike the clothes and the shoes, it didn't quite work.

Molly was also going to the dance, which Natalie found dispiriting. She hadn't realised it was the kind of dance a fifteen-year-old would go to – she took the one and a half years between them seriously. She wondered what Princess Elizabeth would say about dancing. She probably wouldn't be keen, but Princess Margaret would be completely game.

In Mrs Caplin's skirt and top, and with the powder on her cheeks and the lipstick on her lips, for the first time in her life Natalie felt like the belle of the ball and she had no shortage of men wanting to partner her. She danced and was spun around the room by people who didn't mind her Nazi accent, her biblical eyebrows, her chewed nails – they just wanted someone to dance with.

It was a beautiful July night and suddenly it seemed the summer was going to be a good one. She was coming into herself. The band played the liveliest of tunes and she and Molly laughed at silly things. As it turned out, Natalie was glad Molly was there because Alfie and Leah left her by herself all night. At first, they galloped around the room, but soon they just started swaying in the centre while everyone danced around them. You couldn't put a pencil between them. Natalie was content though. That night, she had been reminded of something special: of laughing, of ease, of friendships, of kindness.

She might just be fitting in.

CHAPTER EIGHT

Natty

How are you? Have you got plump on Victoria sponge? I have joined Hakoah Vienna sports club now. They are very good. Yes, I am looking forward to the Olympics. I will think of you listening to it when I do. Mama likes the athletics. She gets stressed at the handover of the baton. Rachel likes the fencing. She says Leo used to fence very well!! She really is in love. It's sickening. (Not really!)

Mama said I could only go to practice today if I wrote to you first (this is blackmail!), so here it is.

Yours eternally,
Your favourite sister
(Libby by the way)

Leah and Natalie were out foraging for berries at the edge of the fields. Natalie had never gone berry picking before, not even in Vienna, but Leah had done everything everywhere. Although they were by a road, barely a car came past and there were no people around. Natalie was relieved. Sometimes, she became quite shy mixing with people out of the house.

They set off, baskets in the crooks of their elbows. Natalie told Leah about Mr Caplin. Not the bedroom bit, she couldn't bring herself to reveal that, but the part about the ex-nanny and the telephone conversation she'd overheard. She had already forgotten the exact words, so she might have exaggerated it a bit, but Leah was satisfyingly shocked. She was disgusted to hear it, she hadn't thought the English were like that, and definitely not Mr Caplin. Natalie responded heartily, 'How do you think I felt?'

They knelt, then walked, then knelt again. Leah reminded Natalie to look deeper within the bushes, and higher up too, and Natalie wanted to say, 'I know that, Leah!' but she swallowed it back and just got on with it. It was so pretty now with the sun beating down on her shoulders, and the different shades of pink of the raspberries off the hedgerows. And the raspberries were perfection themselves. Just like that, no sugar, no cream, no crumble, just simple berry from its stalk to the mouth.

Leah told Natalie about some Austrian swimmers who were boycotting the upcoming Olympics.

'Really? I hadn't heard this.'

Leah sniffed. 'I told you to read the German newspapers, didn't I? The English ones could hardly care less.'

'Oh well,' said Natalie. 'Now I know.'

Natalie told Leah about Mrs Caplin's Juliet audition and how she hoped that Mrs Caplin would get the part. 'She deserves it,' Natalie said warmly, thinking of her boss, the lovely shoes and blouse that she had loaned her, and the fact she had been able to go to the dance at all. She was quite the fairy godmother.

'She works hard. She'd make such a good…' She couldn't bring herself to say Juliet; 'actress,' she said before realising that Leah wasn't remotely interested.

Natalie tried something else. 'And Libby has joined Hakoah sports club. I don't know why she joined that one,' she continued cheerfully. It was a Jewish club. Unlike her, Libby did not look remotely biblical. With her golden plaits and blue eyes, Papa used to say she was more Aryan than the Aryans.

'You don't know why,' repeated Leah darkly. 'Can't you work it out?'

Natalie considered, heart pounding. 'Not… No, not really.'

'They won't let her join the other clubs.'

Leah spoke with her usual conviction, but that didn't mean she was right. And yet it probably was right, and if it was right, that was awful.

'I see.'

'And now there's this fascist Olympics.'

'I don't think it's a fascist—'

'Everyone who supports it is a Nazi.'

'You're being ridiculous, Leah.'

Leah swung around, her lips black with berries. She must have been helping herself to them as she went along, despite telling Natalie not to. Suddenly, it appeared to Natalie as though Leah had blood around her mouth like a lion eating its prey. A hunting animal. It was horrible. Natalie wanted to back away from her.

'No, it's the Nazis who are ridiculous.' Leah was so angry, she slipped into German. 'You underestimate them.'

'What do you want me to do?' asked Natalie impatiently. 'I'm sorry I'm not as scared as you. We all react to things differently.'

Leah put down her basket and wiped her hands on her trousers. She looked exasperated.

Natalie softened. They had been getting on so much better recently. It would be a shame to spoil it over something so stupid as politics.

'I probably haven't been keeping up with the news as I should. I'll find out more when I go back home.'

'You're not ever going back, Natalie.'

Natalie was so startled, she nearly dropped her basket.

'Of course I am. One day.'

'You won't, I promise. And you need to get Aunt Dora, Rachel and Libby out as soon as you can. *That's* what you can do. These Berlin Olympics are going to make things ten times worse.'

It was so over the top that Natalie could only laugh.

'You don't get it, do you? It's *sports*, Leah, not politics… And for goodness' sake, you *know* Mama. When has *anyone ever* been able to tell her what to do? If she wanted to come, she'd come!'

But Leah turned away from Natalie, her head held high. She plucked berries from the bushes and threw them down into her basket like tiny hated things. She wasn't even checking to see if they were ripe any more. When Natalie managed to catch up with her, she hissed, 'This isn't a game, Natalie. This is the Third Reich and they are coming for our people.'

The day after Natalie's disagreement with Leah was the day of the Olympic opening ceremony and Natalie, Mrs Monger, Alfie and Molly all listened to it crammed around the wireless in the kitchen. You could hear the roar of the crowds and the chanting. Mrs Monger made everyone a drink of Bovril and no one said it was disgusting, so Natalie didn't either. She had thought they were having their usual Ovaltine, so it came as quite a shock.

'It's probably a silly question,' Molly said, biting her lip as she did when she was embarrassed. 'But what does "Heil Hitler!" actually mean?'

Everyone went quiet. Mrs Monger collected the cups, then rinsed them. The tap dripped.

Natalie realised everyone was waiting for her. 'Oh, it just means Hail – like Hail Caesar? Hail Hitler.'

'That's not too bad then,' Molly said, and everyone nodded.

The photographs in the newspaper certainly *looked* respectable too. There was a lot of homage to the ancient Greeks. They lit flames on torches. The same part of Natalie that loved the royal family loved this too. She couldn't help but imagine what a thrill it must be to be there. One day, Libby might be able to participate; as Papa would have said, 'Why not? Reach for the stars!' and Natalie would be in the cheering crowd, saying, 'That's my sister!' Natalie kept her fingers crossed and knocked on the wooden table, and later, she and Hugo were allowed to help Mrs Monger make a crumble with the berries. Natalie tried to forget the undisguised fury on Leah's berry-stained face and the way she hissed, 'You're not ever going back!'

Over the next few days, an Austrian canoeist won the gold, an Austrian woman won the bronze foil in the fencing and Natalie was proud – Austria was such a small country now, it was good to see her people putting up a fight. In the end though, the Olympics of 1936 was about one man: Jesse Owens. The Olympics was a chance for the whole world to demonstrate their abilities – not just the Nazis. Surely Leah could see that too?

At the weekend, Natalie arranged a mini-Olympics in the garden for Hugo. For equestrian, she was his horse and he climbed on her back, shouting, 'Giddy up!' Good job he was so light. Alfie found them three boxes, painted one, two and three on the sides, and so they had a podium (Alfie was gruff and unfriendly, but he could be kind). They painted flags and tried to remember national anthems: Natalie was only good for two, but surprisingly, Molly knew the Spanish and the Greek, then Mrs Monger said her father taught her the Russian.

They did running races and the long jump. Hugo wanted to climb trees, but Natalie explained *that* wasn't an Olympic sport. He was the greatest ever English contestant Hugo Caplin – winner!

Hugo loved it. Since there was no sign of Mrs or Mr Caplin, and the weather was so balmy, they stayed in the garden until ten o'clock that evening and Natalie promised they would play it again the following day. Just before bedtime, she told Hugo about weightlifting. This was a mistake, for soon he was lifting everything over his head. But she was in no hurry to be by herself, so she explained further.

'Three seconds, arms straight, otherwise it won't count.'

This was what sports was all about. Forget Leah. Looking forward to the next day, Natalie fell asleep smiling.

As they walked out in the garden on Sunday morning, it was to find Mrs Caplin and a crowd of people there. Natalie wondered if the group had been awake all night; this seemed more likely than that they had been to bed and got up so early. Mr Caplin wasn't there, which was one good thing.

Natalie wanted to go as far away from them as she could, but Mrs Caplin gestured for her to come over.

'You have so much energy, Natalie. I wish I were more like you,' she said, sipping from her glass. The other women tittered. Natalie realised that what was funny was the thought of someone as elevated as Mrs Caplin wishing she was lowly like her. She flushed, wanting to tell them all about Rachel and Leo *Goldberg*, and her papa, Paul Leeman, one of the leading lights in the Viennese social justice movement – but that wouldn't fit the box they had put her in. Here, she was a domestic servant and she supposed it was not their fault they didn't know her, the real her. She might have been the same, were the positions reversed.

'Not really,' Natalie said before realising it was the wrong answer. *Try to be good.* She put down her equipment and, smiled. 'I suppose I do have some energy today.'

One of the women said, 'Did you listen to the Olympics?'

'Ye-es…' But the woman wasn't talking to her, she was talking to her friend, a woman with too much hair for her little face. They both ignored her.

'Did the coloured man win the jumping?'

'Jesse Owens? Yes. And the 100 metres and the 200 metres and the relay.'

'Bet that gave Mr Hitler a start.'

Natalie smiled uneasily. She was still waiting for Mrs Caplin to dismiss her. Fortunately, Hugo was making a nuisance of himself, trying to lift up a garden gnome.

Natalie wondered if this was an actual party. She remembered her etiquette book: *The English people love a garden party in the summer, and they may do an Easter bonnet competition or a competition to see how many sweets are in the jar.*

Mrs Caplin was talking about an actress she knew who was fighting with a producer and a director over 'intimate scenes'. Finally, when she had finished her long account, Natalie asked, 'Would you rather I took Hugo inside?'

'No, we love watching you play. Don't we, everyone? It's sweet.'

Natalie didn't believe everyone found it as sweet as Mrs Caplin did, but they murmured their assent. Unfortunately, Hugo wanted to play equestrian again. This was undignified. Natalie's knees were soon covered in grass stains, then Hugo said she had a caterpillar in her hair.

'She's marvellous with Hugo,' one of the guests said.

'Isn't she?'

'You've been lucky, Caroline,' said one woman, sweeping back her voluminous hair.

'So, *so* lucky. Hugo wouldn't be without her.'

'She's German?'

Natalie kept her head down and pretended she couldn't hear.

'Austrian. A Jewess, of course!' Mrs Caplin said gaily.

'Nothing wrong with that,' agreed her friend.

'Oh, I thought so – it was the nose.'

'And the eyebrows.'

'Oh, you are so good, Caroline,' one of the other women said. 'I hope she appreciates it.'

'Oh, she's grateful.' Mrs Caplin smiled over at Natalie. 'She's a good girl.'

Natalie was surprised no one mentioned what Mr Caplin must think about it.

*

The guests continued drinking and eating all day. Tilly the cat stayed in the drawing room, judging them all through the window. Popping into the kitchen with Hugo, Natalie found Mrs Monger having to prepare a fish supper for ten, and she was incandescent with rage about it. However, when she brought out crab paste sandwiches for luncheon, she was so charming, anyone would have thought she was having the time of her life.

Natalie and Hugo spent the afternoon in the house. Having Mrs Caplin's friends watch their every move was rather off-putting. That evening, just as Hugo was falling asleep, Mrs Caplin came into the nursery. This was unusual.

Natalie put her finger to her lips. 'He's just drifted off, it's been a busy day.'

Mrs Caplin shook her head. She hadn't come for a goodnight story or a kiss on the forehead.

'Come down,' she whispered hotly. 'I want to introduce you to someone.'

Natalie wished she could have changed her clothes. Everyone in the garden had looked sophisticated, even in the morning, whereas she was a mongrel cross between dowdy and rumpled. She smoothed down her frizzy hair – too biblical – and wished she could do something about the size of her nose, anything, just for the evening. She didn't mind it most of the time. She wasn't sure if she was coming down as family member or staff. She should just try to be herself, no labels.

One of the men had put a trilby on one of the gnomes. Natalie was no expert, but the way Mrs Caplin was moving suggested she may have overindulged on the sherry.

Some of the women had taken off their shoes and were dancing on the lawn, in a kind of slow-motion, titillating way. Rachel would have disapproved. Mrs Caplin took Natalie towards a man who was gaping at them. As Mrs Caplin stood next to him, his hand went to the small of her back. Natalie couldn't help thinking he was relaxed, as though he visited there often.

'This is Mr Young,' Mrs Caplin said. 'Mr Young, this is Natalie, my nanny.' She burst into laughter at her own joke. 'Not *my* nanny. Hugo's nanny.'

His eyes were a similar bright blue to Mrs Caplin's. He was her brother or cousin, perhaps?

Natalie went to shake his hand, but he was so caught up watching the dancing women that he didn't notice.

'How do you do?' she said loudly, stretching her hand out further so he couldn't miss. If she had been brought down here for this, she might as well make it count.

He mumbled a reply. His handshake was half-hearted and reminded Natalie of rice pudding. He was too busy watching the women to acknowledge her. There was something compelling, almost animal-like about their dancing – she thought of snakes. Mrs Caplin was gazing at him though, not the dancers, and she was mesmerised, like he was a snake-charmer. He had a dark blond moustache two centimetres thick, no more, and his hair, which was lighter, was long over the ears but short at the back. Natalie wondered why Mrs Caplin seemed so enthralled. Now he pulled away his hand and put the whole length of his arm around Mrs Caplin and muttered something in her ear.

'Good, good,' she giggled. 'Make hay while the sun shines.'

It seemed most unlikely that they were relatives; and Natalie simply couldn't understand why she'd been introduced to him. Then Mrs Caplin gave a deep laugh and flapped her hands at Natalie. 'You can go now, darling.'

CHAPTER NINE

September 1936

My dear girl,

I have something rather important and perhaps surprising to ask. Things are precarious here in Vienna right now. Maybe I have not faced up to it, or maybe I haven't talked to you enough about it – but that's because I have never wanted to worry you. The country is moving politically to the right and we are being made to feel more and more unwanted. It's just small things so far, but I have come to the conclusion it might be better if Libby and I left. (Leo wants him and Rachel to stay for the time being, but even they are now looking at jobs with orchestras in different countries.) I would hate to be a burden on you, sweet pea, you know how important my independence is to me. Papa used to say I was too proud, and he was probably right! But if you could find a way for us to be able to come and work there, in England, then that would be wonderful. Don't worry if not, at this stage, it's just an idea…

Mama

The letter did come as a surprise. A shock even. There was no way Papa would have ever left his beloved Vienna. You would have had to drag him out by his feet and, secretly, Natalie had always thought the same of Mama. And now Mama wanted to come to England? She read the letter again, then looked up to see Mr Freeman there, looming over her. She didn't know how long he'd been there.

'Bad news from home?'

'No,' she said. 'Not at all.' He lit his cigar and looked at her appraisingly.

'It seems you're popular with the boss,' he said. It was hard to tell if he thought that was good or not.

'Oh? How do you know that then?'

His gold tooth flashed as he laughed. 'She's always saying you're better than the last one.'

Natalie clutched her paper tightly and tried to smile.

Mrs Caplin came downstairs wearing her sequinned dress and looking like a modern version of a flapper: her hair was as shiny and smooth as hair could be. It was extraordinary. Everything about her was. As she took Mr Freeman's arm, she winked at Natalie. 'No rest for the wicked.'

Natalie cleaned Hugo's room pensively. That Mama wanted to come to England was a remarkable turn of events. It posed more questions than it answered. For how long? She wanted to work? Not domestic service, surely? Mama was an earthy, practical woman – but cleaning? And Rachel was looking at other orchestras when she had been so proud to land her place with Leo? Could Mama be right about that – was she confused or was it perhaps Rachel who was confused?

Natalie went about her usual routines, but the letter was burning in her pocket. Every free moment, she opened it and read it over again. She had been thinking that she wouldn't go home to Austria for a while yet, maybe not for another year and a half, but it was odd to have the decision made for her. Hugo's affectionate loveliness was a big reason she wanted to stay. And worry about him a little, for his parents indulged him but paid scant attention to him. Her language had come on in leaps and bounds, but she hadn't started thinking in English yet, and she longed for the night she would dream in English. Then she'd know she'd arrived.

Rudi's lack of correspondence was another reason not to rush home. Two measly notes in three months? It wasn't like he'd sworn on his life to write, but he had feelings for her, she knew it, so why had he not followed through?

And it seemed that everyone was just getting on with their lives in Vienna. Not just getting on – things had actually improved for them in her absence: Libby's schooling, Rachel's situation. They were hardly pining for her, were they? But still, Mama and Libby coming to England was a different thing altogether. Mama, here? How would that be? Usually young women left home, their home didn't come after them. She would have to talk to Leah about it. The downside was Leah would say, 'I told you so.' The upside was, she would know exactly what to do.

A few days later, the Caplins went to the West Country. Hugo hid as they were leaving, delaying their departure by two hours. Natalie ran around the house and garden calling for him, but he was in none of his usual places. Eventually she found him scrunched behind the chess set in the drawing room. Going without Natalie was the 'absolute pits' – which Natalie now understood was a colloquialism – and he was refusing to budge. She persuaded him out by promising him she'd be there on his return.

'Always?' he whispered, tears pooling in his eyes.

'As long as you need me,' said Natalie.

'Swear on your life?'

Yes, she absolutely could not go back. He was so vulnerable. It surprised her not only how fond she had become of him but also how fond he was of her. It was clear she was very much part of the family in his eyes. She still felt obliged to scold him though.

'Listen, Hugo, you've made your parents extremely late, and being late is the height of disrespect. It says, *my time is more important than your time*, do you see?'

'They don't like me,' he whispered.

To her shame, the first time he'd said it, Natalie had pretended not to hear but by the third time she had to say something, so she cuddled him and said, 'They do, Hugo, of course they do.'

'Not like you,' he murmured.

The Sandersons were also away, so Leah and Natalie met in town. Leah had submerged herself in English life. She had disappeared into it like an egg in a cake. Natalie knew she was still sticky icing on top. She wasn't essential. She was just a bit of flavour – and not everyone liked that. Even stranger than the fact that in under four years Leah had entirely reinvented herself was that she seemed hardly aware of it.

In the café, Natalie was compelled to analyse Leah further. She couldn't get over it. Perhaps if she prodded and poked, she could find out what lay behind the change.

'I do like it here,' Leah admitted, drinking milky tea like she had been drinking it from the day she was born.

'More than Vienna?' Natalie tried to take the incredulity out of her voice. That Leah could actively *prefer* London to Vienna – well, she was not ready for that. Sure, there were some great buildings here, and the people were kind, but there was nothing like a picnic on a Sunday in the Burggarten or a Mozart concert in a hall with cherubs on the ceiling.

Leah considered. She put down her teacup. 'I feel freer,' she said slowly. 'Since I'm a foreigner, nobody expects much of me – it's liberating to be different. And I like the people here,' she added slowly, 'especially the men.'

Natalie knew what – or rather who – she meant and decided it was best to ignore it. They ordered scones. Scones were another thing Leah had all the opinions about. Fruit scones, cheese scones, plain scones.

'Oh, did I tell you?' Natalie exclaimed, although she knew she hadn't. 'Mama has suggested she might come to England. What do you think I should do?'

Leah's mouth dropped open. 'Oh my gosh!' She was so excited by this news that she forgot her scone and bolted out of her chair to Natalie's side.

'I mean, I do want her to come,' Natalie continued. 'But how?'

'This is amazing.' Leah clutched her so tightly, Natalie could smell her clothes. Then she held Natalie at arm's length and peered at her like a squirrel at a nut. 'Why am I more excited than you?' she asked suspiciously.

'I am! I just… It's not what I expected to happen.'

Leah was staring at her.

'I'm slow at reacting to some things, that's all,' Natalie added. 'Always have been.'

If Leah had known Natalie had been sitting on the letter for almost two weeks she would have had an absolute fit.

The system, as Leah understood it, was that Mama might be allowed a visa for England, but she had to prove to be 'self-sufficient'. Mama would have to prove her ability to pay her way, pay her rent, pay for everything, so Natalie would have to find her a job before she came.

'So, let's make a plan.'

Always with the plans.

Leah borrowed a pencil from the waitress, and then on the napkin, she wrote, 'Ask Mrs Caplin. Ask Mrs Sanderson.'

'That's it?'

'It's a start. Oh, Natalie, I'm so pleased for you.'

*

The Caplins were away for another week. When they came back, Natalie pretended all was usual and wondered how she would inveigle a moment with Mrs Caplin alone. Usually Mrs Caplin summoned her, not the other way around. One evening though, while Hugo was drawing with Molly, she came across Mrs Caplin putting down the telephone. She looked up at Natalie, her expression indignant.

'So, they didn't want me after all. They offered me Nurse instead!'

Natalie's brain scrambled. Then she remembered: *Romeo and Juliet*.

'Will you take the role?'

'God no! I don't want to be typecast. Once they put you in the box of…' she looked at Natalie sympathetically, '*homely*, or "the help", you never get out of it. Damn Freeman!'

Mrs Caplin tucked her arm into Natalie's and walked her into the garden, even though Natalie had been on her way to the kitchen. It was twilight and the sun was blazing red and low. It was a beautiful scene, quintessentially English.

'Anyway, how about you, dear girl – did you miss us?'

'Massively,' said Natalie. They shared a smile.

'Hugo was so tiresome without you. He turns into a completely different person.'

'He's a lovely boy,' said Natalie neutrally. Mrs Caplin bent down at the roses and inhaled deeply.

'I have some news.' Natalie hesitated. 'My mama would like to come here and work.'

'Oh?' said Mrs Caplin. 'Where is she going to go?'

'I… we don't know. I wondered if you could help?'

Mrs Caplin was glaring at the garden gnomes. 'Have one of these been moved?'

Natalie looked. There were three in a row here: Fishing gnome, sandwich gnome and hat gnome, all in the same place as usual.

'I don't think so. Is there any chance of work in this house?'

'Not really.' Mrs Caplin unhooked her arm from Natalie's and walked over to the lawn and tapped her foot around. 'Oh, you're right.' She squinted back at Natalie. 'There is no room here, is there?'

Mrs Monger had a small room downstairs and Natalie had the spare room upstairs. Hugo had his large room, Mr and Mrs Caplin had a room and a dressing room each. Alfie slept in a room at the back of the garage. But there were still a lot of unused rooms.

Natalie couldn't think what to say. She guessed Mrs Caplin meant that her husband wouldn't allow it and she was just covering up for him. *They're certainly growing in numbers.* What else could he have meant?

'I see. Sorry.'

'That's quite all right. Oh, by the way, what did you think of my friend, Mr Young?'

'Fine,' said Natalie timidly, squeezing her hands together. 'Why?'

'Just wondered,' Mrs Caplin said, and she wandered off, smiling to herself.

Leah wasn't impressed when Natalie reported back.

'I thought she was like a fairy godmother. You said that.'

'I didn't say that,' Natalie said uncertainly. *Had she said that?*

'You did.'

'Well, she's right… the house isn't that big.'

'Not that big?!'

'Not as large as some. And there's no work. They're rich but they're not the Goldbergs. And anyway, it's probably not up to her, it's probably Mr Caplin, you know what he's like.'

'But I thought he was hardly ever there,' Leah said. 'Are you sure she's not against Jewish people too?'

'Of course she's not! Anyway, she likes me, and she likes her agent and… *Leah*, it's not her fault.'

Leah sighed dramatically. 'Well then, ask Mrs Sanderson. She's a good person.'

Natalie didn't like the way she said that. Mrs Caplin was a wonderful person too, it was just she couldn't help in this instance.

'And, Natalie, make sure you get across clearly *why* Aunt Dora needs to come. It's not because she wants to improve her English. Understood?'

But when Natalie said she would try this Sunday, Leah had squirmed. This Sunday, she and Alfie had a plan to go to a terrific music hall. A man there could balance ten plates on a stick *on his nose.*

Natalie would have left it, but Leah insisted: Leah didn't have to be there, did she? There really was no time to waste.

Natalie had gone from shock to pleasure at the prospect of Mama and Libby in England. Of course, they wouldn't spoil her adventures – not that she was having as many as she had hoped – they would just be an occasional taste of home. And wouldn't they adore Hugo? And Hugo would adore them! She pictured walks into town and picnics. Would they be allowed to use the Caplins' lovely garden? And Mama would put Mr Caplin in his place and perhaps become grand friends with Mrs Caplin too. There was no reason they couldn't go out together. It raised some complications about *when* Natalie was going back, yes, but they would go back when the time was right. It didn't have to be complicated.

On opening the door, Mrs Sanderson said kindly that Leah was out, but when Natalie explained it was Mrs Sanderson herself she had come to see, she invited Natalie in. She smiled, saying, 'how lovely' and 'well, this *is* a surprise.'

'Now this is what I call perfect weather!' said Natalie and Mrs Sanderson gave her tinkly laugh. The living room was full of books and framed paintings of shipwrecks and fields with horses. Over in the corner was a gramophone just like Uncle David's.

'Is this where the scientists from Cambridge sit and talk about their discoveries?'

Mrs Sanderson laughed until she coughed. She patted her pockets for a handkerchief. Natalie offered one of her own.

When she had recovered, Mrs Sanderson said, 'So tell me, how are things at the Caplins'?'

'Wonderful!' answered Natalie brightly. 'Educational!' she added, since that might appeal to Mrs Sanderson more. She stared at one boat getting battered by waves, and the tiny figures waving for help.

'Mrs Sanderson, I came to ask you a question about my mother. She would like to come here. To work.'

Mrs Sanderson surveyed Natalie closely. 'Is the situation back home deteriorating?'

Even though the letter from Mama confirmed it, even though Leah insisted it was the case, Natalie still struggled to say it.

'They think it will.'

Mrs Sanderson nodded thoughtfully, and Natalie was relieved she didn't ask if Natalie had asked the Caplins first. She probably knew how things were at Larkworthy.

'It must be horrendous. I will see what I can do.'

CHAPTER TEN

On November the fifth, Mrs Monger, Alfie and Molly, Natalie and Hugo went to the Alexandra Palace, where there would be an enormous bonfire. Natalie was waiting for word from Mrs Sanderson. None had come and it had been three weeks. She was running out of patience. What had begun as an idle possibility now had acquired an utmost urgency. Mama *must* come to England. It had to happen.

Alfie explained they were celebrating the burning of the man – a Catholic man – who tried and failed to blow up Parliament. His name was Guy Fawkes.

Ah, thought Natalie, this explained the small children pushing wheelbarrows around town, demanding a penny. She had leaned over one barrow to get a look at its contents and found a scarecrow wearing a Hitler moustache and a comb-over on a sinister mask. She had recoiled in shock.

She watched as the men gathered near the foot of the fire and lit it. There seemed to be something very ancient about this ritual, older even than the seventeenth century, back to the days of hunting and gathering. First, there was a crackling and snapping of twigs, and then the straw effigy began to burn.

Some people clapped. Alfie had brought along a friend, Clifford, and it seemed he had been brought expressly for her. Alfie denied this – *why would I do that?* – but nevertheless, Clifford kept trying to take Natalie to one side, and to talk to her away from the group. Molly nudged Natalie: 'He's a bit of all right, wouldn't you say?' Cliff had freckly eyelids and sandy hair. His teeth didn't stick out, his nose was a good ski-slope shape and there wasn't anything particularly wrong with his eyes or his hair, which curled quite appealingly over his ears, but there was nothing for her. She talked to him politely about the fog that was different from the fog at home and he interrupted, asking if he could take her out sometime, and she shrugged in a way she hoped he'd understand was a no.

'Is it because I'm not Jewish?' Clifford asked, hands in his pockets.

Which would be kinder – to say that was the reason, or the fact that she didn't find him attractive at all?

'It's because I have someone at home.'

'I don't mind if you don't mind.' Clifford picked up a handful of branches and walked over to the fire. He placed them down and threw the last one up in the air. The fire responded and surged up towards the sky.

As she watched the fire, Natalie was suddenly reminded of the photographs of Nazis burning the books of anyone who 'wasn't patriotic' just three years earlier. Pages scorched, little ashes flying around. All the thoughts that had gone into the books, the words and the pages, all gone because the writers weren't the right people or had said the wrong things. It made her feel faint and suddenly desperate to see Mama. She hoped Mrs Sanderson would provide an answer soon – even if it were a no, at least she, or rather Leah, would be able to plan something else.

When Clifford returned, he smelled of smoke yet was more resolute than before. 'I meant, he's not here, is he?'

'Well, let me think about it,' Natalie said, even though she didn't need to think about it. What she needed was to let him down gently.

Hugo clung to her hand. He didn't much like being out in the dark. 'Don't leave me, Nat,' he murmured.

'Never,' she whispered back. It put a big smile on his face.

Back at the house, Mrs Monger said she would teach Natalie another British custom. She filled up her largest saucepan with water, then added six apples: you had to get the apple out. Rolling up her sleeves, Natalie confidently prepared to grab one.

'With your teeth!' added Mrs Monger. 'Lordy, Natalie, you are an odd-bod.'

Ah, so this was the trick. Natalie tried and tried again with her teeth but couldn't. Mrs Monger laughed; naturally, she had removed the stalks to make it harder. Hard to get a grip when the apple was dancing around like that. Finally, she got her teeth into it and managed to lift it into the air. Everyone clapped. Natalie's chin was cold and wet, but she was triumphant: she had done it.

'Just shows, you can do anything if you put your mind to it,' said Mrs Monger.

Molly went next and managed it quickly. 'I've got fangs!' she said, baring her gums. 'Like Count Dracula.'

Every time Alfie tried, they pushed his face further into the water. He came up spluttering, his collar was wringing wet, but he didn't grumble; he stuck his hand in the water and stole an apple that way.

'Cheat!' shouted Mrs Monger. And Hugo joined in too, 'That's not fair, Alfie!' and Alfie let him push his face into the water again.

Natalie said this was one English custom she could get used to. Alfie flicked water at her, which made Hugo laugh until he clutched his tummy.

The next day, Mrs Monger shouted that Mrs Sanderson was on the phone. Natalie galloped for it. She wondered if one talked about the weather with the English even in a telephone conversation. Daringly, she decided not. Mrs Monger was stood by the phone, wagging her index finger: 'This is the last time. If I wanted to be a messenger, I would have gone into the postal service.'

Ignoring her, Natalie pulled the receiver and Mrs Sanderson's voice to her ear.

'It's good news, Natalie.'

'Really?'

'I can be your mother's guarantor. We are allowed a maximum of two women per household. We should be able to arrange her visa.'

'And Libby?'

'And Libby too.'

Natalie found she could breathe again. She put down the receiver. Mrs Monger was retreating into the kitchen, but Natalie threw herself into the housekeeper's arms. Mrs Monger staggered backwards and then, righting herself, stroked Natalie's hair.

'There, there, girl,' she said awkwardly. 'It isn't that bad, is it?'

'They're coming,' she murmured into Mrs Monger's sweet-smelling collar. 'Mama and Libby are coming to England.'

That afternoon, she told Alfie, who was weeding in the garden, and he reached for her hand. 'Pleased for you, Nat, really am.' There was dried mud up to his wrists, but she shook his hand anyway. It was odd, like they were playing grown-ups, when most of the time they just squabbled like siblings. 'It's the right thing,' he said heartily, 'I knew it.' She rolled her eyes and he grinned.

The first thing Mrs Caplin said was, 'But where will they live?', which was a little discouraging but she'd had a few acting rejections recently and perhaps was preoccupied.

'Mrs Sanderson is going to sort something for them.'

Mrs Caplin made a face. 'Beverley Sanderson is such a *good* person,' but the way she said it suggested she didn't think that at all.

Natalie was so pleased with the news that at bedtime she told Hugo even though it might have been better as a surprise. 'Guess what? You're going to meet my mama.'

'Here, in London?' he asked, which made her laugh.

'Well, I can't take you to Austria, can I?'

His face fell, then he nodded eagerly, 'And sisters?'

Sisters? The plural pulled her up short. *What about Rachel?*

'One of them, yes. Libby, the younger one.'

'Not Rachel?'

'Maybe Rachel one day. Not yet.' Rachel was now a Goldberg, not a Leeman. There was no avoiding that. She had thrown her lot in with them. Natalie hoped they would prove worthy of her sister.

That was fine though since Hugo had decided Libby was his favourite. He had a fondness for winners, and Natalie had described at length the shiny trophies and fat medals Libby had collected. She had even imitated Libby's hands-on-knees stance after a big race. The way she hissed 'Water!', then poured it all over her chin.

Hugo was too excited by the news to sleep and Natalie didn't have the heart to make him try. She was excited too. *Her family in England!* They would have such fun. She invented a crazy rain dance and they galloped all around the nursery, hollering and shouting, until they were exhausted. Natalie fell asleep and when she woke up in Hugo's bed after midnight, for a moment, she had no idea where she was.

A few days later, Natalie heard the wheel of the bicycle, the familiar tread then the snap of the letter box. It was a letter from home.

My dear girl,

Would springtime suit you? I'm thinking March. And what should I wear for the journey? Do the English ladies wear hats all the time? Does everything really stop for tea at four o'clock? That's something I'm looking forward to.

Am I too old for the upheaval? Too decrepit for change? What should I do with the house? Should Rachel and Leo move in? Or perhaps a tenant? What about Papa's sketches? It seems terrible to leave it all behind.

Forgive me, I have so many questions. And in answer to
yours, yes, Libby is fine about it so far. She treated the news with
her usual equanimity and will do what she is told. For once!

Mama

Papa had been an amateur artist. His pictures of boats on the Danube
and chalets in the mountains were up on the parlour wall. Natalie
knew that whatever she advised, Mama would endeavour to bring
them with her. She couldn't blame her – Mama didn't have much
of her beloved Pauly left.

Although Natalie didn't know much about the practicalities of
leaving a house, and certainly fashion was Rachel's department, not
hers, she wrote back a letter crammed full of reassurance, enjoying
her new status as 'responsible' daughter.

She told Mama of the German-speaking groups she might join
in London, the shops that sold seeded bread and dried apricots, the
German newspapers she might find. Mama didn't have anything to
worry about, really: she was so likeable and so expressive that she
made everyone understand her – and even if they couldn't, they
generally pretended they could.

You will fit in wonderfully, Mama. If I can, you can! How can
you think you are too old? And you will absolutely love your
boss, Mrs Sanderson. We've been so lucky, Leah and I, and you
will be too. Mr Caplin is the only person I would urge caution
with, but we hardly ever see the strange fellow.

PS. I still haven't had a proper afternoon tea yet, but I will
make sure we have one when you get here.

PPS. The light switches here are very strange too. They go up and
down instead of round, but you will get used to it all, I promise.

CHAPTER ELEVEN

The weather grew colder. Natalie and Hugo could see their breath run away from their mouths as they tramped to and from school. Hugo did wonderful drawings of Father Christmas and made paper chains from newspaper to hang in his and Natalie's rooms. Natalie looked forward to skating and sledging with him. Her room was so icy, she eventually asked for an extra blanket and Mrs Monger gave her two: 'I'm surprised you didn't ask earlier.' Natalie thought, *I'm surprised you didn't offer*, but she didn't say anything.

The Caplins did not have a toaster, something Natalie thought was a little primitive, but Mrs Monger taught her how to use the toasting fork and it became a routine, every day after school, for them to have a toasty snack by the kitchen fire.

Then in early December, King Edward VIII stood down to 'marry the woman I love'. Neither Natalie nor Mrs Monger could believe it. It simply was not possible. It was like stars falling out of the sky. They were glued to the wireless for hours, Natalie pressed as close to the set as possible without being a hog (hog was her new insult, Mrs Monger claimed she overused it). Even the announcers had lost their typical coolness; you could feel their shock, and Natalie's vocabulary was soon overflowing with new long words like: 'Abdication. Primogeniture, constitutional.'

But more than new words, the event raised so many questions. King Edward had given up everything for his woman. A great sacrifice. *Would Rudi do the same for her?* It hardly seemed likely from where Natalie was sitting. She had written him her news: apple bobbing, bonfires, and *Mama and Libby are coming to England*, and how extraordinary that was, and who'd have thought it?

No response. Even writing, it seemed, was too difficult for Rudi nowadays.

In the living room, Mrs Caplin was also permanently attached to her wireless. The King's news seemed to cause her a great deal of emotion. She invited her friends around to talk about it and they gossiped, smoked and laughed loudly with their heads thrown back.

'An abdication party,' said Mrs Monger. 'What an idea!' She was furiously cooking game pie at late notice. Alfie and Natalie had both been recruited to race to the greengrocer for extra supplies.

Mrs Caplin said that she wanted Hugo to perform for the guests later. Natalie thought of the monkeys in Prater Park, who wore human dungarees eye-wateringly tight and tiny shoes, and a man would take a photograph of you with them for five schilling – Mama hadn't allowed it.

Hugo would recite poetry in English, French and German, Mrs Caplin decided. She seemed nervous for once. It didn't matter that Hugo did not like poetry, nor reciting, and would prefer to arm-wrestle, this was what one did.

'Can he do it well?' she kept asking and then replying to herself, 'Oh, I suppose it doesn't matter, as long as he does *something*.'

'Will Mr Freeman be coming?' Natalie asked. Recently, she harboured a strange fantasy that she could divert Leah's attention away from Alfie and towards him. She had always fancied herself a matchmaker and felt Aunt Ruth would be forever indebted to her if she succeeded.

'No, no!' Mrs Caplin clutched her throat. 'And this is a *very* different crowd, Natalie. Please don't mention him in front of anyone.'

Natalie nodded, startled.

Mrs Caplin then seemed to regret the vehemence of her response, for when she spoke next, she was conciliatory. 'It will be a nice surprise when I do get a part, that's all.'

Mrs Caplin asked Natalie to fix the clasp of her necklace. Natalie used to do that for Mama. She strung the shiny pearls around her pale neck, and they made a noise like chattering teeth.

'How do I look?'

'Wonderful.'

'The best?' asked Mrs Caplin, smiling. She loved a compliment.

'Undoubtedly,' replied Natalie and they both laughed.

'You have to be good,' Natalie told Hugo once his mother had left the room. He had built himself a nest on the chest of drawers and was sitting on it, happy as Larry, covered by blankets and cushions.

Alas, Hugo did not want to recite poetry. In English, German or French.

Downstairs, there were a lot of women in beautiful bias-cut dresses smelling of the deep spicy perfumes that Natalie's Great-Aunt Mimi also preferred. Mrs Caplin really was the finest-looking woman there. She was wearing a pale pink dress, her golden hair was fixed by one clasp, but otherwise flowed free, and she had her proportions exactly right. There were lots of men in suits there; they may or may not have been the ones from the Olympics garden party. Unsurprisingly, there was no sign of Mr Caplin; he was away working again.

In the corner, there was a large free-standing globe where the countries stretched out disproportionately long, Britain was the centre of everything and Austria was too tiny even to have its own colour. It was a drinks cabinet and it was one of Natalie's favourite things in the house.

Natalie spotted the man from the garden party, Mr Young, talking animatedly to a man in a purple corduroy suit. He didn't notice her.

'Hugo would like to read tonight,' Natalie said loudly, trying to make the gesture seem spontaneous. Mrs Caplin clapped her hands. 'How wonderful, the entertainment has arrived!'

'What is he reading?' Mr Young asked before Mrs Caplin could respond.

'*Just William*,' Natalie said quietly.

'William Shakespeare?'

'No, Richmal Crompton. Hugo and I are terrific fans of her, er, *oeuvre.*'

Mr Young turned away from them. He whispered into Mrs Caplin's ear. Again, she clapped her hands.

'I've a better idea, Hugo, play something on the piano,' she said.

Hugo didn't want to do that. He buried his face in Natalie's legs. He acted half his age. She tried to cajole him from under her, but at the same time she was thinking, *his piano playing is dreadful.*

'Please, Hugo,' she whispered. 'Just for me,' and Hugo was such an obliging little boy that he sat on the stool and did as she asked.

His performance of 'Twinkle, Twinkle Little Star,' was lacklustre but mercifully short. The audience clapped politely and then turned away from the piano as if to say, 'Fine, we're done here'. Hugo got up from the stool and searched for Natalie's hand. His fingers were clammy. She didn't know if they were to stay or go. She just stood, half-in and half-out, gripping Hugo and being gripped.

'Well, there we have it!' Mr Young shouted, waving around the evening papers. 'Edward is a snivelling, traitorous coward.'

He seemed to be taking this awfully personally. The women near him were a-flutter. One was whispering behind her hand. Natalie saw that Mr Young wasn't well-liked among them.

'Well,' Mrs Caplin said, 'what an insight into British culture we're getting this week!'

'This isn't British culture,' he barked. 'This is what happens when manipulative foreign bitches get involved.'

One of the women backed away from him, shaking her head. Purple-suit man said, 'Steady on, James. No call for that.'

'I'll say what I like,' Mr Young said, and it sounded like a growl. 'I'll say the truth, seeing as everyone else here is afraid of it.'

'James,' Mrs Caplin warned him. The word sounded like 'gems' in her mouth. *Emeralds and rubies.* She stroked the back of his ruddy neck. 'Darling, this is a party.'

'Party, my arse. This is a wake.'

Hugo's eyes were huge. He was trying to look as self-possessed as he could, but he held Natalie's hand so tightly, it was like an unbreakable bond. 'Not in front of the children, thank you,' Mrs Caplin said tartly.

Natalie knew Mrs Caplin meant to be nice – *when was Mrs Caplin not nice?* – but the 'in front of the children' burned more than anything.

And then Mr Caplin came back for the Christmas holidays and there were no more parties. He spent his days at his desk in the drawing room or worrying on the telephone in the hall: sometimes Natalie would find the ladders by the bookshelves had moved and it made her uneasy. Although he was civil, Natalie walked on eggshells when he was there; it felt as though her hold on the house was slipping. She couldn't wait for Mama to come and distract her. Mrs Monger said he was obsessed with work. 'Between you and me, he'll have a breakdown if he's not careful,' she said. Molly added doubtfully, 'Bit he does like a chat. I don't know what on earth he expects me to say?'

'Be careful,' advised Natalie. She could just picture Mr Caplin making a move on a defenceless Molly while she was ironing shirts or hanging out wet clothes. Natalie told Molly that if anything untoward were to happen, Molly must scream with all her might and Natalie would be there.

'Why would I scream?' joked Molly. 'He's handsome!' When she saw Natalie's expression, she said, 'I'm joking, Nat. Gawd, you foreign girls!'

CHAPTER TWELVE

Over New Year, the Caplins went away, Mrs Monger went to stay with her sisters, Alfie went to his mother's, Molly disappeared goodness knows where, so it was just Natalie and Hugo – two dots in the big house, like currants in a steamed pudding.

Poor *Elephant*; there was no time to work on her much-neglected translation and barely any time for reading for pleasure, but Natalie taught Hugo chess – hopefully, she had the rules right – and rolled around the floor laughing with him about frogs and monsters. They hung from the ladders in the drawing room, and Hugo allowed her to read *The Odyssey* to him, sometimes for up to ten minutes a time. The sky made a welcome effort to snow and when it was two or three inches deep, they played angels in the garden. They also made lists of all the things they would do, the games they would play and the places they would visit when Libby and Mama were there. Hugo was most excited about dropping a cushion on Libby's head, and roping Mama in to teach him sewing, seeing as Natalie was so useless at it.

It was, Natalie reflected, one of the happiest of times she'd had in England.

Mrs Caplin came back, but Mr Caplin had too much work and did not. Mrs Caplin launched into a strict soup-only diet. Mrs Monger was disapproving. She reported that Mrs Caplin said she had overeaten and would rather die than be heavy. Alfie and Molly chortled.

'I wonder why,' said Alfie.

Mrs Monger grumbled, 'Hush, Alfie. Ours not to reason why—'

'Ours but to do and die,' finished Alfie. 'Don't I know it?'

At the end of January, Mrs Monger and Natalie watched as Alfie and Mr Caplin carried into the house a gigantic wooden piece of furniture. Alfie's fingers got trapped between box and doorframe, but he carried on gamely. Mr Caplin offered, 'I'll go backwards if you like,' but Alfie, whose face was almost puce with pain, insisted he was fine. They staggered on into the drawing room. Mrs Caplin was out at another audition. Hugo was at school. Natalie didn't know whether she should hang around or not, but Mrs Monger was watching, and Molly had joined, tying back her hair, so she stayed.

Mrs Monger said, 'I must say, Mr Caplin, I didn't think you had it in you,' which to Natalie's ears sounded awful but Mr Caplin didn't appear to notice.

It was a television. Mr Caplin said he'd got it for the coronation. Obviously not the coronation of Edward VIII – who was now gadding about with Mrs Simpson in New York or the South of France or meeting Nazis, no one was sure. But for the coronation of George VI, the brother, the spare.

Mama might be here in time, Natalie thought. She crossed her fingers and touched the cabinet. She couldn't wait to show Libby this.

Mr Caplin was pleased with himself. 'Hard work pays off in the end,' he said, admiring the tiny screen and its massive wooden surround. 'Hugo is going to love this.'

With an air of superiority, Molly advised that no one get their hopes up: 'My sister says televisions are rubbish.'

They turned it on and there was, as Molly had anticipated, that view of a snowstorm, but Mr Caplin insisted that all would be well on the actual day. Turning enthusiastically to Natalie, he put his hand on her arm. 'What do you think?'

'It's fine.' Natalie gazed pointedly at the hand, which he quickly withdrew. Just because he was buying televisions nowadays didn't mean they were friends.

That night, Mrs Caplin called Natalie into her room. At first, Natalie assumed it was going to be about the television – perhaps she wouldn't want Hugo to watch it – but it was for a different reason. She had won the part of Lady Macbeth. 'There is no better role for a woman,' she told Natalie. 'None. And I will make it my own. People will talk about Caro Caplin's Lady Macbeth for ever.'

Natalie bounced from one leg to another. This was good news for Mrs Caplin and she also felt relieved for Mr Freeman, since he had been distinctly out of favour since the Nurse debacle. She managed to be effusive for a good few minutes and Mrs Caplin received her congratulations gracefully. She didn't dismiss Natalie, so Natalie enquired politely, 'So have you seen the television?'

'Uh huh.' Mrs Caplin rubbed night cream into her face. She didn't seem to care for television much. Probably because it was Mr Caplin's thing. 'Jolly good.' Then emphatically, she said, 'You know, Natalie, it will never, never take over from the stage.'

And then, towards the end of February, just two weeks before Mama and Libby were due to arrive, a letter came from Vienna.

My dearest girl,

I have news, Natalie. Rachel is pregnant and she is having the most horrendous time. She is sick, not just in the morning, but all day long as well. We've tried ginger, we've tried herbs, but nothing seems to work.

Leo and his family are sympathetic, of course, but she needs me, especially since kind Dr Schaffer has left. America, I think, or maybe Australia? Many Jewish doctors have gone or are trying to.

I know that you are going to be disappointed, and I am sorry, but we really can't come right now. Maybe next year? You've said that Mrs Sanderson is a good woman – I'm sure she will understand. From one mother to another. I know you'd do the same if you were me. Libby is fine about it. She's come along loads at school recently and with the sports club and it would be terrible to set her back. She does a different activity every night. They are nurturing her. Libby suffered so much after Papa, didn't she? Maybe in time, things will be different?

Papa used to say we had to play the cards we are dealt with, and to be fair, I think we Leemans have been dealt a pretty wonderful hand.

Love,
Mama

Natalie didn't care one iota about ginger, herbs or the whereabouts of Dr Schaffer. And she *didn't* understand. Yes, Rachel being pregnant was wonderful news, but Rachel was with Leo now. The Goldbergs were her family, they were her life. She had chosen them.

Everything, but everything, had been better these last few weeks just knowing Mama and Libby were on their way. Now they were not, she felt flattened and frightened. A dread feeling came over her like a dark cloud in the sky – and she hadn't even told Leah yet. Who knew how she'd react? Far worse than Mrs Sanderson, no doubt.

Why couldn't Rachel have fallen in love with a normal man, a regular guy who would have listened to his wife and would have made good decisions, like not getting pregnant right now? Natalie decided that everything had to be Leo Goldberg's fault. She had never liked him. (This wasn't *entirely* true, but it *felt* true now.) A man who did what his wife told him to do, not what his *parents* told him to do. He was so wet and malleable, but not by Rachel.

For goodness' sake, the rest of them were living in dread yet they were making love, making life and holding Mama back.

Why did Rachel have to always hog Mama? Why did Mama have to be so soft?

After school, Hugo tried to cheer up Natalie with a rendition of the English Country Garden song where you pull down your pants and suffocate the ants, but it was no use, Natalie felt sick to her stomach. She hadn't expected this, she had thought everything was fixed. And it was the worst news, the worst. Everything Leah had ever said about Vienna, Hitler and the Nazis, the anti-Semitism, now weighed down on her, crushing her chest. She hadn't taken much notice before, but now? Now she noticed.

That night, strange dreams about heirs and spares woke her up. She was the spare – that went without saying – talented, beautiful Rachel was the heir. Jealousy bubbled inside her. There was no avoiding how she felt: Mama had chosen her older sister. Not only over her, but over everything. Natalie's brain protested, told her that wasn't true, but her heart told her that it was.

When Natalie next had the opportunity, she cycled over to the Sanderson house. She usually enjoyed admiring the single tree trunks and the split ones like forks en route – the shrubs, the dandelions, the squirrels – but not this time. This time, she noticed only hazards and rubbish: a wellington boot abandoned kerbside, a tipped-over tree, the ashes of a recent fire: she was on a horrible mission and everything was sullied and ruined.

As she came into the kitchen, Leah beamed – as far as Leah beamed – until she read Natalie's face, then she scowled: 'What *now?*'

After Natalie told her, Leah slammed down her oven glove, which showed Natalie she herself was not overreacting by being utterly furious with Mama.

'Dammit!' she said, 'What *are* they thinking?'

But now that Leah was reacting in this way, Natalie wanted to defend Mama.

'It's her first grandchild, Leah. You can imagine how that is.'

Leah couldn't imagine.

'And Rachel really is sick. She hates being sick. She wouldn't let Mama stay unless she was desperate.'

Leah still didn't speak.

'It will be okay, though, won't it?' Natalie asked timidly. 'It shows that things can't be that bad.'

'It shows *nothing* of the sort!' Leah picked up the glove, then slammed it down again. She stalked around the kitchen like she was looking for something to whack. Eventually, she opened a cupboard and started wiping the shelves, which were already spotless.

'Libby's doing much better at school, it says that, so that's good. And she's involved in all the clubs. And a baby in the family? That's good news, isn't it? A blessing.'

'Yes,' said Leah, but she wouldn't meet Natalie's eyes.

'I'll tell Mrs Sanderson,' Natalie said.

'*I'll* do it,' snapped Leah.

Natalie was even more downhearted on the way home. The things she was going to show Mama had attained a sheen, but now that Mama was not coming, everything was plain and rusty. She was getting off her bicycle in the front garden when she nearly ran slap bang into Mr Caplin.

'Ahoy,' he said. For someone so sombre, he did cheerful greetings very well. Perhaps they sapped all his energy. 'Nice day for it. Need a hand?'

'Hello,' Natalie responded warily. 'No, thank you.' She wheeled the bike over to the shed, being careful not to knock over any gnomes. She realised Mr Caplin was waiting for her by the front door of the house, so she took as long as she could, pretending to check the bike was safe, the tyres were pumped, and trying to invent further ways to slow down.

He gave her a semi-smile. Why was he so nervy around her?

'Hugo told me your mother and sister are coming from Vienna.'

Natalie stood stock-still. *Was he trying to be funny?* This was the kind of thing bullies did.

'You must be excited.' He held the door open for her.

'They're not any more. They decided to stay because…' She didn't want to tell him what Mama's reasons were. They hurt so much when she held them up to the light. She shrugged. 'That's it.'

'Oh,' he said. 'How disappointing for you.'

Not for you, she thought.

'Not at all,' she lied. 'I trust them to make good decisions.'

He nodded, forced a smile and said, 'That's the spirit,' or something like that. Whatever it was, she didn't like it. She walked in and up the stairs and, like she had seen Mrs Caplin do, she didn't look back.

CHAPTER THIRTEEN

Leah and Alfie decided that Natalie should be kept busy to get over her disappointment. They invited her to as many dances and trips to tearooms as possible – with Clifford making up a four. Clifford was still keen, and as a reward for his persistence, or out of boredom or something, Natalie let him kiss her. She was seventeen and a half now and the need to kiss someone, anyone, was growing daily. Rudi hadn't written for months. How hard was it to write? Even Libby managed occasionally, and she hated it for good reason. By contrast, Rudi was capable of writing essays of 20,000 words *with* footnotes.

Didn't she have to think about her own happiness too?

Rachel had Leo. Leah had Alfie. Mrs Caplin had… well, Mrs Caplin seemed to have men salivating over her, left, right and centre.

That spring in England daffodils sprouted on the grass verges like in an Impressionist painting. Birds and blossoms wherever she looked. The garden even smelled wonderful. Everything had taken on a brighter, more luscious shade. Natalie knew Mama would have been in her element.

One weekend, Leah suggested a swim at the lido and although it was still too cold for outdoor swimming really, and although Clifford would be there, puppy-eyed and pining, when she found out she was free, Natalie agreed. She hadn't been out without Hugo for some time but Molly was bored today and had decided to take him to the pictures.

The lido was so much more impressive than she had expected. The water was a brilliant blue and sparkling. If only she was there with Rudi, not Clifford. Rudi would have loved this. She thought of writing to tell him about it but couldn't. They were further apart than ever before, and actually she didn't *really* know if he would love it. Did he love an outdoor swimming pool? – she struggled to recall. She did remember the crinkle of his earlobes though. The shape of his mouth. The unrequited advice he gave. Why wouldn't he write?

'Nat, Nat…'

They splashed each other, and of course Alfie had brought along a ball. He threw it to Clifford, who threw it to Leah, who threw it to her. Leah was a strong swimmer and she did lengths while the others played pigs in the middle. They hogged the ball and Natalie grew afraid she'd be stuck in the middle for ever, but Alfie took sympathy on her and let her take a turn. Then they threw a hoop to the surface of the pool and took it in turns to reach it. Natalie hated opening her eyes underwater, so she took longer than the others. She fumbled along the bottom of the pool and had to come up for air. She wasn't going to let it go, though. *Pretend it's Mama and you have to reach her,* she told herself and, just like the apple-bobbing, on the fourth attempt, she finally did it. The others cheered and she threw her prize up into the air. It was one of those surreal moments when Natalie couldn't help thinking, *how on earth did we end up here?* Two girls from Vienna splashing it up in an ice-cold pool with Northern Alfie and Cornish Clifford.

Clifford had brought her a slice of Battenberg – pink and yellow cake. He didn't believe her when she said she'd never had it before. 'It's German, it is,' he said authoritatively. Whatever it was, it was delicious.

When Clifford lunged at her afterwards, on the picnic rug, Natalie tried to imagine he was Rudi or it was practice for being with Rudi. Clifford nuzzled her throat and cheeks, and said, 'You see, it's nice, isn't it?' Natalie supposed it was, but she didn't like the way Clifford kissed her mouth and when he got too handy, she told him off, Battenberg or no.

Being with Clifford, kissing Clifford, was a break from monotony but every time he started up, she found herself yearning to get home. To snuggle up in her own bed or to listen to Hugo's tiny boy snores.

Leah was usually too busy canoodling with Alfie to notice Natalie's discomfort, so Natalie tried to make sure they weren't *always* a four. Sometimes they went out with Molly as well, and sometimes with Alfie's other friends, Frank or Billy. Clifford would eye her mournfully and try to get her alone. She said to Clifford that she hoped he wouldn't get fed up with her. He said, 'For you, I'll wait for ever.'

One night, when Natalie had just got back from a dance where Clifford had pawed her from the moment the music stopped, she saw there was, finally, a letter from Rudi. She couldn't help but feel that by dating Clifford, she had *caused* it to be there.

I was sorry to hear that your mother changed her mind about leaving Vienna. I did my best to persuade her, but with Rachel's baby on the way I suppose she felt she had no choice.

I will keep an eye on them all. And maybe one day everything will be different.

This was utterly confusing. Rudi had done his best to persuade Mama to leave? She had never heard this before. Neither Mama nor Libby had mentioned him – and what did it have to do with Rudi anyway? It was a puzzle. She felt a little jealous, although whether she was more jealous of her family for seeing Rudi or of Rudi for seeing them, she couldn't be quite sure.

And once again, she couldn't help noting there was little of sentiment in Rudi's letter. Had she imagined what had gone between them in her house over the dining table? Was their love affair all in her head? Shamefully, she'd gone further with Clifford now than she ever had with Rudi. But that last line, Natalie read again and again. *And maybe one day everything will be different.*

She couldn't be mistaken on this, could she? That was definitely a hint of something.

*

Natalie didn't tell anyone when it was her one-year anniversary in England, especially not Clifford. He would demand some kissing celebration, no doubt. It was an odd moment. It should have been a happy time – she was achieving much of what she had originally set out to do. She was on Chapter 6 of *Making an Elephant out of a Mosquito* and she was learning so many English phrases and so much about English life: that kings sometimes abdicate and too many cooks spoil the broth. That a man tried to blow up Parliament, that when apple-bobbing, you use your teeth. But she was growing more and more anxious that Mama had made a big mistake. As Mrs Monger would say, 'she felt it in her bones'. Mama, Libby *and* Rachel should be leaving Austria now, no ifs, no buts. It was all very well thinking they might leave later; the opportunity might not be there later. And she felt more abandoned, or isolated from back home, oddly, far more than she had when she first arrived.

Someone did remember her one-year anniversary in England though. As Natalie came back from dropping off Hugo at school, a car pulled up and Mrs Sanderson told her to get in. Natalie hadn't seen her since Mama had changed her mind and felt a cold prickle of embarrassment. As she sat down on the hot leather seat, she apologised again and Mrs Sanderson said in her gentle way, 'No apology necessary, I *completely* understand.'

Mrs Sanderson asked Natalie about Hugo, her work and how she was finding life in England. She said the bouquet of flowers on the back seat were for Natalie because she remembered today was a special day.

Natalie could have wept, it was so lovely, but then Mrs Sanderson said something that suggested that wasn't the *only* reason she had dropped by.

'I did want to ask… have you met with…' Mrs Sanderson shifted uncomfortably. 'Mrs Caplin's journalist friend?'

Somehow Natalie knew immediately who she meant.

'The… the Mr Young?'

'Yes.'

'I have met him,' Natalie said.

'It's just I heard they have become…' Mrs Sanderson seemed embarrassed. 'Very close.'

Mrs Caplin was very *close* with everyone. She called Natalie 'darling' all the time, she stroked Alfie's arm and even Clifford had been squeezed when she met him one time in the garden.

'Mrs Caplin has many friends—'

'I think it might be more than that…'

This was a shocking accusation.

'The thing is, Natalie, I worry about his… influence. His world view is different from mine. He's very ambitious.'

Natalie was speechless for a moment, then she decided, much as she liked Mrs Sanderson, her loyalties had to be to her boss. She remembered that everyone used to call Papa 'ambitious'. They disapproved of it then too.

'There's nothing to worry about,' Natalie responded. 'There's nothing going on and anyway, Mrs Caplin is always perfectly lovely to me. And to Mr Freeman.' As she said it, she remembered that she hadn't seen Mrs Caplin's agent for a couple of months now. Still, she continued. 'There's no problem, no… influence,' she said pointedly, and then because this sounded a little ungrateful, she added, 'I'm very happy at Larkworthy.'

'Then it's nothing,' Mrs Sanderson said. 'Forgive me.' She *was* tired. She had purple rings under her eyes and her skin was pale and bumpy. Natalie wondered briefly if she were envious of Mrs Caplin. That would explain it. 'And I'll always help you, Natalie, you know that. Let me know if your mother changes her plan.'

Natalie guessed Mrs Sanderson had a lot going on at work or at home. And she was glad Mrs Sanderson had made a faux pas – not that this was comparable to Mama's, but still.

'She won't,' Natalie said, 'but I will keep it in mind.'

Back at the house, Natalie couldn't help smiling as she took the flowers in.

'Not your birthday, is it?' said Mrs Monger irritably, searching for a vase.

Natty,

Mama promised me ten schilling if I wrote. I already owe Helga twenty schilling, which means I am down, but I thought I should write anyway, and show off my new pen. Isn't it pretty? I do bubble letters too. You can't borrow it. All your pens have bite marks in them anyway.

Mama says we don't see Rachel enough, but on Sunday, we had a picnic together. She is as big as a cow. She can't take her hands off Leo. Mama said, 'that's young love', and I would be the same one day. Urgh. I don't think so. Are you in love with anyone? I bet our neighbour Arno is saving himself for you. Ha!

I saw Rudi – you remember the boffin who used to tutor you? He was with Rachel's old friend, Flora Lang! She has a very pretty smile. She was wearing a jacket with a fur collar. At first, I thought it was a dead cat. I wonder if they are going to get married. Shall I ask?

I miss you awfully. When will you come home? Will you speak English better than Frau Rascher?! Don't be a show-off like her, please!

The best sister in the family Leeman,
Me – Libby

Natalie knew Flora Lang. Everyone did. Legs like an acrobat, hair like a beauty queen, her family had built half of Vienna and she didn't mind letting you know. She had the pick of all the boys. And she had chosen Rudi Strobl? What could she possibly have in common with Natalie's fiercely questioning Rudi? What jokes would those two make together? It didn't seem possible. It *wasn't* possible. Natalie's eyes searched the page for something, somehow to make sense of this.

No, Natalie did not want Libby to ask Rudi if he was in love with her, thank you very much. She had never written back to her sister so quickly, nor prayed so much to the postal service to deliver promptly.

Flora Lang was everybody's dream girl. Whereas Rudi was, put it this way, Rudi was niche. Rudi was gorgeous but he was an acquired taste. Flora Lang was milk chocolate whereas Rudi was more... olives. With pips in.

CHAPTER FOURTEEN

Something had happened at the Sandersons'. Leah had gone to the dining room as usual to discuss the menu for the day. It was six o'clock in the morning and Mrs Sanderson was sitting at the table like she normally did, but she was coughing. She was coughing up blood. She managed to contain most of it in her handkerchief, but a few vivid drops dripped on the white tablecloth. This seemed to distress her more than anything. Leah told her it was no problem, it would wash out, but she continued to stare at it, then coughed and coughed.

'I'm so sorry, Leah, I'm afraid I'm really rather ill. I'll need you to wire Frances for me and call the doctor.'

When Leah asked, rather impertinently, 'How long have you been like this?' Mrs Sanderson refused to answer, or rather, she was coughing too much to answer, so Leah interpreted that as 'a long time'. Leah said she suddenly was furious with her, which she knew was ridiculous. Mrs Sanderson wasn't to blame. It just was. Mrs Sanderson continued just sitting there, looking frail and pale.

'What do you think will happen?' Natalie asked.

'I don't know,' Leah said. Since Leah always had an answer to everything, it must be bad.

Natalie had wanted to discuss the news about Rudi, but Leah was so distressed about Mrs Sanderson, she could hardly bring herself to order her tea, and so Natalie decided not to mention it. It really was worrying. Natalie liked that smiley and punctual lady, her first English woman friend, very much. She suspected Leah was being overdramatic.

Mrs Caplin had to go out a lot, rehearsing, so Natalie had more Hugo-time. He was doing well at school, he was sporty, just like Libby – they would have got on so well – and he was always up for new experiences. His reading was vastly improving and as for his piano playing, well, he did a fine 'Three Blind Mice'.

Mr Caplin was hardly ever at home and when he was, he just stayed head-down at his desk for fourteen or fifteen hours a day. Mrs Monger said he had been like that for as long as she'd known him.

Natalie thought that as time moved on, she would grow less annoyed with Mama for her change of mind, but instead, she grew more furious with her.

Nothing seemed to settle her. Every time she heard anything about Hitler, in the papers or on the wireless, her heart beat faster. Leah was right: Natalie's family should have left Austria. She tried to concentrate on her *Elephant* translation, but even there she felt increasingly besieged by doubts. It was difficult. Everything was difficult suddenly.

What if they had thrown away their only opportunity to get away?

CHAPTER FIFTEEN

Mrs Caplin said that Natalie could bring as many friends as she liked to *Macbeth*. She was so kind like that. Leah had a ticket – she deserved a treat – and Natalie thought of asking Clifford and Alfie. Now that Rudi was seeing Flora Lang – *if* he was seeing Flora Lang – there was no reason for her and Clifford not to get together. No reason, except she wasn't attracted to Clifford. Yet as the date of the performance drew nearer, she decided she couldn't bear to be at the theatre with those two chaps making crude or stupid comments, so she offered Molly and Mrs Monger the tickets instead.

Mrs Monger said she'd had enough of Mrs Caplin giving her orders all day long, she'd give it a miss, 'thank you kindly', but surprisingly, Molly agreed. She said she needed a good laugh.

Natalie had envisaged a massive theatre, but it wasn't even a real theatre but a community hall with wooden seats and an elevated section at the front for a stage. Still it was pleasing, and Natalie could imagine Mrs Caplin walking around backstage, rearranging her suspenders and telling everyone to 'break a leg', which didn't mean break a leg but was actors' talk for 'do well'. Mrs Caplin had also forbidden Natalie to say 'Macbeth', which was bad luck; she had to say 'The Scottish play' instead.

As they shuffled in, Natalie sniffed cigar smoke. She was sure it would be Mr Freeman but it turned out to be a man who was about a hundred years old with a monocle that kept popping out.

'What ho!' he called to the girls. 'There's room for you fillies on my lap!'

'Thank you, but no,' replied Leah. 'I don't want to kill you.'

'But what a way to go!' he said and everyone along the row laughed.

Molly wasn't a great companion. Once the show started, she sat back with crossed arms, insisting it was all gibberish and gobbledegook and why couldn't they speak proper English?

'Ssssh,' said Leah, before whispering to Natalie, 'she's got a point.'

When Lady Macbeth came on though, it was hard not to squeal with pride.

'There's my boss!' Natalie wanted to nudge everyone. 'That's her.'

Hard to say whether Mrs Caplin objectively was 'good' or not. She looked absolutely stunning, and she delivered her lines correctly and, Natalie thought, with meaning. She and Macbeth got quite *physical* sometimes. Macbeth was excellent – you almost forgot he was an actor – and she enjoyed the witches although something about them reminded her of Leah: she laughed to herself; probably the fact they were always there with their dark prophecies and plans.

At the intermission, which Molly insisted on calling 'half-time', Molly said, 'I'm done…'

'What? There's more!' said Natalie, as incredulous that someone could leave before the end as they could come late.

'Got to see a man about a dog.'

'A dog?'

Molly laughed. 'It's a phrase, silly. No, I'm going to meet a… a gentleman friend.'

'Who?' asked Leah, who never wouldn't blunder into a situation. But Molly went red and touched the side of her nose. Natalie gazed at her uncomprehendingly.

'I have been sworn to secrecy,' said Molly, avoiding meeting their eyes. Natalie's heart raced. She wanted to say something to Molly or Leah, but the bell rang and it was back into the theatre for them. In the second part, her mind wandered horribly. She managed to concentrate when Mrs Caplin was on stage, but when she wasn't, her imaginings flew all over the place. *Surely Molly wouldn't be meeting Mr Caplin?*

Leah didn't want to go backstage or to the rooms that led off from behind the black curtains, but Mrs Caplin had said they must so Natalie marched them there. There were three rooms in a row that might have been dressing rooms and Natalie wasn't sure which was which, but the third door she looked at had a paper sign stuck on saying 'Lady Macbeth', so Natalie knocked and Mrs Caplin's voice called out, '*Entrez!*'

Mrs Caplin was sat in front of a propped-up mirror edged by tiny lights, her long legs stretched out on Mr Young's lap.

'Oh!' said Natalie involuntarily. He had his hand around Mrs Caplin's ankles. His hand was as big as a boxing glove or her legs were very tiny.

'You were marvellous,' Leah said in the obsequious voice she always used with Mrs Caplin. She also bowed slightly.

'Thank you.'

'I thought so too,' Natalie said, trying not to look at Mr Young's thumbs. There was nothing else to say. He didn't look at her once. It was like she was invisible.

While she waited for Leah to first find, then use the lavatory, Natalie leaned against the wall by the dressing room and she could hear their voices, Mrs Caplin's clearly, Mr Young's less so.

'Hugo is in love with her. He would marry her if he could.'

'Awkward, bearing in mind the age gap.'

'Doesn't put you off *me*, does it?'

Sound of laughter. 'I suppose Warwick thinks it's brilliant. He loves a damsel in distress.'

'When did you ever care what Warwick thinks about anything?'

Leah came out from the bathroom complaining of the queues so loudly that Natalie couldn't hear his answer to that.

*

The next day, when Mrs Caplin asked if Natalie had enjoyed the show, Natalie said she had very much. And did she enjoy her performance, and did she catch that bit where she had forgotten her lines? Squirming, Natalie apologised, 'I'm not very observant.' 'You won't say anything to Mr Caplin about Mr Young being there, will you?' Mrs Caplin added in a low voice. 'He was there for the paper, you know. It could be fabulous publicity for me. It's not that Mr Caplin would mind exactly but I don't want him to worry. I'd hate for people to get the wrong idea.'

Mrs Sanderson had got the wrong idea.

Natalie nodded. It was easy to get the wrong idea, she knew that. Fleetingly, her thoughts turned to Molly's coy expression. She tried to ignore it.

'Discretion is important to English people.'

'And to us Viennese.' Natalie was proud that Mrs Caplin talked to her so openly. Proud that she was someone who could be trusted. Flattered that she was being treated as an equal. Rachel hadn't told her she was courting Leo of the Goldberg family for months. That had hurt. Of course Mrs Caplin should have friends. And if she *said* they were just friends, then that was that.

'Of course. Do we understand each other?'

'Perfectly.'

CHAPTER SIXTEEN

Hello Natalie, or should I say, Aunty Natalie?

At last she's here! Hannah Pauline Goldberg (Hannah for Leo's grandmother and Pauline for Papa).

Since lovely Doctor Schaefer left, I had a student – he'd only been studying one year. Can you imagine? He was petrified. He was fine though, Natalie. Thank G-d. Very patient with me. Even so, the birth was a disaster, and I am ruined. Don't ask. Hannah screams all night and feeds all day. Mama is wonderful but Leo's mother doesn't like her here so often so it's a little awkward. Leo and I can't wait to get somewhere of our own, but as you know, Leo is slow at big decisions and I expect he finds things quite comfortable here at home. I suppose I do too.

After the birth, Leo asked the medical student if he would leave Austria – if it comes to it – and he said, 'no, I will stay to the bitter end.' So, Leo now thinks we must too. That's exactly what he said, 'the bitter end'. Make of that what you will.

I must say, Hannah has a permanently angry expression. She's got a heavy forehead, thick eyebrows and dribbles all day long. They say she looks like you! Only joking, Natalie. How I wish you were by my side.

Your ever-loving sister,
Rachel

*

The Christmas of 1937, Natalie's second Christmas in England, was quiet and rather dismal. It did not snow. The Caplins went away, taking a protesting Hugo with them. Mrs Monger went to her old dad's. Leah was either working or wrapped up with Alfie. Natalie remarked that they were like the conjoined twins that had been featured in the *Daily Mail* and Leah put the telephone down on her.

Natalie sometimes noticed Mr Young's name next to a byline in the paper. He once did a scathing report on a minister for trade. Mostly, he did an odd combination of domestic incidents and cricket. Natalie felt glad he didn't do international affairs. He might pretend he knew everything, but she had a feeling he didn't know anything in depth. Nevertheless, she couldn't help rifling through the pages, looking for the articles he had written and signs of his ambition and influence. She never did find a review of Mrs Caplin's Lady Macbeth.

With so much free time, Natalie devoted herself to *Making an Elephant out of a Mosquito*. Here was truth and reason and logic and love. Books were a great hiding place.

One day, Molly came up, sat on her bed and watched her as she was rubbing out parts of Chapter 7, where a baby elephant was learning how to hoot water from its trunk. She loved finding the right words, but sometimes even the simple ones were elusive.

'Why are you doing that?' Molly asked.

'I just want to bring the book to a wider audience, I suppose.'

Natalie explained that translating was harder than she had anticipated. Molly bit her lip and asked if she wanted to go out later. Natalie declined.

'Are you in love with Clifford?'

He had bought her a hair clip for Christmas, and she had got him some tobacco. Love didn't seem the right word, in German or English.

'Not really.'

'Why not?' Molly picked at bits of wool on Natalie's blanket.

'I've got someone back home.' *Did she?*

Of course, Molly wanted to know more.

'Rudi is a funny name. It's like rude. Rude-y.'

She made Natalie feel old. 'Are you in love with anyone, Molly?' If it *was* Mr Caplin, Natalie thought, she really didn't want to know.

'Love is for losers,' Molly declared as she got up. 'Well, these clothes won't iron themselves.'

Mrs Caplin and Hugo came back, but Mr Caplin was working away again. Hugo gripped Natalie tightly and Mrs Caplin, looking chicer than ever in a navy coat that swept to the ground, grabbed Natalie's hands and cooed, 'We missed you so much,' which was unexpected but lovely. Later, she called Natalie into the drawing room and said, 'I wanted to get something nice for you, but I didn't know what.' She blinked slowly. 'You don't seem to care for material things.'

Natalie shrugged. She thought *actually, material things would be quite nice.* Whatever had given Mrs Caplin the impression she didn't like them? They walked around the house to the front garden. Natalie didn't have a clue what was going on. The trees were bereft of leaves. It was chilly and she wanted to go back in to fetch her coat.

'Wasn't your mother going to come to England?' Mrs Caplin asked suddenly.

Eight months. It had taken her eight months to realise.

'The situation changed,' said Natalie.

'Maybe it's for the best.' Mrs Caplin pursed her lips tightly, then released them with a popping sound.

The best for whom? It certainly wasn't the best for Natalie. She was becoming quite annoyed when Mrs Caplin led her to the car, to the door on the driver's side.

'Mrs Monger told me you've always wanted to learn to drive.'

Natalie was speechless. She would be able to take charge of the car and go, go, somewhere, anywhere! She looked at Mrs Caplin, almost bracing herself for disappointment. It couldn't be true, could it? It was the biggest gift she could imagine. Here was freedom. Adventure on the open road. Imagine telling everyone back in Vienna about this!

'Jump in.'

At the wheel, Natalie managed to find some words: 'Mr Caplin won't mind?'

Mrs Caplin winked at her. 'What he doesn't know, he doesn't mind. You're very special, not just to Hugo but to me too, my discrete girl.'

The car vibrated. Natalie felt her toes on the accelerator. Power at her feet. At first, they rabbit-hopped, but Mrs Caplin was a generous teacher, told her it was normal, relax, you can do it. They edged forward and then they were facing the gate and the road.

'Yes,' said Mrs Caplin as though reading Natalie's mind. 'Let's go.' And Natalie was so overwhelmed, she leaned over and kissed Mrs Caplin's soft cheek. Mrs Caplin laughed. 'Eyes on the road!' and soon, they were off.

'You should go and see Leah,' said Alfie, a few days later, on the doorstep, polishing boots. 'She misses you.'

Natalie hated Alfie telling her what to do, but nevertheless decided to pop by to see Leah the next time she went out for a drive. It felt like things had turned again – Natalie had begun life in England feeling slightly overawed by her experienced, more settled cousin, but look at her now behind the wheel of a motorcar! It gave her quite the thrill.

As Natalie pulled up in front of that pretty Sanderson house, Leah came out in a tightly knotted bonnet, but her expression was far from admiring. She looked rather strained. Natalie stopped feeling triumphant and tried to think what she could say to cheer up her cousin.

Leah leaned over the gate. 'Don't come in,' she said. 'We're too busy. We're taking the children to the sanitorium tomorrow.'

And Natalie was disappointed, but she said, 'Oh, but that's marvellous news. I'm so glad Mrs Sanderson is feeling better.'

'No,' Leah said in a voice so quiet Natalie could barely hear. 'She's not getting better.'

A few evenings after, Natalie and Hugo were playing hide-and-seek and Natalie was hiding behind the chess set in the drawing room. She particularly liked this game because she could get a little peace and quiet while Hugo went roaring around, shouting, 'Am I warm?' (he always shouted that, even though she never gave him clues).

But it was Mr Young who came in, followed by Mrs Caplin. And from behind the chess set, she saw Mrs Caplin rear up and kiss first his cheek and then his mouth.

'Don't go yet,' she said. 'Stay.'

'Some of us have important jobs to do,' he said.

This was horrendous. Natalie supposed she should have emerged immediately, but now that she hadn't, it was too late. The embarrassment of it! What if she were discovered? She would just die on the spot.

Then she heard Hugo shouting for her, and Mr Young and Mrs Caplin peeled apart rapidly. Hugo continued yelping while Mrs Caplin snapped, 'Does it *look* like Natalie is in here, Huey?' but she and Mr Young left the room anyway, thankfully; it was the best piece of luck she'd had in ages. Five minutes later, dripping with sweat, Natalie crept out from her hiding place.

She told Hugo that since he hadn't found her, he was to seek her again, just so she could have a moment and take in what she had seen. And Hugo was happy because he preferred to be the seeker anyway.

So, it *was* true. Mrs Caplin and Mr Young *were* having an illicit relationship, a clandestine love affair. Mrs Caplin had lied – well, of course she had – the only surprising thing was that Natalie had believed her. She blushed, thinking of the last conversation she had had with poor Mrs Sanderson. Even when she had seen Mr Young's hands around Mrs Caplin's legs, she still hadn't believed it.

Natalie didn't see herself as *particularly* naïve. She was Viennese, for goodness' sake, they prided themselves on being the most cosmopolitan city in Europe, the most cosmopolitan in the world. Natalie especially regarded herself as someone closer to sophistication than innocence! Having a sister a few years older and a young-at-heart mother, she was privy to 'adult' things before her time. In her family, unlike so many of her schoolfriends', they talked openly about menstruation, about intercourse. They were modern. They might not have a fantastic drinks cabinet globe in the living room, but they had toasters. They even had central heating. They knew all there was to know about the mind, the body, the morphine, the more outré theories of Dr Sigmund Freud. Great-Uncle Ben had been in love with a young non-Jewish woman for many years before he married Great-Aunt Mimi. Aunt Hilda had tricked Uncle David into children and that might be the reason he had left. Adultery, illegitimacy, they should be grist for the mill to this Viennese girl. But Natalie *hadn't* expected it here, not in this house with its beautiful English country garden, and when you don't expect something, often you don't see it, even when it's staring you right in the face. It had been obvious, she knew that, of course it was, but still…

On the one hand, Mr Caplin had clearly philandered first. Obviously. And not with a woman of equal status either, which was worse. Not with a woman who he loved, but with a nanny who had to leave under a black cloud, which was doubly worse. Natalie remembered the hand he once put on her arm. It was pretty clear where *that* might have headed if she had given an inch. *Had Molly given an inch?* she wondered then pushed it from her mind.

Mrs Caplin had been denied love where she ought to find it – now she was forced to look elsewhere. That was the only explanation.

Would Mrs Caplin actually leave Mr Caplin for Mr Young though? Or would she perhaps ask Mr Caplin to leave? This seemed to Natalie the most sensible option, and she wondered if Mrs Caplin had considered it. Should she perhaps suggest it? Or would life continue largely without change, only Mrs Caplin would have the passion she evidently craved and deserved?

Could she ask Mrs Monger? Could she ask Alfie? She could, but she didn't. If they didn't know about it, then it would be a betrayal – and if they did, she would look silly. Perhaps she was the last to know? Could she ask Leah – no, Leah had plenty on her plate right now. Not only was she dealing with the imminent death of her beloved boss, but who knew if her contract would be renewed? Leah's greatest fear was being sent home.

Natalie told herself she wasn't to get involved. Mrs Caplin trusted her. Who Mrs Caplin spent her time with was nothing to do with her. And pretty soon, she too had bigger things to worry about.

CHAPTER SEVENTEEN

In March 1938, Germany invaded Austria. The hardest thing for Natalie was how pleased her fellow Austrians were. Natalie remembered Rudi warning her they would welcome Hitler with open arms, and they did, *we* did. Her people, her Austrians, thronged the streets. The church bells rang out for them. She didn't know what the people expected – although maybe she did. They expected their lives to improve. They expected an economic miracle.

Natalie pictured the scarlet and black armbands, the arms rigidly stuck out. Hitler stood on the balcony of Heldenplatz – their beloved Habsburg Palace overlooking the square of heroes – that little runt of a man, the man who had never kept a promise in his life, and people had decided, arbitrarily and randomly, to believe in him. To love him.

She just hadn't anticipated it.

It was so hard, with hindsight, to say, *how could you not have known*? But Natalie didn't know. She didn't know what she was hearing on the wireless. How could she? It had never happened before. She didn't know where it was going. She hadn't joined up the dots. They chanted Heil Hitler, they embraced it. Two hundred and fifty thousand Austrian people celebrating, 'welcoming Hitler home'.

'It's just like Hail Caesar,' she had said. *No, it wasn't.*

Oh, apparently not everyone who was there felt ecstatic.

Later, Rachel wrote:

Leo's parents were there, in among the crowd, counted among the statistics, but they were 'just looking'. Mama stayed home, but I saw Mary Moser from the orchestra, and she said, 'What a load of old rubbish. I heard they'd be handing out strudel.'

Natalie's friend from school, Elizabet Steiner, wrote:

I was going to the pharmacy to pick up headache tablets but was swept that way by the crowd. Like a giant wave swept you off your feet. Have you ever been in a big wave, Natalie? You are quite powerless to resist. You struggle to stay upright and what a bitter taste was left in my mouth.

No, the welcome they gave Hitler wasn't the hardest thing. The hardest thing was how far away Natalie was. The distance between her and home – two nights, three days – had trebled now. They were separated in some vast unspeakable way. By time, by space, by regime. Everything was slip-sliding out of control. She didn't even know she had control until they lost it. It was like a permanent toothache. How wonderful the world had been before it happened! How could she not have appreciated this?

She had been so sure that the march of time was towards progress, progress and more progress. Could it be that they would go backwards now? That was something she had never contemplated before.

Another hard thing: the English newspapers did not headline with the *invasion, Anschluss, occupation* – oh, whatever you wanted to call it. They were talking about the summer's cricket schedule. The plundering of her country hadn't even made it to page one in the *Daily Mail*, Mr Young's newspaper.

The occupation of Austria was inconsequential news. It was unlikely to affect anyone in England, apparently.

*

Natalie dropped Hugo off at school, then cycled to Leah's. The cleaning would have to wait.

Leah was pickling sauerkraut. The kitchen smelled like a Viennese kitchen. Leah's philosophy was 'When in doubt, cook.' Since dear Mrs Sanderson had passed away, the Sandersons were struggling. Leah was trying to keep everything together but naturally, it was difficult.

'Your family have to come here now,' Leah said as soon as Natalie walked in. She told Natalie that Aunt Ruth had already left. Overnight, she had packed six suitcases and taken the train to her property in the South of France. 'Alfie says we've wasted enough time.'

'What does Alfie know?'

Leah was offended as she always was when Natalie spoke dismissively about Alfie.

'Alfie keeps up to date,' she said as she cleared the table efficiently of mugs and plates. She could do it in five, six motions or fewer. 'He attends all the anti-fascist rallies…'

'Well, what does Alfie propose I do? Mama had her chance. She chose to stay back with…' Natalie could hardly bring herself to say it, 'the baby. With Rachel, Leo and Hannah.'

'But it's worse now, don't you see?'

Natalie nodded slowly. It did look worse, of course, but how bad could it get?

They held the referendum on the *Anschluss* just days after the troops came in. That is, they called it a referendum. There it was, the paper with one big and one little circle. Cheats. Bloody cheats. A guard standing over you, a gun in his hands. A guard seeing you in, a guard seeing you out. That's what they call democracy these days.

But nobody seemed to mind too much.

Natalie wondered how Rudi would take to it. Didn't injustice used to grind his gears? But she didn't hear anything from Rudi. She waited for a letter, for his opinion, his verdict, but none came. She didn't know what had become of him. Maybe he'd just gone along to one of Flora Lang's many summer houses, where everything smelled of roses. She pictured him arranging to meet her outside the polling station. Flora Lang cuddling a pet chihuahua. Did she have a pet chihuahua small enough to fit in her handbag? If she didn't, she should have. Natalie imagined her leaning against Rudi's front door, her long legs like traffic signals. Those slender feet like a courtesan. She was every boy's dream. What was she doing with Rudi? Should Natalie have got Libby to ask him after all?

At night, she dreamed Rudi was laughing at her, laughing at all of them: 'This will teach the Jews. I've been studying my neighbours for years. I used to shine a light at their windows. They've got no idea.'

Yes, that was it. He had given up on her because she was Jewish. And who could blame him? – that was the way things were heading. That was the lie of the land. He knew that. It was only she who had found it all so hard to believe.

The new government in Austria immediately enacted the stringent Nuremberg Laws. It was like Mayor Karl Lueger all over again. No, it was far worse than Lueger. *No Jew can go to university.* Natalie read the newspaper article aloud to Leah. This time the *Mail* had deigned to print it. *There will be separate schools for Jewish children.*

'They can't do that,' Natalie said – at last this was a subject she knew something about. 'So many of the staff of the universities are Jewish.'

'They're doing it,' Leah said. 'Who will stop them?' She was making a pie this time. The flour hung in the air like a fog. 'We've got to get them out.'

'The Nazis? They've only just—'

'Your *family*… Natalie, for God's sake, wake up!'

Spurred into action, Leah rolled up her sleeves and went to Mr Sanderson. Poor Mrs Sanderson had only been buried weeks – it was only six days after the *Anschluss*, the world was unclear.

*

Leah told Natalie she had knocked self-consciously on his study door. Poor widowed Mr Sanderson. Leah wasn't sure what papers he would need to sign but she would get them to him. Leah would help Libby and Mama. She would do it for Natalie.

Mr Sanderson was staring out the window, grief-stricken but always kind. He asked Leah to take a seat, he apologised that it was uncomfortable. He wasn't used to visitors.

'Is everything okay, Leah? What is it now? New saucepans?' This was a household joke. When Leah first arrived, she had despaired at the state of the kitchen and almost every day had demanded new equipment.

She talked to him about how she missed Mrs Sanderson and then she cut to the chase.

'We have family still in Austria. We are worried, especially now.'

'I can imagine,' he said. He kept touching his moustache as though surprised to find it was still there. Leah had reminded herself, *he is in mourning, and he will not be thinking straight.* 'That Hitler is a dangerous little man.'

'You have been so kind to employ me, so kind.'

'Honestly, Leah. The pleasure has been all ours.'

A pause. Mrs Sanderson would of course have read Leah's mind, but Mr Sanderson was unable to.

'I wondered if you could help me. Mrs Sanderson had endeavoured to help get family out once before. She was always so thoughtful. But for complicated reasons, our family changed their minds. I wonder if we could offer another position in the household? A nanny, perhaps, or a housekeeper? Just through this turbulent time.'

Leah didn't say Mrs Sanderson had actually promised to help in the future too – she was saving that up as the punchline – but she didn't get to say it, for Mr Sanderson had already turned quite grey.

'If money is a problem, we could come to an arrangement,' Leah had continued. Plucking arguments out of thin air.

'My dear. I… I suppose this is as good as time as any to tell you. We are leaving ourselves. I am taking the children to India.'

'India?'

'My work is there, the children need to get away. The change will be good for them.'

Leah's face fell. He said quickly, 'I've made some enquiries on your behalf, and it looks like the British government have agreed they won't be sending anyone back, over this difficult time at least. You don't need to worry too much about yourself, Leah. I can't see your status changing for the time being.'

'But will they let more people in?'

'I really don't know, I'm sorry. I suspect no, but no, I don't know.'

So, Leah was now out of a job and possibly a visa. Mama and Libby did not have their ticket out. They would have to think of something or someone else.

Mr Sanderson said he would help Leah find a job, but it turned out he didn't have to. Never one to dally, Leah went straight to the local café, Pam's Pantry, and asked for Pam. Leah said Pam had a face like a wasp sting and she smelled of fried onions. But she was single-handedly running her business, she was overwhelmed and Leah was desperate. But also, more than desperate, Leah was genuine. This *was* the kitchen of her dreams. Leah took along some rock cakes to her interview – and just as the English say the way to a man's heart is through his stomach, the way to a café manager's heart is along the same lines.

'I don't care if you're from the land of make-believe, as long as you're hard-working.' Pam showed Leah ankles swollen like great tree trunks. 'Can't stand on these much longer. You can do a proper English breakfast, right?'

'The English and their breakfasts!' said Leah later. 'It's like a sickness! They feel the same way about it as the royal family.'

Since the royal family was one of her favourite subjects, Natalie's ears pricked up.

'They worship it.'

'Really?'

'They want bacon and eggs, mushroom and tomatoes, at seven a.m.' Leah kept saying it. 'They've just woken up and they want all the lard they can get their hands on!'

Natalie thought this sounded pleasant. At the Caplins', she sometimes had boiled egg and soldiers with Hugo. A lot of soldiers ended up face-down on the floor. Mrs Caplin, who was endlessly watching her figure, only had fruit.

On Pam's menu was macaroni cheese. Scotch egg. Steak and kidney. And the astonishingly named bubble and squeak.

Leah had proposed an Austrian dish of the day instead, but Pam apologised. 'Maybe when Mr Hitler's come off his high horse, but until then we don't want anything to do with him, we don't want people reminded of him. They'll choke on their treacle puddings and then where will we be?'

Leah made her and Alfie's favourite schnitzel but because *feelings were running high*, they agreed to call it 'escalope'. Pam was afraid the word 'schnitzel' was too provocative for her customers.

Leah told Natalie that Pam's Pantry was like Café Central – the most beloved café in the whole of Vienna. Where chess-players argued politics and politicians argued over chess. Where the obedient pony and traps lingered outside waiting for customers, where Trotsky and Stalin – and some say Hitler – stacked up espresso cups and talked about the merits of communism until they were blue – or rather red – in the face.

It wasn't until Natalie went to visit Pam's Pantry in Wood Green High Road that she realised Leah was joking. And the joke was: Café Central could not have been further from Pam's Pantry in design, customers, menu, ANYTHING. It was, Alfie explained, 'a greasy spoon.'

Leah's accommodation, rooms above the café, was included, so she was happy. And sometimes, Natalie noted, Alfie came back early in the mornings with a wry grin on his face. Down in the kitchen, she would find him whistling some dumb tune, with a distinct whiff of fried onions about him.

CHAPTER EIGHTEEN

Natalie decided to ask Mrs Caplin about Mama again. That's what Leah had told her to do and after all, Mrs Caplin and she had become great friends recently. Mrs Caplin had said no last time, but she hadn't realised what was at stake – mind you, neither had Natalie. This time would be different.

All those things that were merely bothersome last year were now becoming deeply significant and polarising this year. Rachel and Leo probably had the chance of getting out through connections of the Goldberg family or the orchestras – whether they liked it or not, Natalie had to find a way out for Mama and Libby. She was their only hope.

But before Natalie had the chance to ask her, Mrs Caplin instead invited Natalie for a 'talk'. And Natalie knew from her etiquette book that 'a talk' as opposed to 'talk' entailed serious and private conversation. They walked out to the garden. It was spring and unseasonably warm. On the lawn in front of them, Hugo was having a tea-party with his two favoured gnomes. Natalie had worried that his parents wouldn't approve of tea-parties, but one time when Mr Caplin had seen him, he had joined in and pretended to have tea from the tiny cups and saucers. Molly came over to join in too and it was a rare moment of fun.

Mrs Caplin also shrugged when she saw it. 'If he's a fairy, he's a fairy. He'll just have to get a job in show business.' Then she added, 'Mr Young says sports are more important than languages and music anyway, fortunately, Hugo is no slacker at either of those.'

Natalie got chairs for them both. The garden was looking even more wonderful than usual. The stripes of the lawn were beautifully uniform. A butterfly occasionally landed or lifted off. *This is the best of England*, thought Natalie. *I do love it here. Even though I miss home, if Mama, Libby and Rachel could be here, I will never ask for anything else again.*

Mrs Caplin pulled her chair close, closer until their knees were nearly touching, and Natalie waited for what she was going to say.

Mrs Caplin put her hand out for Natalie's.

'You must think I'm amoral.'

'Amoral…' Natalie played with the word in her mouth. 'Amoral?' It began with an A – she should know all the As – but she was still unfamiliar with it. 'How do you mean?'

'A bad person!' She peered at Natalie from under lowered lashes. 'Because of my… because of Mr Young.'

'Never,' said Natalie vehemently.

Shockingly, Mrs Caplin was *crying*!

'What on earth is wrong?' Natalie asked. This was not the direction she had expected the 'talk' to go.

'You're too kind, darling. Hardly anyone's nice to me now.'

There *had* been fewer parties recently, fewer lunches out, now that Natalie thought about it.

'I'll always be nice to you,' promised Natalie.

'You would, wouldn't you? That's why you're so precious. The thing is…' Mrs Caplin paused dramatically, 'I'm truly deeply in love with Mr Young.'

'Oh! I see.'

It was hot, hot in the garden with the sun beating down, but this was something else. Natalie regretted her woollen jumper, but she didn't have many summer clothes that fitted any more.

'At first, it was just a diversion, a distraction, but it has become something else. Something deep. Something incredible. Do you know what I mean?'

No, thought Natalie. Shamefully, she could smell her own sweat. Mrs Caplin never smelled of sweat. But she nodded. 'I think so.'

'He is my everything.' Mrs Caplin squeezed Natalie's hands tighter. 'Oh, I can't tell you what a relief it is to talk about it. We've been so careful. No one else knows, you see.'

Natalie thought that might not be quite correct, but she let Mrs Caplin continue.

And Mrs Caplin was so relieved that she talked about Mr Young for some time. 'He is passionate for the good of the country. *All* the countries, even yours and Germany's. And he's a superb writer too. Actually, you would have so much in common, I know you like books too and he's so keen to do well at the paper. They don't pay him enough, and sometimes they give him the most ridiculous stories to cover, it's really not fair when you've got a mind as sharp as he has, but he works day and night for them, for all of us.'

Growing bored of Mr Young's brilliance, Natalie stared at the garden gnomes. Mrs Caplin watched her looking at them.

'They were my father's,' she said. 'They're all I have left of him.'

'You have something. That's the important thing.' Natalie wondered whether to mention her own father – she missed him a lot lately, and after all he was *another* man passionate about his country – but Mrs Caplin didn't ask. She didn't know *anything* about Natalie. The differences between her and Mrs Sanderson felt very apparent then.

'What about your mother?' Natalie asked. *Anything but more Mr Young.*

'Never knew her,' said Mrs Caplin abruptly. She stubbed her cigarette out on the ground. 'James wants us to get a garden swing and a swimming pool there.' She pointed. Natalie gulped.

'He is not moving in, is he?'

Mrs Caplin laughed. 'No, but we sometimes dream about it, you know? It helps.' She lit another cigarette, inhaled deeply. 'We're so trapped, Natalie. You can't imagine what I'm going through. One moment I'm in paradise, the next it's absolute hell.'

Mrs Caplin let her head loll back for the sun to shine down on her beautiful face. She had finished with the subject. She closed her eyes, looking utterly serene.

Natalie's mouth was dry. Was this her moment? Not really, no. *But if not now, when*? That's what Papa used to say. *If not you, then who?*

Natalie's voice was squeaky. 'I wondered if you'd think about getting some extra help,' she said, 'for the cooking and ironing. Mrs Monger and Molly are marvellous but an extra pair of hands…?'

Mrs Caplin's eyes snapped open. 'We manage, don't you think?'

'My family need to leave Austria.'

Mrs Caplin sat up. She screwed up her nose pensively. 'Do you know, I'm sure you asked me this once before?'

Oh God, she did remember.

'I… yes. The situation has changed now though. For the worse.'

'Is it since the union with Germany? "More living space", wasn't it? Such a funny thing to say. Everyone wants a bigger living room. James and the German correspondent for the *Mail* are great friends. He thought about going over for a bit to see it for himself, but can't bear to leave me. Anyway, James says the Austrians are delighted.'

'Not *all* Austrians.'

Mrs Caplin paused, then slapped her own arm, leaving a red patch.

'It's a bit like *Macbeth*, isn't it? Intrigues, comings and goings…' She hesitated, obviously trying to think of more similarities. 'Battles?'

Natalie realised she had to be patient here. Patient and clear. 'It's my mother and sister. They wouldn't have to live here. All they need is an offer of work. And then they can come. You see, the Nazis don't like the Jewish people at all.'

Mrs Caplin stretched. 'Isn't there an agency or something for aliens? You might be able to sort something out there.'

Aliens? Natalie nodded slowly.

'Let me know how you get on.'

'I will. Thank you.'

'No, thank *you*, darling.'

'But… but if we could send for them… You'd love Rachel and Leo too, I know you would.'

Mrs Caplin grabbed her hand and kissed it, silencing her.

'You're such a good confidante. I don't know what I'd do without you. Kill myself probably.'

Mrs Caplin rearranged her parasol to get her face out the sun, then lay back down. Natalie was dismissed.

The next day, Leah came round. Natalie was reluctant to see her since she didn't want to relate the conversation she had had with Mrs Caplin. Leah would be angry and Natalie would end up defending Mrs Caplin again. But for once Leah didn't have that on her mind. She was clutching a cardboard box close to her chest.

'It's for you, from Mrs Sanderson,' she said. 'It was in her will.'

Mrs Monger clucked at this, then called Alfie and Molly into the kitchen to watch. Natalie had no clue what was within the box. She was so nervous that her fingers shook. Mrs Monger had to get the bread knife to break the string and then there was all the tissue paper to get through as well.

It was a hat. It was the hat Mrs Sanderson was wearing when Natalie first met her. The hat Natalie had so admired. The furry hat with a hint of paper boat.

Among all the other business Mrs Sanderson had had to take care of in her rushed final weeks, she had taken the time and effort to bequeath Natalie her hat.

It was the kindest thing. Even as Natalie gingerly picked it from its box, she knew this present was meaningful not just for what it was, but what it represented. Mrs Sanderson had listened to her, she had remembered her opinions, she had gone out of her way to thank her. Now tears filled Natalie's eyes – what a loss.

'Put it on then,' said Leah.

When Natalie did, Molly gasped. 'You look like royalty!' And Mrs Monger slapped her hand to her mouth and proclaimed, 'Ye gods, if she isn't the spit of Princess Elizabeth!'

The next day, a letter came from Rachel.

Natalie,

Leo was attacked in the street. Don't be alarmed – he's okay, but it's shaken him, as you can imagine. This situation is intolerable. The Nazis are everywhere now. We must leave Vienna. We have to think of Hannah's future. I have to ask: is there anything you can do? Have you some connections in music or orchestra or the arts perhaps?

I'm sorry this letter is so sparse with nothing hilarious to report. Things are changing so quickly. It might be that soon our letters won't get out any more. Can you help, dear sister? Please, please ask for us.

All my love, Rachel

CHAPTER NINETEEN

There was a German Jewish aid agency, a refugee coordinating committee, a labour relief agency and the passport office. Leah suggested Natalie try the labour relief agency first.

You could tell the office wasn't used to this number of visitors. It was an inhospitable place: one mahogany desk, with its ink-pad, in the centre of the room, looked like a permanent fixture but it seemed someone had hurriedly pulled in lots of other tables and small chairs that didn't belong there. On some of the tables there were Underwood portable typewriters, some with the papers in, some without. On others, there were large piles of papers, some telephones, the same dull black as the one at the Caplins' and copper hand-bells to the side. And more wooden chairs all the way around the edges of the room as well.

The tables were manned by English women, yet the room was full of foreigners. Now Natalie saw them all together, she understood how they stuck out. When she was on her own, or in the house or in the to and fro to Hugo's school, she forgot. Natalie found herself hoping it wouldn't be the woman in the green suit, with the grey hair in a bun, the small pinched glasses and the small pinched expression, who she'd get sent to. These were the kind of English women who quietly and without acknowledgement organised a nation. Emotional as marble, affectionate as machines.

'Next!' green-suit woman bellowed, voice like a foghorn. Games mistress on a wintry morning.

'My name is Natalie Leeman. I am from Austria and I would like—'

The woman held out a form, but then said that before Natalie could have it, she needed to explain the system.

Natalie didn't hear much beyond the first lines. She interrupted: 'You are making it more difficult for people to come here now that Hitler has invaded Austria? Am I correct?'

The woman scowled. 'No, not exactly.'

'What then?'

The woman leaned back in her chair. She seemed at the end of her tether already.

'It's not like they didn't welcome him, is it?'

'*My* family didn't. The Jewish people didn't.'

'Well, I don't know what to say.' The woman looked like she didn't care much. 'It's because there are so many. That's how it is. Sorry. But the good thing is we're not sending anyone back to Germany or Austria now, so you should be okay.'

Had Mama left it too late?

'So, just as I said,' Natalie persisted. 'Although the situation there is worse, *you are actually making it harder to escape?*'

The woman sighed. 'Fill this in for your family, then bring it back. We'll see what we can do.'

Natalie had to do the writing on her lap. She tried to rest the paper on her bag and proceeded without success. Her pencil was blunt, and she had to turn it on its side. It seemed that – like her family in Austria – pencil would be all too easy to erase.

Next to her, a man perfumed by cigarettes, noticing her troubles, said, 'Do you want to lean on me?' She said no at first, but then, as she couldn't make progress, agreed. He got up and graciously turned around, loaning her his back.

'A'right?'

'That's better…'
She didn't talk, she concentrated. This was serious.

Age:
Sex:
Place of Birth:
Date of Birth:
Religion:
Profession:
Skills:
Other:

Did she tell them that Mama was not religious? Was this an advantage or not? Who knew nowadays? Natalie watched everyone at the desks lean towards the English women. She listened carefully. Maybe something they said would be a hint, a clue to the right answer.

The woman on the right of her, with no accent at all – she was as English as the day is long – was trying to get her parents out:

'My father is a lawyer, but he is good at carpentry.' She showed the woman opposite her hands, trying to convince her. 'Look, these are very big practical hands. From my father.'

The man on the right was bouncing a cooing baby on his knee. 'Her name is Anna. A-N-N-A. My wife's little sister. That is right. She is still in school, but she can clean. She can do anything.' His voice trailed away and he buried his face in his baby's woollen cap, suddenly embarrassed about the words that were spilling from him. 'In the family she is famous for her love of tidying.'

What could Natalie tell them about Mama? Mrs Dora Leeman was loving and wise? Cheerful and generally happy with her lot? She was a non-conformist who got on with everyone, her smile made everyone feel good. After they'd seen her, the milkman went off whistling, the postman went off smiling, the newspaperman went away chortling. (Natalie knew she did not take after Mama.) If you made a mistake, Dora Leeman didn't make you feel ashamed; she would ask if it was an accident – although if you had a success, it was *all* yours. The greatest pride of her life was her three girls.

What could Natalie say about Libby? Strong at sports, self-contained, disciplined, cool-headed, imaginative. A dislike of dairy products, a fan of the harp.

What about Rachel? Voted school's most beautiful girl, superb musician *and* composer, petite, smiley, secretive about herself, a gossip when it came to others, and so in love with Leo Goldberg, it made you wonder what he had that all her other suitors didn't.

What about Hannah? A baby, just a baby – didn't she deserve a chance?

Would that persuade them, these cool-headed women? Was that what she was doing here? Trying to *sell* her family to these women? She thought of the stallholders at Petticoat Lane market, which she had visited with Leah: 'Come over and look at this. You'll love this. Three for a pound!' She had to make her family appear like a special bargain or desirable, something anyone would want.

If that's what she had to do, she would do it – and it wasn't hard to do, because it was true.

The man Natalie was leaning on tilted his head around and shifted his back slightly. It was like trying to write on an animal, or perhaps writing at sea. He had deep dark eyes fringed with long, dark lashes, a bit like Rachel's.

'Are you finished yet?'

Natalie realised she had been taking a long time. She tapped his shoulder appreciatively. 'Nearly. Thank you.'

'My mother is Jewish,' she said to herself as she ticked the boxes. 'She is forty-six years old.'

Is this how a gambler feels? Putting it all on black.

Must she start all over again? Yes, yes, she must go to the back of the queue. She inserted herself at the end, waiting for an English woman to meet her eye. She liked the look of one, she was dressed dowdily but had a spark in her eyes that gave Natalie hope. Something of a Mrs Sanderson about her features. Something whimsical and dreamy.

Natalie was nearly running out of time if she was to get back for Hugo at school. (She *had* to get back for Hugo at school. She had never *not* got back for Hugo at school. How many times had she drilled into him the importance of punctuality?) A woman was standing at the door, telling late arrivals they couldn't come in, not today. No more.

A woman cried out, 'I can't get from work earlier than this. I ran all the way!'

The woman this side of the door was firm: 'We're finishing up for the day.'

And then the person behind her pushed her forward. One woman was free. A different one. Neither whimsical nor harsh. She ran through the form with Natalie, repeating, clarifying, wasting time:

'Skills?'

'I have put nursing,' Natalie said, flushing, thumbing the paper. 'Here. And sewing. Like a… a… seamstress.'

'She does both?'

'She could.'

'Is she a *qualified* nurse?' Pretty, fair eyebrows raised.

'She nursed my papa.'

As Natalie spoke, she realised, suddenly, belatedly, that this explained her mama's great and terrible attachment to Vienna and the house. It wasn't just Rachel's baby, her lack of English language skills, that kept tugging at her to stay in Austria. It was the family home she was born in, the home she lived in with Natalie's grandparents, the home Natalie's father had died in. The home where Papa's ashes were kept in a jug on a shelf.

This was why Mama had never wanted to leave. Of course – how could Natalie have been so slow to understand this? This was where Mama had loved and was loved in return.

But you can't live in the past, Mama. There's no future for us in Vienna. Not while the Nazis are there. Leah is right.

'Married?'

'Widowed.'

'Well, that's good,' said the woman, then covered her mouth. 'I'm so sorry, I meant for *these* purposes.'

She apologised again, told Natalie it had been a long day. They were only open to the public for three hours.

'How long has it been busy like this?'

The woman looked up, as if glad to talk about something different. 'Ever since the *Anschluss*.'

Two weeks ago? Natalie should have come earlier. Why hadn't she come sooner? Why had she been so bloody complacent? Leah knew. Leah had known all along.

'This is what is needed: money. A guarantor. A job. A visa.'

'Thank you,' Natalie said. So, all was not lost.

'No,' said the woman. 'We don't… we can't do that. *You* need to arrange that, and when you have arranged that, we will help process it for you.'

'So, the best chance is to apply for domestic work – um, cleaning or nannying?'

'Not any more, no.'

'I don't understand.'

'The problem is things have been closing down for refugees for some time now. There is worry that refugees are…' she paused, 'flooding into the country too quickly.'

'Flooding?' Natalie thought of Noah. She thought of building a big ark. Is that what they wanted them to do? Get in an ark two by two and let all the others perish?

The woman hesitated. She crinkled her nose. 'It means, "pouring into".'

Natalie thought of Mr Caplin's '*infested*' again.

The woman straightened her pile of papers with the palms of her hands. The stray ones slotted obediently into place. 'They think the refugees are skiving – lazy, living off working people.'

'But they also think we are *stealing* the jobs?'

'That too,' the woman said. She gave a little laugh. Natalie was unsure what she was laughing at.

'But how could we be both? Stealing jobs and living off others' work?' Natalie leaned forward. She was getting angry now. Half with the woman. Half with herself. *How had she been so blind?*

'Unfortunately, it's not about the *facts*, Miss Leeman, it's the perception.'

'So, the perception is that Jewish women are stealing jobs and lazy.'

The woman pursed her lips. She didn't like her own words spelled out for her. And Natalie thought, *why, why I am picking a fight with the only person who can help me?*

'Excuse me,' Natalie said. 'I am being far too emotional… sorry.'

'I appreciate that it's very trying,' the woman said. She fumbled around one of the desk drawers and produced a piece of conciliatory liquorice. 'Please,' she said. Natalie took the peace offering and they moved on to Libby's paperwork.

Another woman was waiting behind her. It was like being at a café when someone else wants your table. Studiously, Natalie avoided the waiting woman's gaze. She told herself that she would never be complacent again. She would never be lazy again. She would do this….

'I'll be back next week,' Natalie promised the desk-lady, her new friend. She wanted the woman the other side of the desk to say the situation would improve, maybe she had insider knowledge, but she didn't.

'I know you will,' she said instead.

Natalie had barely vacated her seat before the girl behind her had inveigled her way in.

'My name is Berta and I am from Berlin, Germany.'

The man who had lent Natalie his back was outside, cupping a cigarette from the wind, the collar of his mackintosh up like the walls around a castle.

He had had the most dragon-like of the women in the room and there had been raised, irritable voices – his mostly. The colour of his eyes was the first thing she had noticed, but now Natalie saw he had dark stubble around the chin, halfway to a beard. Rudi used to lament he could never grow a beard. He wasn't hairy enough. This man needed a shave. If Natalie had known him better, she would have told him: *The English don't like the demi-beard look. Bad etiquette. For them, it's all or nothing.*

'How did you get on then?'

He shook his head. Those soulful eyes. At another time, another place, you'd call him handsome, but for the downward set of his mouth and the exhaustion in his cheeks. *Why do we all look so tired*, Natalie wondered. *Was it the dull English lighting? The overcast skies perhaps?*

'No progress since last week,' he admitted.

'I don't know what we have to do.'

'How many are you trying to get out?' he asked, gazing at her.

Natalie found it difficult to meet his eyes. Eventually, she responded, 'My mother and my younger sister. My older sister, her husband and the baby…' She paused. She would do her best to help Rachel, of course she would. 'Although they have other people, hopefully, who might be in a better position to help them.'

Leo had better manage something for Rachel and the baby soon. It seemed impossible that he, a Goldberg, one of the most influential and highly regarded families in Vienna, would be unable to get them *somewhere*.

The man nodded; this was a language he understood. She was quickly at home with him in a way she had not been with most of the men she had met in England.

'And you?'

He counted on his fingers. They were long and brown. 'My younger brother, my parents, three grandparents, three aunts and two uncles.' There were too many to fit on both hands.

'Eleven,' he said finally with a sigh. His eyes were very unusual.

'All reliant on you?'

'Just me, yes. It's a big responsibility.'

Natalie thought, *no wonder he looks tired.*

He handed her a cigarette without her asking. He told her where he lived in Vienna and where he went to school. She said she knew it, although she did not particularly. She hadn't intended to dally, but it was pleasing to speak in her mother tongue with this pleasant-looking man. She enjoyed the sensation of the smoke in her throat. Small pleasures. Something about him compelled her to stay.

Natalie couldn't say this fellow was a barrel of laughs, though. A barrel of worry more like. He flicked the cigarette, then had to kick the ash off his own shoe.

'I gather the chances of bringing people here right now are less than zero.'

'No,' Natalie said, suddenly buoyant in the face of his pessimism. 'We can do this.'

'No money, no guarantor, no job, no visa. How?'

They talked about Hitler and Natalie told him a funny anecdote she had heard about Hitler's application to the finest art school in Vienna – she was proud that the Viennese had turned him down – and Hitler's patently absurd inability to paint faces. He didn't laugh.

Nothing would make this man laugh. He was frozen in dismay. He asked Natalie what she missed most about home, and she said, 'My family of course,' although she was thinking of Mama mostly, her championing of her and the way she'd wrap her in a warm blanket after a hard day at school and say 'my lovely girl', and he said he missed 'the glass of water you get with your coffee, and the newspapers in the streets.'

Natalie decided either he had an eye for detail or he was even more of a cold fish than he at first appeared. Although Natalie wanted to talk, talk, talk, she tried to hold back a little. Be less Natalie, more Rachel. Less overfriendly puppy, more English nanny. His name was Erich and he said he had been in London for five years: came in 1933 and worked in diamonds—

'Diamonds!'

'In Hatton Garden.'

'A garden!' Natalie said. Well, this *was* perfect. Stripy lawns were her new favourite thing. 'How wonderful that your workplace is in a garden. The English love them, don't they? What do you think of the gnomes?'

At this, he burst out laughing. 'It's not a garden any more. It is a business district. And no, I don't like the gnomes.'

'I do,' Natalie said boldly, although she hadn't, right up until that very moment, but she wanted to hear him laugh again. Such a nice sound. 'They remind me that there might be a hidden magical kingdom out there, that everything is going to be all right.'

When he smiled, the whole shape of his face changed. 'Well, there's no magical kingdom here. I'd better get back. No work, no pay. I'll see you around, Natalie gnome-lover.'

'I've been called worse!' Natalie shouted over her shoulder as they turned to walk in their opposite directions.

'I can believe it!' he said, still laughing.

*

There was another letter when she got home. Natalie had started dreading letters: they never brought good news. This one from Mama was no exception.

Helga has gone. I don't know where. She was forbidden to work for Jewish people.

Did I tell you my bicycle has been taken?

Great-Uncle Ben is training to be a butler. Great-Aunt Mimi is smoking eighty cigarettes a day. She'd have two, three at a time, if she could. My old friend from school, Anna Wolf, is working as a volunteer at a Jewish centre for the elderly and will not even contemplate leaving.

I saw our next-door neighbour Arno in his uniform, sauntering around like he owns the world. He pretended not to see me, but I know he did. His mother had the cheek to wave. No, I haven't seen Rudi Strobl, not since his poor mother died. I expect like most young men, he has joined the Nazi Party too.

Natalie swallowed. She hadn't heard about the death of Rudi's mother. She hadn't heard anything. As for joining the Nazis… *Not Rudi*, she thought. Please, not Rudi. *Surely of all people, Rudi wouldn't?* But Flora Lang *and* Rudi might. And what about Helga? Helga who warmed their jumpers, who Mama said couldn't be trusted to comb their hair because she was far too gentle to get through the knots, who insisted on running the things they had forgotten to school. Helga had gone?

Over the next week, Natalie received two more letters from old schoolfriends: Elizabet Steiner and Lena Schwartz.

I am not bad at baking, Natalie, do you remember those cookies I once made?! With the raisins? If you know anyone who needs a cook, please, please, please pass on our information…

Elizabet

And:

We don't have much money, as you know, but once we are working, we would of course pay you back. We can do anything, Natalie, anything. Please ask for us. I always remember how kind your mother was. My little sisters love you.

Thank you in advance.
Lena

Leah had always been the more prepared about the developments back home than Natalie was. She pondered what it said about her. Natalie was the one who – on paper – had more *tragedy* in her life – the premature loss of her young, dynamic father. Surely, she shouldn't have been surprised how quickly things can turn? But she hadn't expected it, while Leah had.

Was it that Natalie had a sunny personality and Leah's was darker? Or did Leah have more imagination, more understanding to picture it? Neither idea seemed to explain it.

Natalie would never know how Leah understood the ramifications of what was happening before she did. Somehow, Leah knew the dark depraved depths people go to, perhaps before they even knew it themselves.

CHAPTER TWENTY

Natalie went to see *Pygmalion* at the cinema with Clifford, Leah and Alfie. The George Bernard Shaw story about the girl who is trained to become posh was the kind of thing Natalie would usually enjoy, but she was far too preoccupied with what was going on in Vienna and by another fruitless day, this time at the passport office. Back home, Jewish people were no longer allowed to visit the cinema. Natalie could only begin to imagine Rachel's fury at this and hoped it would propel her and Leo to *do something*. Why did Rachel have to marry an impractical musician? Someone with more of a foot in the real world would have been far better equipped to cope with this crisis.

She thought of Mama watching Helga pack up her things. The only time Natalie had seen Mama cry – not the tipsy crying she did at parties – was when they were bringing Papa's ashes home. In the street there had been a gust of wind, which nudged the lid off; poor Papa had nearly blown away. Natalie must hold onto that. If there was one thing she knew, it was that emotionally, Mama was as strong as an ox.

She was also blind as a bat without her glasses.

The girl in *Pygmalion*'s catchphrase was 'Not bloody likely!' On one side of her, Clifford was scratching around on her thigh. He did this a lot, and when she complained, he said he couldn't help it, he found her irresistible. On the other side, Leah and Alfie were slurping and grunting at any fallow moments in the film.

Not bloody likely, she thought.

'I can't concentrate,' Natalie whispered to Leah. 'I can't stop thinking of Mama and Libby.'

Leah wrinkled up her nose. Natalie thought she was going to say, 'It's not that bad.' But she whispered, 'We'll get them out, Natalie,' and offered her a humbug.

How had she not acted with more urgency? She should have been like Hansel and Gretel and laid breadcrumbs to get out. How could she be here, watching wretched films, when they were suffering so much? The gap between her world and theirs seemed so great and so brutal. It wasn't fair.

When they were outside, Leah and Alfie recommenced snogging. Clifford put his freckly arm around Natalie, and she braced herself. His lips loomed towards her, landed on hers. She found she couldn't respond, not even the little that was required.

'I'm sorry, Cliff, I'm not in the mood.'

'You never are, are you?'

Not bloody likely, she thought. 'Not really,' she admitted. Usually, Clifford took it with equanimity, but this time he took his scarf and gloves from her and stalked away down the Old Kent Road.

Alfie peeled himself away from Leah and sighed. 'We'd better head back.'

A few days later, Natalie was buying fruit for Mrs Monger when the greengrocer asked her if she was German. Natalie couldn't quite detect his tone, but she could see his half-leg. War wound. She knew people wondered, but being asked outright was a rarity. English people were usually awkward about where a person came from. It was like they didn't wish to uncover anything uncomfortable.

'I'm Austrian,' Natalie said, thinking, *it is still a different country, no matter what Hitler and the Nazis say*. No matter what the *world* said, for hadn't they just let it happen?

She put the apples on the metal scales and watched the pointer swing to the right. The greengrocer put them in her bag. He held more than she could at one time. She did the same with the bananas.

The Empire had gifted the British stranger fruit than Natalie could have imagined. Leah loved all the fruits from the Caribbean – another reason she preferred England to home – but Natalie was still suspicious around pineapple and she refused to try coconut.

'Like that Adolf Hitler?'

'What?'

'Hitler is Austrian.'

'I don't like Hitler. I probably like him less than you do. I am Jewish from Vienna,' Natalie pronounced cheerfully while the grocer packed her peaches in the bag. He was fast but careful, Natalie noted approvingly. Mrs Monger would tell her off if any were bruised.

'Like Sigmund Freud?'

'Exactly.'

He was persistent. 'Did you know Sigmund Freud?'

It was Natalie's turn to laugh. No, she did not. 'Vienna is quite a big place, you know.'

He didn't catch her tone. 'I was in Belgium,' he said. 'And France. In the hospital I was friends with a German. His name was Hans Klein. I wonder what he's doing now?'

Natalie and Erich met near the historic Tower of London, where the young princes had been imprisoned and where the ravens wouldn't leave. It was impressive but Natalie was distracted. She didn't want Erich getting any *ideas*, so she decided to tell him about Rudi, 'her boyfriend', straight away, and in elaborate detail. As he was telling her some anecdote about some poor folk who were beheaded, Natalie interrupted and told him about Rudi. About their fun shining torches into each other's windows, his commitment to his studies, their private lessons. She skipped over Rudi's encouraging her to go to England, the recent lack of letters, his having been seen with the beauty Flora Lang, for she feared it might be transparent to Erich – as it was to her – that Rudi had fallen out of love with her, but she told him almost everything else.

'He's more myself than I am,' she finished.

'Brontë,' Erich said, to Natalie's surprise. 'Now is it Emily, or Charlotte? Or Anne? It couldn't be underestimated Anne, could it?'

'Emily,' Natalie said coyly, caught out.

'In that case, it must have been Heathcliff and Catherine?'

'Yes.'

'Nice,' Erich gave her a half-grin. 'That ended well, didn't it?'

They started laughing. For someone very serious, Erich could be quite funny.

Erich led them down some steps at the back of the Tower to a sandy patch of beach filled with couples and families enjoying the sun. Natalie was delighted. They took two deckchairs, one red striped and one yellow, and Erich insisted on setting them up clumsily by himself.

Natalie showed Erich the photo of her family that she now carried everywhere in her purse. She explained that Mama didn't really look like Mama in the picture at all, but Erich said he could still make out her dancing dark eyes, the lovely smile. Erich liked that Mama and Papa were political. He said his family were not. He had an uncle who was a Zionist and a cousin who was a communist, but his family liked to keep their heads down. 'If they have a motto,' he said, 'it is probably – don't make a sound.'

Erich was so easy to talk to. Natalie told him about *Making an Elephant out of a Mosquito* and he made exactly the right comments.

'Translation strikes me as extremely hard.'

'It is,' she admitted. 'Harder than I'd thought, to be honest.'

Ever since the *Anschluss*, she had found herself unable to write anything but letters home. Erich nodded. He said he understood that.

Some children started digging a hole near them. One threw sand into the other's eyes, then ran off crying.

Natalie told Erich that the year before it had all been planned for Mama to come to England. 'Unfortunately, she… she changed her mind.' Her voice was croaky. She pretended she had sand in her throat.

'Why?' He looked shocked.

'My sister, the new baby… you know.'

'What about the people who were going to sponsor her?'

'The wife is dead and the husband is leaving the country.'

Erich took a sharp intake of breath. 'That's a shame.'

'I wish Mama had come,' Natalie said in a tiny voice. *Why didn't she come then? If only they'd come then.*

'What about your employers now, won't they help?'

Natalie tried to pull herself together. 'They have, I mean, *she* has. Mrs Caplin gave me some connections and things. She's done as much as she can do, I think.'

She looked out to the boats that were forging through the river, creating slipstreams of white foam behind them. A young man came around selling chilled drinks, then Erich knelt on the sand and made a tiny castle complete with stones and a feathery flag.

'You're an engineer!' Natalie laughed.

He grinned. 'Mama would be so proud!'

Later, with red, sandy skin, they walked slowly back to the station. For once she was in no hurry to get home. Erich didn't take her hand, and Natalie was pleased, if a little disappointed, that he didn't even try.

Before the Sandersons left for India, Mr Sanderson asked Leah to come back to the house. Leah told Natalie this made her so anxious, she didn't sleep for three nights in a row. Mr Sanderson had already asked her if she would like to go to India with them. He had said she would learn *the* most amazing things to do with lentils and cumin. Now, she wondered if he was going to ask her to marry him.

'Mr Sanderson wanting to marry you?' Natalie repeated. 'What? Why?' *Where did this come from?* Sometimes Leah could be so arrogant, it took Natalie's breath away.

'Well, quite,' Leah said primly.

But then, Leah *was* pretty now. Natalie didn't know how it had happened, but she was. Twenty-four, tall as an Amazonian and shapely like a dress-shop model. Her eyes were clear and bright, her gaze was gently benevolent, she had strong unbitten nails, and she *did* make the best rock cakes. Mr Sanderson, perhaps more than anyone, would know that.

Anyway, it turned out it wasn't a proposal; at least not a proposal of marriage.

He got her to sit by the fire, tartan blanket over her knees. It was so cosy in his study that Leah thought it might be hard to ever leave. There was a cross-legged wooden Buddha on his desk, with very long earlobes and a cheeky smile, and then there were all the books, books galore. Every shelf was stacked high with them, and they were all higgledy-piggledy, as though arranged by someone who was not interested in the books themselves, but merely the ideas contained within.

Mr Sanderson talked about how impressed he and Mrs Sanderson had been with Leah and it can't have been easy, blah di blah, to up sticks, make a new life in a new country where you don't speak the language.

Leah reported this all slowly, and Natalie thought, *really? He invited her over just to say that!* But then eventually, he got to the crux of it: 'I wanted to leave you something, something I know Beverley, Mrs Sanderson, would have wanted you to have too.'

Very slowly, tenderly as though it were something exceedingly precious, he gave her a black-and-white photo of two skinny dogs. These dogs were so skinny, it was like they were all bones. One dog was facing the camera, too close; his eyes were bigger than his body. He was all nose. The other was further away. She recognised one of them. Mrs Sanderson had talked about it.

'You want me to have this photo?'

Mr Sanderson laughed. 'I want you to have our racing hounds.'

*

Natalie and Leah went over to the kennels together. Natalie brought along Hugo since he was fond of animals. The smell of that place though! A sturdy woman in green boots came over and when Leah explained who she was, she was delighted, explaining with great animation the background of the two dogs in the photo as she led them to the animals. And the dogs woofed at them, at each other, and started bounding around. It was quite a welcome.

Tiny Tim was older, Rosie was a bitch. This seemed rude to Natalie, but apparently it was the appropriate word when it came to dogs. They went to meet them. The dogs came forward. Tiny Tim was lively and wanting to sniff. Rosie loped over more reluctantly.

'They're like something from a graveyard.' Natalie surveyed Tiny Tim's back and legs while trying not to look shocked. 'It's like they are skeletons wearing stockings.'

'These aren't actually that thin,' the woman in boots corrected her. 'They're all muscle, they are.'

Hugo was delighted. Once he got over his nerves, there was no stopping him; he ran his hands across their ribs and nuzzled into Tiny Tim's face.

'He feels like a load of plates in the sink.'

'How would you know how that feels?' Natalie nudged him.

'Where will you keep them?' All Natalie could think of was Leah's tiny rooms above Pam's Pantry. That was no place for a small dog, surely, never mind two of this size? Tiny Tim was nothing like his namesake.

'They'll stay here at the kennels.'

'Who'll pay?'

Leah scowled at her. 'It's sorted, Natalie.'

Hugo loved them. 'Tiny Tim!' he kept shouting. 'Rosie!' He didn't want to go back home. Ever. And eventually, Natalie had to half-carry, half-drag him out, which was horribly undignified. She promised to bring him back the next week and yes, Hugo, if you like, the week after that and the week after that too.

'Can't we keep them, Nat? I'd look after them, I promise!'

'Look what you've done,' Natalie laughed to Leah.

'The poor boy,' Leah whispered so Hugo wouldn't hear. 'He just wants to be loved, doesn't he?'

Meeting the dogs put Natalie in a better mood than she had been in for some time. Mrs Monger was in a good mood too when they got home, because Mrs Caplin was dining out (with Mr Young, no doubt). Hugo was also in great spirits: he was too excited to settle, so Natalie let him stay up and draw pictures of the dogs. He did one of Rosie racing, with skid marks behind her. They showed it to Molly, who held it upside down. 'It's amazing, Hugo! Is that Tilly the cat being sick?'

'It's Rosie winning a race!' he said, snatching it away. 'Obviously.'

Hugo had no patience with Molly.

Natalie only had to read two pages of *Just William* that night before Hugo was snoring away nicely. She went down to the kitchen and told Mrs Monger about the trip to the kennels, although she didn't dare mention that Rosie was a bitch. Mrs Monger told Natalie that greyhounds only lived to the age of eight, which didn't seem right, but even when Mrs Monger was in one of her better moods, it was best not to argue.

CHAPTER TWENTY-ONE

The next morning brought another envelope from Austria with two sheets of paper inside. The first letter was from Libby.

> We've moved in with the Goldbergs. They make us take off our shoes at the door. They don't like sharing their food.

It didn't make sense. Natalie pulled at the second paper from Mama.

> Our house has been taken from under us. They smashed Papa's jug. I'm sorry, I couldn't stop them. I begged them to let me take Papa's paintings, but they wouldn't.
>
> All our possessions are gone. Have they been borrowed or stolen? I don't know. My sewing machine too. Surely, we will get our home back some day?
>
> Leo's parents are kindly putting us up until we find somewhere else to go. Not just us. Five other families, Natalie, five! We are twenty-four in total! I can't complain because it is so good of them, but it is a terribly tight squeeze. Mind you, Baby Hannah loves it. We pass her around like a pudding. Libby loathes it. You know how she hates to speak to people sometimes. She now hates to speak to people *all* the time.
>
> I have heard they send people to prisons and camps. There is talk that they will shut the borders and we won't ever be able to leave. Sending you all my love, dearest girl, please send any

news about work or visas, anything at all. The not knowing is terrible.

'It's not too late!' Natalie wrote back to Mama at the new address. 'I'll keep trying.' She had a recurring image of Libby racing. She'd pass on the baton to them. *She would. She could.*

One Sunday morning, Natalie was in the kitchen helping Mrs Monger when Hugo came in, looking sheepish. He went over to the sink and washed his hands.

'What is that man doing in Mummy's bed?' he asked.

Natalie and Mrs Monger looked at each other.

'He might be poorly?' said Mrs Monger, eyeing Natalie helplessly.

'He doesn't *look* poorly,' Hugo said.

Natalie took a breath. She didn't know what was going through Hugo's mind, but she didn't want to plant anything there that shouldn't be there.

'I don't know if that's any of our business, Hugo,' was the best she could do.

Shaking her head, Mrs Monger grabbed the milk jug off the table so forcefully that it dripped onto the cloth.

Later in the garden, Hugo mentioned it again, as she knew he would. He was like a dog with a bone sometimes.

'Does Mummy love that man?'

'No, Hugo,' Natalie paused. 'She loves you the most.'

Hugo made a face.

'Not everything is as it seems, Hugo,' said Natalie desperately. 'Shall we play tea-parties?'

Mrs Caplin had brought Mr Young into the house? Into her bedroom?! What was she thinking?

*

When the Caplins went to their summer house, initially Natalie was relieved for the respite. Not from Hugo so much as Mrs Caplin and the drama that accompanied her. Hugo was even more despondent about the trip than usual. He kept asking for Natalie to come. He asked so many times it became embarrassing. Mrs Caplin explained they employed a local girl to care for him, and it was 'out of the question'.

'But she's not half so much fun as Nat,' Hugo protested.

'Yes, yes,' Mrs Caplin said vaguely, 'but fun is not everything.'

'I want Natalie,' he persisted and Mrs Caplin rolled her eyes. They took Molly though, because there were parties there and Molly was so good at clothes and cleaning. Natalie didn't think Molly would be keen, but Molly said she was excited for a bit of country air.

Without Hugo filling her days, Natalie felt unstructured and useless. She planned to go to the agencies or the passport office every single day, but infuriatingly even they took summer holidays. There was nothing to do. Hugo's schedule was her scaffolding – without him, she flopped. She dwelled on what was happening in Vienna and waited every morning for letters or news. All was unsatisfactory. She looked at the photographs of the princesses Elizabeth and Margaret in the newspaper and wondered what it would be like to be them instead of her, a helpless refugee-nanny from Austria. She looked out for Mr Young's bylines in the *Mail* yet, whenever she found them, felt herself recoil in a mixture of admiration and revulsion:

Car accident kills two pedestrians.

Woman shoots husband in suspected love triangle.

She also couldn't help wondering why Mr Freeman had disappeared. Had he gone of his own accord? And if Mrs Caplin had had to fire him, did that mean she might be next?

Rachel's next letter was even more painful to read.

> I never wear anything new. I know that sounds disgustingly trivial, Natalie, under the circumstances, but everyone else looks so wonderful. It's just us Jews who must walk around drab and uninteresting. Leo will go off me, I'm certain. Many shops won't serve us any more and the Jewish-owned ones are barely allowed to exist. What are we supposed to do? Please send news, dearest sister. I'm not ashamed to say we'll do anything now.

That night, Natalie dreamed her family were hanging from one of the gondolas of the big wheel in Prater Park. Only she was at the bottom, at ground level. They were all shouting at her, the same thing, *save the baby, save the baby.* And she didn't know what to do. They weren't going to throw it overboard, were they? She woke up, covered in sweat, and for a moment she couldn't work out where Hugo was.

Erich asked Natalie if she wanted to go for a walk with him. He said he sometimes couldn't face going into the tiny jewellery workshop with its naked lightbulbs and its copulating flies.

'At least some things are having fun,' Natalie said, then blushed furiously. He didn't seem to hear – she hoped he hadn't.

'It must be hard for your eyes?' Natalie said more loudly, contemplating the purple-black shadows of his face. He looked so tired, but then she had never met him not tired.

'My fingers suffer most.' He stretched them to show her. 'They're blistered.'

'Who needs fingers anyway?'

He laughed. She felt like she had a special skill in making him laugh.

Natalie asked him if he remembered the big Ferris wheel in Prater Park.

'Of course I remember it,' he said, like, *are you crazy?* 'Is this your way of saying you want to share a gondola with me one day?' He arched one dark eyebrow at her. He was good at that, the one-eyebrow thing.

Natalie poked him in the side. 'No, Erich. It is not.'

She decided not to tell him her nightmare. No point bringing him down.

She was walking with Erich. Erich in England. Not Rudi in Vienna. It was nothing like walking out with Clifford – who chatted endlessly as though he were panic-buying words – or Alfie, who was monosyllabic except when it came to Leah or Nazis. She was so relaxed with Erich, it was like he was a member of her own family. He talked just the right amount. He told her about the diamonds, the process, the men he worked with who came from Antwerp, South Africa and Amsterdam. He understood her stories about Great-Uncle Ben and Great-Aunt Mimi, Uncle David and Aunt Ruth. They had a shorthand, an ease in communication. It was not just that they spoke the same language; it had the same rhythm or tone. They knew so many of the same places in Vienna it seemed impossible they'd never met there before.

He was also the most melancholy person she had met in her entire life. He made Leah sound like Pollyanna.

In the café, they reminisced about strudel back home. Those layers of flaky wondrousness. He told her his mother was a superb cook.

'If I still lived in Leopoldstadt, I would be as heavy as an ox by now.'

Natalie laughed at the idea of a chubby Erich. It was impossible to picture since he was stringy as a wire hanger.

'I write and tell her I'm eating. That's all she ever wants to know. My father writes: *are you working hard, Erich? Do the people like you? Is it secure?* My mother writes: *what are you eating? That terrible English food! I hear they have kidney and liver. What do they do with the rest of it?*'

He smiled wryly, but as Natalie grinned back, his eyes filled with tears. He wiped them away quickly. 'You didn't see that.'

As they walked, he pulled her down an alley. 'Come here, Natalie,' he said in a voice muffled by his scarf and collar. He grabbed her and before she had a moment to breathe, he kissed her. His tongue whipped between her lips. Warm and wet.

It wasn't Rudi, but it was... magical. Natalie moved her hand to the back of his neck. It was far, far better than being kissed by Clifford and pursued by his tentacles.

But then it was not Rudi and that in itself was wrong. Natalie pulled her head back and wiped her mouth. With Clifford, it had always been strangely meaningless. Natalie was always aware of how detached she was when he touched her. Like a marionette.

This was different.

'I'm sorry, Erich,' she whispered.

Erich was sorry too. He looked more ashamed and shadowy than ever. His blue eyes looked rain-cloud grey. He stepped back out the alley, back into the main street, almost knocking into a passing man, wearing a bowler hat.

'Forgive me, Natalie.'

'There's nothing to forgive – it just... this won't help.'

'I know.'

She wanted to mention Rudi, and hadn't Erich remembered what she said just the last time they'd met? How had he forgotten? – *he's more myself than I am*? But she found she couldn't say Rudi's name just then. She couldn't say his name without the extra name, Flora Lang, squidged up alongside it.

Erich looked downcast. He wrung his hands. His face was a picture of misery. 'I just wanted to forget about everything for five minutes,' he said.

'*Thanks!*' Natalie said, smiling. 'I'm *so* flattered.'

'Oh, and I suppose you're very lovely too,' he added sorrowfully. He looked at her from under his eyelids. Was that a glimmer of a tentative smile?

'That's better!'

She reached for his hand and kissed the bony back of it. Oh, his fingers were so thin and veiny!

'I think we both need a friend right now.'

Tears came to his lovely eyes again and how she wished they wouldn't. Seeing them made her want to hold him, to press herself against him even. He wiped them with his sleeve. She wanted to ask him if he'd noticed that some Englishmen kept their handkerchiefs up their sleeves and could he explain why?

He said, 'How am I going to bring them all here? It feels impossible.'

He was a top-heavy fraction. She was only four over one. And the Goldbergs might have other avenues. They *must* have other avenues. She squeezed his fingers. This made him worse. The tears fell.

'It's okay…'

'I don't think I can take it any more, Natalie. Mama is going out of her mind with fear. I can't sleep because every time I close my eyes, I have a terrible premonition of what might happen to them.'

'What? What do you think will happen?'

What could be worse than what was happening now? Mama and the twenty-four guests squeezed into Leo's family's apartment. Helga sent away. Mama's bike missing. The jug of Papa's ashes. They had even stolen her papa's paintings. Did they think they were worth anything? Fools. Natalie liked the idea of Nazi officers going to a prestigious auction house, trying to get Paul Leeman's paintings valued and finding out they were worthless.

Of sentimental value. Only.

Erich shook his head from side to side as though wanting to rid himself of his vision. 'I imagine terrible things; crashing bombs like in *War of the Worlds*. Lost limbs. Spectacles smashed and teeth broken.'

'They're all going to be okay,' Natalie told him. 'The Nazis aren't Martians. I even know some nice ones.'

She thought of Arno, her Nazi neighbour who Mama had encouraged her to befriend. 'Such a sweetheart,' she'd said. His dumpy nervous mother with her hearing issues now waving at Mama in the street!

Erich looked at her, the way she imagined he would study a dud diamond. *How many carats did you say?*

'It's true. My neighbour Arno, for instance, wouldn't hurt a soul. He taught my little sister how to skip. Never. Impossible.'

'Hitler is a maniac and he's got everyone eating out of his hand.'

'Then we'll get our families out. We will.'

She thought how she had left one foreboding male face in Vienna and found herself looking at another in London.

As she lay in bed that night trying to sleep, she was pleased she hadn't kissed Erich back properly. She didn't want him to have false hope on that score. *Rudi. Rudi was still in her heart.* Rudi – minus Flora Lang – equalled enough for her. But when Natalie woke up in the middle of the night, her thoughts went straight to one person, and it wasn't Rudi. She touched her lips where Erich's lips had been, surprisingly sweet and surprisingly passionate. She wished she could take all his troubles and fears away from him.

His eyelashes had brushed her cheek. If only she could have returned that kiss, just for a little longer.

CHAPTER TWENTY-TWO

Sometimes, it was possible to pretend that nothing had changed in Austria at all. This was a great psychological trick that Natalie would sometimes play upon herself. In this *nothing-has-changed* universe, Mama was sewing, laughing, batting off unsuitable suitors like Odysseus' Penelope; Libby's treasure chest of medals and trophies was expanding and she was making super, if slow, progress with her writing. Rachel and Leo were working in their orchestra and happily complaining about the conductor. Little Hannah was thriving. They were even thinking about having another baby! Leo's parents took Hannah in a big trundling pram every Sunday to Kahlenberg, from where they admired the views of the city. The great-aunts and -uncles would be arguing, Uncle David would be studying Esperanto, Great-Aunt Mimi would be chain-smoking at the theatre.

In the nothing-has-changed universe, they all think of her in London and they can't help but feel slightly sorry for her. Between themselves they worry: 'poor Natalie out on a limb, stuck out there, a gnarly branch that has moved away from the family tree. Why would you do that?'

Rudi, in the nothing-has-changed universe, has not moved on. He was faithful, he was true; he was waiting for her.

So, nothing like real life at all.

The Caplins returned from their summer break with their car so crammed full of trunks it was a wonder it could move. Hugo flew into Natalie's arms. Great heavy monkey he was, Natalie had to grab the banister to stop herself from falling.

Mr Caplin was there, in the shadows. He gave his half-laugh. 'She's here, Huey. I said she would be, didn't I?'

'I *was* worried!' said Hugo, nuzzling Natalie closer.

'Don't you trust me?'

Hugo didn't answer. Natalie kept her eyes down. *Trust that man?*

'I missed you so much.' Hugo buried his face in her shoulder. 'It was utterly pointless without you.'

'Hugo!' warned Mr Caplin. 'That's too much.'

'Well, it was BORING listening to you and Mama argue all the time.'

Mrs Caplin's face was stony. Natalie smiled weakly at her, trying to tread the fine line between sympathy for her and betrayal of Hugo.

'Real life *is* boring, Hugo. I'm sure Natalie understands that all too well. Take him upstairs, please, darling.'

Natalie grabbed Hugo's hand, intending to head for the stairs. Before he had left, he had taught her the song 'Ten Green Bottles'. And he sang it now: 'And if one green bottle should accidentally fall…'

Mr Caplin said, 'It's good to see you, Natalie. You look healthy.'

'Good grief,' said Mrs Caplin, 'stop sucking up to her, for goodness' sake!' She turned to Natalie. 'You always look beautiful, darling.'

Natalie laughed politely. But Mr Caplin persisted. It seemed he was trying to win her over.

'Natalie, I hear things are difficult for the Jewish people in Austria now.'
Who was he, trying to kid that he cared?

'I hope your family are well.'

Natalie stared, but Mrs Caplin snapped at him, 'Anyone would think she was the boss and you were the nanny.' Mr Caplin looked as though he'd been punched. As she and Hugo finally took their leave and went up the stairs, Natalie could hear Mrs Caplin saying, 'Why on earth are you bringing all that up?'

The next day, Natalie and Hugo went to the kennels to see the dogs. Hugo had missed them so much. After he had petted, kissed, and stroked them, he looked up at Natalie and said, 'I love you, Tiny Tim and Rosie in that order,' and all thoughts of Mr Caplin's strange comments were forgotten.

On her next day off, Natalie went to Pam's Pantry. Leah was talking so animatedly to the customers – about Tiny Tim and Rosie – that Natalie found herself almost doing a double-take. Leah somehow managed to look and sound more English than the English. Some people become themselves in a foreign country, Natalie supposed, better versions of themselves. But Leah always said that while her passport, background and accent said Austrian, her heart said British.

'I'm so excited to see you,' Leah said, which surprised Natalie, until she clarified. 'I heard Dr Freud is in England now. Go and see him.'

'Dr Freud? *The* Dr Freud?'

Natalie thought of the poor greengrocer and how she had laughed at his fanciful idea that everyone in Vienna was somehow acquainted with each other.

'You actually *know* him?'

Leah lit a cigarette. She blew out the match tenderly like she was blowing a kiss. She liked to keep Natalie waiting sometimes. 'He's in Hampstead now. It's not far.'

'*How* on earth do you know him, Leah?'

Leah didn't answer for a moment. And then with her head lowered and a voice so quiet that Natalie had to lean closer, she said, 'I don't really, but he used to treat my mother.'

Natalie tried not to look too shocked, for she knew it cost Leah to make such an admission.

'Aunt Ruth? Really? Why?'

'For many years,' Leah made her face look matter-of-fact. 'For her... her hysteria.'

'I didn't—'

Natalie thought of Aunt Ruth's gout. The cures Mama sent. The recipes especially chosen for their 'healing properties'.

'No. Well, one doesn't… one can't advertise these things, Natalie.' Leah was back to her old impenetrable self. 'Anyway, go see him. The family has connections. They might be able to help.'

Natalie had an envelope from home and Hitler was on the stamp. It was a shock to see him there, in profile, mid-rant. Hitler had forced his way into her life. He was in her hand.

The letter was from Arno, the sweetheart who once so impressed Mama. The neighbour Mama secretly preferred to Rudi. (Not so secretly really.)

You will have heard about the *Anschluss* by now, Natalie, but have you heard I have joined the division of the Nazi Youth? It is very exciting. It reminds me of the boys' brigade. Some people say it isn't right, but they are the crazy ones. If you could see us you would understand. It's fantastic that we young people are finally getting a chance to shine. And we will shine. Don't be afraid. Please come back, we need more and more young people to rebuild our homeland. Austria will be strong once again.

With love, your dear friend, Arno

Hugo bounced into her playfully, trying to grab the envelope.

'STOP!' Natalie shouted at him. 'For God's sake, this is serious!'

Hugo shrank away. Natalie regretted her temper immediately and ruffled his hair affectionately. The boy deserved so much better than what he had.

'I'll just take this to my room then we'll go out and play. Yes?'

*

Mrs Caplin wanted help packing for a weekend away.

'Will Mr Caplin be here?' Natalie didn't want to be left alone with the man, especially now. Who knew what he'd try to do if he had free run of the house? He liked 'damsels in distress'. That's how he probably saw her.

'No, Warwick is working away.'

Mrs Caplin folded silk nightgown after silk nightgown into her case.

'It looks like you're going to be spending a lot of time in bed,' Natalie said brightly, then turned beetroot as the implication sank in.

'Naughty!' Mrs Caplin waggled a painted fingernail at her.

'I was just wondering…' Natalie said. 'Whatever happened to your agent? Mr Freeman? I haven't seen him—'

'Nothing *happened* to him,' Mrs Caplin said.

Natalie waited.

'Freeman just mightn't be a good fit for me after all.'

A good fit?

'And it's not like he got me any work, did he, darling? Lady Macbeth is all down to James.'

'I didn't realise,' Natalie said.

'Now, tell me,' Mrs Caplin continued, 'I want to get Mr Young a present. What would you advise?'

'I'm afraid I have no idea.' Natalie would have loved to be able to click her fingers and advise Mrs Caplin on a present for Mr Young that he would love but it was not easy to pick presents for a man she knew next to nothing about – except that he was ambitious and liked cricket.

'Oh, you do, you must do.'

'A hat?' Natalie suggested eventually.

Mrs Caplin made a disappointed face. 'I might as well ask Tilly the cat.'

*

Mr and Mrs Caplin both being away was an opportunity for Natalie to visit the Freud family. It wasn't ideal – she would have to take Hugo with her – but it was better than nothing. Leah called on her behalf, and whether out of obligation, curiosity or desire, they invited her that Saturday afternoon.

Hugo was wide-eyed and talkative on the bus. The only way Natalie could get him to stop singing 'Ten Green Bottles' at the top of his voice was by bribing him with some old sherbet lemons from the bottom of her bag.

The Freud family residence wasn't far but it was awkward to get there and Natalie worried they would be late. She told Hugo they were visiting old friends because she was slightly concerned that Mrs Caplin would mind them going. You never knew with her. When Natalie was a child, adults had seemed so predictable. Now she was an adult, it seemed to her that people were entirely unpredictable.

It turned out they weren't late, but it wouldn't have mattered anyway. They were swept into a house where everyone was talking German loudly and the women looked like her or Rachel or Mama. Natalie relaxed immediately. Dr Freud was much older than Natalie had imagined and quite poorly. He was in the courtyard garden, in a bath chair with a white blanket over his knees. When they were led outside, he said, 'More guests, what are they all for?!' and his daughter, Anna said, 'Sometimes a guest is just a guest, Papa,' and everyone laughed. Natalie joined in, but she didn't understand it. A few of the younger girls liked the look of Hugo and grabbed him to play in the garden.

Martha Freud, Dr Freud's wife, was distant and preoccupied. She said she remembered Natalie's Aunt Ruth, 'what a *talented* woman', but Natalie thought she was just being polite. What talents did Aunt Ruth have other than her penchant for putting people down and inheriting large properties?

It was an afternoon of lace tablecloths, dogs and cats, the sun dappling the trees.

It was like being at home in Vienna on a Sunday afternoon. They sat in the back garden and drank black coffee and ate fat pastries. With cream. And talked in German and argued and discussed. Dr Freud's voice was going, and he dozed off sometimes, letting out loud snores that made some of the younger guests laugh. It had been a terrible journey across Europe and taken such a lot out of him. He was too old for this.

Natalie told him her name and he grew confused; he thought she was a third or fourth cousin. Anna said gently, 'I don't think she is, but she does look a little like your beautiful cousin Naomi, doesn't she?'

Then he made a joke about the Gestapo. He had been made to sign a statement to say they had treated him well.

'I wrote down that I highly recommend them,' he rasped. And everyone laughed, and one man slapped his knee at the comedy of it, *the Gestapo, I highly recommend them*! Everyone, that is, except Anna, who shook her head sadly as he spoke and patted his hand when he finished.

Dr Freud invited Hugo to sit on his lap and to stroke his long beard. Natalie thought Hugo would refuse, he wasn't much given to physical affection, but he approached shyly. 'It's like a dog!' Hugo called out.

Dr Freud said, 'Did he say dog or God?' And the women laughed and said, 'Oh, you are naughty, Sigmund.' He slapped his thigh again.

'An Affenpinscher!' he said, and then, 'So tell me, little boy, do you know who I am?'

Everyone waited. When he spoke, it *was* like he was God. Hugo mumbled shyly, then hid his face in Freud's waistcoat.

'I'm Doctor Sigmund Freud,' Dr Freud continued. 'Say it.'

Dutifully, Hugo repeated it. 'Doctor Sig. Man. Froud.'

Everyone clapped.

'Like a medical doctor?'

Natalie held her breath, but everyone laughed.

'Like a medical doctor, yes.'

Anna stood next to Natalie at the buffet table and watched her dish up smoked salmon. 'The Sandersons are good people, educated. You've fallen on your feet there.'

'I'm not with the Sandersons, that's my cousin Leah. I'm with the Caplins.'

'I don't know them.'

'I do,' said the woman next to her, who smelled of chopped herring and had dangly earrings. She muttered something to Anna.

Anna nodded seriously. She slopped beetroot on Natalie's plate, then added a slice of seeded bread. 'Hmm… They are an *interesting* couple.'

'Interesting,' Natalie repeated, not quite sure what she was saying. 'Mrs Caplin is a wonderful actress.'

'Has she been in anything I'd know?'

Natalie stared. How was she to know what this woman knew? 'She was in… The Scottish play.'

'Macbeth?'

'Yes, she was very good.' *Good?* She tried again. 'She played the part with aplomb,' she said, which was what Mrs Caplin had told her the director had said.

'Lady Macbeth?'

'Yes.'

'Interesting.' This time the woman laughed.

The woman took a plate stacked with food over to Hugo and told him to sit up and eat nicely, which to Natalie's relief, Hugo did.

Natalie helped to carry the dishes back in the kitchen, where she hoped to corner Anna alone. Anna was the brains behind this operation – and what an operation it must have been to extract this entourage from Vienna and get them to Paris and then London. If she could do that, she was a woman who could do anything.

Anna was at the sink telling the two young maids that they must take home leftovers for their families. They were protesting but she was insisting, while pulling out bags and grabbing containers.

When they had finished, Natalie enquired politely, 'May I ask you a question?'

Without even looking up from the dishes, Anna Freud said: 'My love, I know exactly what you are going to say, and I have to tell you this: we have a list as long as your arm of people we are trying to get out from Germany and Austria. I feel like a real-life Sisyphus.'

Natalie understood and was ashamed. The Freuds didn't even know her from Adam, yet she was asking for their help.

Anna wiped the plate until it made a squeaky noise. Her hands were red compared to her pale arms. She set that plate on the side and began the next.

'Even my father needed a guarantor. Things are upside down. How do they put it: through the looking glass? We have no power here, you must understand that. All our money, status and reputation we used to get out of there and now we are bottom of the pile.'

Even as she worked at the dishes, she kept moving her head from side to side, and her neck made an actual crunching noise. 'All Papa's sisters are still in Austria.' She took her fingers out of the water again, and this time counted on them: 'Dolfi, Mitzi, Rosa and Pauli, their families, their children. I am trying to get them out. I write letters, I attend meetings, I put money in envelopes.'

'I'm sorry.'

'Don't be sorry. I would do the same, I *have* done the same.'

She put the wet plate down and then looked at Natalie properly, as though seeing her for the first time. 'Your mother would be very proud of you. How old are you?'

'I just turned eighteen.'

Anna leaned forward and touched Natalie's cheek. Her hand was damp and had tiny washing-up bubbles on it, but Natalie was grateful for the touch. 'Only eighteen. So young for all these burdens. We were lucky to get out. You were smart to get out.'

Natalie nodded uncertainly. Was she smart? If so, it was the first time she had seen it in that way. If something wasn't intended, was it still smart? No, she decided, she had been lucky. And her family had not.

'We should have gone earlier.' Anna rubbed the back of her neck, wincing slightly as she did. 'We didn't know how bad it would get, of course. Well, it *is* bad. If I can think of anyone, anything to help, I will let you know.

But then she thought, and she seemed to backtrack a moment. It gave Natalie some hope.

'Tell me about your mother.'

Natalie spoke quickly. Perhaps she *could* find something for them after all? This funny, brilliant, *important* family, surely they hadn't lost *all* their influence? 'Mama grew up in Innsbruck. She and Papa lived in Vienna. Papa died a few years ago, from cancer. Mama is forty-seven and she sews and takes care of people wonderfully. She's trustworthy, loyal and deserves a chance.'

But when Natalie looked up, she saw tears forming in Anna's eyes. This threw her. Everyone was crying around her. First, Erich, now Anna. Natalie couldn't find any more words.

'I know.' Anna squeezed Natalie's hand. 'I know.'

'She's still going to get out,' Natalie continued confidently. 'They all will… because… they will.'

'And what about you? What do you hope to do when you're older?'

Natalie told Anna that she wanted to be a translator.

'What a wonderful idea!' Anna said, but rather than cheering her, Natalie immediately felt the fool. She had not achieved anything in two years, yet here she was, bringing it up as though she had won a prize. Anna studied her. 'Although if it doesn't work out, maybe you'd consider working in therapy, perhaps with children? You're a good listener and a fine communicator, and excellent with that little boy, I see how much he trusts you. It's difficult with the traumatised ones.'

'Traumatised?' Natalie asked quickly. It wasn't a word she would associate with Hugo. Libby maybe, after Papa, but not Hugo.

Anna nodded. 'Anyway, tell me about your translations.'

Natalie's heart swelled. She said, 'It's a children's book. Not many people know it, but the author Kurt Brunner once wrote a story called *Making an Elephant out of a Mosquito*, about an elephant who thinks he is—'

Anna interrupted, 'I know that book. And I know Kurt Brunner.'

'Perhaps I should write to *him*,' Natalie thought aloud.

Anna looked doubtful, but then she seemed to have a change of heart. She put her arms around Natalie and squeezed her as though she were a small child. She whispered in her ear, 'Leave no stone unturned, child. Do you understand me? This Mrs Caplin, does she have lots of connections? If she's a good a woman, as you say, then she will surely help you. Then use every chance you have, every connection, every lead, everything you have, to get your family out.'

And then the two dogs ran into the kitchen and whipped about her legs. Hugo came chasing after them, shrieking. Anna reached into the cupboard and said that because he was such a good boy, he might be able to give them each a treat. Very slowly, he held out a treat in the palm of his hand and carefully, one after the other, they reached for it.

'You've got them completely under your spell,' Anna said.

'I do, don't I?' Hugo said proudly. 'Dogs like me.'

It was growing dark by the time they got back. Hugo dragged his feet, then fell asleep on the bus, his head heavy on Natalie's shoulder, his body ready for bed. They found Mrs Monger agitated and striding. The kitchen smelled wonderful, but Mrs Monger had on her most put-upon expression.

'Where *have* you been?' Before Natalie could explain, she said, 'I don't want to know. Mrs Caplin is back.'

'She's meant to be away.'

'Well, she's here with her friends and she wants you both to have dinner with them tonight.'

'Which friends?' Natalie asked, although she knew who it would be – it would be Mr Young and his crowd. It always was nowadays.

Mrs Monger shook her head disapprovingly. She went over to the range and stirred the pot with her great wooden spoon. 'They're waiting.'

Hugo ran ahead of Natalie to the bathroom. Side by side, they washed their hands. The mirror was smeary. She wondered if she should say anything about today, tell Hugo to keep it a secret – but she knew, from experience, that keeping a secret can make you obsess over something. Best to ignore it. She could still see the top of his head, and her own, anxious reflection. He flicked water and she flicked it back, laughing. 'I'll get you next time.'

It was fine, wasn't it, though? What were the odds that Hugo would mention it? What were the odds anyone would mind? It was just Hampstead. A sunny day. A tea-party. Two friendly dogs.

Ten of them were already sat at the table and Natalie had a sudden vision of that scene in *Macbeth* when the ghost of Banquo visits. Here were beautiful creamy-skinned women, with their hair piled high like cream on cakes and whisker-thin straps on their dresses. The men were in blazers and shirts without ties, which meant it was not a formal supper. Mr Caplin was not there, of course. He was probably bedding down some unwitting domestic servant.

Natalie and Hugo took a seat each at the small table set at the end for them without the gleaming tablecloth. They tucked in. It was a delicious goulash and when Mrs Monger came to collect it, Natalie thanked her; she winced and shook her head.

'It's stew, Natalie.'

'Well, it's still wonderful.'

When Natalie was nervous, her accent was stronger. She grew horribly self-conscious. She had a sensation that her voice was like a voice calling for prayer from a synagogue. Or a peasant shrieking at the Cossacks to let her family go. She wondered how Anna Freud would analyse this.

'Where have my favourites been today?' asked Mrs Caplin gaily from four seats down.

Don't say anything, Hugo.

'We went to see friends.' Natalie squeezed Hugo's little hand under the table. He squeezed back. He was singing 'Ten Green Bottles' under his breath.

Natalie tried to keep her expression relaxed. She concentrated on the peas. In England, you don't scoop the peas into your fork; instead, you lay them on the back of it. Natalie didn't see the reasoning behind this but was determined to master it.

'What did you do there?' asked one of the kindlier-looking women, in pearls and a peach cardigan that was slightly too small for her full bosom.

'We played with dogs,' Hugo said.

Hugo wouldn't remember Freud's name, she was sure of it. Natalie smiled warily at him and attacked the peas again.

One of the women laughed. 'I love dogs too, Hugo.'

Mrs Caplin barely ate any more. She pushed her plate away. 'Thank you, Mrs Monger, give us a few minutes before dessert.'

'Whose house did you go to, Hugo?' asked Mr Young.

Don't say anything, thought Natalie.

'What weather we are having!' she said.

'Dr Sig Man Froud,' Hugo said loudly, tapping his spoon. 'DOCTOR SIG MAN FROUD's house.'

Natalie thought suddenly of Odysseus and how he had to tell everyone his name after he killed the Cyclops. *For goodness' sake.*

Mrs Caplin carried on smiling. 'I don't know what on earth you mean, Huey?'

'I love the way small children speak,' the kindly lady in peach said. 'It's a complete mystery to me.'

But it was no mystery to Mr Young. Natalie watched as his cheeks reddened.

'What did you say? What did he say? Did he say Sigmund Freud? That old Jew? The doctor? The nutter?'

Natalie didn't know which of the three he thought was worse. All of them perhaps.

'Sig-man Froud?' said Hugo less confidently now. He eyed Natalie nervously. Her fork was mid-air and the peas plummeted to the floor. 'Sig man froud. Doctor,' he whispered.

At this, Mr Young was so incensed he got up and strode over to Hugo, who was now pushing all the carrots to the side of his plate in a little pile of unwanteds. Mr Young knelt by Hugo's chair. The kindly lady and Mrs Caplin exchanged glances. Natalie picked up her runaway peas.

'Did you go to his house?'

'Ye-es.'

'Did he touch you? That filthy old man! Did he?'

Silence in the room. Peach cardigan lady bowed her head as though in prayer. Mrs Caplin stroked her own cheek.

'I sat on his lap,' Hugo said quietly.

Natalie could feel the horror rising around her. It was like being caught in a huge wave.

'It was fine—'

'Wha-at?' Mr Young bellowed. Natalie was trembling now. She wanted to scoop up Hugo. She had done this to him, she had got him in trouble.

Mrs Caplin now joined Mr Young on the floor next to Hugo. She put her hand on Mr Young's shoulder – restraining him? Steadying him? 'What happened, Hugo? Answer us, please.'

Hugo looked up innocently. 'The dogs licked my fingers.'

'And you liked the dogs. And everything was all right.' Natalie spoke quickly.

Mrs Caplin seemed to be enjoying this. She got up, raising her eyes and flicking her hair at her female friends as though Mr Young was just a joke and not a bully.

'So, she took you to see Sigmund Freud?' demanded Mr Young.

'James, I believe we have already established that fact,' Mrs Caplin said idly. She made a face at her friends as if to say, *he does go on.*

'The psychotherapist?'

'You're not digging around for a story now, my love.'

He glared at her. 'Story? Shame on you. I'll protect your child even if you won't. What else does she do?'

'What do you mean?' whispered Hugo.

He bent down to Hugo.

'Tell me, my boy, has Natalie ever hurt you?'

'I'd never hurt Hugo!' Natalie began furiously. Mr Young put his fingers to his lips. He was in command of the room. In command of the house. Natalie couldn't help thinking of Hitler and his rallies. Some people have charisma, others don't. Charisma doesn't tell you anything about if they are good or bad or right or wrong. It means they're powerful. Whatever their size, they have reach.

Everyone turned to look at Hugo. This was a kangaroo court and he was the witness.

It was rotten. She didn't know what she wanted him to say. She wanted to spirit him – and herself –away from this humiliation. She remembered Mrs Sanderson.

'No!' said Hugo. And there was a collective sigh of relief.

'Get them out of here,' Mr Young said, as though it was his house, his child and his staff, but Mrs Caplin did nothing to defend Natalie or Hugo. It was like she was under a spell.

'Shoo-shoo, you two,' she said, 'up you go!'

*

The next morning, Mrs Caplin came into the kitchen to speak to her. Mrs Monger, who had probably heard the fracas but had not asked about it, made a face. Natalie sat as Mrs Caplin pulled out a chair. She seemed awkward but also determined.

'Everything is under control, darling. I know how much Huey loves you.'

'I didn't know I couldn't go there, Mrs Caplin.' It seemed important to get this across even if she had guessed it might be frowned on. 'You never said.'

'Oh, he really put the wind up you, didn't he?' Mrs Caplin said. 'Don't worry, *I'm* the boss here, not Mr Young. James just wants to defend our people, but he needs to learn to pick his battles.' She laughed. 'It's not personal,' she went on. 'It's not about *you*.'

Natalie nodded. She thought maybe she should tell Mrs Caplin that, excellent though the agencies and committees were, she hadn't made much progress. However, she couldn't seem to find a way in. Mrs Caplin managed not to give anyone the space to deliver bad news.

'Anyway, that's not the only reason I came down. Did you hear it, everyone? Mrs Monger!' she called, 'And Alfie. Big story!' She slapped the newspaper down on the table and proclaimed, 'Peace for our time.' She was reading from the headline.

'What is this?' asked Mrs Monger as Alfie crowded in to have a look. 'Mr Young wrote it,' Mrs Caplin told Natalie proudly. 'That's probably why he was so overexcited yesterday. It's a big day for the newspapers.' She coughed slightly. 'And for all of us, obviously.'

'Read it then.' Molly nudged Alfie but it was Mrs Monger who read aloud. 'Premier says, "peace for our time – give thanks in church. It is Peace Sunday". Tumultuous crowds throng Downing Street as Mr Chamberlain speaks from Number Ten window. Pact with Hitler is only a beginning. Duce asks Premier to Rome.'

'What does tumultuous mean?' asked Molly.

'Oh, big…' said Mrs Monger.

'Very big,' corrected Mrs Caplin.

'Exactly,' agreed Mrs Monger.

Natalie didn't know what to say. She shifted the paper to where she could see it better and read on, waiting for someone to take the lead. Fortunately, Mrs Caplin did. 'It's wonderful news. There won't be another European war. Peace has been signed. Give thanks to Mr Chamberlain and Mr Hitler. This is a historic day. James and I will certainly be raising a glass tonight!' At this, she left the kitchen, smiling triumphantly.

The remaining four looked at each other.

'This is a disaster,' said Alfie, putting his head in his hands.

Natty,

Mama gets dressed up every day and goes out without fail at ten to nine. She won't tell me where she goes. She says it's important but she won't let me go with her.

Do you think she could have a boyfriend? I hope not. Please write soon.

Libby

CHAPTER TWENTY-THREE

Leah looked glamorous in a fur coat from goodness knows where. She had persuaded Natalie to wear her best dress – the one from Rachel's wedding. Natalie felt uncomfortable but Leah said it was 'just right'. Erich was in a crisp white shirt, dark braces, and when he kissed Natalie hello, she could smell his cologne. He could wear a paper bag and he would still look handsome. He said, 'You look lovely,' to Natalie and she glimpsed Alfie just behind him, raising an eyebrow.

It was the dogs' first race night. There were crowds of people, far more than Natalie had anticipated, some in hats, some without, and you could feel everyone was in a great mood, all the way from the Underground station, as they walked to the stadium. Relief at 'peace for our time': even if those feelings were mixed with scepticism: war was off the cards for the time being at least.

Natalie had promised Hugo a blow-by-blow account of events, and he had promised to be a good boy for Mrs Monger and to draw his best pictures.

They took their place in the owners' area, where it was blessedly quieter and less squashed. Waitresses in white aprons came around with platters of food. Alfie tucked in without a moment's thought. Shrugging at each other, Erich and Natalie copied him. Over the last few months at the kennels, Leah had got to know lots of people and there were plenty of warm introductions, kisses and hugs; they were all included and welcomed. Natalie couldn't help noticing that Erich was watching her more than he was watching the track.

She smiled at him, and he smiled shyly back. She was relieved that Clifford hadn't been able to come and she'd been allowed to draft Erich in as his replacement. Leah and Alfie seemed to like him well enough too. And she was relieved she didn't look out of place in her outfit – in fact, she seemed to be getting plenty of admiring glances.

The starter gun went off, and then there was the thunder of the dogs whirring around the track, the whole place seemed to shake, and there were triumphant cheers and roars for the dogs to 'go on, GO ON!' The dogs were chasing a— what were they chasing? A mechanical hare. The dogs were so driven, so focused; they didn't know it was mechanical, obviously; they had the scent, their bodies straining, the single-mindedness. The speed, too fast really; if you looked down at the programme, just for an instant, you wouldn't see them fly by.

I should be more like a greyhound, thought Natalie, *get more things done.*

Yes! Tiny Tim had won. Natalie didn't realise it at first – they were all so close, weren't they? How they could tell between first and sixth? But Leah was jumping up and down, Alfie was jumping and yelling, and suddenly Erich was embracing her too. *Don't let go*, she thought suddenly, *it feels nice.*

Leah counted her winnings.

Then it was Rosie's turn. Leah was optimistic (overly optimistic, Natalie thought) about Rosie's prospects. Beautiful Rosie never seemed that bothered about anything, she had that easy-going lope to her. Natalie considered her 'louche'. Alfie said she had a touch of Wallis Simpson about her.

'She will win,' Leah said with her usual certainty. 'She's just a slow starter.'

Natalie thought of Libby and the way she always surprised them all near the finish line. Maybe it was possible.

They were off, flashing past, their numbers on their backs. It was so fast, Natalie couldn't help wishing there was more to it, but it was exhilarating when they steamed by. Why, they were like machines – so different from the Rosie she knew, who lay on her back for Natalie to tickle her belly sometimes. Rosie didn't win, but she came a brilliant second in a field of eight, which meant more money for Leah to collect.

They were exuberant. The owner of the winner, Topsy Turvey, bought them all gin and tonics and the owner of poor Saint Nicholas, who had refused to run, asked Natalie out: 'You're very exotic,' he kept saying. 'I like that in a woman.'

They laughed all the way back home.

Natalie and Alfie were still going over it all in the kitchen one hour later. It had been an excellent night, the best.

'You want to watch out with that Erich.' Alfie already had something in his mouth. He must have swiped something from the larder as soon as they got back. A pork pie, even though there had been all that food at the races. He was a gannet.

'How do you mean?'

Was he going to say something about Erich being bad-tempered, violent or something? She was ready to argue. Despite his dark looks, the unfashionable stubble around his chin, Erich was the gentlest of fellows.

'I mean he's in love with you, Natty. You must know that.'

'No, he isn't.'

But something ticking in the back of her head told her Alfie might be right.

Then, in November, more cruel news. Things had got even worse in Germany. *And* Austria. They called it Kristallnacht. The Night of the Broken Glass – only it wasn't just one night, and it wasn't only glass that was broken. Jewish properties were attacked, Jewish *people* were attacked.

The day after she heard, Natalie took Hugo to school early, then headed straight for the bus, and rode one hour to the Labour relief agency. She wasn't alone with that idea. There was already a queue halfway down the street. It was like the queue for the Christmas concert at the Kursalon although the atmosphere couldn't have been more different. She looked out for Erich, but didn't spot him.

'We'll never get seen,' the woman next to her in a blue trouser suit sighed.

'We'll all get seen,' a tall man in army uniform confidently said.

'The British government will look after us,' a woman in a pretty frock like she was going dancing said.

'Us maybe, but not my brother in Berlin,' another said.

'My father is a professor at Leipzig University,' said blue-trouser-suit woman. 'Do you think they want him in? Do they hell!'

By midday, the line had hardly moved. If Natalie had thought it was slow previously, she was to find out what slow really was now. Mama had told her how terrible it was during the Great War, and how they waited hours in line for bread, so she stayed put. But by one thirty, she had to give up. She didn't stand a hope of doing this and getting back to pick up Hugo by three.

On the way to the school, she remembered other family stories. How Mama had met Paul Leeman when he was standing for council and she had avoided him because despite what everyone said about him, her first impression was that he was arrogant. He had asked her for dates but she kept turning him down until the evening she saw him give a speech to a workers' co-operative and she saw that he was a caring, thoughtful man. Then Mama fell for him, hard. He was ambitious, not for himself but for everyone. No one had been more committed to the working people than her Pauly. No one was more of a patriot. No one more dedicated to his city. He would be rolling in his grave if he could see what was happening to his beloved Vienna now.

'I thought we were the future,' Mama used to sigh. 'And we were for a while.'

And Rachel? Rachel was a child of melody – a spoon was a drumstick, a comb was a whistle. At ten, her violin teacher declared he couldn't teach her anymore. She was too good, she must try for a scholarship, a special place at an academy. She succeeded and was four years younger than the previously youngest person there.

What about Libby, her long-rangy sister who refused to engage in small talk but could throw a stone to whack a post two hundred yards away with a triumphant ding?

And all the cousins and the uncles and aunts and the great-uncles and the great-aunts?

Why were they doing this to them?

Natalie tried to call Anna Freud. She wanted to speak to someone who she guessed might be feeling a similar level of pain and anxiety. But the Freuds' telephone just rang and rang. Natalie told herself they were probably out, but part of her was paranoid and wondered if they were ignoring her.

It was pointless anyway. Anna wasn't the chance she had hoped for and Natalie needed the powerful now, not the powerless.

Natalie did as Anna had suggested though and wrote to Kurt Brunner. She tried not to let it come across as fan mail but it did and it felt faintly embarrassing. He probably received hundreds of letters a week too. If only she had struck up a correspondence with him earlier, they might have been enormous friends by now and he wouldn't see this for what it was – a beggar's note.

I love Making an Elephant out of a Mosquito. *It's true, isn't it, that we shouldn't worry about the small things but…?*
Natalie chewed her pencil. She started again.

It's true, isn't it, that we need to look after each other. Can we, is there any chance you might be an elephant for me?

She crossed that out. Too soppy.

Could you use your influence to help my mother and sister leave Vienna?

Your most faithful reader…

Hugo had started having nightmares. Every shadow was a ghost. Every creak a monster. It was since Mr Young had shouted at them; Natalie was sure of it. He begged Natalie to stay in his room, by his side, until he was asleep. When Natalie mentioned to Mrs Monger that maybe Hugo and she should swap rooms, she snorted.

'And have Hugo in the room right next to his mother? I don't think she'd be that keen on that idea, do you?'

Sometimes, Natalie found herself hoping Hugo wouldn't be able to sleep. She liked it when he would rush in next to her, his sticky child's breath like wind rustling in her ear.

Hugo had long since stopped asking for his parents at night, and he stopped looking for them in the day too. He still drew them in his lavish pictures, but mostly they were in the background. He was devoted to Natalie and she to him. *Is that wrong?* wondered Natalie. It didn't *feel* wrong and yet… If she backed away from him now, he'd have nothing.

Mr Caplin was grave and absent, Mrs Caplin was obsessed with her *James*, and between the two of them, Hugo was quite forgotten. *Was* he traumatised? thought Natalie, remembering Anna Freud's words. She didn't know. Hugo was just Hugo. He wasn't sad when he was with her, and he wasn't sad when he was at school. All was well, as long as she could hold onto his little hand at night, and she was more than happy to do that.

*

A postcard from Rudi. Egon Schiele's painting *Room in Neulengbach*. It depicted a sad little room. Why had Rudi chosen this one?

I'm so glad you got away, Edelweiss.

That's all it said. The words combined with the sorry-for-itself picture made it feel like he was talking in code. Did he have to be so cryptic? So obscure? He had never called her Edelweiss before. NEVER. Was this something he had picked up from Flora Lang? Natalie wanted to tip him upside down and shake him for more words to come out. *Wouldn't he tell her anything?* Every day, she was slipping away from their love story and she hated herself for it. Lying in bed at night, she couldn't conjure up Rudi any more, even with his strange notes. He was like a television with no signal, just a spoil of grey fuzz. Nowadays, the only one she could picture clearly was Erich.

Even Mrs Monger took pity on Natalie after Kristallnacht. One day, Natalie got back from the agency, and Mrs Monger insisted on taking her to the cinema to see the latest hit comedy film, *Climbing High*.

'It will give you a good laugh,' she promised.

Natalie managed not to laugh, not one single time, while Mrs Monger found it so funny she wept. Mrs Monger also whispered that the actress was the spit of Mrs Caplin and then cackled that Mrs Caplin would never get into film because she was more wooden than a tree. Natalie thought that was a bit spiteful.

Afterwards, they sat on a bench outside a fish and chip shop. Mrs Monger didn't like shop-bought, she always said, 'I can do better at home,' but she wanted to treat Natalie. But even there you couldn't get away from the terrible news, because the newspaper they ate from was full of: *Looting mobs defy Goebbels, Jewish homes fired, women beaten.*

The chips were so swamped in the malt vinegar that the English love, they made Natalie's eyes water and her nose run.

'You said there had been the people who didn't like the Jewish people for ever and it will go away as quickly as it came.' Mrs Monger never could bring herself to say the word *anti-Semitism*.

'What if I'm wrong?'

'You wrong? Natalie? Never!' Mrs Monger chortled and Natalie wasn't sure if she was laughing with her or at her. She tried to join in, but she felt as though she had forgotten how to laugh.

Mrs Monger had a photo of the King on her side of her chips. 'That's lucky, isn't it?' She looked at Natalie. 'See here, everything that's important today is less important tomorrow and even less important the day after. It all disappears eventually.'

Natalie nodded, still tasting the sharp sting of vinegar on her lips. *Women beaten?* She missed Libby, Rachel and Mama so much. If they had come to England and not her, they would have managed to get everyone out. Rachel especially would have been able to do it. Her mixture of good looks, charm and common sense won people over everywhere. A smile from Rachel was worth ten of anything Natalie had to offer. And Libby? Well, people liked helping quiet Libby. They always did. Anyway, she was earnest and dedicated enough to achieve things without other people.

'My sisters are capable, beautiful and strong, and I am a nothing.'

'You're a fine young woman,' Mrs Monger said, without pause. Then, when she realised that didn't quite hit the mark, she added, 'We like you, Natalie, and I can tell you – I didn't at first. Not one bit. Come on, cheer up, girl. I've a new phrase for you.'

Natalie nodded tearfully. Even in her darkest moods, she was always up for learning an English saying. 'It ain't over 'til the fat lady sings,' Mrs Monger said. 'And I'm not singing, am I? So, it's not over.'

*

The next day, as Natalie chased Hugo into the house after school, she saw Mr Young looking at her with his strange mixture of interest and disdain. He straightened his tie in the mirror and smoothed back his hair as if she weren't there. He had a folded newspaper under his arm.

'You still here then?'

Natalie ignored him. It was obvious she was still here, no?

'It!' shouted Hugo.

'Got out just in time, didn't you?' He had a strange expression on his face. It was a smile, but it wasn't. Natalie was again struck by how cruel he seemed. What on earth did Mrs Caplin like about him?

'I don't know what you mean…'

'It's all kicking off over there now, isn't it?'

But then Mr Caplin's car pulled up to the front of the house. The look of terror on Mr Young's face was worth everything.

'Daddy!' shrieked Hugo. He was already half upstairs, his school satchel left on the hall floor. 'Daddy's home!' He bounded back down.

'Stay calm, everyone.' Mrs Caplin appeared at the top of the stairs. She was beaming. 'James, you *really* had better head off now.'

Mr Caplin opened the front door. He surveyed the scene. Mr Young reached out to shake his hand, Mr Caplin automatically shook it. He seemed in a kind of speechless daze. Mr Young left. He looked like a man trying not to look like he was in a hurry.

Flushed and beautiful, Mrs Caplin marched down the stairs. She made to hug Mr Caplin, but he backed away.

'Who on earth *was* that?'

'He's a friend of the nanny's,' Mrs Caplin said in her most bored voice. 'Of Natalie's.'

Oh God. Mr Caplin turned to Natalie: 'He's a friend of yours?'

Natalie nodded quickly. She had to defend Mrs Caplin. What would Mr Caplin do if he found out?

'Was that a yes?' Mr Caplin asked. It was the first time he had addressed her so impatiently and it made her tremble.

'It was a yes.'

'Is that right, Huey?'

Hugo shrugged and then punched himself in the head. Mr Caplin gazed at them all, then pulled Mrs Caplin to one side.

'You let him in the house?'

'What do you expect me to do with her guests? Keep them in the garden shed?' Mrs Caplin's voice was loud and high. 'Come on, Warwick! *Mi casa es tu casa*, no? Or doesn't it apply to staff? Or staff from certain places?'

Mr Caplin stared at Natalie and then stalked off up the stairs. It was terrible.

Mrs Caplin's shoulders were going up and down. Natalie drew closer, thinking to put her arms around her, but then she realised it was laughter. Mrs Caplin was shaking not with fear but with laughter. 'Now that was fun!'

'Mrs Caplin?'

'There, that was brilliant! Thank you, Natalie.'

Natalie didn't know what to say to her. She wanted to say, *why are you taking risks like this? Why are you involving us?* But she couldn't, she couldn't. Somehow, she knew, the risks were part of this. Mrs Caplin – or Mr Young – was looking for a little more excitement and Natalie was just a pawn in the game. But what if Mr Caplin decided he wanted to get rid of her? What would happen then? Could she trust Mrs Caplin to protect her? She would have loved to have answered yes, but something told her that was far from assured.

CHAPTER TWENTY FOUR

Erich put his arm around her. Natalie told herself it was in friendly, brotherly fashion and she thought he told himself that too. She thought of Rudi and she thought of Erich. Between the two of them, she felt so lost and so tired. Between them and London and Vienna, she closed her eyes. He closed his too. A tear slid from the side. They had been talking about Kristallnacht again. Hard to talk about anything else.

'I'm so exhausted with it all, Natalie,' he whispered.

'I know.'

Her passion for him was growing, even though she did her best not to water it, she did not feed it, she did not want it; yet it wouldn't go away. She was helpless. She wanted Erich to kiss her. More than that, she wanted him to make love to her. Like a man and a woman. The desire just coursed through her. It made her want to weep. What was the matter with her? She tried to think of Rudi, but he gave so little and his letters were so infrequent and so short that she couldn't even picture him any more. She tried to think of the conversation she had over two years previously with Mrs Sanderson, *he is mine and I am his,* and it just seemed like childish declarations now.

They had all moved on.

Mrs Caplin had someone. Leah had someone. Even Molly had a secret someone. But she mustn't. *She mustn't.*

She thought of Erich's calloused fingers, thought of putting them to her lips, she thought of touching him. She knew he would respond; she knew it. But should they?

She had always been so certain about Rudi. It was hard to break out of that way of thinking.

Natalie felt like Odysseus approaching the sirens. Someone needed to tie her up to the mast of a ship else she would drown. She had been so good. So true. *Don't turn into someone fickle or disloyal.* Mrs Caplin had good reason to go astray; she didn't.

Natalie even tried to pray about it, but it did no good. Each time she saw Erich, she couldn't help herself. Resolutions flew away like birds after a gunshot, and she wanted nothing more than to be his. He wasn't more herself than she was – he was someone totally different to her in every way, but they fitted together, hand in glove. They understood everything about each other.

They watched a family fly a kite. It took ages for it to lift, to be free, but then when it did, how beautifully it dipped and twisted in the sky. The father started running with it, and the daughter chased it gleefully as that old kite managed to stay up there; the kite was pulling away and the father was pulling it in, and Natalie thought of her family and how she had to hang on, however much forces were pulling them apart.

She nearly declared her feelings to Erich that day. She nearly told him she was in love with him, but she didn't. She couldn't.

'When I first came here, I thought that Mama was being unusually relaxed to let me come. Now, I think she only let me because she was growing nervous about the rise of the Nazis.'

'Weren't *you* worried?'

'Not really,' admitted Natalie. It was only because it was Erich that she felt she could say the truth about her blind spot when it came to the Nazis. 'I didn't see that it could have anything to do with me.'

'I would have come anyway,' said Erich. 'But I wouldn't have this…'

'Heavy load?'

'Exactly. This constant feeling of guilt, shame and worry.'

'I wish I could go back and get them out,' Natalie said wistfully.

'I wish I could shoot some Nazis.'

'Erich!'

'Well, I do. I feel such a sense of coming catastrophe. Natalie, I'm sorry but I do.'

They parted with a hug, not too much contact; they kept a decorous distance between them. Why did they have to be so sensible? They made a promise for next week. Next week was too far away, but then they had to be good.

Erich walked away and as he did, she saw two men push into him. Natalie thought it was accidental at first, and then she heard them.

'Nazi scumbag.'

'Dirty Kraut.'

Erich kept on going, though; he just carried on trudging down the road towards the crossing, the wind lifting his beautiful black hair from the back of his collar. Natalie loved the sight of him then, even from behind. He was perfect.

My dear Natalie

It's agony to leave Mama and Libby, and everyone, but everyone insists it is for the best. Is it though, Natalie? I know you did it. You were so brave. I wish I could be as courageous as you. I wish you were here to advise me. I wish we were back in our room, with nothing more serious to worry about than who is the most handsome, Arno or Rudi Strobl.

You know the Nazis have taken over everywhere? Can you imagine – Nazi soldiers sleeping in our beds, their heads on our pillows, their hands on their guns?

We needed work, you can't imagine Leo without work, like a bear with a sore head, can you? So, he has managed to join an orchestra in Amsterdam. It is a good one – you know Leo, he wouldn't want a step down, even if wild crocodiles were snapping at his heels! They don't have a place for me at present but maybe in six months, who knows?!

So, Hannah will be a little Dutch girl!

We will be safe there.

Natalie could breathe again. Finally, *finally*, some good news.

'Hugo,' she called out, 'listen to this!'

CHAPTER TWENTY-FIVE

They met Alfie and his friends in The Rising Sun pub before they were to go dancing together. Much as she was keen to experience a fabled place of ill-repute, Natalie hadn't wanted to go, but Leah insisted she needed to take her mind off things.

'Won't we stick out like sore thumbs?' Natalie didn't feel like taking her biblical hair and her Jewess's nose to dances at church halls now. She seemed to attract the wrong kind of attention.

'No,' said Leah, but then she didn't care even if they did. Sore thumb was fine by her. She was buoyed by her weekly trips to the races. Her friendships with the owners, trainers and veterinarians. Her dogs were never less than third or fourth place. Tiny Tim never let her down. Rosie was a trooper. Leah was learning and learning. She had switched their diet to raw meat – so much better apparently. She had deep discussions about spaying and neutering. She was a woman on a mission.

Natalie had to rush since, as usual, she hadn't known if she was free until the last moment. She was wearing a fitted dress of Molly's that Molly said she may as well keep, and lipstick from Woolworths that Leah had persuaded her to buy. It was a mistake: while it looked pretty with Leah's complexion, it made Natalie's cheeks look redder than ever.

By the time they arrived at the public house, it looked as though Alfie and his friends had been installed there for some time. They were shiny-lipped, lolling about on the upright chairs. One of them had a cute dog with a wet nose curled up on his lap so Natalie went over and made a fuss of him. His name was Charlie or something, his dog was Snowy. It was easier to talk to a dog than with the rest of them. But Leah had to include her:

'Everyone, everyone, Natalie has some good news!'

'Your mother?' Alfie looked up at Natalie, bleary-eyed and foamy around the mouth, which always made Natalie think of a rabid dog she'd once seen when she was out canvassing with Papa. She knew now this meant he'd been drinking. What she didn't know was how Leah put up with him.

'No, not Mama, not yet. My older sister Rachel and her husband are going to Amsterdam.' Natalie smiled at Leah. 'And the baby, of course. Little Hannah.'

'Holland?' Alfie sneered, wiping his mouth with his sleeve. 'What the hell are they going there for?'

Natalie hadn't expected that. There was nothing wrong with Holland. Unless you didn't like windmills. Did Alfie not like windmills? Had he an aversion to clogs? She scowled at him. 'Well, Alfie, I'm sorry Holland is not good enough for *you*.'

His friends laughed. Snowy, unsettled, jumped up and barked. One of the men sniggered. 'That's you told, Alf.'

But Alfie was undeterred. 'They should have come *here*. If there's a war—'

Natalie interrupted as viciously as he had. 'There's *not* going to be another war, Alfie.'

'If there's another war, Hitler will have them in days, hours even.'

'For goodness' sake.' Natalie grew tearful again. Tearful and overdone in this silly dress of Molly's that was too tight at her arms, and with her over-bright lipstick. No amount of fitted dress and Woolworth lipstick could cover up what she was – an outsider – and the efforts she made to conceal that made it somehow all the worse. None of *them* were wearing lipstick, after all.

'We can't do anything right, can we, Alfie? You tell me they have to leave and when I tell you they've left, you tell me they've done it all wrong.'

He paused. The pub seemed to go quiet. The man ordering at the bar and the barmaid both looked over warily. Leah put her hand on Alfie's arm. She said something to him with her eyes. Natalie could see him slightly shrink back, change his mind.

'I'm sorry, Nat,' he said eventually.

'And stop calling me Nat.'

'Truce?'

He reached out for her hand. Natalie dodged it. She wasn't going to forgive him that quickly. She looked down at his ugly inebriated face and wanted to slap his chops. She couldn't believe Leah didn't feel the same.

'You're right, Nat-a-lie. They've done well. It's a start, isn't it?'

The church hall was done out in red, white and blue flags, and there was a band of young men inside who looked no older than high-schoolers, and a table of soft drinks manned by some church elders. Leah was completely happy and at home in this world of English dancing. Look how she snuggled against Alfie's hairy arms. The once-snobby cousin, who liked everything and everyone in its place.

Leah went whirling off like a teapot at the fairground. Natalie stood to one side and danced with the occasional elderly fella who took sympathy on her. She knew it was sympathy because one of them said, 'My wife sent me over,' and the other said, 'I thought you'd get rigor mortis standing there all alone like that.'

Natalie had been slightly relieved Clifford wasn't there and so was a bit disappointed when he arrived, just after ten o'clock. It wasn't just his wandering hands, but that he tended to monopolise her and act as though they were long-term partners. But there was no getting out of it. He asked Natalie if she wanted a drink and she supposed she might as well. He was gone a long time and when he came back, it was with some strange-tasting cordial that couldn't have been from the soft-drink table and made her want to gag.

She drank it down.

'Like it?'

She made a face. It didn't really matter whether she liked it or not, she decided. She was feeling quite heady all of a sudden. He pulled her up to dance. He was actually quite the dancer for once, and in her dreamy haziness, she was glad he had turned up. Clifford wasn't a bad guy, was he? He wasn't Erich, but Erich was out of bounds really. He had rough worker's hands, and his thighs kept knocking into hers, in quite a sexual way.

'I've missed you,' he said.

'I've had lots of work,' lied Natalie.

He got her more of the strange cordial and her head grew fuzzier, but it was a pleasant kind of fuzzy. The tension about her family she had been carrying around for the last few months seemed to dissipate. Everything was fine – no, everything was very amusing.

When the music sped up, she saw Alfie twisting his arms, trying to get them over Leah's head, and she looking down on him, doe-eyed. Natalie was still annoyed with Alfie, although she tried not to be. She was feeling everything strongly. All was exaggerated in her head. She focused on Alfie and her anger. What did Alfie know about continental Europe? Nothing, that's what.

Clifford asked Natalie if she was all right.

'Alfie hurt my feelings,' she said timidly. Why was her voice like that? It wasn't just foreign-sounding. It was… the words ran into each other like custard.

Clifford leaned in. 'Don't worry about Alfie, he thinks he knows everything.'

Natalie grinned. That was exactly it. Clifford was an absolute genius. How had she doubted it? Searching the room, she saw Alfie again, holding Leah tightly to him: 'Well then, he's found a good match in my cousin.'

This made Clifford laugh. 'You're gorgeous,' he said, clutching her closer, and for once, Natalie didn't mind at all.

*

After the dance finished, they lingered in the garden, smoking and making jokes. Clifford had his arm around Natalie's waist but as long as there were people there, he wouldn't try to kiss her. Natalie contemplated what she would do if he tried this time. She usually would rather not, but then, it was a small price to pay to keep him on-side. Besides, kissing Clifford didn't seem too much of a bad idea that evening. To have someone warm to burrow and escape into.

No one seemed in any hurry to get back and since Alfie had promised to walk Natalie home, she had to wait for him.

'Is this how you dance in Austria then?'

'Oh no!' Leah said delightedly. 'Let's show them a traditional dance, Natalie.' Even though it was only Alfie and his friends, even though it was so dark you couldn't see much, Natalie didn't want to. Still, Leah, with her boundless enthusiasm, hauled her to her feet. The men formed a circle around them. There was no escape.

Natalie tried to imagine an accordion and a cello. Leah faced her, bowed, and then twirled her around. Their arms met over her head and then over Natalie's. Leah was so much taller she had to crouch. Finally, Natalie let out a laugh. Then they did it again a little faster, more serious-faced.

Natalie was transported back, remembered learning the moves at school, taking them to a fete. Rachel, now in Holland; Arno, now a Nazi; Rudi, now a mystery; her sister, Libby, trapped.

She remembered one time, dancing at a school event, Mama watching and clapping along, laughing arm in arm with Papa on the walk home: *Bravo! All our children can dance. We might be the luckiest family in the whole of Vienna!*

'I feel sick,' Natalie hissed suddenly. In an instant, Leah had let go of her hands. Natalie retched into a bush. Alfie went over to see if she was all right, and she threw up again and some of it splattered over his shiny black shoes. He didn't say anything as he walked her home – he was his old sullen self.

*

That night, Natalie woke to the sound of her door opening. She assumed it was Hugo. He sometimes came in when he couldn't sleep. No one came in, but she was sure she saw Papa looking at her from the doorway. He didn't say anything; he just stood there. He was in a jacket, shirt, his dark hair. It was definitely his beard with its touches of grey. Soft, he looked so calm. Like he had before the tumour got to him. Before the bedridden months. Before his ashes were tipped into a jug in a house Mama had been made to leave. And his presence made everything all right. He didn't speak, he didn't need to. Everything about him was reassuring. Everything would be all right in the end. He was here. She was safe.

Natalie fell back asleep.

CHAPTER TWENTY-SIX

The next Saturday she was free, Natalie decided to drive to Pam's Pantry. She put on Mrs Sanderson's hat – her lucky hat – and Mrs Monger said she could take some herbs from the garden. They collected cuttings of rosemary, thyme and sage. Tilly stared at Natalie as she put them in the passenger seat, as if she had stolen them. 'It's fine, Tilly, I got permission,' she told the cat, before sneezing. *Damn cat.*

She set off nervously, the car smelling like a vegetable patch.

Just as she approached the front gates, she saw Mr Caplin's car coming towards her. Right in front of her. She saw his shocked face, the dark round 'O' of his mouth, and she braked as hard as she could. The car screeched in protest.

Of all people, it had to be him.

She signalled that she would go backwards. Mr Caplin couldn't be expected to reverse, of course. *No one says no to Mr Caplin*, she thought resentfully. She struggled with the gearstick, then started to reverse. As she put her foot to the floor on the accelerator, she heard a terrible sound. A searing sound and then a thud. A horrendous thud.

Oh no. She'd killed the cat. She'd killed Tilly.

When she didn't move, Mr Caplin got out of the car and rushed over to her. She just sat there. She didn't think she would get up. If she didn't see it, it wouldn't have happened. If he weren't there, she might have got away with it. He didn't know yet, she realised. Could she pretend it hadn't happened or could she just slam on the pedals? She could drive to Southampton and catch a ship to New York. No one would know she murdered the cat.

'Are you okay?'

She was frozen. Her fists wouldn't undo from the steering wheel. Her knuckles were white.

'NATALIE!' Mr Caplin said loudly. 'Are you okay?'

When her voice came, it was like it came from a different part of her. 'The cat's dead, Mr Caplin. I killed her.'

He looked at her, then ran behind the car. He ducked out of view. How bloody would it be? How mangled? She had reversed, gone forward, and reversed again. It didn't get much worse than that. He straightened. He was laughing, cradling something in one arm. He banged on the window.

'It's a gnome, Natalie. It's not the cat. Tilly's over there, look!'

He pointed at Tilly standing on the front wall, staring at them both disdainfully. She couldn't have looked more disappointed if she tried.

The relief! Natalie couldn't stop laughing.

'Come.' He grinned. 'He's not in great shape.' The gnome was in four or five pieces. 'Let's see if we can save the poor bugger.'

Mrs Monger was doing the weekly shop so there was only Alfie in the kitchen. He raised his eyebrows at them both, then left, apologising that he was late to start the windows.

Mr Caplin poured her a glass of milk. He laid the gnome out on the table as if he were about to perform surgery. It was one with a fishing rod and satchel. Surprisingly, the rod and satchel were still intact.

'You have to drink,' he said. Natalie gulped the milk down and slowly, her steadiness returned, but also her fear. She was so relieved that it wasn't the cat, but even so, Mrs Caplin loved those gnomes. If she found out, she'd be furious.

Mr Caplin seemed quite unperturbed as he gathered a magnifying glass, glue and scissors.

'How are your family?'

'Very good.'

He looked up as if he hadn't expected that.

'My sister is going to Amsterdam.'

'You're pleased?'

Natalie nodded. 'Very.'

'Excellent. And how is Hugo getting along?'

'He is marvellous,' said Natalie.

'He is rather, isn't he?'

Natalie smiled at him. She couldn't have anticipated what he would say next. Not in a million years. She expected he might tell her off about the car; perhaps he would forbid her from it, or ask how she even came to be driving it. Instead, he said, 'You know, Hugo is not my son.'

'Oh!' she said.

'I love that boy though with all my heart.'

'I didn't know,' Natalie said. And why was he telling her this now?

'I met Caroline when she was five months pregnant. The other fellow was a scoundrel – wouldn't marry her. She asked me. I thought if I worked hard enough, we would be able to have a good life together, a beautiful home, a family, I could provide everything she needed.'

Natalie nodded. Hugo was not Mr Caplin's child. This changed nothing, but at the same time, it changed everything.

'Does Hugo know?'

Mr Caplin reddened. 'I did explain it to him once, but I think he may have forgotten. Or maybe he doesn't think it's important. I don't. But I suppose I wanted you to know.'

Natalie nodded. She imagined he was telling her to pre-empt her thoughts that he was a bad father.

He gazed at her for a moment. 'That hat… it reminds me of…'

'It was Mrs Sanderson's,' Natalie said, quickly adding, 'She left it to me,' in case he thought she had come by it nefariously and was about to rip it off her.

He smiled warmly. 'I know Beverley was very fond you. Did she ever tell you we were sweethearts?'

Natalie shook her head.

Mrs Sanderson?

'We were very young.' He was concentrating on the gnome, his eyes scrunched up to apply the glue. 'After the Great War, she married Gordon… He's a lovely man, and well, there we are. We remained good friends. It was her idea that we get you, of course, our girl from Vienna. And like everything she does, I think it worked.'

The little gnome had lost his broad grin but was still managing a faint smile. His left cheek was cracked and there was a big line down his leg.

'Adds a bit of character, don't you think?' he said. 'As good as new.'

Natalie found she was trembling again. 'Almost.'

CHAPTER TWENTY-SEVEN

Kurt Brunner, the author of her favourite book, *Making an Elephant out of a Mosquito*, was a Nazi. The book that spoke to Natalie throughout her childhood, that seemed to embody her values, her philosophy, was written by a fascist-lover.

This hurt. This really hurt.

Natalie had tried to ignore her suspicions at first, but when she came across an interview with him, a double-page spread in a German newspaper, there was no pretending. The dreamy writer who used to run poetry workshops for deprived children was now a bright star in the new Austrian regime. 'Kristallnacht was not a big deal,' he said. 'The only Jews that were attacked were criminals, conspiring against the state. They were corrupt bankers; they were bleeding Austria dry and a boil that needed to be lanced.'

She took the book downstairs and stuffed it behind some others on a high-up shelf where she'd never have to see it again. Mr Caplin was the only one who looked at the bookshelves and she doubted he would notice.

Back to the labour relief agency and the refugee coordinating committee.

'The situation is terrible. There must be more help available.'

'There isn't!' the woman the other side of the desk said, twirling her pen.

Does this woman know what it's like to advocate for someone far away when you don't even know what they want? Mama *said* she would come, but would she *really* pack up her trunk and dare get on a train? Everything was petrifying and Natalie could sense day by day, Mama was becoming paralysed with fear. In the newspaper, there were photos of people being forced to kneel in front of Nazis. Forced to clean the streets with toothbrushes. Leo's older brother, Nathan, had. Nathan, the world's leading specialist on the clavichord, reduced to scrubbing doorsteps. And what was his crime? Being a Goldberg. Being a Jew.

She had to get Mama out. Mama who taught her how to throw stones so they jumped across the Danube, saying, *Not throw, dearest girl, skim.* Perhaps that's what she'd be saying now: *Not so heavy-handed, child.* Some things need a light touch.

'Isn't there *anything* I can do?'

Guarantors. If she hadn't known that word one year ago, by God she knew it now. More paperwork. *Keep trying. You never know.*

Natalie cycled back to Larkworthy, wishing Erich had been there.

When she next saw Erich, some weeks later, he told her a friend of his brother's had been executed in the street. A nineteen-year-old, made to kneel, shot, then left to die on the cobblestones.

Natalie didn't know why Erich had told her that. *What purpose did it serve?* She hated him then. Why was he including her in this… this horror? Natalie told him it wasn't true. It must be a lie. That man must have been doing something wrong.

'He was trying to walk his little sister to their grandmother's house.'

'That *can't* be right. I know the Nazis are terrible but they're not that terrible.'

The Jews were not allowed to study. They were not allowed to play in orchestras. They were not allowed to race. They were not allowed to have staff. Homes and shops were being taken from them. But this?

'I'm sure it wasn't… it wasn't how you say it was.'

'Are you saying I'm lying?'

'No, I'm saying you've probably got the facts wrong.'

They walked to the Lyons tearoom in silence.

When they talked about things other than the news from Austria, they got on better. Erich told her stories from his work – who ordered what, which gems were fashionable; and he had a story about a cousin of the Queen, an engagement ring that would not fit, and a groom who ran away.

When he was animated, Natalie couldn't help admiring the contours of his face. He really was quite – not just handsome, beautiful in a way. As he talked, out of nowhere, Natalie imagined him kissing her, reaching out and touching her breasts, and she had to shake herself.

She thought of what Alfie had said after the dog races, 'He's in love with you.' Sometimes, she suspected it might be true. Erich had *fallen for* her. She wouldn't hurt him, she mustn't. Life was complicated enough. But Erich was looking at his shoes again, not her, and maybe she was being vain or silly again.

Natalie couldn't get Erich's story out of her head. She imagined a small girl watching her brother murdered by men in uniform. By men you thought you could trust. There was something about it that didn't add up. It *couldn't* add up. It was incomplete. A piece of information had to be missing.

Pam had asked Leah to help do up the Pantry and Leah was keen to oblige. There was a new framed photo of Walthamstow racing track, and posters of victorious dogs and events from its past. When she was next there, Natalie told Leah and Alfie what Erich had said, they gazed at each other, and she knew straight away, *they* believed it. It wasn't a stretch for them, it was at eye-level.

'We've heard stories like that too,' Alfie said finally.

Leah turned round the sign on the door, so it read 'CLOSED' to those outside.

Dusk was falling and the sky was flaming pink. On any other day, Natalie thought, she might have found it wonderful. But now her heart was gloomy. The man with the ladder had come to light the streetlights and she watched without watching as he worked efficiently, climbing, lighting, descending, moving on. He must have done it thousands of times before.

'They don't talk about it in the papers here, but it's happening all the time.'

'Why don't they?' she said.

Alfie grimaced. 'Because then everyone would know that Chamberlain's stupid appeasement policy is wrong. They would prefer to pretend that Hitler is not a dangerous tyrant.'

Natalie sighed. This was too much.

'Why do you find it so hard to believe?' Alfie asked finally.

'I just can't believe people *hate* that much.'

These weren't *any* people; that's what Alfie – for all his doom-and-gloom prophecies – didn't understand. These were *her* people. These weren't Martians landing from outer space or monsters rising from the deep, these weren't ghosts from dank cupboards or skeletons from the spooky graveyard. These were Arno and his family next door. This was her favourite author since she was nine. Her friends at college, her teachers, for goodness' sake.

They wouldn't do this.

These were the people she stood next to every day. The people she smiled at on the tram. They wouldn't do this. It was impossible.

CHAPTER TWENTY-EIGHT

By the spring of 1939, Natalie had been in England for nearly three years. If she had stayed at home, she might have been at university. If she had applied herself to translation, she might have had a proper career. Instead she had done nothing over the past three years apart from waste time and bite her nails.

Mr Caplin was distant. Mrs Caplin was charming, but far more besotted with Mr Young than even Rachel had been with Leo. Alfie, Leah, Clifford and Natalie still double-dated occasionally, but it was irksome and made Natalie bad-tempered. She would go through the motions, dance the dances, but she wasn't really there. Being with Clifford made her feel disloyal not only to Rudi but to Erich too nowadays.

One evening over dinner, Mrs Monger was pale-faced, Molly even more so. Molly was in trouble. Molly was in trouble meant that Molly was pregnant, a fact Natalie didn't realise until the stewed pears. Molly, dear old Molly, who slipped out to meet secret beaus was having a baby. This was surprising, but, when you thought about it, not that surprising at all.

'Whose is it?'

Molly scraped her bowl and wouldn't say. Mrs Monger pursed her lips. It was hard to tell if she knew or not. Yet it was because they were so secretive that Natalie was able to work out whose it was. Mr Caplin's. It had to be his. Had Molly actually *wanted* to do it with him though? She had made it clear that she wasn't interested... but Molly, she was so young, so vulnerable. Poor, poor Molly.

'Do you want me to say something?' Natalie chose her words carefully. 'Perhaps to Mrs Caplin?'

'God, no! Don't tell *her* whatever you do.'

'What are you going to do then?'

'I'll have it adopted,' Molly said neutrally. Mrs Monger thumped the dishes into the sink. It was a wonder nothing cracked.

'You don't want to keep it?'

'*He* doesn't want to keep it.'

I'll bet he doesn't, thought Natalie furiously. *How could he get away with this?*

She thought about the gnome incident and how she had just started thinking Mr Caplin kind. More fool her to be conned so easily.

One afternoon, Natalie and Hugo were playing hopscotch at the front of the house when Mr Young's car drew up. He came by three times a week nowadays, if Mr Caplin was away, maybe more. Natalie had drawn a chalk grid on the concrete slabs by the door. She swallowed fearfully. No doubt he would find something wrong as usual.

Hugo was after a seven. He threw his stone, but it was distracting having an audience and it went on the nine.

'Dammit,' he said.

'Ssh!' The last thing she wanted was for Mr Young to know that she let Hugo swear.

Natalie's turn. She threw. She got a six – bang on – which was what she wanted.

'Not fair!' said Hugo.

'I'm still behind you,' she consoled him, and did the jump and hop to the end and back.

Mr Young watched her. He squinted. He chewed.

'Nice game, hopscotch,' he said, half to Natalie, half to the air. And then he winked at her. 'My favourite number is three.'

He walked to the front door as though he were the master of the place.

No one is *all* bad all the time.

I go to the consulate every morning now, I am there as soon as it opens. (Don't mention it to Libby, she will only be afraid.) I feel like I am hunting, visas are our prey. But we are also the hunted, Natalie. A man waiting outside was pelted with stones by a group. For no reason, no reason at all. I even knew one of the men who did it. He was friends with Papa in local government. Papa would have been devastated by all this. In one way, I am glad he is not around to see it. They were telling him: 'go – go, leave,' they were chanting at him. I would say they were animals, but it's not fair to animals.

Don't they know? That's what we are trying to do.

How is your translation coming along, dear girl? I have started to think that cross-cultural communication is the answer to all this damn mess. What greater way for people to understand each other than by reading books, by understanding others' ideas, their lives? I should have told you before, it *is* a noble calling, Natalie, and I know if anyone can, you'll do justice to Kurt Brunner's fine words.

Proud of you, my love, hope you are still smiling.
Mama

Mr Caplin knocked on the door of Hugo's nursery while Natalie was cleaning. There was no avoiding him. She had let her guard down during the gnome incident, but she wouldn't let herself forget that he was a philanderer, he was the one who didn't want her here, who thought his country was 'infested'. She clenched the duster, a poor weapon, and decided she could throw Hugo's collection of stuffed bears at him, if necessary.

As usual, Mr Caplin commented on the weather, enquired after her and Hugo, commented on how happy Hugo seemed. Natalie nodded and continued polishing furiously. If he thought they were going to be friends now, then he was very much mistaken. 'What about poor Molly?' she wanted to shout into his faux-meek face. *Don't think we don't know what you do.*

'Natalie,' he said. 'This is a little awkward for me.'

Natalie blinked at him. She couldn't imagine what he was about to say. She pulled the sides of her blouse a little further together; it was slightly undone at the top, because she and Hugo had been playing hula hoop in the garden.

'That man who was here, was he really a friend of yours?' The words seemed to rush out of him. Natalie didn't know whether she was relieved or not. Relieved that he wasn't about to make a pass at her, not because she had to decide whether to lie or not.

'Yes,' she said finally, for her loyalties would never not be with Mrs Caplin.

She watched as he seemed to unclench slightly and this told her that it was the right decision too.

'How do you know him?'

'I just do,' she said with her eyes on Hugo's horse, whose expression was suitably serious.

'Does… does Mrs Caplin ever bring men here at night?'

'M-men?' repeated Natalie as though unfamiliar with the term. *How are you defining 'men'? And what do you mean by 'night'?*

Mr Caplin licked his pale lips. 'My wife, Caroline, does she ever have male friends to stay?'

What to say? Whose side was she on? What about you? she wanted to retort. *You're hardly innocent here.*

'She gets picked up sometimes, in a car, for auditions and things, but she comes home alone. Is that what you mean?'

Mr Caplin's shoulders relaxed in their blazer. He let go his grip on his tie.

'I don't actually know what I mean. I'm an old fool. People talk, you know. You're a good girl, Natalie, thank you. I'll get to my work. That's something I am good at.'

Natalie backed away from him. She wondered if he was saying this for sympathy. Maybe he was still readying himself to make a move on her. But he wandered off in the other direction, muttering, 'I'm sorry.'

A few days later, there was another party and another lot of friends calling out for their glasses to be refilled. Natalie was waiting for the nod for poor Hugo to do whatever they wanted him to do. He was the entertainment, but they were still talking politics – at least it meant Hugo mightn't have to thump 'Jerusalem' out on the piano. Natalie watched Mr Young pontificating.

'All the Jews are trying to come here now.'

Natalie wondered if it was the drink making him less inhibited about sharing his opinions but he seemed quite sober.

'Who can blame them?' asked an older woman with bright red lipstick, but Mr Young didn't like that.

'If they're so worried, and I don't know why they are, they just don't like giving up their money, then why not do something about it, instead of living off other people's goodwill?'

One of the men tried to pacify him. 'Don't know if it's as simple as that, James.' He chortled, but Mr Young didn't laugh when he was talking politics.

'Course it's bloody simple,' he snapped. 'Stay and fight then, don't weasel yourself into other countries where you're not welcome.'

Natalie thought of Mama sewing buttons onto a blouse. *Fight Nazis?* Really? Squinting into the distance, asking someone to pass her her 'seeing' glasses. Fumbling for her purse? She wouldn't even see the Nazis until they were upon her. The thought was so absurd it very nearly made her laugh.

And poor Erich's family. That tapestry of elderly people, what were they expected to do? Take up arms, get the sandbags in?

Should Erich's brother fight – his younger brother? Maybe. Without guns, without training, perhaps he should still take on the might of the Nazis. Maybe he should try an assassination? The Nazis might well take out a few hundred people as reprisal, but still… Is that what they wanted them to do?

The next day, when Natalie got on the bus, the conductor said, 'Thought you lot had your own cars.'

Natalie didn't get what he meant at first, maybe it was more of that British anti-Semitism? But the conductor was smiling broadly at her, including her in the joke.

'First time we've had a princess on board,' he continued. 'Welcome, your Maj'.'

Natalie caught on. She laughed. 'Sometimes we like to mix with the common people, don't you know,' she said, imitating Mrs Caplin's special telephone voice, and she did the charming little wave she had seen the Princesses do. The conductor saluted, chuckling, and it made her smile all the way to Pam's Pantry.

Each time Natalie visited the café it looked more stylish. Not Vienna-level stylish, but not far short. Apparently, Pam and the customers were delighted with the change in décor.

Alfie and Leah were holding hands across the Formica. It was still such an incongruous sight, Natalie wanted to laugh.

'Do you think I look like Princess Elizabeth?' she asked.

'Not at all,' Leah said dismissively, never once taking her eyes off Alfie's sweaty face. 'By the way, Natalie, I've asked Alfie to marry me.'

'And I said yes!' Alfie said, no doubt thrilled at the prospect of an endless stream of strudel and boiled chicken.

Natalie was reeling. She suddenly thought of Rachel and Leo's engagement party – the first time they had been to the Goldbergs' mansion on the prestigious Ringstrasse. She and Mama had exchanged shocked looks as staff upon staff had called them down endless grand corridors. These people, these people were different to them. Now the Goldbergs had no staff and their house was filled with families and now Leah was marrying too. All the people she loved were moving away from her and into the arms of men who were not their equals. Somebody should stop them.

Leah was waiting for a reaction. It was as though Natalie were at school and hadn't been paying attention to the lesson. Now the teacher was coming around, showing off his cane.

'Congratulations!' Natalie finally mustered. 'That *is* news.'

Alfie went back to Larkworthy; he had work to do in the garden. He gave Leah a squelchy kiss – did he have to? – before he left. A few customers came in, workmen in overalls, wanting their sausage rolls and their milky teas. Natalie made herself a black coffee and sat in the corner, trying to collect her thoughts. She thought she had worked out what was happening.

When the last customers had left, and Natalie finally had Leah alone, she said, 'This is amazing news. But Alfie has no money.' What she meant to say was worse than that – Alfie has no *chance* of getting money. He had what Aunt Ruth would call *no prospects*.

Leah shrugged. Her cheeks were flushed and her hair awry. 'He makes me feel happy. More than that,' she added, 'he makes me feel like I'm home. Me, him, Rosie and Tiny Tim. We are a family. A family of four.'

Home. That's what it was about then. Natalie put her arm around her. 'Come on, Leah, I know what this is…'

'What?'

'A visa marriage.'

Leah peered at her as if she was trying to solve a mystery. Natalie wondered if she should stop talking, but something compelled her to continue. Wasn't honesty important? 'I know how much you hate Austria – and I also know you are petrified of being sent back—'

Leah sprang away from her.

'How dare you?'

'It would solve that problem for good!' Natalie persisted stubbornly. 'So, I can see *why* you're tempted. They definitely won't be able to throw you out then – but really, *Alfie*? Couldn't you do any better? I don't know what you—'

'Get out!' Leah bellowed so loudly that the newly-hung pictures shook on their hooks. 'Out! Natalie Leeman, you're a snob.'

'I'm not a snob!' Natalie was breathless with incredulity. 'But Alfie is a gardener!' She couldn't bring herself to say, 'odd-job man.' It was a phrase that gave her an uncomfortable feeling in her stomach.

'And I'm a cook and you're a bloody nanny!' yelped Leah. 'For goodness' sake, Natalie. How could you be so prejudiced? You're everything I hate about Vienna.' Leah pointed her finger right in Natalie's face. She jabbed. 'That's the main reason I'm glad I'm not there. Go. Now. Go.'

Such a dreadful, dreadful day. After the row, Natalie's head was throbbing. Leah thought she was a snob? This was so far from how Natalie saw herself that she could hardly believe it. Leah had gone utterly mad. She wished she had asked Leah to elaborate. In what way exactly was Natalie prejudiced? Just because she didn't agree that Alfie was a good match. Natalie wished she had expressed her misgivings better.

There was a letter on the mantlepiece waiting for her. Mama was writing less now. Rachel wrote more. Libby wrote about the same. This one was from Libby and was even shorter than usual. Natalie braced herself. There was *never* good news from Vienna now.

Mama sleeps late and has stopped going out at all. We miss you and talk about you lots. Mama wants to come to England. Can you hurry up and get us out, please?

Natalie tucked it into her pocket. Too painful to read again. *Oh Libby, sweet girl.* She *was* trying. Or was she? Was she trying hard enough? Should she chain herself to the railings of Parliament like the suffragettes did? Should she jump out in front of a horse race – no, better than that, the dogs? Perhaps that's what was needed – a grand gesture. But she didn't feel capable of a grand gesture and she would only get trampled on, or she would hurt the dogs and their skinny legs, and then she would be taken down to the police station, and probably Mr Young's newspaper would talk about what a criminal she was. Then she'd be sent back to Austria. Grand gestures were often the most futile of them all.

She remembered Mrs Monger's threat, *back to Mr Hitler for you*, and how at the time it had seemed ridiculous.

In the kitchen, Hugo was drawing football matches: his new thing. 'GOAL!' he shouted when she came in, and ran over to hug her. It was heart-warming, especially after such a day, and she clutched him back.

Mrs Monger looked up at her, tight-lipped. She'd been cooking mackerel.

'Mrs Caplin is in a bad way.' Apparently, she had asked repeatedly for Natalie, and would Natalie go up to see her now?

Now? All Natalie wanted to do was lie down and cry. Or sit down and eat a currant bun. Bad news from Vienna and she had just upset her biggest ally in England. The person who knew her most. The person who was her best friend. Why hadn't she just bit her tongue for the peace? How hard would that have been?

Natalie dallied a little with Hugo, thankful for his unquestioning loyalty, but Mrs Monger's eyes were burning into her, willing her to get a move on.

Reluctantly, Natalie left the sanity of the kitchen with a slice of Mrs Monger's lemon drizzle on a decorated plate. She didn't feel like Mrs Caplin's company today. Why had she reacted like that to Leah? Had she learned nothing? She hated herself, yet also felt irritated by

Mrs Caplin. It was horrible to always be at someone's beck and call. And what was up with her now?

'Good luck,' Mrs Monger said, before adding hopefully, 'never know, she might be asleep.'

The curtains in Mrs Caplin's room were drawn, and the top of the bedside table was awash with balled-up handkerchiefs, miniature whisky bottles and glasses. Mrs Caplin was but a lump in the bed, buried under the covers. Phew! The room smelled of sweat and sheets. The glass ashtray on the bedside table was bulging. Natalie moved some of the things onto the floor and found a place for the cake with its tiny fork. She grabbed some of the dirtier-looking handkerchiefs, turned towards the door and began to tiptoe out to freedom. *Don't wake up, please don't wake up.*

'Natalie,' Mrs Caplin called out, 'Wait!'

Natalie stood still as Mrs Caplin pulled herself up to a seated position. She was wearing a silk dressing gown, cream, and her hair, now loose, looked darker than usual. It needed a wash. Somehow though, she was even more gorgeous and glamorous in her despair, if that was possible.

'Sit and talk with me a moment. You're my friend, aren't you? My special friend.'

'Of course.'

Natalie hovered at the side of Mrs Caplin's bed nearest the door. The last thing she wanted was to chat. She wished she were in the kitchen drawing goals. She wondered if Mr Caplin had found out about Mr Young? If he had, that wouldn't be Natalie's fault.

Mrs Caplin sighed. 'I'm in agony.'

'Has something happened?'

'I seem to have been broken up with – *is that how they say it these days?*'

Natalie covered her mouth with her hands.

'Mr Caplin?'

'No!' Mrs Caplin said it so sharply that Natalie wanted to back away, but then Mrs Caplin burst into hot uncontrollable tears, her knuckles pressed into her eyes. 'Mr Young.'

Natalie took a breath. She couldn't find the words, in English or German.

'But… Mr Caplin?'

'Forget Mr Caplin for one minute,' Mrs Caplin hissed. 'It's James I'm talking about. He says unless I leave Warwick then he will never see me again.' She covered her face in her hands. 'Oh God, Oh God. What am I going to do? He says I've broken his heart.'

Natalie tried to imagine the cruel Mr Young suffering from a broken heart. She didn't expect he had a heart to break. It was hard to feel sympathy for him, or with Mrs Caplin come to that, but she should try.

'I… Have you talked to him about it?' It seemed pathetic against the magnitude of the problem, but what else could she say?

'Repeatedly.' Sighing, Mrs Caplin threw herself sideways on to the bed. Natalie couldn't help wondering if she was playing the part of the lovesick *femme fatale* rather too well.

'I can't let him go, Natalie, I can't. He is my world.'

Licking her lips, Natalie tried to think of the words Mrs Caplin would want to hear. What would Mrs Monger say? No, that was no good. She put her hand on Mrs Caplin's shoulder. What *should* she have said to Leah? Finally, she ventured, 'Could you divorce Mr Caplin, and then you would be free to be with Mr Young?'

'I can't!'

So that's settled, thought Natalie. But as far as Mrs Caplin was concerned, it was not.

'I don't want to be left destitute, I can't. I won't.'

'I thought Mr Young was doing well at the paper?' It was a bit odd to be standing up for Mr Young, it was not as though Mrs Caplin was proposing to run off with a gardener/odd-job man.

At that moment, Natalie registered that yes, she might be a snob.

'The thing is…' Mrs Caplin lowered her eyes. 'Mr Young is not a wealthy man. At all. Quite the reverse.'

'Oh?' said Natalie. Now this *was* surprising. Everything about Mr Young, his arrogance, his accent, his gait, his clothes, seemed to point to wealth.

'If I left, I wouldn't be able to have this house and this life, and Hugo and you!'

'I see.'

'But he wants me to himself. I know it's agony for him, it's shameful, it's humiliating, but what about me? He can't leave me like this, he can't.'

'Well, if he won't accept…'

'*Why* won't he understand? I give him everything that I can. More than everything.'

'If you love him that much then maybe you should consider… I don't know?' Natalie said helplessly.

'I am not leaving, Natalie. It may seem strange to you, but my life is fine. Warwick is perfect for me. He doesn't interfere. He gives me space.'

'But you're not really free,' Natalie said in a low voice. She found herself wanting to shake Mrs Caplin to wake up. The world was on the edge and Mrs Caplin thought the most important thing was which man she'd rather take up with.

Mrs Caplin crumpled down again, cigarette in hand.

'Why won't he just love me as I am?'

Natalie considered. She tried to put herself in Mr Young's position. She should try to walk in his shoes. 'Maybe he wants a family of his own, Mrs Caplin,' she plucked out of nowhere.

'He *doesn't*,' Mrs Caplin hissed. 'I know him, and I know exactly what he wants. He's just… I have to keep him, Natalie. Do you understand?'

And Natalie did understand this. 'Maybe he'll be back,' she said helplessly. 'People change their minds…'

'No, this time it's the end. He's tried this before but never with so much fury. It's definitely over.'

'Well, I...' Natalie scratched her head. She was lost for words. She tried to think of what Mama would say now. Something gentle yet encouraging, no doubt. The words came to her: 'I know you will deal with this, Mrs Caplin, in your own indomitable style.'

Mrs Caplin looked up at her, nodded meekly.

'I can, can't I?'

'Absolutely you can.'

Mrs Caplin seemed to be waiting for more.

Natalie thought of the posters on the walls of Pam's Pantry. 'Once a winner, always a winner,' she said, thinking of Wee Katy, canine winner of the 3.20 at Walthamstow.

'I like that,' Mrs Caplin purred.

Natalie took Mrs Caplin's limp hands as a tear rolled down Mrs Caplin's cheek. She sniffed loudly and they both laughed.

'Shall I ask Mrs Monger to make a cup of tea? It will go nicely with this lemon cake.'

'Please.'

Mrs Caplin swivelled out of the bed. Her legs were long, shiny and immaculate. Mr Young was a fool, there was no doubt about it. Maybe all men were. In which case, it was more important than ever to be as strong and as good a friend as she could possibly be.

'And Natalie, you won't breathe a word of this, will you? To anyone?'

'Not a soul,' Natalie promised. 'Trust me.'

As Natalie went to fetch the tea, there was a definite spring in her step. No more Mr Young? Well, that was a small piece of good news to come out of the darkness.

CHAPTER TWENTY-NINE

Sometimes, the hands of the labour relief agency clock moved around so slowly Natalie wondered if invisible forces were holding them back. Yet other days, the time just flew. Every week, Natalie queued outside, she waited inside, queued inside, waited outside. She wanted to have all the options available. She had to. What if there were an opportunity, a job or a contact offered here? There might be, there might, there might… Mama mustn't miss out.

It was a miserable rainy day and the queue did not move. When cars went by, they splashed puddle water into the people waiting. It felt like an added insult. One man had ripped his shirt. 'They're dead, they're dead, you're killing them!' he was wailing. But he still had to wait in line. Another woman shouted, 'We're all in the same boat,' and someone else shouted, 'No, we're not, mine's about to capsize!' Natalie wanted to laugh, but the woman next to her was crying. Erich would have calmed the situation, but Erich had been coming to the agency less and less. He didn't say it, but she knew he was losing hope.

By two o'clock, Natalie still hadn't got inside to speak to any of the ladies and she had to decide what to do. She could go now, having wasted her day, and possibly miss precious opportunities for Mama, or she could persevere and be late for Hugo. Late – the thing she hated being above all else. Late was worse than snob or prejudiced. Sometimes, she thought the one thing she had going for her was her punctuality. She was the on-time sister.

She stayed for fifteen minutes longer but when they didn't move forward an inch, she gave up. As she left, she saw the woman's face behind her break into a broad beam.

Natalie raced down to the bus stop. She had given herself a small amount of spare time for the connections, but somehow, she still missed the bus. What would Leah say? Well, Leah wouldn't know because Leah wasn't talking to her.

As Natalie ran up the hill to the school, *late, late, late*, a motorcar chugged up behind her and she prayed it wasn't Mr Caplin. *Late, late, late*. The car drew alongside her. She saw with relief it was Mrs Caplin, and waved but continued to run, ankles twisting in her heels. She and Mrs Caplin both arrived at the school about the same time. Natalie was sweating and her hair clips had fallen out.

'Where on earth have you been?' Mrs Caplin snapped as she stepped out the car, narrowly avoiding a puddle.

'I'm so sorry, it won't happen again.'

'No, it won't.'

Natalie couldn't tell if Mrs Caplin meant because Natalie would never get the chance again and she flushed bright red. Mrs Caplin wouldn't get rid of her, would she? Not for this, surely? It was a first offence.

While he was waiting with his teacher, Hugo had drawn a large picture with crayons. Recently, he had been less enthusiastic about his drawings; the gap between what he envisaged and what he achieved seemed to stall rather than spur him on and Natalie suspected he had been forced into this. Nevertheless, it was a beautiful piece of work. There he was, in the centre of the page, smiling broadly in shorts with mucky knees, tufty hair and uneven socks, quite a good likeness, and he was holding her hand and she was smiling and holding, yes, that's what it was, Mr Horsey on his strings. Her hair was far too curly – Hugo, did it *really* look like that? – and her eyebrows were black rectangles like twin Hitler's moustaches, but it was recognisably her and quite flattering in a way. Further away in the top right corner was his mother in an evening dress, one that Natalie knew she had, gold and strappy, and she was holding someone out of the picture's hand. His father was nowhere to be seen.

'What a picture.' Natalie hugged him tightly. 'You're an artist! I'm so sorry.'

'Get in the car,' said Mrs Caplin.

As she drove, Mrs Caplin seemed to get less annoyed. Maybe she had seen the state Natalie was in. Or perhaps the picture had softened her. She *did* look pretty in it. Natalie started explaining what had happened, but now Mrs Caplin simply lifted her hand, leaned her perfumed head close to hers.

'You've not been having an assignation, have you?'

Hugo was sitting in the back, staring at his artwork, pretending not to pay attention.

'Good God, no, I—'

'Oh, don't be so shy, Natalie. We all need some passion in our lives.'

'I wasn't!' Natalie was outraged but Mrs Caplin was smiling to herself. She turned her blue eyes on Natalie and winked. 'Don't worry, darling. I am having the time of my life!'

Natalie's heart fell. She should have known it couldn't last.

'So are you and Mr Young…' *How to phrase this?* '…back together?'

Mrs Caplin nodded her head. 'I can't let him go,' she explained matter-of-factly. 'I can't. He is my everything. He is the only thing I have. And he says I am the same.'

When they stopped at a traffic light, Mrs Caplin leaned over again. Natalie leaned away but then realised Mrs Caplin wished to show her something. It was a brooch of an eagle with its wings outstretched. Its beady head twisted to one side, to the right. It was silver. It wasn't the kind of thing Natalie liked; nor would she have expected Mrs Caplin to like it, but it was clear she adored it.

'It represents long life, great strength and majestic looks.' She chuckled to herself. 'He's a good man,' she said, fingering the bird. 'He's ambitious, passionate, a patriot, a nationalist, and there's nothing wrong with that.'

'The lights are green,' Natalie said. What was she supposed to say? It was an eagle, she had realised, a Nazi eagle. She rubbed her arms and stayed quiet.

As soon as they got home, Hugo asked, as Natalie anticipated he would, 'Nat, what's an assignation?'

'An assignment?' Natalie was still trembling from it all. 'Oh, maybe it's like something you are assigned to do for work.'

Hugo seemed satisfied with this evasive answer but Natalie had no nails left to bite. She wished she could have talked to Leah then, but Natalie was *not* a snob and she wanted an apology from Leah too. Yes, Natalie had said the wrong thing, but so had Leah and she was determined she wasn't going to shoulder all the blame.

CHAPTER THIRTY

When a rare envelope with Rudi's unmistakable handwriting on it turned up, Natalie was engulfed in shame. What if he knew she was going off him – what if he sensed it? She certainly hadn't been as effusive recently as she used to be. Most of the time she hardly even cared. Yet they had only been apart three years – was she that fickle? She didn't see herself as fickle. What would Catherine Earnshaw have done? She opened the envelope slowly, hating herself, but this letter was not as bad as she feared. *What exactly did she fear?* This was longer than his usual letters but there were no declarations of love or anything. It was as matter of fact as an encyclopaedia. More so. She had nothing to scrutinise. If you didn't know *he was more herself than she was*, you wouldn't have guessed he ever was from this note. It was like a message from one office clerk to another. Office clerks who weren't overly fond of each other.

Only in the final paragraph did Rudi become cryptic.

Do you remember Flora Lang? Probably not, but I am in part of a group with her. We share a cause, I suppose.

We have arranged for your mother to go on a little holiday, if necessary. I hope you understand what I am saying here, dear friend.

At first, Natalie did not understand this: Rudi's girlfriend had arranged a holiday for Mama? Good grief! She had to read it a good two or three times before she realised what it actually was. If she couldn't get Mama to England, Rudi was suggesting Mama would be going into hiding. That was it. That was what Rudi was trying to do.

And then Natalie realised belatedly, three years after the event: she had been put in hiding too. Only she hadn't even known it. She had had no idea. Rudi did this; Rudi had arranged this. Those conversations with Mama on a Wednesday evening while Mama was 'looking for her purse'. The whole *you need to be a translator, you need to go to England*. It was all part of a bigger plan after all. He just hadn't thought to explain it to her. They might as well have swaddled her, put her in the reeds and pushed her down a river. She was just a puppet in this, no different from Mr Horsey; everyone was pulling her strings. The realisation made her feel so light-headed that she had to sit down.

And now the only person Natalie wanted to speak to about it hated her.

As Natalie listened to the wireless in the kitchen that evening once Hugo was in bed, the news got worse. The Nazis had invaded Czechoslovakia. They'd gone and done it. The Nazis were taking over the world and no one was stopping them. Hitler said it was to protect the Germans there, but everyone knew this was just a pretext for this huge act of aggression. Of occupation. Of colonisation. They'd promised to stop at the Sudetenland. Had they? Well, *of course* they hadn't. They drove their troops in, their tanks in, even little Mr Hitler drove in, in his open-top car, and some people – who were they? – threw bunches of flowers at his tyres. The swastikas were hung in the streets and from the buildings. That unforgettable red, black and white branding everywhere. It must have been petrifying.

Molly raised her voice. 'This isn't good, is it?' She put her hand to her belly reflexively.

Alfie raised his voice and said to no one in particular, 'I told you. I *told* you that he's not interested in peace. This is it.'

Everyone sat there in silence. Natalie thought of Libby's friend Mina, whose family were Czech. What would they be thinking now? Someone was jiggling the table but there was so much tension in the air, Natalie didn't dare ask them to stop. She thought of Mrs Caplin upstairs, combing her gleaming hair and touching her eagle brooch. Would she be pleased?

And she couldn't help thinking, selfishly, might there be more competition for jobs and visas now? So far, it had been mostly Germans and Austrians trying to flee. Would they now be joined by people with family over in Czechoslovakia? Wouldn't this make it all the more difficult for Mama and Libby?

Mrs Monger poured out golden cider for them all and the smell of fermented apples filled the kitchen, but Alfie pushed his glass away.

'I'm going to see Leah.'

He tugged on his coat as though fighting it.

Natalie called out impulsively. 'Give her my—'

'No,' he snapped back, his face dark and angry. 'She's going to be devastated. That fool Chamberlain, look what he's done. She doesn't want to hear from you ever again either and I don't blame her.'

'That's not fair,' she said. 'I'm *not* a snob.' Why had that word hurt her more than anything? Because she hated snobs. Papa always hated snobs too.

Alfie laughed. 'She thinks you're *pathetic*, that's what. You've got to fight for your family instead of always pandering to her-upstairs, like she's a bloody queen. Can't you see what's right in front of your nose?'

'That's enough, Alfie!' shouted Mrs Monger and he left the room, slamming the door behind him.

My dear girl,

The Nazis came to the Goldberg house. They beat the men, it was terrible what they did to Leo's father. I don't know why, Natalie. No one does. They threw him around the room and kicked him, even when he was lying on the floor, pleading with them to stop. This was in front of us all. In front of Libby. A terrible thing for a child to see.

They have taken the antiques, Natalie, the musical instruments, they have taken everything. We are just left here, rattling around in this empty shell, like prisoners. I don't know why.

Rudi visited – he is trying to help us, but I fear he will get himself into trouble. Much better than that Arno, who I see strutting around town in his uniform. He won't even meet my eye now.

It might be that our letters won't get out any more. I will keep trying and I hope, my love, you also will keep trying. Is there any news?

All my love,
Mama

CHAPTER THIRTY-ONE

'Please,' said Mrs Caplin. She sat next to Hugo as he refused to play the piano. 'Just one little tune for Mama.'

Hugo puffed out his cheeks as Tilly stared suspiciously at them all.

'How about "Morning Has Broken"?' Natalie suggested tentatively. 'We could do it together?'

Mrs Caplin stood up so Natalie could take her place. She and Hugo did a terrible rendition of the song. Rachel would have despaired. She hated what she called 'plinky plonkers' or 'weekend pianists'.

'You see?' Mrs Caplin said. 'There you are, not too bad, was it?'

Hugo skipped out. Natalie stayed. She had to speak now. She had to try again. Mrs Caplin picked up the *Daily Mail* from the smallest coffee table and sat down to read. She smiled at Natalie: 'Mr Young is all over the paper today.'

This was a good sign – Mrs Caplin was open to a conversation at least.

Natalie admired the feature about a man falling from two storeys yet surviving the incident. He had lost his memory and at the end it was suggested that readers who had any knowledge of his provenance should write in. 'Poor man,' said Natalie, so that Mrs Caplin knew she had read it, and, 'He really can't remember anything!'

Mrs Caplin had moved on. She was very proud of Mr Young's career and often read aloud his articles, even if it was just 'Poetess Weds Lion Tamer' or 'Cricket cancelled due to flooding'. And even if they didn't say his name but just '*Daily Mail* Reporter'.

'Mrs Caplin, I wonder if you could help...'

'Help?' Mrs Caplin repeated the word like it was one she was unfamiliar with and Natalie wished she had used a different approach.

'I mentioned before that my mother and sister would like to... they have to... leave Austria. I wondered if you could look over these application forms I have from the labour relief agency and another from the coordinating committee and... They're about visas and guarantees and—'

Mrs Caplin sighed. Her sigh encapsulated so much weariness. She couldn't believe Natalie was bringing this to her attention again.

'It's really not too complicated. And it would mean so much. Things are terrible there now.'

Mrs Catlin stretched to stroke Tilly.

'Has she been fed recently?'

'The cat? Yes, I think so.'

'She acts like she's never seen food in her life. Cheeky Tilly!' Mrs Caplin waggled a polished finger at her. 'We all know what you're up to.'

Natalie laughed but her trepidation was mounting, and she really didn't want to talk about the cat.

'So, I have forms and—' she repeated.

'Forms?'

'For my mother and sister, so they might come here.'

'Why don't you ask Mr Caplin? He mostly deals with things like this. He's in charge of good works.'

'Is he?' Natalie did not know *anyone* was in charge of good works at Larkworthy. Although her antipathy towards Mr Caplin had lessened, she still worried she could not trust him.

Mrs Caplin picked up the paper and buried her face in it.

'How it must feel to have your words in print! Just when everything feels so...'

Natalie waited. She couldn't imagine what Mrs Caplin was about to say.

'Precarious. He's moving up, Natalie. And fast. What a rise! He'll be chief editor soon, don't doubt it.'

Natalie gazed at Mrs Caplin's fur stole, her dresses that were so silky they were like South American rivers, the hair that glowed in any kind of light. *Precarious?* She of the pale eyebrows in a country of pale eyebrows. What was the worst that could happen to her right now? And still she waited uncertainly.

'My mama,' she began, her voice trailing away.

'We do want to do our best for your people, Natalie,' Mrs Caplin announced suddenly, 'but I have to admit, Mr Young and I are feeling quite honeycombed, as they say in the newspaper.' Here, Mrs Caplin giggled slightly. 'Very honeycombed sometimes.'

Natalie took this in. Honeycombed? Was this about bees? Perhaps not; Mrs Caplin seemed to be suggesting surrounded, or overwhelmed? She had a feeling Mrs Caplin was repeating this, whatever it was, like a script she had learned. But why? She didn't see why. They *were* friends, Natalie told herself, whatever this meant. Natalie advised Mrs Caplin on outfits and Hugo. And Natalie kept her secrets for her. Mrs Caplin gave Natalie shoes, tickets, and let her drive her car. And how Natalie loved driving the car. She had grown in confidence and now drove to the corner shop and to the station. She had even driven to the woods one Sunday with Hugo bouncing on the back seat, insisting she go faster. And Mrs Caplin might be in love with a Nazi-lover, but she was also a great friend of the Jews. Remember Mr Freeman? Mrs Caplin even felt Jewish, or at least she said she did! Natalie was a cherished member of the family. She had to say something.

'I'm not sure I understand you, Mrs Caplin.'

Mrs Caplin sighed. 'Mr Young says Jewish people will end up taking over if we're not careful. It isn't about you though. You're a good girl.'

'The other day Mr Caplin did ask me if you have men here.' Natalie spoke very slowly, enunciating each word very clearly so there was no doubt as to her meaning. She waited until Mrs Caplin met her eye. 'I told him that you did not.'

Was she threatening her own boss? Natalie couldn't believe the words that were coming out her mouth. Mrs Caplin narrowed her eyes and stroked her golden hair. Natalie waited.

Whatever it was, it worked. Natalie wasn't pathetic, whatever Leah thought. There was fight in her yet.

'Leave the forms here, darling,' Mrs Caplin suddenly said brightly. 'I'll see what we can do.'

CHAPTER THIRTY-TWO

When Natalie next saw Erich, it was a pretty afternoon and even the sky seemed optimistic. Since her last conversation with Mrs Caplin, Natalie was feeling emboldened. She had been walking on air from the moment she left Mrs Caplin's side. She had danced around her room and in the kitchen– she couldn't quite believe she had done it – and she had kissed and hugged Hugo even more than usual.

The River Thames made a rushing noise as though hurrying towards something. They sat on a bench overlooking the water, and skimming stones. The ducks came along and looked at them, unafraid. They didn't have to be afraid, because neither Natalie nor Erich were good aims, Erich said they should get prizes for being so bad. Then they threw stale crusts at their favourite ducks and gave nicknames to those who elbowed their way in and managed to grab something meant for another.

'It's a metaphor,' Erich said, while Natalie thought to herself, *I am in love with this man. I am. I am.*

If you had seen them, you wouldn't have known the despair or the turmoil they were in – or at least Erich was in – Natalie wondered, cautiously, if she *might* have turned a corner since the conversation with Mrs Caplin. Life was like that, wasn't it? You couldn't see someone from the outside. They were china containers, not glass jars, and that was a pity.

That morning, Natalie had had another letter from Rachel, which had also lifted her spirits.

Dear Natalie,

I have not managed to get work in Amsterdam which, considering the cost of finding someone to look after Hannah, was to be expected and is fine, really. I manage to practise much of the day with Hannah plumped next to me. She is better than a metronome. Our neighbour is an elderly deaf woman – how perfect is that? – and she grows herbs in window boxes so the flat smells beautiful too. I feel lucky. I have almost mastered Liszt's twelve *Transcendental Études*. I think Papa would have been proud.

We took Hannah to the photography studio, where they insisted on putting her in a sailor's frock and clogs. She looks like she is having a terrible time, but she loved it, and wept when it was time to go. She still looks like her Aunty Natalie and behaves like her sometimes too!

The orchestra Leo plays in does European tours, sometimes they play London venues. Leo says, if that happens, I will be allowed to come with him. Can you imagine – me, Hannah and you, together walking the streets of London? I can't think of anything better.

Hold on to that thought,

Your ever-loving sister, Rachel

The tiny girl in the photograph did look like Natalie. A more adorable version, of course. She had a furrowed, heavy brow and even in black and white, you could see her cheeks were flushed. It seemed baby Hannah was as overcast as Natalie (whereas Rachel was never less than sunny). Natalie showed the picture to Erich and he cooed appropriately. He didn't have any photographs of his family. He said he kept asking them to send some, but they were too afraid to go out and get stamps.

Then Erich asked after Leah. He liked Leah ever since they met at the dog races.

'We're still not speaking,' Natalie had to admit.

Erich didn't make her feel bad about it though but said, sympathetically, that even great mates fall out sometimes: 'Friendships rise and fall.'

'Like the big wheel in Prater Park?'

'I wasn't going to say that, but okay,' he chuckled. He laughed so much more now. She secretly wondered if she had fixed him, then hated herself for being so arrogant. They had just got to know each other better, that was all.

Erich's bright eyes clouded over though when a violinist set up near them. And Natalie felt a little teary when she realised that he was playing Rachel's beloved Strauss: *Der Rosenkavalier*. It was a sign, a lucky sign. It had to be. She looked for signs these days like you look for water in the desert. When the violinist had finished, they clapped and called 'Bravo!'. Natalie hurried over from the bench as Erich shuffled a few steps behind.

'Where are you from?' Natalie knew he wasn't English; she just knew it: hard to say how. The shape of his face, the cut of his clothes.

'Germany,' he said warily.

She sympathised. *I probably answer in that tone too.*

She replied in German, 'Been here long?'

'One month,' he responded.

'You see?' Natalie said, smiling over at Erich. 'There are still people getting out.' She repeated it to make sure Erich got what she was saying. You never could tell with him if something went in or not. Less reserved now he knew they weren't haters, the man said he was working as a chauffeur. Natalie asked if he liked it and he said, 'It could be worse, much worse.'

'What's your name?'

He grimaced. 'Adolf.' He raised his shoulders as though to say, *what-can-you-do?* 'My parents wanted me to have a nice German name. I may change my name soon, I just can't decide to what.'

Natalie liked this man. 'The little boy I look after is called Hugo.'

'Hugo!' he repeated. 'That's nice.'

They talked a little about their experiences, the strangely named food, the too-milky tea. He picked up his bow, smiled at them. 'At least you two have each other.'

Natalie was embarrassed, then warmed. But then she thought of Rudi. She thought of the letters she kept under her pillow; the occasional sweet lines committed to memory.

'No,' she said quickly, 'No, we don't, we're not together, you see.'

Erich didn't say a word.

'My mistake.' The German reddened, dipped his head. He nodded at them both, then began to play again.

If they didn't know what was going on back home, how perfect this slow London courtship might be. The scenic walks through the park and by the river. The sense of more intimacy to come. Natalie couldn't imagine being with Erich in Vienna though. Would they have ever met – would they have become friends if they'd both stayed there? Natalie thought not, but then considered the effect his smile, his laugh, his dark eyes had on her... *why wouldn't they?*

But they only met because of the terrible situation back home, so ridiculous to even idly speculate on anything different.

They went for tea, then walked and walked until her feet ached. She didn't want to say goodbye, but they managed it quickly, and abruptly. She thought he might have tears in his eyes again.

The following day, Natalie went to Pam's Pantry by bike. She felt nervous about facing her cousin, but it had to be done. And yes, she did want to tell Leah what she had said to Mrs Caplin. Not to show off exactly, or not *just* to show off, but to seek reassurance that she had done the right thing. Leah had been strangely prescient about all this; she probably was right about other things too. The international situation had got worse again. Plus, on a more trivial note, Natalie wanted to chat with her about Molly's big news. Leah's take on Molly's trouble with Mr Caplin would be interesting.

Natalie had been missing her cousin. It was only now – with a few weeks' distance – that she could see what a crutch Leah was. More than a crutch. Good grief, if it weren't for Leah's intervention, she too would probably have been trapped in the Goldbergs' house desperately searching for a way out. Leah helped save her, yet Natalie was avoiding her. Natalie had also worked something out: she *was* jealous of Leah. Not of Alfie personally, *obviously*, but the fact Leah had someone. Leah's engagement only reinforced the fact that Natalie didn't have a family here. Leah was not her enemy and it was time for them to be friends again.

But when she arrived, Leah refused to come out of the kitchen.

Pam came forward, clutching menus over her chest. 'Leah doesn't want to see you.'

Natalie was dumbfounded. This wasn't how their reunion was supposed to go. Leah was meant to forgive her, welcome her; maybe they'd have coffee and walnut cake together. Pam looked at her sympathetically, which was worse somehow than if she were angry.

'I want to apologise. Please tell her—'

But Pam shook her head. 'Go now, we mustn't have a scene. Not in front of the customers.'

And so Natalie cycled back home.

When she got home, Mrs Caplin was wandering around the house in only her dressing gown and crying. There had been another argument.

'I need to keep him, do you understand?'

Natalie inhaled deeply. It was hard to sympathise with Mrs Caplin when she was so consumed with worry about other things, but she didn't have much choice.

Mrs Caplin fumbled with her cigarette tin. She was drinking in the day nowadays too; you could smell whisky on her breath sometimes. None of her friends visited any more. The kindly lady from the dinner party had called around a few times, but Mrs Caplin had refused to come downstairs and she had given up.

'James has grown bored of me. Can't he see that it's like a prison for me too?' Mrs Caplin grabbed her hands. 'What am I going to do, Natalie? I would do *anything* for that man.'

It probably wasn't the best time to ask, but Natalie hadn't seen her for a week and thoughts of Mama and Libby were pressing on her temples. 'Did you do the forms?'

'What forms?' Mrs Caplin looked annoyed.

'The forms for me. For my mother and sister to leave Austria,' she said. How could Mrs Caplin be so obtuse? 'You promised.'

'I think so,' she said vaguely, then, looking at Natalie's face, she said, 'Oh I did, I definitely did. But what shall I do about James?'

Hugo couldn't sleep recently. Natalie tried not to let her anxieties spill over to him, but maybe they did. He cuddled up to her in bed two nights out of three. Natalie felt bad for letting him, but worse when she turned him away. One night, Natalie heard her bedroom door open. She heard muffled laughter in the corridor. The door shut again. Was it Mrs Caplin asking for advice? Or Mr Caplin even? He was the one with the history of such things. She must have been dreaming though and very soon, Hugo's snores helped her back to sleep.

'How's Leah?' she asked Alfie a few days later.

'Not happy with you.' Alfie blew his hair out of his eyes. He wore it longer now and it suited him better: less ear on display. Natalie thought how honest he was, how kind. *Had she been* really *rude to Leah about him?*

'What can I do?' she asked. She wanted to cry, yet she felt aggravated too. For goodness' sake, she didn't have the capacity to deal with Leah's moods on top of everything else.

He shrugged unhelpfully.

Molly was still washing and ironing, although she did things a lot more slowly than she used to, and she made a hupping noise when she got up from a chair. Her baby bump was quite noticeable now. Natalie suspected that the *I only just found out* thing was a lie. Natalie was no expert, but Molly looked ready to pop at any moment.

One lunchtime, they were eating toad-in-the-hole, which disappointingly had nothing to do with *The Wind in the Willows* and was quite surely one of the most flavourless dishes ever to have been invented, when Molly made an announcement.

'Change of plan! We're getting married!'

Natalie nearly fell off her chair. 'Married? No!'

It was impossible. *How could that be?*

Mrs Monger looked pleased, while Alfie continued to stuff his face.

'We'll do it in Cornwall. He's got family there.'

'Oh, yes?' said Natalie, scraping bland pudding off the sausage. *How was this going to work?* If Mr Caplin married Molly that meant Mrs Caplin was free to be with Mr Young, and this would be the worst outcome for her and Hugo. Surely?

'He sends his love. I think he feels guilty about you.'

'He's got nothing to feel guilty about on my account.'

'We're so happy. Clifford is already making a cot.'

'Clifford?'

'Ye-es.'

'What's it got to do with Clifford?'

The man who had spent much of the last year or so trying to squeeze Natalie's breasts. *That* Clifford?

'Quite a lot, don't you think?' Molly cupped her hand on her stomach. 'Hope baby looks more like me. It's a right fidget like him though.'

Finally, it began to dawn on Natalie. This wasn't what she thought it was. She had been such a fool. Clifford? Clifford and Molly? It made sense, and yet it still didn't.

'I thought... I thought... Not Mr Caplin?'

'Mr Caplin?' yelped Alfie at the same time as Molly.

'Wha-at?' Molly laughed hollowly. 'No, why would it be his? Mind you, if it *was* his, I'd expect a bloody nice cot from Harrods.'

'Oh.'

Natalie couldn't have been more confused. She had never felt much for Clifford, but he had sworn to be hers eternally and she had grown rather used to his attentions – although she realised it had been months since they'd met up. It was like having a safety net. And Mr Caplin – it *wasn't* his? She had been so certain it was another case of the master and the maid. She surveyed Molly closely, but she was as insouciantly bright-cheeked as ever.

And Alfie was still chuckling to himself. 'Mr Caplin? I don't think Molly is quite his type, Nat!' Natalie squinted at him. What *was* he trying to say?

'You don't mind, do you, Natalie?' Molly interrupted. 'I know you were fond of him.'

'I don't mind,' Natalie said. 'He's all yours.'

Natalie got up. Molly looked very relieved, but she was laughing too.

'I can't believe you thought I'd be having Mr Caplin's baby, Natalie. What *are* you like?'

CHAPTER THIRTY-THREE

Hugo and Natalie made daisy chains in the sunshine. They play-fought with swords cut from card. Natalie drove to town and back with Hugo jumping around on the back seat. It might have been an idyllic time if the war drums weren't beating in the background: if what was going on back home wasn't going on.

'Why didn't your sister come?' Hugo asked one time.

'She couldn't then, but she might do soon.'

'I hope so,' Hugo said, then jumped up, dusting himself down. 'Race you to the gate.'

Since Leah was still not speaking to her, Molly was too weary with pregnancy, and Mrs Caplin was out, presumably with Mr Young, Natalie spent most of her weekends either with Hugo or alone.

Natalie considered translating something else: her beloved Just William books into the German maybe; but she was feeling less and less inclined to write or even speak German if she didn't have to. She thought of other books she had known and loved as a child, but none of them seemed relevant any more.

Her pen was now only used for the long letters she wrote to her friends and to her mama. She never heard much back, but it was important to persevere.

Sometimes, the gap between what she knew was happening in Vienna and the blue sky and spring sunshine in England was too great. It was obscene to enjoy herself in any way, she should stop herself. But Papa had always said she must throw herself into life: *if not now, when? For life can be nasty, shortish and brutal.*

Other times, she had this strange urge that something nasty, shortish and brutal should happen right now, something, anything, because then at least there would be no more of this uncertainty, there would be an end to the limbo. It was like the urge to smash the car into a tree.

She saw Erich a couple of times at the labour relief agency and once at the coordinating committee but he didn't ask her to go with him to the beach or to the tearooms, which was a shame but strangely a relief too. Being around Erich made her heart ache worse sometimes. So did letters from Libby.

I offered Mama ten schilling to write to you, but she just cried. I am not allowed out any more. I did run up and down the stairs twenty times – they are incredible! – but Mr Goldberg asked me to stop. He is sweet, but he gets terrible headaches since the beating and needs 'absolute quiet'. He told me that English people eat sandwiches all the time; they would even eat bread as a filling. Was he joking? Mrs Goldberg asked me when our 'damn visas' are coming through. I said you're working on it. Mama said not to pressure you, but it won't be long now, will it, Natalie?

Love Libby

Mrs Caplin was making hay while the sun shone once again, by having a party in the garden. There was a long trestle table covered with a white cloth and little candles flickered at every place. Mrs Caplin was wearing a brand-new dress, flared and bright, showing off her tiny waist: a happy dress for a happy occasion. Mr Young was just wearing a shirt, no blazer, and was striding around, telling everyone it was time to take their seats.

It looked so pretty; Natalie imagined Rachel here. Wouldn't she love it? And Libby, she could just imagine Libby's eyes widen at this. She would be shy, she would nudge Natalie, *you didn't tell me it was so posh!* And Mama… well, Mama had that ability to get on with everyone. Natalie could imagine her crossing the lawn, smiling serenely: 'A party? Well, I do love a party!' and then getting just a little tipsy, wobbling on her heels and laughing even louder than usual.

Natalie sat next to Hugo at the end, on a separate trestle table for the children – although he was the only child. 'Did you wash your hands?' she whispered as he tucked into his clear soup noisily, although she knew he hadn't. She decided she would ask Mrs Caplin about the forms again tomorrow. This wasn't a time for coyness.

There were speeches. There was gratitude at Caroline and James' unrivalled hospitality. Mr Young acknowledged them with a curt nod. He was stretched out like a cat, his arm along the back of Mrs Caplin's chair. *He really thinks he is the master here*, thought Natalie resentfully. Perhaps for the first time, she felt sorry for Mr Caplin, dashing around the country working, trying to keep Mrs Caplin in the style she was accustomed to. Weren't the parties and the goings-on here humiliating for him, or did he really not know? And the thing Alfie was suggesting, was that true? She had asked him outright the next day: 'Is Mr Caplin a homosexual?' and he had laughed again and said that stupid saying he liked winding her up with, 'Ours is not to reason why, ours is but to do or die…' which probably meant he had no more idea about it than she did.

Natalie thought of the evening she had returned from the Freuds' and the pleasure Mr Young had taken in humiliating her. But that wasn't going to happen tonight. Tonight, the air was too sweet and the table too elegant. The garden was a credit to Alfie too, she supposed. He had lots of skills, really.

The guests were on the dessert course when Natalie attracted the attention of the people on the other table.

'Hugo, tell us some secrets about your nanny!' Mr Young bellowed across the guests. He tapped his glass with his spoon and the

conversations stopped. 'Listen up, everyone. Hugo is going to talk.
HUGO?'

'Don't,' said Natalie quietly to Hugo.

But Hugo was delighted at the attention.

'She eats peas like this.' Hugo elaborately scooped like he was
shovelling coal. Everyone laughed as though this was brilliant.

Hugo was wearing his pyjamas and, for some reason, a beret he
had discovered in the back of his wardrobe. He gazed around at
everyone. His teacher said he had a tendency to play the clown when
he was uncomfortable or didn't understand something.

Natalie suddenly thought of the park where she and her sisters
had played in Vienna while Mama sat on a bench, crocheting. At
Christmas, the mobile organ truck came with its fat cherubs and
Libby and Natalie counted them, six or eight or ten, blowing their
tiny trumpets, and in the centre a golden woman, statuesque, like
the figurehead on a ship, that Rachel always said looked like Mama.
And Mama saying, 'It is hard work being an organ grinder. Here,
give a few pennies from me.' Libby and Natalie were transfixed, and
Libby had danced; she was only a baby back then, still in nappies.
Natalie didn't know what reminded her of this, but she could see
it so clearly in her mind's eye, hear it, smell it too, as the exchange
between Hugo and Mr Young went on around her.

Mrs Caplin was clapping her hands. 'Go on, Huey, tell us!'

Hugo seemed to search for something else to say. He played to the
audience. 'She talks about her mama all the time.' Natalie winced.
The women tittered. One of them said, 'Aww.'

'Come on, Hugo,' said Mr Young impatiently. 'We want more
than that. Dig deeper. There must be something juicy.'

Hugo shook his head.

This was utterly horrible. Natalie was so heartsick, so homesick,
she thought she might drop down and die, there in the beautiful
garden, in front of all these posh people. If it weren't for the embarrassment of it, she would have, she was sure.

'What else does –' Mr Young persisted, flicking a glance at Natalie – 'our resident *Jewess* do?'

Hugo spoke to his bowl. 'She knocked down Mama's gnome with the car.'

Mrs Caplin leaned forward to Natalie. 'You didn't, did you?'

Natalie couldn't tell whether she was joking or not. She spoke up. 'We fixed it. You can't see the crack…'

'Who is we?'

'Mr Caplin and I.' Natalie found her voice was squeaky.

Mrs Caplin didn't like this. 'Mr Caplin and I?' she repeated, 'Did you indeed. I'll have you know I love all my gnomes very much and if one of them has been injured—'

Everyone else seemed bored. This game was over. They turned away from Hugo and Natalie and poured their wine and they drank. There was so much drink on the table, and so many empty glasses and bottles.

Mr Young didn't let up though. 'C'mon, Hugo. Surely you've got some stories about your little friend?'

Hugo balanced his spoon on the back of his hand.

'Any boyfriends?'

At this, the spoon dropped. Hugo grinned at it.

Mr Young said, 'Aha, ladies and gentlemen, we have a scoop here! Stop playing with the spoon, Hugo.'

'She likes two men.'

'No, I don't!' said Natalie, horrified. She heard Mrs Caplin distantly say to the woman next to her, 'I can't believe she knocked down my gnome. She knows I love them.'

'Does she now?'

'You do!' Hugo gazed at his reflection in the spoon defiantly. 'And I even know their names.'

Natalie protested. 'No, you don't.'

'Let the child speak,' said Mr Young as though she were the bully here and he the friend. Hugo peered down the table at Mr Young and then back at Natalie, his eyes the size of pennies.

'Their names are Rudi and Erich,' he said in a tiny voice. 'Rudi is in Austria, but Erich is here.' He put down his spoon and it wobbled again.

'Rudi,' Mr Young repeated. 'And Erich. How very *Germanic*. It seems Miss Purity is not Miss Purity after all.' Mr Young squinted at Natalie and then dabbed his moustache with his napkin. 'Interesting. Well done, Hugo. That's a good boy. Now scoot, you two.'

Natalie could hardly bring herself to speak to Hugo as she took him up to his room. He was subdued as he trotted up the stairs and unusually, he didn't ask to stay up longer. He was ashamed. He knew better than that. He *was* better than that. He brushed his teeth without prompting and asked if he could wear his beret to bed. Natalie said no. Then he asked if she would hold his hand as he fell asleep. She did that sometimes.

'Not tonight,' she said. Strains of jazz came through the floorboards. The party must have moved inside. *When would they stop?*

Hugo peeped up at her. 'Are you angry with me?'

'I'm sad with you,' she said, picking his clothes up from the floor. This is what Mama might have said. She hung Mr Horsey on the wardrobe. All his strings were tangled, and his teeth were wobbling as though he'd had a hard three years.

It wasn't Hugo's fault. He was eight years old and he had been wound up like a clockwork toy. But at that moment, it felt like it was.

'You're sad with me?' he repeated. Then after a few minutes had passed, and he had his head on his pillow and his dark hair spread out behind him, he whispered, 'You won't go back to Austria, will you?'

'Maybe,' she said. She was being cruel – he was a child, a helpless child – but she couldn't help it. 'Probably not. It's no good for people like me any more.'

'I'm sorry, Nat.'

Natalie took an intake of breath. Sweet boy, he was led to it. Mr Young was the one she should be angry with. Mr Young was the one who knew better. Hugo didn't *want* to hurt her: she was his world.

'Everything is fine.'

'You're still angry.'

'I'm not.'

'Promise you won't ever leave me,' he said sleepily.

'Promise,' she said, as she took his hand and waited for him to fall asleep.

The party continued. Natalie slipped away to her own room and got in her bed. She was trembling and covered her ears with the blankets, but Mrs Monger knocked loudly.

'They want you down again.' Her expression, as she looked at Natalie, was sympathetic.

'Can't you say I'm ill?'

'You know Mrs Caplin.'

Reluctantly, Natalie pulled on her clothes – which were helpfully lying on the floor – and tiptoed down to the drawing room, where she hovered by the door. There were only five people left now: Mrs Caplin, Mr Young and three men in suits, playing a drinking game. One was very fat, his watch chain stretched across his belly. The other two kept slapping him on the back, making him spill his alcohol, and shouting names at each other. For the first time, Natalie wished Mr Caplin were there. Maybe he wasn't such a bad egg after all.

One of them got up, holding his hat and coat, and Mrs Caplin lunged for him. 'I won't let you go!' But he pushed her from him quite aggressively, so she had to right herself, and he said, 'Not enough action here for us, Mrs C. We're going up town.'

The three men started to leave, still gabbing away, and Natalie pressed herself against the wall in the hall, hoping they wouldn't see her as they noisily left the house.

Mrs Caplin poured more drinks from the crystal decanter, then sorrowfully asked Mr Young, 'But why have they all deserted us?'

He threw himself down on the sofa, his legs wide, his collar open. He looked a state. 'Get me another drink, Caro. Make yourself useful.'

Natalie tiptoed away before they noticed her.

At first, Natalie thought the scuffling sound outside the door must be a dream, but it sounded again, and then there was a knock. She knew it wasn't Hugo; he would have started rattling the knob by now.

'Who's there?' she called out. It must be a mistake. *Surely she wasn't being summoned again?*

The door opened. When she saw them both standing there she realised the interruption was deliberate. Mrs Caplin was now in her silk dressing gown, her hair loose and shiny. Mr Young was more than usually pink-cheeked and wet-eyed. Mrs Caplin was smiling, but there was something unsettling about the set of her mouth. They were self-conscious, posing there, as if for a photograph. Natalie stared at them for a moment. If for one second she imagined they had come to apologise, very quickly, she realised she was wrong.

'Let us in, darling,' Mrs Caplin said. Natalie thought her eyes looked unfocused, almost glazed.

Perhaps she didn't know where she was?

Mr Young hiccupped and laughed. His eyes searched the room, looking past her. Natalie glanced behind her, hoping to see what he was looking for. She wished she'd tidied up.

Now Natalie saw Mrs Caplin was wielding a bottle of Brut champagne. The doorframe was helping to keep her upright.

'Come on, Natalie.' Mr Young's moustache quivered as he spoke and all you could see was a thin wisp of lip beneath. 'She promised me I could have a go.'

Mrs Caplin covered her mouth and half her face with her mani-cured fingers, but she kept her eyes on Natalie. 'You don't have to say it like that.'

'How should I say it?'

'Having a cuddle?'

Natalie looked at Mrs Caplin. *What was happening here?* Awful thoughts went through her mind. *She couldn't be, couldn't be...*

Mrs Caplin let go of the doorframe and lunged towards Natalie, engulfing her in a cloud of her sweet perfume. She whispered, 'Just one time, darling. Just to keep him interested. I can't have him leave me, not now, I can't.'

'Mrs Caplin?' Everything was upside down. Natalie still couldn't believe what was happening. 'What do you mean?'

Before Mrs Caplin could reply, Mr Young had grabbed Natalie and wrangled her against the bedroom wall. Natalie was trapped. She dodged away from his mouth as it came at her like a runaway car. He was up against her, pushing at her, pressing into her. His face was hot and angry, his moustache scratchy and the pressure was terrifying. He mumbled into her collarbone, 'I like a bit of resistance,' and she could taste the alcohol on his breath.

Natalie broke one, then both hands free, got them between her and him, and slammed at his chest. She heaved him back, but he was upon her again. She knew she had to stay upright; she knew his drunkenness was a point against him and she knew – at least she thought she knew – Mrs Caplin wouldn't let him go too far... would she?

Mrs Caplin's tone was increasingly desperate. 'Oh, it doesn't have to be a big deal, darling. Please don't turn this into an issue.'

Again, Natalie pushed him back with all her might and this time he staggered backwards. He seemed absolutely shocked.

'You know how good we are to you. Be nice!' Mrs Caplin helped restore Mr Young upright. 'What do you want to do, James?' She clucked around him as he wiped his slobbery face with his sleeve furiously. 'What shall we do now?'

Natalie had never seen people so damaged in her life. This man who loathed her wanted to have sex with her. This woman, who she thought had liked her, seemed to think that was more than all right.

Natalie pushed Mrs Caplin towards the doorway. Mrs Caplin shrugged her off, but half-heartedly. Her face was still incredulous, as if she were the one who should be shocked. As though she were the one who had been insulted. And Mr Young followed her out, but as he passed Natalie, he spat a great globule of spit onto Natalie's foot. And then they were outside the door and Natalie could slam it shut. She did so and stood there, holding the knob as tightly as she could.

'Natalie, NATALIE… you can't do this!' Mrs Caplin began to hammer on the door, but it felt different now. She didn't want to come in. It was for show. Then she kicked it. 'I'm the boss here, darling. DARLING!'

'Leave her.' Mr Young's voice was slurry. 'Silly Jew bitch.'

'After all we did for you, Natalie. You just aren't grateful, are you? I did so much for you and all you do is take, take, take. Ungrateful child.'

She heard the clattering of shoes along the corridor. Mr Young must have been striding away, and Mrs Caplin was chasing after him. There was a scrunch, the sound of a fall maybe, then a cry: 'James! James, wait for me! Please. It doesn't matter, *she* doesn't matter. You've still got *me*.'

When it had been quiet for long enough, Natalie crept down the corridor into Hugo's room. He was fast asleep in his little bed, like a boy in a fairy tale, tucked up and warm. The puppet horse was hanging from his wardrobe bathed in moonlight, and now its face seemed to be looking questioningly at her: '*What are you going to do now?*'

She kissed the boy, her lovely boy, and he stirred slightly. She shushed him and told him she loved him and always would and nothing was his fault. In his sleep he smiled. And then she did something that she knew would be deeply hurtful, but she couldn't help herself. She unhooked the horse. She held it in her hands, careful not to get tangled up. It seemed very important to her right then that it came with her: it was hers, it was the last thing she bought with Mama.

But then Hugo woke up. Always a smart boy, he understood quickly what was going on. He shook his head so violently she feared he would do himself damage.

'You said you wouldn't leave. You promised you wouldn't!'

'I have to.'

'No, no, NO! You said you wouldn't. Let me come with you.'

Natalie unpeeled his fleshy little hands from her back and spoke to him more sternly than she had ever spoken to him before. She said, 'I have to go, Hugo, I'm sorry. I love you, but I have to go.'

She would never forget the terrible howling sound he made as she left.

CHAPTER THIRTY-FOUR

The shutters of the shops were down, and the upstairs were in darkness. Natalie thought about just walking on and on to the station, taking a train somewhere, anywhere, but she was so weary, and her suitcase was so heavy now, it was so full, it almost hadn't done up. She rang the bell instead. As she waited, a fox appeared and turned its orange eyes on her. She gazed back, unsteadily until it scuttled away.

Leah took one look at her, at Mama's suitcase, and led her up to her tiny rooms. Straight away, the kettle was whistling, and she served up tea with milk, even though Natalie said she didn't want anything. Leah said she would have to make do with the sofa, even though Natalie didn't want to stay.

Leah said that she knew this would happen all along. She bloody knew it.

Natalie was still shaking. Shaking legs, shaking hands. Unbelievable. Violated. Humiliated. How far would they have gone? What was it they wanted? Surely not? How could she do that to her?

'It's all right.' Natalie was trying to be brave. 'I am going back home.'

'Back? Not to those depraved bastards, you won't.'

Natalie looked at her in dismay. *Was Leah so far gone that she had forgotten where they came from?*

'No.' Over the past few months or so Natalie had really started to believe Larkworthy was her home. How wrong she had been. 'Back to Vienna.'

Leah made a snuffling sound. 'You can't do that. You would be going to certain death. When the hell will you understand this?'

'No, I wouldn't. I would be going to Mama.'

Natalie whimpered, then started to cry. She hadn't cried in such a long time, she must have stored it all up, a cupboard full of tears, and now that door was unlocked, yanked open wide, the emotions pouring out. She thought of the fox who had stared at her and then ignored her as though she were nothing.

How amazing it would feel to have her mama's arms around her, the clean smell of her hair, rocking her in her chair, whispering sweet things in her ear, all the things she wanted to hear. 'You're a wonderful girl, a clever, kind, brave girl, they'll learn that soon enough, just be yourself, everything will work out.'

'I would lock you up before I let you go back.' Leah took the untouched cup and went over to the sink. She rinsed the cup under the cold tap.

'But how can I afford to, how can I live?' Natalie whimpered. She had saved some money, yes, but she doubted it would last more than three or four months. And she had to find a job and a place to live while trying to get Mama and Libby out… Everything seemed utterly insurmountable.

'I'll help,' said Leah. 'And you'll have to help yourself. Can you peel potatoes?'

'Le-ah, yes, yes, I can.'

'So, you will work here and stay with me above the shop. We'll be fine together.'

Natalie nodded helplessly.

'And you are wrong about me and Alfie,' Leah added, stern now. 'So wrong.'

'I know,' said Natalie in a low voice. 'I'm sorry.'

And then Leah's arms were around her, drawing her in. 'It's okay, Natalie, it's going to be all right.'

*

Angel Underground station was on the black line. Natalie had to change at King's Cross. Angel sounded auspicious somehow. This was a long shot, but maybe it would work. Not everything would be a dead end. There had to be a way out somehow.

She was still surprised when Mr Freeman answered the door though. She hadn't expected that, she hadn't expected anyone to be home.

It was eight o'clock in the morning and some horses and carts were still on the streets. It looked like Mr Freeman was on his way out; he stood there in a full black coat with a fur collar that subliminally echoed his black moustache. A tie, that same swept-back hair. When he saw Natalie, he startled slightly, but covered it up. He was a man who didn't like to show surprise. She saw she was an unwelcome sight to him. And he spoke in a low voice, so she knew she was secret, 'What *are* you doing here?'

He wouldn't let her enter the house. There were several people inside; she could feel their presence. They had quietened down to listen to them.

'I need your help,' she said.

'What could I possibly do for you?'

She hadn't expected the conversation to take place so quickly, without preliminaries, without talk about the weather, but here they were.

'I need to get my mama and sister over from Austria.'

He stared at her, and the stare seemed to say, *what has that got to do with me?*

'You're an agent, aren't you? You could say Mama is on your books; she could perform in a show.'

He lit up a cigar pensively. He was listening to her at least.

'She sings nicely. And if she weren't good enough, she could do backstage work surely? Sewing, costumes, or something…'

At that, Natalie thought Mr Freeman was going to let her in the house, but he didn't. Instead, ungainly, he lowered himself on the doorstep and patted for her to sit beside him. Mrs Monger said *never sit on a cold step, you'll get the piles*, but Natalie was weary after the stress of the journey, after the headache of the nights before, so she sat down. Somehow sitting there with their knees almost in their faces, sitting like children, took her back to her and Rachel side by side, plotting at the top of the stairs.

'Let me explain something to you.' He spoke clearly and slowly, as if he thought she was a halfwit. 'If they let in millions of refugees from Germany, from Austria, from Czechoslovakia, anti-Semitism will rise here.'

Was this his argument? Dear God. 'No, it won't,' Natalie interrupted. 'Why would it?'

He ran his hand through his slick hair. It must get sticky doing that. Now his voice was weary. 'Of course it will. You've only been here, how long? Two or three years?'

'Three…'

'Three years! That's nothing. You don't know what this country is like. They'll turn at any minute, with any excuse. Never doubt it. If there's an economic downturn, it's the Jews, if there's a war, it's the Jews, if there's a crime, it's the Jews, if there's a plague, it's the Jews. We're only one step away from fascism here as well. We can't help everyone.'

'I'm not asking for everyone.' Natalie lowered her voice, for she knew it was a betrayal of Erich's family and her old schoolfriends, and she hated herself for it. 'I'm asking for your help for two people.'

'No can do, I'm afraid.' Mr Freeman made a show of looking at his wristwatch. 'Look, doll, I'd try if I could – I'm not completely heartless – but you've got this wrong. I'm *not* someone of influence. No one is going to listen to me. I'm on the edge of society; you want someone in the thick of it.'

'You're my last hope.'

He laughed.

'No, I'm not. The one you want to ask is your boss, Mrs Caplin. You're "great friends", aren't you? She always said that.' He put on a high voice. '"My Jewish nanny and I are the best of friends."'

He squidged his cigar out in the flowerpot next to him. He smiled at Natalie as if everything were simple. 'She told you she's feeling "honeycombed" yet? She likes talking about that. And "all the Jews coming in through the back door..."'

'I *thought* we were friends,' Natalie said in a tiny voice. She thought but didn't say, *I was mistaken.*

Mr Freeman sighed. 'Look, have you heard there's a plan to get some children out?'

Natalie scowled. This wasn't the encouragement she wanted. How would this help her family? Mama? Or Erich's family who she wanted so much to help too?

'It's no good. I need to get adults out as well.'

'Take this anyway.'

Natalie hadn't noticed he had a bag by his side, a leather briefcase. He dug into it now and pulled out a newspaper, one of the smaller ones. 'Page sixteen, girl. You can't miss it.'

'I'm not interested,' she told him and went back to Angel.

CHAPTER THIRTY-FIVE

'I'm happy to have you stay,' said Leah, 'but for the love of God, Natalie, you have to learn to be tidier.'

Compared to Larkworthy, the flat above Pam's Pantry was a hovel. It had a bricked-up fireplace and a dreadful painting of a woman smoking, a gypsy maybe, whose dead dark eyes always reminded her of Mrs Caplin, hung over it. There was a clock in a sunshine shape with squiggly rays, only it didn't feel sunny, it was demented. Every time Natalie looked at it, she felt slightly nauseous. Then there were the nicotine-stained lampshades with their pointless tassels. The lace and the curtains, the trinkets everywhere. It was so unstylish. The sofa where she slept that was too narrow even to sit on comfortably. Mama's suitcase took up most of the floor.

Thank God for it though. It was home and she was safe, and she could sleep at night, for a few hours anyway.

'Do you hate me, Leah?' Natalie asked one time, plumping the thickest cushion of the slim bunch. She would have guessed Leah would say, 'That's a ridiculous idea,' or 'I don't mind you at all.' Instead, Leah looked perturbed. She lowered herself onto the too-small sofa and it was as if the question had sunk her.

'We don't have to get on all the time, do we?' she asked searchingly.

'No,' agreed Natalie.

'I never knew what it's like to have a sister,' Leah's voice was gruff. 'I always envied you for having Rachel and Libby, but I suppose I see you as mine now, if that's all right with you, of course?'

'Of course,' said Natalie, and since they were being so polite, she added, 'Thank you.'

'I always thought Clifford was soft on *you*,' said Mrs Monger incredulously when she came to visit with a basket of gooseberries and two letters: one from Rachel in Amsterdam and one from Libby in Vienna.

'I know!' said Natalie helplessly. But she didn't want to say anything out of line. Mrs Monger was Molly's aunt after all.

'We miss you,' Mrs Monger said awkwardly.

'I miss you too.' Natalie still could not get that last terrible night at the Caplins' out of her head. Over and again she played it, from Hugo publicly revealing her confidences to the way they had pressed in at her door. And the awful things Mrs Caplin had spat at her.

'Does Mr Young still come around the house?'

Mrs Monger made an indecipherable face. 'Less so.'

'And Mr Caplin?'

Mrs Monger shrugged carelessly. She was more concerned about what Natalie planned to do with the gooseberries, they could be so bitter. She recommended a tart. 'He works all the time then goes away to work…'

Natalie considered. 'Whatever happened to the last nanny? The one who was caught coming out of Mr Caplin's room?'

'Oh yes, she was a toerag, that one,' said Mrs Monger. 'A thief.'

'Wha-at?'

'You had to nail everything down when she was about. The things that went missing, I can't tell you. She was a magpie for shiny things.'

'I see,' said Natalie thoughtfully. 'I see, yes.'

The next morning, Natalie slept late and when she hurried downstairs, she saw a sheet of paper on the counter of the café. Leah raised her eyebrows.

'I should have got better notepaper maybe, but I thought it best not to waste any more time. The sooner the better…'

Everything was *the sooner the better* now.

Natalie read, blushing.

Natalie Leeman's mother and sister desperately want to come to England, but they need visas and jobs. We the undersigned ask the Home Office to relax the rules for this broken family to be reunited.

'Thank you,' Natalie said. She wanted to grab her wonderful cousin and hug her, but even anglicised Leah didn't like displays of affection. Instead, Natalie got peeling potatoes and felt Leah's warm approval like sunshine on her back.

Whenever Leah took customers their bill, she took the petition too. Natalie didn't know quite how she dared. Wouldn't they feel furious or at least put-upon? But most of the customers knew Leah by now and understood her and Natalie's story. Most of them signed. A few even tipped their caps at her and wished her good luck.

But Leah was out shopping for emergency bread rolls when the man with the unkempt beard came in. He was dressed in boots, filthy fella, with spittle around his mouth, and bags under his eyes. He fumbled with his coins. He barely had enough money. He thumbed the petition paper on the counter, and Natalie couldn't help thinking, *Please don't*. She didn't know how she was going to handle this.

'This is you?' he asked. 'You're Nally?'

'Natalie,' she corrected him quietly.

'And your family?'

Natalie nodded, telling herself, *treat him like everyone else.*

Natalie got him some tea and he was pleased with it. He liked it extra-milky. She gave him a glass of water too, force of habit, although he looked at it in surprise.

He kept looking over at the petition on the counter. You would think it was a plate of juicy teacakes. It was like something waiting to go off between them.

'Will you sign?' Natalie finally asked.

'No,' he said as she flushed. Another hater. She thought of Mr Young's eyes on her from the bedroom door and shivered. The way he tried to reach for her. The things Mrs Caplin said. Feeling 'honeycombed' wasn't in her dictionary but she had worked out the sense and she understood well enough what 'ungrateful child', 'be nice' and 'having a cuddle' meant.

She went to pick up his cup and plate but as she did, he tapped the inside of her wrist; it shocked her and she shook him off instinctively.

'I can't write, you see. I can read, just, but,' he held up his hands, 'these won't obey. Ma thinks I'm a leftie and they should have let me be, but that was then…'

Her heart went out to the poor fella. How could she have had such bad thoughts?

'A cross will do.'

'A cross will do, aye?' he muttered. He laboriously filled it in. 'Wish you luck, pet. Awful situation. Just awful.'

This man who she had been feeling sorry for was sorry for her. Natalie blushed as she thanked him again.

It was a beautiful sunny afternoon the day Natalie took the petition to the Passport Office. She wore Mrs Sanderson's hat, hoping it would bring some of her positivity. It worked and she played the 'after you', 'no, after *you*', game with a lady wearing a similar hat as they got on the bus.

'What is this?' the woman asked as she pushed it across the desk.

'Thirty-seven names,' Natalie said proudly (and a small stain of egg yolk).

Ten had seemed ambitious. The fact there were thirty-seven had surpassed all her expectations. Natalie was in love with England, in love with the English. The awkward man with the grimy hands had changed her view of the world.

'I can't submit this, dear,' the woman across from her said gently.

'But could you send it to Parliament maybe?'

'We just need money and a job-guarantor now. That's all.'

'That's all,' Natalie repeated dumbly. The woman said it as if it were nothing, but it was the whole world to Natalie.

CHAPTER THIRTY-SIX

No news came from the Freuds. Natalie hadn't dared hope any would. What could the Freuds do? They were no longer powerful people, they weren't the benevolents any more, they couldn't bestow their largesse on people; they had been forced to become takers, cap-in-handers. Dependent on the goodwill of others. How unhappily did they carry that burden?

Dearest girl

I have heard of the transports, but it is not possible for Libby. Have Libby travel across Europe by herself? I don't think so. It was hard enough letting you go! – but Libby is so so… young. You know Libby. She can't be trusted. If there was someone to go with, if you could have come to meet her maybe, but even if you could do all that, it isn't free. It is expensive and we have so little money, now. We really are living hand to mouth.

I'm sorry I haven't written for so long. I have been feeling low, but today I am stronger again. I won't give up without a fight.

The queues at the American Consulate were even worse than the British, but yesterday, I made it to the front. I filled out an application and it seems we are finally on a list: 7052 and 7053. I know that's not great, but it is something. I think it's best we stay together.

All my love,

Mama

As well as missing her family, Natalie missed Hugo too, and it was even more painful to think that he might miss her. It was horrible to think that he might blame himself. She should have told him what was going on. She should have written. And yet she found she could not.

Alfie wasn't much help. 'Yes, he's furious with you,' he shrugged. 'why wouldn't he be? You're the only one who ever bothered with him. Don't worry, Mrs M and I keep an eye on him.'

Working in Pam's Pantry was quite enjoyable though. Leah said she peeled and chopped vegetables as well as anyone and no one said her bread-cutting or toasting was inadequate, so presumably that was fine too. Natalie cooked, boiled, roasted and grilled as required. She was fine with the customers, if a little withdrawn, Leah said, before adding, 'It's nothing, you've got a lot on your mind, I know that.'

The door rang whenever anyone came in. One morning, Pam herself made the bell ring. She wore a paisley-patterned silk scarf tied up at the chin and dark sunglasses, and was holding a newspaper open in front of her. Usually Pam didn't have much time for Natalie, as Natalie tried to prove her worth by frantically sweeping, dusting or mopping. But for once, Pam trod heavily over to her and not Leah.

'Have you heard of this?'

Natalie wrinkled her nose up at the article. It was a different newspaper, but it was the same story that Mr Freeman had shown her. Some children, Jewish children from Berlin and Vienna, were coming to England without their parents.

'It's no good for us.' Natalie picked up the cups from the table. *Really, people were filthy buggers, weren't they?*

But Leah had come out of the kitchen, dishcloth in hand. She read it over Natalie's shoulder, her lips moving as she did.

'How wonderful.'

'It's children only.'

'Maybe Aunt Dora could come too?' Leah said, although she must have known she couldn't.

They shouldn't even let children travel on their own, thought Natalie. She had managed it, but she had been sixteen at the time. Imagine Libby trying the same trip! She was so young. Making the right connections, having the ticket when she needed it, not eating all the pastries before the train departed the Südbahnhof (as Natalie herself had done). Getting to the dock, boarding the ship. Yes, Libby was twelve now, but she was immature, frighteningly so. And she didn't speak much at the best of times. What if she needed help and couldn't ask?

Pam and Leah looked at each other. It was like a secret message passed between them. Now Leah put her hand on Natalie's shoulder. She smelled faintly of milk.

'Write to your mother and tell her she must get Libby on one of those trains.'

Natalie didn't like this: Mama and Libby should not be separated. What's more, it was ridiculously unsafe. And it was ridiculously unfair. She was not going to have Mama left behind. That's not what this was about. She was not going to bring Libby out without Mama. That would be the very definition of failure.

But she said, 'Maybe,' mostly to shut Leah up.

Leah gazed at her. She picked up vinegar, salt and plates. She always carried a lot at once. 'That's how you get things done,' she always said. 'Never leave a room without bringing something with you.'

A philosophy for life.

'Actually, don't worry, Natalie, I'll do it.'

It was busy that day in the café. When a small boy who looked like Hugo came in with his young mother and ordered an apple turnover, Natalie's heart ached. It was obviously a big treat, a birthday maybe, or a reward for a success at school. He ate silently and contentedly, the pastry dropping around him like snowflakes. His mother watched him and laughed, said there was more on the table than in his stomach.

Exactly, one week later, when Natalie was having a five-minute sit-down with a coffee at her favourite table (nearest the counter), Leah laid out another newspaper in front of her. Natalie didn't want to see more articles about the terrible Nazis or even the hopeful Kindertransport, but it wasn't that. It was something in the small ads. Leah had pencilled around it to make it stand out from all the other ones.

Tiny Tim. £30 ONO

'OH-NO?' Natalie read aloud. 'What does that mean?'

'Or nearest offer.'

Leah was selling Tiny Tim? Her winning dog?

'That's how we're going to make your money.'

Tiny Tim had been meant to raise the funds for Leah to buy a café herself one day: a Viennese café, one in the centre of London, not on the fringes, one where she might serve schnitzel outright, wear a dirndl, and serve a glass of cold water with every hot drink, and no one would ever dare say a word against it.

'It's all right, I still have Rosie. And Rosie is going to breed and honestly, it's fine.'

A wave of exhaustion came over Natalie. She almost swooned from it. 'It's too much, Leah.'

'You think it's too much for my little cousin's life?'

Natalie may as well have been punched in the stomach. She covered her face in her hands. Leah got up and put the closed sign on the glass door even though there were ten minutes to go and even though she was scrupulous about timekeeping. Some things were more important than the hours on a clock. She came back and sat by Natalie and she didn't need to say another word.

It was decided. If Tiny Tim sold, Natalie would borrow the money from the sale to pay for Libby's place on the Kindertransport. Leah would put her own name as a guarantor. They wouldn't give up.

*

Tiny Tim sold the very next day. And a few days later, a telegram came.

Dearest, Libby will try to get on the train in May.

Thank you,
Mama

CHAPTER THIRTY-SEVEN

It didn't feel reasonable to go to a concert when so many people were suffering, but Erich had been given expensive tickets from a customer at the shop and, they agreed, it was silly to let them go to waste.

The Queen's Hall reminded Natalie of the Kursalon back home, where Natalie's father had hoisted her on his shoulders, and she could smell his rich cologne and he kept whispering, 'Don't kick my chest, sweetness, that hurts.' It was *The Gypsy Baron* by Strauss. She remembered the conductor slipped slightly at the end, making her and her father giggle. And that the harpist was wearing a red dress and it kept slipping off her shoulder.

They went to the bar for pre-show drinks. For once, Erich was in brilliant spirits. He was happier perhaps than she'd ever seen him. Uncharacteristically, he was resolute and clean. He was freshly shaved. For the first time, she thought he looked *properly* handsome. She always thought he looked lovely but today, she thought, everyone would.

He took her hand. 'Do I scrub up all right?'

'Not bad.' Natalie stuttered. *Not bad? He looked gorgeous!* She was completely in love with him. It was painful to keep her hands from him. *Didn't he know?*

'I have news,' she began. 'My younger sister might be able to get out.' She couldn't wait to talk about it, she was bubbling over with it.

'On the Kindertransport?'

The chandeliers made the foyer so bright; Erich narrowed his eyes to adjust to the light after the darkness outside. She suddenly worried that he wouldn't be pleased for her. That it would be too painful, given that his own family were still stuck.

'I think so, I hope so. If it happens, yes. They've already done a few. There should be more, yes.'

Erich let out a big sigh of approval. 'You've done so well.'

But of course he was pleased for her, of course he was. Erich adored her. She knew it. She felt it. But not like that maybe. Not in the 'girlfriend' way probably. These days he presumably saw her as a sister.

'It wasn't anything to do with me, Erich,' Natalie admitted. 'Leah raised the money and Mama managed to arrange it their end. We're lucky she's young enough.'

He nodded. 'You succeeded, Natalie.'

'I didn't—' she began, but he wasn't listening.

'I wish I had.'

'Don't say that. There's still time.'

'I failed.'

'It's not true. We're all doing our very best.'

They queued at the entrance to the stalls, among the English people in their finery, and they were mostly ignored. Natalie could feel people noticing her and Erich, noticing and noting they were 'outsiders'. These people wouldn't be the type to throw rocks at them in the street – no, any racism would be far subtler here. It would involve calling over a manager and letting him do it. Everyone was wearing pearls and emeralds, bow ties and cummerbunds.

Their chairs were in the middle of a row where people had already been seated. For them to get past, the occupants of the seats had to stand up for a few seconds and this they did so resentfully. Did they object to it because Natalie and Erich were speaking the hated German? Natalie shuffled past, trying to avoid bodily contact. Erich found their seats. Either side of them were one large woman and one large man.

'Which would you prefer?' he said out of the corner of his mouth. 'Tweedledum or Tweedledee?'

*

As soon as the orchestra filed in noisily and began warming up, Natalie was at home. No matter what anyone there thought, this was her world, this was familiar, and it was personal. So what if a couple of idiots didn't think they should be there, didn't get it; *she* got it. Natalie looked through the programme at the foreign-sounding names and gleefully pointed them out to Erich.

'This one must have got out; this one got out too. You see... Could your brother not come... on the Kindertransport, I mean?'

The woman next to her said *shush* very pointedly.

'It's not started yet!' Natalie hissed back, suddenly empowered. To her surprise the woman sank back in her chair. This felt like Natalie's territory. That violinist sitting there, the cellist, these were her people. They might not all be Austrians or German-speakers, they might not all be foreigners, but they were musicians, they were performers, they were creatives. They would understand.

'It's children, Natalie,' Erich repeated wearily. 'Only children.'

'But your brother... He is young enough surely?'

'Eighteen. He is over the age limit.'

'He could—'

'Pretend?' he whispered. 'Yes, but he is over six-foot-tall and he has had too much of my mother's cooking.' He held out his arms at his stomach to illustrate. 'He also has a beard like a Russian fighter. He won't pass.'

'I heard there is a scheme for young people to go to Palestine.'

'Full up.'

'And another for America?'

He rubbed his thumb and finger together. 'You need this.' He meant money. 'Plenty of it.'

'Keep trying.'

'I *am* trying. Every day I am trying. I am sending letters to everyone I know. I wrote to Mr Chamberlain himself.'

'What did he say?'

'He didn't reply. I wrote to my MP, I wrote to the mayor.' He blushed. 'I even wrote to your Freuds. Nothing.'

'I'm sorry, Erich.'

She remembered a conversation they had had, not long after they had met. She had said that if only her family were not Jewish, or if only they could *pretend* not to be Jewish, then they might be safe. Erich had said that it was all so unfair, but you couldn't deny reality, and even if they tried, the Nazis – and their allies – would never let them.

Then the music started and Natalie was swept away. It was Mahler, her Mahler, Austria's Mahler, Symphony No. 1 in D major. Rachel had always loved it, called it depressing but 'in a good way'. Natalie watched the orchestra, the faces of the musicians, the incredible way they used their arms, the trembling of their legs, but she was with Libby and Mama in her mind. Libby was packing her bag. *What suitcase would they use?* she worried. Libby would be clamming up and Mama would be trying to get her to talk. It never worked. Libby would be exasperating everyone. Mama would decide instead to concentrate on food. That was something she could get right.

Erich's hand somehow found Natalie's, and she closed her eyes. His hand was warm and safe, and she loved him. This was her reality.

In the interval, Natalie felt suddenly, stupidly euphoric, even though she told herself, *not yet, not yet*. It was too early to be excited. Libby was not out of danger yet. Anyway, what of Mama? It was a strange situation, like an unfinished painting or a partially written symphony. Leah said it was better than nothing, but was it?

Erich patted her shoulder as they stood in line at the bar. 'You've done well.' She wished he would grip her around the waist, clutch her to him. Tell her he too was being driven mad by desire.

If he was jealous that Libby would soon be on her way he didn't show it.

'Remind me of your sister's name again? Libby? Like liberation?' He smiled shyly, letting the word play in his mouth. 'Well, of course she is coming, I would expect nothing less.'

He drank his wine and gave her his heart-warming smile. '"And when I die, I want to go to heaven and have a little hole among the stars to see my Vienna, my fair Vienna".' Do you remember that?'

Natalie did, but she couldn't concentrate on what he was saying. She just wanted to grab him and kiss him. To kiss him hard with all her heart and soul. With all her body. She was so hungry for him, she wanted to bite him like a… like a… Wiener sausage. She couldn't believe Erich didn't know it, that he couldn't feel the heat, the want and the need coming off her. She wanted to say his name over and over. She nearly called it out. She wanted to lean into his ear and say, *love me, please*. She wanted him to put his arm around her, to put his hand on her thigh. They should run away, and find some secret place and make love there and then. It had to happen soon, didn't it? It had to happen.

The bell rang for them all to return and, both politely determined not to make those poor souls go through the indignity of having to stand up again, Erich and Natalie rushed to get back quickly.

Leah had left a note for her at home: 'Clean up this room PLEASE'.

As Natalie felt her way in her open suitcase, she found an inside pocket that she hadn't known about before and, in there, a tiny rolled-up almond sweet in paper, squidged up, more than three years in hiding, and a note Mama must have wrapped around it all that time ago. 'Very proud of you,' it said in Mama's swirls. 'I hope England is everything you hope it will be.'

CHAPTER THIRTY-EIGHT

The next week, Natalie did not see Erich at the labour relief agency as they had arranged. He was working more hours for more money to help towards visas or guarantees or promises. It was a busy time of year for him too. Summer was wedding rings. Natalie told herself this wasn't a bad thing. Without meaning to, Erich made her frustration about the situation worse. And her desire for him embarrassed her. She could no longer think about him without getting ridiculously hot. Even his name evoked in her such peculiar feelings. Her desire must have been so obvious. She might as well have a streetlight flashing over her head, saying: *She loves you.*

At Pam's Pantry, Leah was stirring a vat of tomato soup. The English love their tomato soup. She served it with flat rolls. Natalie told her other English words for rolls – butties, buns, cobs – while Leah added salt and pretended to be interested.

Leah had other things on her mind. She said, 'You used to talk about Erich all the time.'

Had she used to talk about him all the time?

'You don't anymore.' Leah spooned up the soup and tasted it with the tip of her tongue like a frog. Shaking her head, she added more salt. 'Is anything wrong between you two?'

'No, no, everything's fine,' Natalie told her. *Oh God, was she so obvious?*

'You'd tell me, wouldn't you?' Leah insisted. 'If anything changed. If you got together or anything?' She smiled shyly. 'I'll do the catering for the wedding…'

'Le-ah!' Natalie said weakly. 'That's not going to happen.'

Natty,

Mama has decided I must come to England! By myself! I said
I wouldn't, not without her, not ever, and she slapped me on
the face then cried for hours. She has never hit me in my entire
life! Has she ever hit you? Or Rachel? I bet she has not! I am
very annoyed. The Goldbergs asked what happened to me and
then they told me I had to go too. They were kind to Mama,
even though she hit me.

I wish I had studied English at school. It's all Frau Rascher's
fault. I never liked her. I wish I had studied with Rudi Strobl
like you. Does anyone even speak German there? What am I
supposed to bring?

Your fed-up sister,

Libby

It still didn't seem possible. Natalie tried to picture it, could not.
And Libby crossing the borders? It would be far worse, far more
dangerous, than the trip Natalie had done three years earlier. What
if Libby told someone what she was doing? For someone so shy, she
could sometimes blabber with the best of them. What if she were
taken somewhere else? What if the train was attacked? Who would
defend the children?

And Natalie knew she still had to try for her mama. She wouldn't
give up on her, ever. There were still other ways out, surely?

That week, her lady at the coordinating committee was a stern-
looking woman with a pressed flower on her coat. She was talking
about Edward's Mrs Simpson – 'a floozy' – to the woman next to her

when Natalie came over, and she didn't seem keen to be interrupted. Desolately, Natalie filled out some new forms. She no longer felt any shame about lying about what Mama could do. Yes, she could drive a bus. Double-decker? No problem. Yes, she could fix a leaky pipe. The woman across from her didn't seem to care either.

But when Natalie didn't see Erich at the labour relief agency or the passport office the following week, she was surprised. They didn't have so many places that would listen to them and she knew if Erich had managed to find somewhere else, another possible connection, another possible chance for a prized visa, he would have told her right away. There might have been competition for places, but Erich was never mean.

In Pam's Pantry three days later, it was quiet. Only a few workmen came in for shepherd's pie. Leah impulsively let Natalie have the afternoon off work. Afterwards, Natalie wondered if Leah had had some kind of instinct.

At first, she considered going to meet Hugo at his school. She missed him so much. Would he be pleased to see her and throw himself into her arms like he used to, or would he be too hurt? Or too angry? Hugo usually forgave easily, but you never knew. She had abandoned him to a distracted mother, her intimidating boyfriend and a distant father. Oh, she knew Mrs Monger and Alfie would be keeping an eye on him, but still… And what if Mrs Caplin were there? She couldn't face her. Not now, and she doubted ever.

Instead, Natalie took the Piccadilly line to Holborn and walked to Hatton Garden. She knew it would not be actual, literal gardens, although she was convinced there must be *something* of nature left over. A flower or a pretty tree creeping through the pavements at least. She was proud that she had remembered the name of the establishment where Erich worked – Gems of London – and she smiled to herself. She could navigate her way around London like the best of them nowadays. She knew which Underground lines to take and which colours got you where. She was becoming a proper London girl. Almost as proficient as Leah.

Relieved and a little breathless she had got there so smoothly, Natalie dallied a short while outside the workshop, looking in. So, this was Erich's place. His English home. Through the glass window she saw workstations, desks full of machinery and benches, but there was no one around, which was odd. Or maybe it was lunchtime – yes, maybe that's what it was.

She had to tell Erich she loved him. She knew that then, that instant. Seeing the place where he spent his days was like a confirmation of it. Dear Erich who worked so hard, who just needed a break. It was nearly the 1940s; she had to offer herself to him. All this waiting, what was it for? The world was upside down, insane, so they needed to hold on to all that was good.

And Natalie wanted nothing more than to live an *authentic* life. That was one thing Rudi had taught her. And the fact was, she wanted nothing more than to lie in bed with Erich and to make love. He was her one. He was her North Star in a topsy-turvy universe. She wanted him so much, it took her breath away to think about it. Anything. She would do anything, *everything* with him. *Everything*, like in all the books on the top shelf, the Lady Chatterley and the rest.

And if he said no, he said no. At least she would have tried. And, if the train did bring Libby to her, well, practically speaking, she was going to be super busy over the next few months, settling her sister in. This was the best time to get things moving. She had to declare her feelings soon or she would burst, it was as illogical and yet as simple as that. 'Do you want to lean on me?' was the first thing he had said to her. *Yes, Erich, I do, very much.*

Gulping, she rang the shop bell.

Today was the day.

An old man in full religious garb stood in the doorway. 'I've come to see Erich—' she began in English, but he replied in German.

'Wait a moment, please.'

He wouldn't shake her hand; some religious people didn't, which Natalie understood, but the way he pulled away from her for a moment made her feel contaminated.

The first man called for someone else – Harry, or 'Arry, or Arlo, Natalie wasn't sure. She saw a man with a pleasant jowly face, rolled-up sleeves and a white butcher's apron look up and over to her. He hesitated for just a second, as though steeling himself, then came over, wiping his hands.

'I've come to see Erich,' Natalie said again. 'He works here?'

She was oblivious. Utterly oblivious. She did not read that room. (After that, she would never be so surprised about anything ever again.)

The jowly man shook his jowls. 'I'm so sorry, my dear. Erich is no longer with us.'

The world shifted on its axis. 'He's moved?'

'He's dead, may peace be upon him.'

She had missed the funeral by only one day. The jowly man apologised many times: 'You know how quickly we do it.' He said they had heard of the Miss Leeman, but so sorry, he didn't know how to reach her.

Natalie had stared at him, gobsmacked. *Erich, dead*? In this country, this country where you did not expect people to die?

'Was he sick?' she whispered, although she knew in her heart he was not.

'He lay in front of a train, my dear,' the man said softly.

When Natalie heard this, there was a rush of blood to her head, a thousand questions, although none of them were ones she wanted to know the answer to.

Leah kept saying, 'You've got to be strong. Don't give up hope.'

Was Leah saying Erich was in the wrong? That he hadn't been strong enough?

Natalie started a letter to Erich's mother, but she found she couldn't find the words. His family were desperate to leave – might they think, wrongly, she had some power here? They might look at her in the same way she had looked at Anna Freud. She couldn't bear for them to transfer their hopes and expectations from Erich on to her. These would be very false hopes and very unmeetable expectations. The idea that she would let them down was so painful she took the easy way and let them down in that way that would affect her less.

Over the next few days and weeks, Natalie went over and over Erich's last movements. What had he been thinking? Where did he go? How did he feel? Why didn't he tell her? She knew Erich and she *knew* he didn't want to die. He just wanted *this* terrible agony, this unresolvable burden, to end.

Leah said Natalie could take a few days off work, but Natalie refused. Better to work than do nothing. But when she caught a glimpse of her reflection in the metallic tea urn she hardly recognised herself: wild-eyed, wild hair, her face collapsing with sorrow. This would not do. She would frighten the customers away. One day, Natalie promised herself, she would unpack this experience and look at it closely, she would allow herself to feel and grieve the dreadful loss of him, but she could not afford to do that now. She could not let herself fall apart, not while Mama and Libby were waiting for her, relying on her; not while she needed to work for Leah. She needed to be strong.

But every night, her heart told her: she and Erich should have made love. She would never not regret that. She would never not regret that she didn't get to tell him she loved him. *Oh, Erich.* Even if it had just been for the one time. Even if it had just been one kiss. One proper, reciprocated kiss. If only she had let him lean on her.

CHAPTER THIRTY-NINE

Platform 6 at Liverpool Street station. Liverpool Street was not in Liverpool, as Natalie had once imagined, but was on the east side of London. It was not far from Hatton Garden, nor from where Erich was buried in the Jewish cemetery in East Ham, and it was not far from Cable Street where in 1936, a fierce battle between the local people and Oswald Mosley's fascists had taken place. It was near the docks, near where the River Thames meets the sea. The train was coming from the port of Harwich. A fine place for her sister to arrive.

If she arrived.

The train was expected at 16.08. Natalie arrived at 14.03 – just in case.

May 1939, three years after Natalie had done a very similar route, on a very different journey.

The station café was so small and confined, it was like an afterthought. In Vienna, the station cafés were double the size, sumptuous and grand, with chandeliers sometimes and brass fittings. Here, the only shiny thing was the tea urn and the tea came automatically with milk. Oh well… 'Down the hatch,' as Molly liked to say. The serving woman wiped the counter clean, then dropped her own cigarette ash onto it.

Natalie had begun to want to disguise the way she spoke – her accent seemed to be a clarion call for all sorts of discussion – but the tea lady didn't seem fazed by it. She was probably used to all sorts of voices coming through here.

Natalie kept looking at her watch as if by looking at it she might speed up time.

'Going anywhere nice?' the tea lady asked as she put some biscuits on a patterned china plate in front of her.

English people like to talk about journeys and difficulties travelling herewith (Chapter 8).

Natalie shook her head. 'I'm meeting someone.'

Natalie remembered how happy and excited she'd been on the train here. She'd been such a simple soul, coming here to improve her language and to impress her friends back home. Wanting to translate books about elephants and mosquitos and everything in between – submitting to a little nannying as a means to an end. What a naïve creature she had been. She remembered the pastries she had bought at the stations where she changed. The children she had waved to as the train crossed Holland; they were selling trinkets and she would have ended up buying one if the whistle for the train hadn't blown and she'd had to run, dragging Mama's honeymoon case behind her. And on a misty window she had drawn the outlines of rabbits and the backs of pigs with curly tails, and pretty girls' faces, and one time, she had tried out a swastika – oh, not for the Nazis, just for its appealing shape or its repetitive pattern maybe – then she had rubbed it out with the side of her hand. It was a lifetime ago and she barely recognised that girl on the train.

Will Libby be on the train?

It was 16.00 and the platform started filling with organisers, some wearing Red Cross armbands, and she thought of the army of women in the refugee and labour agencies who she had never exactly been friendly with, and she hoped they would forgive her.

Most of the children didn't have relatives here and they would be onward-bound to Wales or the Lake District. The ones who did have family would be packed off in cars or taxis to go to their new homes in the same way she had been whisked away by the gentle, generous and surprisingly prompt Mrs Sanderson. Natalie knew then – silly to dwell on what-ifs – but she knew, if Mrs Sanderson were still alive, how very different things might have been. She remembered that car journey, the thrill at driving on 'the wrong side', the way, embarrassingly, she had showed off the many words for rain… Well, it turned out, a large vocabulary was not so important after all.

Come on, Libby! Be on the train.

Then it was 16.06, 16.07, 16.08 and the train was pulling in, screeching brakes – that horrendous sound couldn't be more welcome – and those choking steam clouds were her best friend for it was here, it was here, was Libby here?

She thought of poor Mama slapping Libby. How at the end of her tether must Mama have been, for she would never, ever, condone violence at normal times, and especially not towards her own beloved daughters. Slapping Libby for saying no?

She had to stay strong. Erich would want her to. The thought of him made tears fill her eyes. Had he torn a little hole among the stars to see his fair Vienna? She hoped so. Unbearable to think he was not on earth anymore.

There were little ones – so tiny – staring out the window at her. They were climbing down from the train, so tiny, *too tiny*, it was unbelievable really, that they had been wrenched from their parents and stuffed into packed train carriages. Their clothes – there was something undeniably Austrian about them, you could only see it if you had been in England. She couldn't put her finger on it, the colour palette maybe, the materials, the fact that they were overdressed – clearly some of them were wearing their clothing allowance. And lots of shorts – which Hugo wore too, but the length was different, and the length of the socks was different. And the girls tended to have bobbed hair with clips and the girls here tended to have bunches or plaits. But Libby loved plaits too, so that generalisation didn't work either, so…

Natalie waved at the children and they waved back automatically. *Where's my girl? Where's my sister? Where's my Libby?*

There was an elderly couple standing near her, and they were so anxious; they began crying and blowing their noses even before the train pulled in and they were still crying as they held a small boy – he couldn't be more than three – and his older sister – only about seven – and as they carried their luggage down the platform.

'This is all you have?' the grandfather kept repeating. 'This is all they let you have?'

'It's all I could carry,' said the bigger girl apologetically. 'Mama said.'

Another woman grabbed a child and stuffed an apple in his face. 'Eat, child! You must be starving.' But the child shouted, 'I don't like the green ones!'

Out they came, a shy crocodile. Some spectators had gathered, English people, a man with a camera, possibly a journalist.

One child carried another child. 'He's broken his leg!' he shouted apologetically. A man ran forward and picked up the injured one: 'It's all right, sonny, you're in England now.'

Two children, identical twins, must have swapped mittens for they were strung together by a length of wool. They curtseyed.

Natalie smiled at them, and they waved back in unison with their enjoined hands.

A boy with glasses in a tank top, no coat – his mother would tell him off for that – jumped down (Hugo hated wearing his coat).

Two more children, brother and sister maybe, with a bear each tucked under their arms, serious-faced and keen. Natalie heard one say to the other, 'Don't tell them we're Jewish. They'll send us back.'

A teenage boy, his face streaked with tears, trying desperately not to cry, wiping his cheeks with the back of his hand, helping unload the train. His face set. It was the older kids who looked most distressed. She guessed they were the ones who understood what this was. The younger kids had bewildered but adventuring faces. Natalie was drawn to the stoic boy as he grappled with luggage. *You're a brave boy*, she wanted to tell him. He couldn't have looked more alone. *Your family will be proud of you.*

'Where's my Libby?' Natalie said it aloud to no one in particular.

What if Libby didn't get on the train? What if she had got *off* the train at the wrong stop? What if she couldn't come? *She gets stomach cramps now*, Mama wrote, *I think they are women's things.* What if that had stopped her? What if she were on the loo when the train had left? What if Mama had changed her mind? What if Natalie didn't recognise her little sister?

Another trunk appeared, then, closely followed behind it, there she was. Natalie needn't have worried; she would have known her anywhere. *Anywhere.* The last three long-drawn-out years vanished in a blink of an eye. White knee-high socks, that uniform, the plaits dangling down – neat though; Libby couldn't bear it if her plaits didn't align.

Finally, she was there. She was holding hands with a small girl with an expression of utter confusion.

She was nearly thirteen years old now and Natalie had been looking for a nine-year-old. She had lost three of her sister's years.

She would never let Libby go.

Natalie signed off her sister with a flustered Red Cross woman with a clipboard. She was trembling so much, she didn't see how she could travel, so, wobbly-legged, she took Libby back to the station tea shop, where they could calm themselves. She was thankful for the steam rising from the urn. She didn't want Libby to see how emotional she was, but Libby seemed impervious to everything.

But then when their drinks arrived, 'I didn't want to leave Mama,' Libby kept saying. 'She threw up in the toilets. I wanted to stay with her.'

'Mama will come soon,' Natalie said and Libby nodded, wide-eyed. Natalie realised she was petrified, beneath the bravado.

'The girl next to me cried non-stop,' Libby explained irritably. 'I had to put my hands over my ears.'

Natalie thought this didn't sound very nice, but she couldn't tell Libby off. Not now. She was a fragile thing, she needed to be wrapped up in tissue paper.

'Is it bad back home, Libby? LIBBY?'

Libby took a sip of her coffee. Natalie remembered that coffee was once a big cause of disagreement in the family. Mama and Papa had fallen out over it: 'It will stunt her growth.' 'It will feed her mind.' Well, it didn't seem to have stunted her growth at least. She was taller than Natalie and definitely taller than Rachel. She looked up from beneath those pale lashes. The skin under her eyes was blue and thin. *Poor tired girl*, thought Natalie desperately. *Another of us, deep-down tired.*

'It's worse than you know.'

Natalie paused. *It's worse*, the words reverberated in her head. *It's worse, it's worse.*

Libby stared out of the window, her hands hugging the cup. She didn't say anything.

'They have some good running tracks and coaches here,' Natalie told her. She wanted to give something to this poor tired girl. Some glimmer of hope, of future. 'I can get you some plimsolls—'

Libby shook her head. She met Natalie's eyes properly this time. 'I'm never running again.'

The lady at the counter brought over large slabs of cake on plates with napkins. She must have worked out where Libby had come from because she leaned over to Natalie and said, 'The cakes are on the house,' then she plucked at Libby's immobile cheek (Libby hated being touched) and said, 'You've come a long way, girl, well done.'

Libby ignored her. She told Natalie a joke. It involved a truckload of horse manure falling on the town hall. Libby could hardly tell her for laughing.

It didn't make sense. How could manure fall on a building?

'I don't get it,' Natalie said. She wanted to get it, desperately. She wanted to laugh at this joke.

'I guess you had to be there.' Libby's eyes were flinty cold.

And that was the problem, Natalie understood. She had *not* been there: she had escaped. Even before escaping had been a thing. She had got out. Her family had not. Whatever difficulties she might have experienced in England, her loneliness and loss were on a different scale to what Libby and Mama had endured.

And then Libby said, 'I saw Rudi Strobl before I left.'

Natalie kept her mouth closed, her expression light.

'Rudi?' Much as she tried, her voice sounded squeaky and oversized. 'You saw him?'

'I just said.' Libby's mouth was full of sponge and buttercream. Natalie had forgotten this: *her younger sister ate like a horse.*

'And?'

Libby swallowed, but then took another large bite. 'We were not able to get much food in Vienna,' she explained with her mouth full. 'They wouldn't serve us any more, it would be un-Germanic. There was one small grocer shop, do you remember the Konig family – the shop on Mariahilfer Strasse?'

'Yes?'

'They served us until someone smashed their windows in. But then they delivered food to Mama secretly. Nice people.'

Natalie smiled at the thought of these good people. *Thank heavens for the good people.*

'But do you remember the Lackners?'

'Yes.'

'Mrs Lackner spat at me and called me a filthy Jew.'

Natalie wouldn't have said Mrs Lackner was a particular friend of theirs but never in a million years could she have pictured her doing that.

'Libby, you were saying – Rudi?'

'I forgot,' she said listlessly. 'He persuaded Mama to let me leave.'

Natalie thought he might have. Libby blew on her drink, spraying spots of coffee across the table. If Mama were here, she would have told her not to, but she would have laughed too.

'Did he give you a message…?'

'Oh yeah.' Libby dug in her pocket, found nothing, then tried another. She was full of pockets – she hated clothes without pockets. After much rummaging, she came up with a handkerchief, an Austrian coin, an English one and a scrubby little book of stamps, a wrapper of something unpalatable, but no message from Rudi.

'I remember now, Natalie, it's in my suitcase. Rudi said I had to hide it. Pass it over.'

Natalie,

Flora Lang and I have found some places for Jewish families – and your mother will go, if necessary. I am staying here. I had everything lined up for a university job in America, but with Mama gone and Papa so frail, I can't leave him. I will work here. I should be safe, but you never know. The cruelty is unimaginable.

I have always hoped you would just get on with your life without me, Natalie. In every way. You know what I mean. There really is no point hanging on for me, although I hope that you will think of me sometimes. And I'll never stop loving you, sweet, funny, clever Natalie, and I wish I could shine a light through your window and see your lovely face, just one more time.

Yours for ever,
Rudi

Natalie put it in her pocket. She could not think about this now. These sentiments would have been so welcomed last year or even just a few months ago, but now everything was clouded by the loss of Erich, poor Erich. She had let both of them down.

She had to focus on Libby and stability was what Libby needed now. Stability was what Natalie would try her damnedest to give her. This was what Mama wanted; this was what Mama had sent her for. It was summer 1939, the whole world was precarious, and didn't they know it.

Friday evening, they sat beside the fire in the flat above the Pantry. Libby had been in England for almost one week and she had tried bubble and squeak, porridge, pork chop and shepherd's pie and was an unexpected convert to Scotch eggs. Nothing much seemed to make sense to her, but Rosie the dog did; a trip to the kennels had done more for her in an instant than anything else Natalie had tried. Now Alfie was drawing with her at the table. They could hardly communicate, but the language of sketching dogs was fairly universal.

Leah had lit the Shabbat candles. She had said a prayer. She didn't mind picking and mixing parts of the faith she was interested in, parts she was not. Natalie watched her. She used to think Leah was the inflexible one. The stodgy black-and-white one. The one who liked dogma and plans. Now Natalie saw that Leah was the one most able to bend.

CHAPTER FORTY

It was the end of August and in the café, Leah's face was tight with anxiety. She nodded her head curtly towards one of the tables towards the window. 'Over there,' she mouthed.

Natalie looked and there was Mr Caplin, looking completely out of place in Pam's Pantry, like an elephant made out of mosquitos. He was wearing a dark hat and dark suit, and looked ready for a day's work in the City. Natalie continued wiping tables. *Maybe he hadn't seen her?*

It was another hot, grey-skied morning; the window cleaner and the meat boy had just been, Leah had already been contemplating a change to the menu several times. Fish balls or not fish balls – that was her question.

Natalie drifted towards Mr Caplin's table, where he was nursing a cup of tea. When he saw her, his face lit up, but then returned to an expression that was more neutral.

'I hope you don't mind me coming here, Natalie.' He took off his hat and held it out between them like a peace offering.

'It's fine…'

'It's another warm day,' he said.

She nodded.

'Mrs Monger told me where I might find you. I hope you don't… Sorry… Would you please take a seat? Just for a minute.'

Natalie glanced over to Leah, who was watching them both beadily. Leah lowered her chin: permission granted. Natalie sat down opposite him.

'I'm so sorry you left us. Was it something I did?'

'Not you,' Natalie said nervously. There was a thrumming in her head, a beating pulse. She met Leah's eyes and guessed Leah was thinking the same thing. *Maybe he can help?*

'Was it Hugo?'

Natalie shook her head and smiled at the thought. *What could that lovely boy possibly have done to make her leave?*

'How is Hugo?'

He offered her a cigarette, then lit one for himself. 'Quite broken-hearted, I'm afraid, but he will get over it. This is the way of things. Perhaps you could visit us sometime?'

Natalie made a non-committal sound. While she missed Hugo so much it ached, the thought of seeing Mrs Caplin made her feel, depending on mood, either prone to violence or horribly sick.

'Was it something my wife did?'

Natalie sighed. She picked up the salt and pepper pots. Leah hated her fiddling but right then, Natalie needed something to do with her hands.

'What are *you* going to do?' she asked eventually.

He shrugged his shoulders. 'What *can* I do? I love that boy with all my heart. I can't leave him with her. Who knows what will happen?'

Natalie excused herself. Even the sight of him was painful to her. She hurried to the kitchen, remembering that Leah had asked her to take her mutton stew off the heat. There were apples in the colander in the sink waiting for rinsing and Natalie was suddenly reminded of apple-bobbing. She remembered ducking her head down and plucking the apple out with her teeth. Of course, it would be easy without the water making the apple bounce and float. Of course, it would. But then there would be no game. She suddenly remembered Anna Freud's advice: 'Leave no stone unturned.'

When she came back to the table, Mr Caplin was reading the menu. His cup was empty. He looked at her expectantly.

'Some time ago, I asked Mrs Caplin if she would help get my mama out of Austria...' Natalie began.

He didn't say anything.

'Do you think she will have done the paperwork? Maybe she took it to the agency directly, or to the Home Office or...'

He took a long time to answer and when he did, his tone was slow and mournful.

'I... I think you have to realise something about my wife. Caroline doesn't care about much apart from herself, that is. I've found her word generally means nothing.'

Natalie had guessed it, but she still couldn't stand to hear it. 'She might have?' she said weakly.

'She won't have. Not if I know Caroline.'

Natalie understood that everything Mrs Caplin had given her had been at no cost to herself, that she had given her leftovers, crumbs, and that when it came to something that mattered, something that cost, she would not and could not do it.

Later, she would wonder if it had been too great an ask – but no, however she tried to rationalise it, Mrs Caplin had let her down. Later, Natalie would come to despise Mrs Caplin even more than she despised Mr Young because at least he had never pretended to be her ally. His hatred was written all over him. Caroline Caplin's was harder to read. She had not been a friend and it was Natalie's mistake to believe she was. The signs were there all along, but Natalie had failed to read them.

'I took Hugo's puppet when I left,' Natalie said abruptly in a small voice. She was not worthy of anything. She had not been a good nanny. She had failed at everything she had touched – from translating, to Rudi, Erich, Hugo... every single thing. 'The horse. I'm so sorry.'

It was a ridiculously small thing in a world of cruelty, but it was an act of cruelty, nevertheless. Yes, it reminded her of Mama, but Hugo loved that horse. It wasn't like she could pretend that she didn't know how much he loved it. She *did* know it and yet she had still done it. She knew what Mama would have said.

'I've done too many things I regret.' Mr Caplin breathed loudly. 'Perhaps it's the things we don't do that we regret the most.' He paused and looked at her intently over the table. 'That's why I came, Natalie, I take it that even though your sister is here, you still need a guarantor?'

'For Mama, yes.'

'Could you use our address? And for a job, we could say she would be Hugo's new nanny?'

'I don't know… I thought, I thought you didn't like people like me either,' she said dolefully. She remembered that phone conversation so long ago. *'Infested'. 'They're certainly growing in numbers'.* It was a phrase that had somehow imprinted itself on her brain.

She couldn't have misremembered what he said, could she?

'Whatever gave you that idea?' he asked incredulously. 'And no, I have nothing against people like you. Not at all. Ever.'

Natalie couldn't bring herself to speak.

Oh God. She realised suddenly. He mightn't have meant the Jewish people – he might have meant something or someone else. He might even have meant fascists. Perhaps he was referring to the far right, people like ambitious Mr Young. For weren't they growing in numbers and power too? And weren't there a lot of people they hated, not just people like her, enough that it meant they had lots of enemies.

Mr Caplin met her eyes. 'I don't know exactly how it feels but I might have an insight into feeling like I don't belong.'

She put her hands on her cheeks, felt her skin on fire with mortification.

'I can't promise anything, but it's worth a try,' he said. Then he smiled. 'Bring the puppet back to us when your mother is safe. Deal?'

'Deal.'

How had she had never noticed it before? Mr Caplin had very kind eyes. They shook hands on it. He stood up and placed his hat on his head resolutely. She knew now he would help. She might have saved herself a whole lot of pain if she had asked him years ago.

*

That night, trying and failing to sleep on the sofa she now hated, Natalie remembered the time she was at school and the headmaster had called her out of the classroom. It was only seven years ago, seven years next month, but it was a lifetime, several lifetimes ago. She knew it was going to be something bad by the unexpected warmth in the headmaster's voice and his subdued, grim air. Mama was in the office and before Natalie could take this in, Mama had shaken her head and said, 'He's gone, Natalie, Papa died.' And she had put her arms around her. Natalie was in shock. She knew her father was ill, but she had thought he was going into hospital for a minor procedure; that's what they said. Was it not minor? Did they know? Did Papa know? And what were they going to do now? And then Mama said: 'Natalie, this is going to be tough on you in particular because you were always Papa's precious girl, weren't you? You were always so, so alike, but believe me, I will do everything I can to make you feel as loved as your papa did.'

And Natalie had wept and wept until the headmaster had 'ahem-ed' several times, then emitted a 'sorry' and 'it's just the office and...' and for the first time Natalie had seen her mama without her lovely ship-sinking smile. For one moment, she looked utterly desolate, and it had broken Natalie's heart. She had sworn to Mama that she didn't need looking after, she would look after Mama instead. Mama was not alone: they would take care of each other and everything would be all right.

Two days later, Germany invaded Poland and all borders were closed.

CHAPTER FORTY-ONE

1946

After

Natalie was working as an ambulance driver, based at St George's Hospital in Tooting, south London. The Northern line. She did shift-work. It was long and dreary, but mercifully uncomplicated. There was rationing. She wore flat squeaky shoes and spoke her English quietly. She lived in a shared house with three nice English girls, who travelled home to their nice parents or their nice boyfriends from Friday evening to Monday morning.

She didn't mind the house, but it was amazing how much you could miss a garden. Natalie went to parks a lot now and looked up the names of flowers, but parks hardly ever had the beautiful stripes of a freshly mown lawn or that special smell that she had grown to love. Leah was working in a municipal kitchen in Manchester; something about it reminded her of Austria, she said ambiguously. She and Alfie had two adorable boys and three large greyhounds – the original Rosie, Rex and Amadeus – and they were making her money. Leah didn't say how much, but her buying her third property was a big clue. Alfie had joined up at the start of the war and was nearly killed at Dunkirk but had crawled into a fishing boat from Hove. He and Leah were more in love than ever.

Libby was still working in Suffolk at the farm where she had been sent as a land girl. The outside and active life suited her down to the ground. She only ever wore trousers and had her hair cut into a short bob. When Natalie saw her, every six months or so, she had to stop herself saying anything about sport. Libby had moved in with her good friend Stella. She hardly ever wrote to Natalie, but they telephoned each other once a week and for days after the call, Natalie always found herself smiling at the stories Libby told her.

It was another dull Thursday; the weather was nondescript and they had been several days without sunshine. Natalie was near the end of a quiet shift when a man came into the hospital looking for her.

'Ooh!' said one of the girls, who had Natalie down as a loner. 'A male friend!'

As soon as Natalie heard someone was looking for her, she had this strange feeling, this intuition, about who it was.

Hugo Caplin would be nearly sixteen now, and she imagined him slaying the ladies with his easy charm, his laconic wit and the dark curls of his hair. She had wondered if he wondered about her. If he feared she had been sent back or if he never gave her a second thought. Did he want his marionette back? Did he want an apology or the full story? He'd never get the fullest of full stories, but she had an approximate one ready. Natalie had imagined their reunion a hundred times: Hugo would tell her that he and his father had finally thrown Mrs Caplin out of Larkworthy. She had lost Mr Young, her looks, money, everything she valued. Perhaps it was her punishment to be honeycombed by the drunks and the homeless on the streets. Natalie would go back to the house and the garden that she loved most and play hide and seek with her favourite boy among the gnomes, or hopscotch or pretend tea parties.

But as soon as she saw him, the messenger, she knew instantly that this had nothing to do with the Caplins. They wouldn't have sent someone like this. This someone was so grey and emaciated, the stubble seemed to cover his entire face, but his head was toddler-like, far too large for his body. The suit that didn't fit, the eyebrows that were knotted and too thick. Her heart was thumping as she strode down the corridor to him, her stupid shoes making their stupid song, the left somehow squeakier than the right. Here she came, her soles announcing: *Here I am. I am Natalie Leeman. That is me.*

'Yes?'

He looked her up and down.

'I thought you were Princess Elizabeth.'

Natalie smiled, hoping the smile conveyed that she couldn't help it and nowadays she preferred Princess Margaret anyway.

The man held out a hand. Between his yellowy fingers an unlit cigarette waited. 'But other than that, you are exactly how he described you.'

Natalie's indulgent smile vanished.

'Who? Who sent you?'

He grinned at her. *Bad teeth, terrible teeth.* She had thought he was old, but revise that, he was someone who hadn't been looked after, someone who'd maybe seen terrible things.

'Rudi Strobl.'

Deep breath. Breathe, Natalie.

'Is he… is he alive?'

'Yes.'

'Rudi is? Rudi Strobl? Are you sure? Is there a message?'

'No.'

Natalie was so dizzy, she needed to sit down. These were the chairs where people were told the bad news. She had been there once when a man had been told his daughter had been killed in a V2 attack. When a woman learned that her husband had been crushed in a collapsed Tube station. She put her head between her knees and breathed slowly. When she next looked up, he was still looking at her, smiling. He seemed amused, still teasing his unlit cigarette.

'There's no message?'

There was no message, but there was an address on a lined and scrappy paper. The man handed it over, grinning at the same time. He was a Cheshire cat. The grin was so fixed it was unnerving. She still thought this might be a joke, an elaborate one, but it was Rudi's handwriting. Definitely. She'd have recognised his handwriting anywhere.

Natalie walked to the bus stop, took the number 9 to Earlsfield and then walked again. Could it be true that he was only fifteen minutes from her? They might have passed each other in the street! They might have queued together in the same line for bread or posted letters at the same letter box. Strangely, she did not feel hurried or rushed. Rather, she was on some higher level of calm. Suddenly everything was settled. After all the years of non-stop motion, it was time to stop, to regroup, to redirect. The cake was made, they just had to put it in the oven to rise. The scarf was knitted, they just had to take it off the needles and wear it.

A feeling of peace. That the work had been done.

She had stopped getting letters from Mama in 1940, Rachel and Leo in 1941. She had nothing after 1939 from Elizabet Steiner and Lena Schwartz. Old schoolfriends – Annie and Marguerite Rose – wrote in 1942 that Flora Lang had been publicly executed against a wall in the street, but Rudi had been arrested for subversive activities and was being sent to a labour camp.

She wondered what their first words to each other might be. She had wondered it before, but now it came to it, she couldn't remember what she had decided. Would they greet each other as they were in Vienna or as the people they were now? Who were they now? Would they know each other again? Would they *like* each other again?

She rehearsed – 'Nice weather, isn't it, for the time of year?' You had to be polite.

Nearly ten years had passed since they'd set eyes on one another. In those ten years, Natalie had lived all over the place: at the Caplins' lavish house, in Leah's tiny flat; she had been interned on the Isle of Man for eight months and she had been in three separate hostels for ambulance drivers. She had been a non-person for much of the time; she had become an alien overnight. Libby had kept her going, Libby and Leah, Alfie and their children, Mrs Monger and even Pam, but a darkness had gnawed at her, lapped at her edges constantly; its tide never went out. Sometimes, she would look down at her legs and almost be surprised that she was not wading in thick dark mud – because that's what it was like, getting through every day.

It was such an ordinary English house with ordinary windows and an ordinary roof missing ordinary tiles. It was not a place for dramatic reunions. No gnomes in the garden, two silver rubbish bins overflowing. Weeds poking through the slabs in the path. One empty milk bottle. A red door that had lost its redness. A knocker that could do with a shine. Natalie knocked. All her expectancy, fear and love were there in that knock.

Muffled voices then footsteps. A fleeting thought: *What must she look like? Still in her uniform, in her driver's hat.* She hadn't even paused to look in a mirror. That was odd of her. She was usually vainer that that. There was no make-up, no hairstyle that could compensate for the ten years that had passed.

Ten years.

'Rudi Strobl.'

'Natalie Leeman.'

The face. The same face that she had left behind. The eyes were the same. Not the hair – no, that had all gone, he was now sporting a close crop or a baldness, hard to tell which. His smile was different too. He used to be all teeth; now, although he was smiling, yes, he *was* smiling fit to burst, yes, he *was* pleased to see her, his mouth stayed clamped shut.

'I didn't know if you'd want to see me,' he said.

All thoughts of sunshine and clouds had left her head. She couldn't think of anything but the man before her.

'You came,' Natalie whispered.

'I'm here,' he said.

Rudi was a changed man, but Natalie gradually realised that she had never really known him very well, not really. And, well, she was a changed woman too.

That evening, that first evening they were reunited, they stood in the narrow kitchen of his lodgings and drank milky tea. They couldn't take their eyes off each other. He was like a mirage in the desert. Within seconds of seeing him, she wanted to say, 'Take me to bed,' but she couldn't, not yet. He said he wanted only to speak English from now on. He had been three years in a camp; he didn't want to talk about it. He had managed to survive, that was all. She told him she would be ready to talk about it when he was. He shook his head. *That's not happening.*

Later, they went upstairs to his bedroom, a tiny room with drawing pins on the wall and notes, notes from her, and by his bed, a small cut-out picture of her in that kimono with her 'what the heck is going on here?' face.

She was nervous, excited, ashamed, angry: all the emotions she had ever experienced were there all at once, in that room, in her head, churning around inside her at that moment.

'How did you know I hadn't met someone?' she asked him, hoping he would come up with a satisfactory answer.

She thought shamefully of Erich. Poor dear Erich. Even if not Erich, then there was Clifford, who she had let kiss and feel her on some Friday nights, and then there were other men during the war, a serviceman here, an American there. But Erich was the only one really.

'I just knew it,' he said.

'And you?'

Natalie would remember the phrasing because even at the time it struck her as ambiguous. 'No one came close.'

Later, she found out that there was another woman who Rudi had loved. Her name was Clara Tilmann and she died of typhus in Ravensbrück, April 1945, thirteen days before the end of the war.

They didn't tell each other their histories that night though. They fitted together back in place, but they were wary too. It was the strangest thing. Maybe like a lock and a key that works most of the time but sometimes, for other people, it has to be jiggled?

Later too, she wondered: did he really know she'd be alone, or did he just hope it? And Rudi smiled, nuzzled her cheek and said, 'it was a bit of both, of course', and 'wasn't she the same?'

They turned off the big light. Rudi flicked on a handheld torch and faced it to the wall, where it made a big yellow moon.

Pieces came together gradually. She found out that when the Nazis invaded the Netherlands in 1941, Natalie's brilliant sister, Rachel, her husband Leo and their adored daughter Hannah hoped to go into hiding in Amsterdam with some other Jewish musicians. But before that happened the Nazis came to collect them to put them on the trains. Wet, soft, privileged insubstantial Leo fought like a tiger, fought not to go. He was pushed to the ground and kicked in the head. He was a bloody pulp after they'd finished with him, he was unrecognisable, and he was dead.

Rachel and Hannah were murdered within hours of their arrival at Auschwitz.

Rudi had secured Mama a hiding place in a basement within a family home. Or rather, Flora helped Rudi, who helped Mama.

Mama was smuggled there one night from Leo's family home towards the end of October 1939. Leo and Rachel had already left Vienna, of course. One of Leo's brothers, his wife and their two small children went with Mama. Leo's sister went into hiding somewhere else. Another brother was in America. Leo's parents refused to leave. They were soon put on trains that went directly to a concentration camp. Rudi didn't know what had happened to Mama after the basement, but he told Natalie to prepare for the worst. Natalie whispered she already had, but it was horrible to hear and she hadn't prepared for the worst, not really – how do you?

A few months after Rudi found her, a French woman called Jocelyn who had lived in Vienna came to London with news. Jocelyn had beautiful black hair and pale powdery skin. She was as thin as a sparrow, and she had a smile that slipped when she thought you weren't looking at her.

Rudi had handed Natalie the baton and now, Jocelyn told her another part of Mama's story: how they had managed, eight of them, underground. They were starving hungry and they were bored. 'Strange to say bored,' Jocelyn said, 'but we were, we knew everything about each other, but we wanted stimulation. We wanted nature, the world, culture.' They were frightened too, but mostly bored. There was less and less food, they had less and less energy, and then they became less bored and more depressed. One of them, a boy about Natalie's age, tried to cheer them up with daily questions and answers, quizzes, but they ran out of pens and papers too quickly. And they were so hungry, they could hardly concentrate.

In 1942, the husband and the wife of the home they were staying in had a terrible quarrel over rations. They often argued over the provisions, but this night it was worse. It started in the kitchen, travelled through into the living room, escalated into the evening, into the night. They would not be quelled. They would not be contained.

'We were all starving,' Jocelyn whispered. 'You have to understand that.'

They covered their ears. The argument turned violent. Things were thrown. Books, ornaments, pictures.

'She's a pig, honk, honk, no, she never, it wasn't her, it was him…' Jocelyn paused. 'Then the police came.'

'The neighbours had reported them?' guessed Natalie.

'No, the husband was so furious with the wife, "my thieving wife", that he went to the police himself. He betrayed himself, his wife, and all the families they were hiding,' Jocelyn said to Natalie. She kept holding onto her smile. 'I don't know what the moral of the story is.'

'There's no moral, is there?'

Mama became ill on the train to Byelorussia. She was feverish, delirious and cried out for her own mother. Desperately, Natalie asked if she called for her or her sisters, and Jocelyn told her, 'You were never far from her thoughts, Natalie. I can promise you that.'

It wasn't enough. 'Did she never ask for me?'

'I'm sorry,' Jocelyn said. 'By then she was in the most terrible pain, she was in her own world already.'

'And the angry father and the pig mother? What of them?'

'Both shot for collaboration.' Jocelyn held Natalie's hand. She said, 'Natalie, you, Rachel and Libby are all she talked about in the basement. I feel I know you as well as my own children.'

Natalie pressed her hands against her ears. She thought she could hear her from here: *Natalie will come, my Natalie will get us out.*

Natalie and Rudi Strobl married in March 1947. Libby, her friend Stella, Leah, Alfie and their two children were loud enough, colourful enough, to fill in the gaps in the audience. Mrs Monger came along wearing an enormous hat, but although they were invited, Molly, Clifford and ten-year-old Cliff Junior did not, which was perhaps for the best. Libby gasped when she saw Natalie in her bridal gown and uncharacteristically, she swooned, 'I've never seen anyone so beautiful in my life!' For some reason, that reminded Natalie of the first time she saw Mrs Caplin and both how she had been so deceived and how she had failed. Mama had told her to be good. It wasn't that she had been bad, it was that she had not been wise.

The registrar had gone out for a moment and, shyly, Natalie had turned to her Rudi and she couldn't not ask him the thing she had been wondering about for so long. She had to know.

'Why didn't you write?' she whispered while Leah fussed around the children and Libby looked at her watch – Libby always appeared to have better things to do.

Rudi was more handsome than ever in a borrowed suit, his father's tie and a hat they'd bought together down Petticoat Lane market. Looking him in the eyes made Natalie blush.

'I did!'

'Not much,' she said. He nodded and she was relieved he wasn't going to try to deny it. He really *hadn't* written much. Foolish to say otherwise.

'I didn't want to tempt you back to Austria,' he said softly. 'I knew if you came back, it wouldn't be safe, so I knew you had to not come back for me...'

It was what she had guessed, but it was good to have it confirmed. He loved her. And she loved him.

They kissed slowly, tenderly, until Alfie yelled, 'Oy, yoy! You're not married yet.'

And then the registrar came back, and they got going.

All the ghosts, Rudi's and hers, were in the registry office, with them as they whispered their vows, with them in the hotel restaurant afterwards: a flicker of Aunt Ruth's green satin dress here, the wheels of Rudi's mother's bath chair, his father's Great War medals, the clap of Rachel's beautiful musical hands, Leo pontificating about Beethoven or Strauss, a baby gurgling in a Silver Cross pram, Uncle David explaining Esperanto, Great-Aunt Mimi telling everyone they'd got it wrong, all wrong; Great-Uncle Ben telling everyone not to listen to her. Mama's pretty hair pulled back in a bun for special occasions: she would be worrying about the food and if there would be enough cheesecake to go around: 'Don't let Uncle David have any more slivovitz. His nose is already scarlet,' she might say. 'Uh oh, too late!' and then she would cry, as she always cried at parties.

EPILOGUE

2012

'You're on time!'

This dear boy, this old man, is it him? Really him? Hugo Caplin?

'Of course. You drilled the importance of punctuality into me!'

He is curved like a comma, and his hair is shaved, but there is still the warm set of the face. The fun and humour in his eyes. Oh, he'll not be throwing cushions and beanbags at her today!

'I remember I got you in trouble about Sigmund Freud,' Hugo is saying. 'But I can't remember much else. I can only remember you were there, and then you weren't.'

Oh yes.

'I tell everyone that I once sat on Sigmund Freud's knee and stroked his beard and played with his dogs.'

Natalie would have stroked Hugo then if she could have. Why, he was every bit as lovely as she remembered. Patricia had done well. It was only six days after Natalie had made the request. The girl hovering nervously nearby looks more like the Hugo she remembers than this stooped old man. She is his granddaughter, Chantelle. She stares at them bewildered as Hugo and Natalie do their secret handshake, the one they used to do at the school gates. Chantelle has dark hair, dark skin and large, nervous eyes. Natalie, who is used to spotting teenage issues from a hundred metres, wonders what is wrong.

Hugo uses a Zimmer frame and needs to sit. Patricia jokes with them about the security, 'You managed to get in Fort Knox then?', but Natalie misses their reply.

'Here is the only other man – apart from your father,' she says to Patricia, 'who wanted to marry me.'

He did become an Olympian – in 1954 – Natalie was right about that. He *was* that rower. They got bronze, beaten by a German and American, he said. Missed the 1958 because his wife was heavily pregnant 'with the mother of this one'.

Chantelle blushes, cuddles her grandfather, then sobs into his collar.

'What's the matter?' Natalie asks, alarmed.

'There, there,' Hugo soothes the girl, and Natalie can see he is a lovely grandfather, of course he is, full of warm affection. He smiles at Natalie. 'Her boyfriend has just left for school in America. He'll be away for a year.'

'Nine months,' Chantelle corrects him.

'Long-distance relationship, huh?' Natalie says kindly. 'It can work. Patricia's father and I were separated for many years.'

Patricia says, 'Come into the kitchen, help me make the tea,' and Chantelle goes gratefully. Natalie is alone with Hugo again, like they were for all that time, every day, before school, after school and most weekends.

When they are out of earshot, he leans forward. 'You're still with us then?'

She laughs. 'Just about.'

He takes her hand, like he used to when he was six and she was sixteen, and she is back there, in the garden of the house, jumping around the gnomes or in his room, laughing about monsters, bears, or plagues of frogs.

'Was it my fault you left Larkworthy?'

'No!'

'Dad told me it wasn't, but you know, he was never that convincing even when he was telling the truth.'

'It wasn't,' she says firmly. Poor Hugo. She feels the weight of all the mistakes she had made press down on her.

'I was frightened you'd gone back to Austria, that's what I thought for years. I only found out very recently, funnily enough, when I saw a photo of you in the paper about a TED Talk?'

'Ah yes,' Natalie nods.

'I wasn't sure at first, but underneath it said: Dr Natalie Strobl from London, born in Vienna, 1920. I doubted there could be more than one of you.'

'Yes. I married Rudi.' Married twenty-six years until a heart attack took him, in bed next to her while she slept.

'And became a doctor?'

In 1950, Anna Freud had found her. She had visited, all efficient and determined, a pen behind her ear. 'You are going to come to work with us,' she had told Natalie and Natalie had gone and worked at her centre for traumatised children and studied for her qualifications in the evenings once Patricia was in bed.

'Indeed. I gave up the dream of being a translator and went into psychotherapy instead.'

'The girl who loved to talk became a listener?'

'Something like that.' Natalie smiles. 'A skill I should have picked up much earlier.'

'I'm happy for you, Dr Strobl.'

'Strobl is a mouthful,' admits Natalie. She had never got on with the name, but women didn't keep their own in those days. 'So, tell me, Hugo, about your family?'

For years she had thought of them at least every day. He pauses. 'My mother and Mr Young split not long after you left; Mother quickly moved on to someone else. He wasn't much better. Unfortunately, she didn't seem attracted to the... the normal fellas, and she was killed with him in a car accident in early 1940. One of the first casualties of the blackout, the papers said.'

'Oh, I'm so very sorry, Hugo.'

All that energy wasted, wishing terrible things on her, all those counselling sessions, and she had been dead all this time.

Hugo continues.

'I heard Mr Young was involved in some fascist groups in the 1950s. For a time, I had a few worries that he might have been my father all along. I couldn't bear the idea.'

Natalie nods. She had wondered too. Not back then, but Anna Freud had once suggested it, and the idea had pinged.

'He wasn't though…' He makes a praying motion with his hands. 'Thanks be.'

They both laugh.

'That's one bit of good news.'

Natalie sniffs. 'I wish I hadn't stolen that bloody puppet.'

Hugh smiles. 'That was a blow.'

'You didn't hate me for it?'

'Never! It was always more yours than mine.'

'I want you to have it back.' She fetches it from the cabinet, where it is flopped against the glass. A shabby thing from a shopping trip in Kartner Strasse, still has its own teeth and hair, but only just 'Maybe Chantelle will be able to do something with it?'

He nods, holding it aloft. 'Ah, my old friend,' and she's not sure whether he's talking to Mr Horsey or her.

'So, *your* family, Nat? Tell me.'

She points to a photo on a sideboard. A couple in the sunshine – two smiling elderly people in sunglasses, both pleasingly plump – stand in front of an alligator with its jaws clamped shut. The sign above them says: 'Welcome to Gatorland'.

'Leah and Alfie celebrated their golden anniversary in Florida last month; they're still going strong.'

'Ah, I always liked them.' Hugo places down his cup and she knows what he is going to ask next and she knows she is going to have to tell him. She has a polished, practised version she uses with strangers and when she talks about it to the therapists she still – well, up to six months ago – occasionally trains, but she knows she won't use it with him.

'And your family from Vienna?'

'My younger sister, Libby, yes. She came out on the Kindertransport. She lives in Norwich.'

'The sporty one? I'm glad.' He pauses. 'And the others? You had an older sister – the musician, I remember?'

'Rachel.' She shook her head. 'And her husband and baby – murdered.'

'I'm so sorry.'

Natalie shakes her head. She isn't going to cry. Not today. There have been too many tears.

'And your mother?'

'I couldn't save her.'

Even after all these years, even now, it burns her, all the things she did wrong. All the things she failed to do. She had underestimated the Nazis and overestimated herself.

She remembered when she had to explain it to Patricia for the first time. Rudi was no help, he left the room, and she had tried to tell her daughter in a way that wouldn't break an eleven-year-old's heart. 'Try to remember the good people,' she had said.

'But there weren't enough?' Patricia had asked.

'Not enough *did* enough,' Natalie had said, 'but there were plenty of good people. Most people are.'

It seemed to satisfy Patricia.

Over the years, Natalie had had three mental collapses – they called them 'nervous breakdowns' back then – one when Patricia was born, which was filed under post-natal depression. The second, when Patricia went on that school trip to Austria – and the third in 1986 when ex-SS officer Kurt Waldheim was voted in as president by 53.9 per cent of the Austrian public.

Other than that, she had got on with it. Got on with life. With work, with family. What else could she do?

'You saved me, Natalie,' Hugo says now. 'You saved *me*. You know that, don't you?'

Natalie shakes her head. The tears are coming. *No*, he was another she had failed. She was a spinning top of failure. *Mama…*

He explains. 'You were there every single day for three years. Every time I fell over. Every time I had a bad dream. I had never known love or security until you came along. These were… how do you say it? The formulative years of my life, and you were there, embracing my hobbies, my love of the outdoors, sports, wrecking things, and letting me off my hated tasks. If it weren't for you, I would be nothing today.' He pauses. 'It wasn't easy. But you, you were my constant. Thank you.'

Hugo has tickets to the Olympics. It is 2012 and the Olympics have come back to London. Oh, there is some interminable debating about whether Natalie is strong enough to go. Mark, Patricia's husband, does not think so, of course, but Anthony and Sharon think it is fine. Anthony is going to drive them and the great-grandchildren and they are going to shop all day long in Westfield shopping centre while they wait for her. The great-grandchildren are delighted.

It is a beautiful day. They walk through a pathway of volunteers: game-changers. The fuss they make; Natalie feels like a bride. She is wearing her favourite hat, Mrs Sanderson's furry hat which Patricia has never liked, but Patricia didn't say anything about it today because she is determined 'It is Natalie's day' and she is trying really hard to hold her tongue. The stadium is magnificent and if Natalie had worried that the size of the crowds would remind her of the braying hordes of Berlin, or of Nuremberg, she needn't have done. There are a hundred different languages, a hundred different-colour skins here, a hundred different flags. Everyone is taken care of. The food vans aren't cheap: 'Five pound for a Coca-Cola!' she repeats, but Patricia thoughtfully brought smoked salmon and cream cheese bagels and the queues for the loos aren't as bad as they had feared. Hugo and Libby get on like a house on fire – she always knew they would – and are talking about who won what when and who they are most looking forward to seeing. Natalie has time to look around.

Are they perhaps the oldest people in the entire place?

She has wanted to see this ever since Berlin, 1936. A girl, she can't be more than seventeen, a tall, rangy thing, is attempting the high jump. After the first jump, she asks the audience to clap for her. The audience obliges, they clap, clap in time, and then as she runs, they clap faster. She doesn't make it. When it's her third, final attempt, she asks the crowd to help again. Natalie is spellbound. She claps with all her might, everyone does, it sounds like a storm, but it's not enough; she jumps but doesn't make it. She picks herself up, thanks the crowd, then walks off in her tiny knickers. She is utterly glorious in failure and Natalie is overwhelmed at her fearlessness.

Patricia is next to her, Libby the other side of her. Hugo is holding her hand, and with the other, she is waving a British flag. Against all odds, she is here. This is her country, these are her people: she is home.

A LETTER FROM LIZZIE

Hello there,

I hope you have enjoyed *The Wartime Nanny*. Until recently, I didn't know that 20,000 Jewish women came from Germany and Austria to Britain to work as domestic servants between 1933 and 1939. Their experiences were mixed but the vast majority stayed in the UK and after the war, they went on to work and train in different fields. When I found out, I knew I wanted to tell a story about them and I am hugely grateful to Bookouture for giving me the chance to do so. I hope you find this period in history as fascinating as I do.

If you want to keep up to date with my latest releases, just sign up at the following link. I can promise that your email address will never be shared and you can unsubscribe at any time.

www.bookouture.com/lizzie-page

Readers who've read my books before will know I can't resist putting real-life remarkable women in my stories. Natalie and Leah were a fictional composite of different stories I heard and imagined. However, you'll find Anna Freud here, who is based on the real Anna Freud, the refugee, who founded the National Centre for Children and Families and worked tirelessly towards better mental health for adults and children.

It's always fabulous to hear from my readers – please feel free to get in touch directly on my Facebook page, or through Twitter,

Instagram, Goodreads or my website. If you have a moment, and if you enjoyed *The Wartime Nanny*, a review would be very much appreciated. I'd dearly love to hear what you thought, and positive reviews help to get our stories out to more people. I love writing reviews myself – I've put some of my favourite recommendations on Goodreads.

I'm currently working on my next books for Bookouture. They are going to be a slightly different direction again, but there will definitely be drama, family conflicts and women will, once again, take centre stage.

Thank you so much for your time,
Lizzie Page

lizzie.page.75

@LizziePagewrite

@lizziepagewriter

lizziepage

AUTHOR'S NOTE

In *The Remains of the Day* by Kazuo Ishiguro, a butler, Stevens, gradually realises all he missed out on in life, out of pride and a sense of duty. It is a beautiful story (and a great movie!); heart-breaking as Stevens comes to see the mistakes he has made. In one episode, his boss, Mr Darlington, sacks two refugee domestic servants because they are Jewish, and Stevens goes along with this. Those sacked maids, Ilsa and Irma were one of the reasons I wrote about Natalie and Leah here. I wanted to see a story from their point of view.

I had a fabulous time reading some wonderful books for research, especially:

Other People's Houses by Lore Segal

Whitehall and the Jews 1933–48 by Louise London

Servants: A Downstairs View of Twentieth Century Britain by Lucy Lethbridge

Aprons and Silver Spoons: The Heartwarming Memoirs of a 1930s Scullery Maid by Mollie Moran

The Hare With Amber Eyes by Edmund de Waal

I was fortunate to see Tom Stoppard's mesmerising play *Leopoldstadt* at Wyndham's Theatre.

I also went on a trip to Vienna, where I took some fantastic walking tours of the city and immersed myself in the story of the Jewish communities in Austria before and after the war.

I'm also very grateful to two friends of young people who escaped. from Vienna – Mary Forsdyke and Richard Kurti. Thank you for sharing your stories.

Just as with evacuation stories, the experiences of refugee domestic servants were very mixed, and I hope I captured some of that mixture in Natalie and Leah's stories. Some young women were welcomed, and became closer than family, leading to lifelong relationships. Others were mistreated, sexually, financially or verbally abused or isolated.

In this story, Natalie's sister Libby escapes via the Kindertransport. This was an immense and remarkable operation. Ten thousand Jewish children were brought out of Nazi Germany and occupied territories. They were brought to safety in England, where they were able to build new lives free from persecution. For the majority of the children who escaped, it was the last time they saw their parents.

ACKNOWLEDGEMENTS

Huge thanks to the Bookouture family, especially my brilliant editor, Kathryn Taussig, who is so good at trusting me, nudging me and decision-making for me. She always gets it spot on.

I usually forget to thank the copy-editors and proof-readers, but not this time! Many thanks to you all for your hard work on my terrible grammar. I know I overuse the dashes – I can't help myself. I love what you do.

Huge thanks also to my agent, Thérèse Coen of the awesome literary agency Hardman & Swainson. Thank you for being such a fantastic agent, mood-booster and fabulous advice-giver.

Thank you to friends in real life and online, especially anyone who has ever asked after *The Wartime Nanny*. The story has been so long on my mind that it does now feel like I've just given birth after the very longest pregnancy ever! I appreciate your interest and encouragement.

Thanks to my family. Lockdown has meant we have been together more than ever. I think it's fair to say I'm not a natural home-educator. Thank you for your patience and your love – I'm a lucky one.